Without a Flaw

a novel

MICHELE
ASHMAN BELL

Published by Covenant Communications, Inc.
American Fork, Utah

Printed in the United States of America
First Printing: May 2002

09 08 07 06 05 04 03 02   10 9 8 7 6 5 4 3 2 1

ISBN 1-59156-017-9

Library of Congress Cataloging-in-Publication Data

Bell, Michele Ashman, 1959-
    Without a flaw : a novel / Michele Ashman Bell.
       p. cm.
    ISBN 1-59156-017-9
    1. Diamond smuggling--Fiction. 2. Abused wives--Fiction. 3. England--Fiction. I. Title
PS3552.E5217 F56 2002
813'.54--dc21   2002023759

This book is dedicated to
my daughter Andrea.
They don't come any
sweeter than you!

Chapter 1

Isabelle Dalton's stomach knotted with fear. Glancing at the clock, she calculated how much time she had left before her husband, James, got home from work. Turning down the vegetables to let them simmer, she gave the gravy one last stir. She still needed to change her clothes, put drinks on the table, and light the candles. She'd have to hurry. The last thing she wanted to do was keep him waiting.

Racing up to her room, she quickly took off her jeans and sweater, hung them up, then pulled on the clingy black jersey dress that her husband liked so much. She hurried to the bathroom, where she brushed her mane of long blonde hair, then twisted it onto her head and fastened it with several glittering rhinestone clips.

She touched up the bruise on her right cheek with some base makeup and glossed on a light coat of lipstick. Checking her watch, she realized she only had ten minutes to get back downstairs and have everything ready in time.

Shoving her feet into her shoes, she scurried downstairs and filled James's crystal goblet with wine and hers with ice and water, set them on the table, then lit the candles. She wasn't much of a drinker, preferring to keep her mind and reflexes sharp, especially when James was home.

The timer on the oven buzzed, letting her know that the dinner rolls were finished and that James would be pulling into the driveway anytime now. Her stomach lurched as she poked the vegetables with a fork, hoping they weren't overdone. He hated it when the carrots were too soft.

A flash of headlights passed the kitchen window, telling her James was home. As she always did before he came through the door, she prayed he would be in a good mood and that she wouldn't do anything to set him off. She'd made his favorite: pork roast with mushroom gravy, new potatoes along with steamed broccoli and carrots, and her delicious dinner rolls.

Taking their dinner plates, she began dishing up their food. James liked to have his meal on the table, waiting and ready, when he got home. After five years of marriage, Isabelle finally had the routine down, but having things just the way James liked them, all the time, was no easy task. And when she disappointed him or didn't measure up, the price was too painful to have to endure very often.

Her nerves tensed and she froze when she heard the doorknob turn and click. Pasting a smile on her face, she waited for James to enter the room before she greeted him, because that was how he liked it.

"Good evening," she said when he finally appeared. She anxiously searched his expression to determine what kind of mood he was in.

"Good evening, Isabelle," he replied.

She walked to him immediately and gave him a kiss, then stepped away. "I hope you're hungry," she said cheerfully, trying to keep the mood light. "I made your favorite."

He glanced over at the stove, then back at her. "I thought we'd decided to have lasagna tonight," he reminded her.

"I know, but, . . ." she swallowed, hoping with all her heart that he didn't get angry, ". . . I was hoping—"

"Isabelle," his voice was impatient. "I give you a menu at the beginning of every week. I expect you to follow it."

"I'm sorry, James," she apologized quickly. "I won't let it happen again."

He nodded sharply, setting his briefcase and the mail—which he insisted on collecting himself every night—on the counter.

"Did anything come for me today?" He looked at her with a piercing gaze that made her stomach curdle.

"No." Her tone was even.

His gaze penetrated deeper. Beads of perspiration broke out on her forehead, and her palms grew clammy.

Without a word, James spun on his heel and left the room to wash his hands.

Isabelle pulled in several deep breaths to calm her jumbled nerves. James received packages from Federal Express at least once, if not twice, a week. She didn't know what was in the packages; she never asked. She didn't care. But sometimes when something he expected didn't arrive, he made her feel as though it was her fault it hadn't.

With the plates of steaming food on the table, Isabelle stood by her chair, waiting for him to join her, which he did moments later.

He helped her into her chair, then sat in his own chair.

Placing the linen napkins on their laps, they picked up their forks. Isabelle waited for him to take the first bite before she began. This was their routine, night after night. This was how James liked things. He was happier when things went as he wanted them to, and Isabelle was much happier when he was happy. It wasn't worth trying to change the way he liked things.

He nodded after taking a bite of the tender, juicy pork roast. "Very good," he said.

Isabelle relaxed a little and smiled. "I'm glad you like it." She took a small bite of her own slice of meat. Under James's encouragement and tutelage, she had become an exceptional cook. There were few things he allowed her to do, but cooking was one of them. He liked having a wife who could prepare gourmet dinners, especially when he entertained people from his law office.

"So, how was your day?" She asked the same question she'd asked every night for the past five years.

"Fine," he said, taking a sip of wine. He told her about a couple of his clients, and how brilliant he'd been in court that day. She smiled approvingly and said the appropriate words at the appropriate times.

She didn't have much of an appetite; she usually didn't at dinnertime, but she managed to take a few bites of the food on her plate. When James was finished, he placed his napkin beside his plate and told her he'd be in the den watching the evening news while she cleaned up the dishes.

Putting the last pot in the dishwasher, she shut the door and turned the knob for the cycle to begin. Giving the sink a quick scouring, she rinsed the sponge and wiped everything with a paper towel so the chrome faucet sparkled and the porcelain sink glistened.

She was just about to hang the dishtowel to dry when she jumped. James was standing in the doorway, watching her.

Holding her hand up to her chest, her heart beating wildly beneath her fingers, she said with a laugh, "You startled me."

His eyes narrowed in an intent gaze.

"Did you need something?" she asked nervously. She hated it when he stared at her like this. This was a look that frightened her. She scanned her mind quickly for something she might not have done to his liking or how in any way she might have angered him.

"I was looking for my evening paper . . ." he said, eyeing her.

Her heart stopped beating. She'd forgotten to get the paper. He liked having it beside his leather recliner in the den. She'd been so busy getting dinner she'd forgotten to get it off the porch. She was just about to apologize when the phone rang.

She jumped to get it, but James answered it. Grateful it was for him, she rushed to the front door. Grabbing the paper off the porch she took it inside and to the den, hoping James would forget it wasn't there earlier.

Picking up a novel, she tried to read as she waited for James to return. But it was impossible to comprehend anything she was reading. She was too nervous worrying about what he would say to her about not having the paper next to his chair.

Finally, she heard footsteps coming her direction.

"That was Mother," he said. "She wants us to come over for dinner on Sunday." He sat in his chair and picked up the paper.

The only thing worse than trying to please James was trying to please his mother. Mrs. Dalton was as nitpicky and critical as a person could get. "How nice of her to invite us," Isabelle lied, watching closely for a muscle to twitch in his cheek, or his hand to clench, to indicate he was going to flip out about the paper. "Did she mention if she'd like me to bring anything?"

He always read the business section first. "No," he replied, getting lost in his reading. "We just need to be there promptly at six."

"I'd better go write that down so I don't forget," Isabelle said. Relieved that her forgetting the newspaper hadn't turned into a big deal, she went to her planner and wrote down their dinner appointment. It was bad enough to suffer James's wrath, but adding his mother's to it was the truest form of hell on earth.

The evening was quiet, and as usual Isabelle was grateful to climb into bed that night. Most nights James stayed up late doing work he'd brought home from the office. She was grateful she could slip into the privacy and safety of her dreams. There she was happy and carefree again, as she had been before she'd married James.

Lying in her bed, Isabelle waited for her dreams to overtake her as she considered that her marriage was nothing like she'd imagined it would be. James had a side to him that she hadn't seen before they were married. A dark side. And sometimes, a violent side. He'd been attentive, protective, and involved in her life when they were dating. For a girl whose parents were both now gone and whose older brother had left home when she was a young girl and hadn't been seen or heard from since, she liked having someone to protect her, take care of her.

In the beginning James had swept her off her feet with all his attention and devotion. She'd been flattered by his near obsession to be with her or know where she was at all times. She hadn't understood what his demands really represented. She didn't realize the extent to which his "obsession" would grow.

James's love was anything but gentle and nurturing. It was controlling and dominating and robbed her of her freedom: freedom to associate with others, to pursue her dreams, to be herself. He told her how to dress and wear her hair, whom to associate with, what to do each day, where to go, what to buy, and even whom to talk to on the phone. She knew she'd grown paranoid about his obsession, but she honestly wondered if the occasional reverberation she heard on the phone meant the phone lines were bugged.

With each year they were married, his control seemed to grow stronger, more obsessive. At times she caught him staring at her, as he'd done earlier that night, with a look in his eye that rattled her nerves. And she wondered what exactly that look in his dark, pensive eyes meant.

The next day Isabelle woke to find it raining. She'd hoped to have sunshine so she could work out in the yard, but the drizzle kept up well into the afternoon. March had been a particularly wet month with sudden downpours, even blinding ice storms. When the weather was bad she spent her time indoors, playing the piano, losing herself in nocturnes by Chopin or concertos by Mozart. James didn't like her leaving the house unless she had specific errands to run or unless she worked out in the yard. She longed to go for walks in the woods behind their house, or down to the local gym and exercise. But he didn't like her going alone. So she didn't.

Finally, the storm broke and sun peeked through the clouds. Grabbing her windbreaker Isabelle went outside. She needed a breath of fresh air, so she walked down the lane toward the main road, thrilled to see the tips of crocuses and daffodils peeking through the soil. She kept the cordless phone with her in case James called, as he sometimes did at odd times during the day, just to check on her.

Turning back to the house, she stopped to look up at the beautiful Tudor-style home she lived in, but that strangely didn't feel like home. To her it was just a house where she lived. She had no sense of peace or love there. In a way it was like a prison. A beautiful, five-hundred-thousand-dollar prison. For anyone outside looking in, Isabelle appeared to have a life of luxury. James was a partner in the law firm of Harper, Calhoun, and Dalton, a prestigious firm in Boston. He was highly regarded in his field and well known and respected by every attorney on the East coast. He dressed impeccably, and was incredibly handsome with smooth dark hair and deep, dark brown, mysterious eyes. His tall, six-foot-three good looks, Harvard law degree, and wealth and power made him a community icon. The Dalton name dated back to the city's founding fathers and represented both money and power. Isabelle was considered the beautiful, devoted, dutiful wife. She was poised, gracious, soft-spoken, and always at his side.

But no one in the community knew what happened behind closed doors.

"Isabelle," a voice called to her. "Oh, Isabelle."

Isabelle turned to see their neighbor Cynthia Twitchell calling her. Cynthia had come outside to get her mail.

"Mrs. Twitchell," Isabelle waved. "How are you feeling?" Mrs. Twitchell had been recovering from a bout with bronchitis.

"Much better, thank you. I haven't seen you all winter. How have you been?" The woman walked toward her, smiling her sweet, warm smile.

From the few conversations she'd had with her neighbor, Isabelle gathered that the Twitchells had two children. One of them was grown and married with a baby; the other one had been living in the United Kingdom for a while. Cynthia didn't look old enough to have a grandchild.

"I've been well," Isabelle said with a friendly nod. "I'm glad spring is here. I've missed working in the yard."

Cynthia looked at Isabelle with interest. Isabelle always got the impression that her neighbor somehow knew what it was like for her at home with James. The woman never pried or asked, but her eyes held such great understanding and sympathy that Isabelle couldn't help but wonder.

The sound of a car coming down the street caused both of the women to turn and see who it was. To Isabelle's complete horror, it was James.

The stone-cold look he gave her as he pulled into the driveway turned Isabelle's blood to ice. Had he thought she was getting the mail?

"I have to go—" Isabelle left Mrs. Twitchell behind and ran back to the house. She got inside before James did and quickly hung up her coat.

"Isabelle!" James yelled as he came through the back door.

She jumped when she heard her name and raced to meet him.

"I was just asking Mrs. Twitchell how she was feeling after her bron—"

"I need to drop off the car at the shop so they can repair the dent in the door," he told her.

Relieved that he didn't reprimand her for being outside talking to the neighbor, she said, "Do you need me to follow you in my car?"

He looked at her as 'though she were a complete idiot. "Of course I do!"

She flinched but steeled herself. "Would you like me to change my clothes first?" She knew that whenever she went out in public, he liked her to look her best. She was in jeans and a button-down oxford shirt.

"You won't be getting out. You're fine," he told her.

The ride to town took about fifteen minutes. Isabelle didn't mind the drive though; she enjoyed having a chance to get out of the house for any reason.

She waited in the car while James went into the shop to take care of business. She remembered how livid he'd been when he'd discov-

ered the ding in the door of his Jaguar after work one day. He'd
threatened to sue the parking attendant and the garage, but no one
knew anything about who could have done it. James kept his Jaguar
in immaculate condition, and any defect or damage was intolerable.
The dent had happened on Tuesday, today was Thursday.

James emerged from the repair shop and approached the car.
Isabelle jumped out to allow him to drive.

"You drive," he ordered. "I've got to call the office."

It made her nervous to drive when James was in the car with her.
But today he was so busy talking on the phone and writing in his
Palm Pilot, he wasn't paying attention to what she was doing.

The road to their house followed a river which had become
swollen with early spring rain. She followed the twists and turns in
the road, but as she came around a sharp bend, she had to brake
quickly to avoiding running into the tail end of the car in front of her
that was moving too slowly.

"Isabelle, you know how dangerous this road is!" James exploded.
"Every year people die on this turn because they drive too fast. What
are you thinking?"

"I'm sorry," Isabelle replied. "I was going the speed limit." She checked
the gauge often, especially with James in the car. She wasn't speeding.

He didn't reply but she dropped her speed considerably, not
wanting to push her luck any further.

The next day Isabelle was grateful a warm sun was shining. She
looked forward to spending the day outside, cleaning out flower beds
and working in the soil. Being outside gave her a sense of freedom she
rarely felt. It also gave her a nurturing, caring feeling which she
longed for. A feeling that often made her think of how much she
wanted a family, and children of her own. But James was opposed to
having children. She'd never expected they would have a large family,
probably only two children, but James had told her in no uncertain
terms that he didn't want any children, or pets, for that matter.

It was probably for the best, she reasoned, as she fastened a rubber
band around the end of her braid, which hung down her back
between her shoulder blades. James wasn't her idea of an ideal father.
He wasn't exactly tender and loving. But her life seemed so empty and

meaningless. Her days were filled with mindless housework, cooking, and cleaning, but even that wouldn't fill up all the empty hours of every day. She had more time on her hands than she knew what to do with. James was adamantly opposed to her getting a job, even though she had a degree in early childhood education. He didn't like the thought of her being around strangers, especially men, when he wasn't around. Not that Isabelle had ever given him any reason to mistrust her. But that didn't matter.

There was still a cool nip in the air, so Isabelle slipped on her windbreaker before going outside. With the cordless phone in one hand, she headed for the garden shed, where she kept all her tools. The rosebushes needed a good pruning, so she decided to start there first.

As she clipped and pruned she felt the calming effect of being outside: the warmth of the sun on her back, the freshness of the breeze on her face. Her sheltered life left her little to find pleasure in, and she had learned to find happiness in small delights.

"Yoo-hoo," a voice called to her from the side of the house.

"Mrs. Twitchell, I'm in the back," Isabelle replied, pushing herself to her feet. She removed her gloves and smiled warmly at her neighbor.

"Hello," Mrs. Twitchell said. "I had an inkling you'd be outside on such a lovely day." She handed Isabelle a plate of cookies. "I made a batch of applesauce cookies. Thought you and your husband would enjoy some."

Isabelle was touched. How thoughtful of her neighbor to bother. Isabelle lifted the plate and smelled the spicy, appley scent of the warm cookies. "They smell wonderful. Thank you."

"Oh," Mrs. Twitchell remembered something else. "I almost forgot. The mailman put this letter in my mailbox by mistake."

Isabelle took the letter and thanked her.

"Well, I guess I'd best get going." She hesitated, as if she wanted to say more, but didn't. "By the way, I have a gardening book you might enjoy looking at. It has some wonderful ideas and tips in it."

"I'd like that," Isabelle told her. "And thanks again for the cookies." Ever since her own mother died shortly after Isabelle and James got married, Isabelle had missed having someone to talk to, someone who would listen to her, counsel her, support and strengthen her, much like a mother would. In a way Mrs. Twitchell was the closest thing she had, but Isabelle didn't dare confide in her or anyone else. If James found out she'd said anything to anyone, she was certain he would beat her within an inch of her life.

"We ought to go out to lunch one day," Mrs. Twitchell suggested. "Since we're both home all day, we could go to the country club for lunch, then go shopping for the afternoon."

Isabelle would've liked nothing more than to spend an afternoon with her neighbor. But she knew it would never happen. With a smile she said, "I'll have to check my schedule and get back to you."

The woman bid her farewell and headed home. Sadness filled Isabelle's heart as she watched her leave. She appreciated Mrs. Twitchell's offer of friendship, and would have loved to have a friend. Someone, anyone, to fill the emptiness in her life, an emptiness that sometimes felt as though it would consume her entire being.

Her stomach growled. It was past lunchtime, and she hadn't eaten breakfast. Taking the plate of cookies inside with her, she poured herself a tall glass of cold milk and sat down at the counter to sample Mrs. Twitchell's baking.

Out of curiosity, she turned the letter over that Mrs. Twitchell had brought to her and gasped. It was addressed to her.

Chapter 2

Isabelle stared at the letter. She rarely ever got mail anymore. Any letters she did get James usually intercepted and read first before he gave them to her.

She noticed the return address was from *S. MacGregor*, in Westmoor, England. A surge of excitement sent her heart racing. She had a great-aunt in England, her grandmother's sister. Was this letter from her Aunt Sophie?

Her father had been born in America, but his family went to England when he was a young boy and he'd grown up there. Her mother had been Irish and English.

Ripping open the envelope, she read the contents.

My dearest Isabelle,

After the countless letters I've written to you without receiving any reply, I suppose I should assume you wish to have no contact with me. But I just can't seem to forget those beautiful green eyes of yours, like your mother's, and that gorgeous head of curly red hair. Of course, that was many years ago when you were just a child, but still, you are my grand-niece and I have not forgotten you.

I am therefore making one last attempt to contact you, in hopes that you will drop me a short note to let me know how you're getting on. Your grandmother and your mother were all the family I had, and you and your brother are all I have left. I am growing old, and I am hoping that before I pass on, I can bestow upon you what is left of their legacy.

I would love to hear from you, but even more, I would love to see you and your beautiful, smiling face again. Perhaps you could come to England on holiday. You would be welcome to stay as long as you wish. My home is your home.

I must get this in the post, but I enclose with it my love, prayers, and best wishes to you.

With love,
Aunt Sophie

Isabelle stared at the letter, her breath coming in short, quick gasps. Her Aunt Sophie had been sending letters to her and she didn't even know it. But why hadn't she received them?

James. There was no doubt in her mind. Because she was forbidden to collect the mail, he could have easily intercepted the letters and gotten rid of them as part of his need to keep a tight rein on her.

A warm feeling in her stomach quickly filled her entire body. Her great-aunt still loved her and cared about her. The woman thought about her and wanted to see her.

To know that someone, an actual family member, wanted to have contact with her, even spend time with her, lifted her spirits. She'd been so isolated, so imprisoned by James, that she'd forgotten she did have at least one relative left in her family. A relative who loved her and wanted to see her.

By the sound of the letter, Isabelle gathered that at one time she must have been to her Aunt Sophie's home. But for the life of her Isabelle couldn't remember being there, nor could she put a face to the name.

Isabelle thought of her brother, Ryan. She hadn't heard from him since she was a teenager. How she wished he'd contact her. Since he chose to stay away from her, it was out of her hands. But her Aunt Sophie cared. Knowing someone was thinking of her made her feel warm and wonderful inside.

But how would she ever be able to visit her aunt? James would never take her to England, nor would he let her go alone. In fact, judging by the way he'd kept her aunt's letters from her, she wasn't sure he would allow any contact with her.

Isabelle glanced around the room as if to make sure she was still alone. James had her so spooked and nervous that she felt as though she were being watched constantly by some unknown eye.

The doorbell rang, scaring Isabelle out of her skin. Cautiously she crept toward the front door, wondering who it could be. She never had visitors during the day.

When she looked through the window, no one was there. She went to the door and opened it. On the porch was a package delivered by Federal Express.

Bringing the package inside, she shut the door and locked it. The letter from her aunt was still clutched in her hand. She had to keep the letter from James. He couldn't know she had it. She would put it away in her special hiding spot where she kept a few pictures of her parents and brother and all the money she had in the world. Money she'd saved over the years, from grocery money and other spare change she'd acquired. Why she hoarded it, she didn't know, but she liked knowing it was there and that it was hers alone.

Walking up the stairs to her bedroom, she thought about how wonderful it would be to visit her aunt in England. To talk to someone who knew her mother and father and had a connection to her. James shouldn't keep her away from her family. It wasn't right. Yet she knew, right or wrong, he still would. And to bring it up, to even ask, was an invitation for his anger, something she never triggered intentionally. Despite her constant vigilance, she still managed occasionally to do things that upset him. She wasn't about to bring up the subject of her aunt or all her missing letters.

Still, she longed to see her Aunt Sophie. She had a vague recollection of her aunt, but that was all. Her past, especially her childhood, seemed to have slipped into a thick fog in her mind. Perhaps it was because it took every ounce of willpower, strength, and conscious effort to cope with the life she now had. Dwelling on the past only made her discouraged and frustrated.

Inside the walk-in closet in her bedroom, she pulled out a suitcase that was tucked back in a corner, behind racks of shoes and handbags. Fishing the suitcase key out of the bottom drawer of her jewelry case, she opened the suitcase, pulled out a carry-on bag she had stored inside, and pulled out a shoe box from the bag.

Inside were pictures of her brother and parents, her passport showing dual nationality, English and American, and money. The box was full of bills: ones, fives, tens, and twenties. She made piles with the money and began counting, curious to see how much she had saved. By the time she finished counting, she could see that she had close to seven hundred dollars. After five years of saving, she was amazed she had so much.

At first, when she began saving the extra cash, she'd intended to use the money to buy a special gift for James. But she'd never found the right time or right item to spend it on, so she'd just kept saving.

She put the money back in the box, then looked at the pictures of her parents. Her father had been killed in an automobile accident by a drunk driver when she was nine. Then her older brother had run away from home when she was sixteen, breaking her mother's heart.

Isabelle had met James after she graduated from college. Her mother hadn't cared much for James from the very beginning. She didn't trust him, even if he did drive an expensive car, was darkly handsome, and lavished them both with gifts. There was something about him she didn't trust. Isabelle had imagined herself to be truly in love for the first time and had paid no attention. She regretted not following her mother's instinct.

Isabelle and James had been married barely a year when her mother had died. Isabelle was already realizing the full extent of James's obsessive and controlling behavior, and her mother's death had hit Isabelle hard.

But this letter from her aunt gave her new hope. She still had someone who loved her and cared about her. And maybe, somehow, it might prove to be a link to her brother. The chances were slim, she knew, but she didn't want to let go of the possibility.

Reading the letter one last time, she placed it inside the box and put everything away, just as it was before. She then went to the computer and logged on to the Internet. She was curious to see how much airline tickets to England were.

After some scouting around, she located a fare for three hundred and seventy-nine dollars one way, out of Boston.

An idea flickered across her mind, but she quickly banished the thought. She knew she would never dare go to England by herself. Not unless she was willing to leave James for good. She'd thought of leaving James many times. Especially after the times he'd beaten her. But where would she go? Seven hundred dollars wasn't enough to start a new life.

Besides that, she was afraid of him. Not only of what he did to her when she was with him, but what he'd do to her if she ever left him and he found her again.

No, she thought sadly as she disconnected from the outside world and turned off the computer. The only way she'd ever be free of James would be in death. He'd told her many times that the thought of her being with anyone else nearly drove him mad. He claimed he loved her passionately, but his way of showing his love and devotion was through his possessive control. It wasn't normal and it wasn't healthy. Isabelle knew that. She just couldn't do anything about it.

Her thoughts continued as she began to prepare dinner. Tonight James had scheduled grilled salmon. She would make baked potatoes and a green salad to go with it. A nice evening meal was important to James. And if it made him happy, Isabelle was willing to do it.

A colleague had given James a ride to and from work that day, and as usual Isabelle's stomach was in knots when he arrived home. But dinner went well and James actually seemed to be in good spirits. He'd won a big case in court that day and even promised Isabelle that he would take some time off this summer and they would go on a vacation, perhaps to a secluded island getaway in the Caribbean.

While Isabelle cleared the dishes, James went to the den to read his newspaper. Everything seemed to be going well until she heard him call her name.

Chewing her bottom lip nervously, she went to the den. James was standing, holding the Federal Express package in his hand.

"What is it, James?" she asked.

"This package," he lifted it for her to see better. "It came today?"

"Yes," she said, wondering what the problem was. "This afternoon."

"Tell me about the delivery man, Isabelle." He stepped closer to her, the muscles in his jaw clenching.

"The delivery man?" She was confused. "I didn't see the delivery man. He just left the package on the porch."

"Of course he did." James lowered his voice, reaching out for her arm, but she pulled it away.

"I'm telling you the truth. I didn't even see who delivered it." She tried to speak convincingly.

"Why don't I believe you?" He grabbed at her arm again, this time latching onto her elbow. He dug his fingers into her flesh, his manicured nails biting into her skin.

"James, please." She pulled her arm back, but he gripped it even tighter. "You're hurting me."

"Oh, I am, am I?" His eyes narrowed and he smiled cruelly. With a sudden jerk, he threw the package across the room and grabbed her other elbow, taking Isabelle completely by surprise.

Isabelle whimpered, dreading what was coming. She'd never, ever given him reason to doubt her fidelity to him, but he became so insanely jealous over the most ridiculously innocent things. Isabelle had learned that there was no convincing him otherwise.

Pulling her closer to him, he held her tightly, his eyes burning into hers. Just then, the doorbell rang.

James swore. "Who could that be?"

Peeking through the curtains, he saw who was on the porch. "It's that pesky Mrs. Twitchell," he told Isabelle. "Get rid of her."

Chapter 3

Isabelle didn't want to see Mrs. Twitchell right now. She was afraid her face would give her away.

The doorbell rang again. With a tremulous smile, Isabelle answered the door.

"Hello, dear," Mrs. Twitchell addressed her. "Harold and I were just on our way to a movie and I thought I'd drop this by." She handed Isabelle the gardening book she'd promised earlier that day. "Take your time; I'm in no hurry for it."

"Thank you, Mrs. Twitchell," Isabelle said as she started to close the door.

"Oh, and don't forget, we're doing lunch at the club soon," Mrs. Twitchell reminded her just before the door shut.

Isabelle wished Mrs. Twitchell hadn't said anything about lunch. It wouldn't matter to James that she had nothing to do with Mrs. Twitchell offering, nor that she had no intention of going with her. Isabelle knew James too well. She knew he wouldn't believe her.

When she went back to the den, he looked at her with a malicious scowl.

Isabelle held out the book for him to see. "Mrs. Twitchell let me borrow her gardening book," she told him innocently.

"You seem to be spending quite a bit of time with Mrs. Twitchell," he said. "Why is that?"

Isabelle responded quickly in her defense. "No James, really. I—"

"What is this about going to lunch?"

"She suggested it, but I have no intention of going," Isabelle assured him.

"But you've thought about it, haven't you?" He stepped nearer, closing the gap between them.

She stepped back. "James, please."

"When will you learn, Isabelle?" He grabbed both of her wrists and jerked her toward him. "You bring all of this on yourself."

"I'm sorry, James. I won't talk to her again. I promise," Isabelle pleaded.

"It's too late for promises," he said, raising his hand.

Isabelle didn't get out of bed until almost noon the next day and then, when she did, she could only hobble to the bathroom. Avoiding the mirror, she turned on the water in the tub, hoping a long soak in a hot bath would soothe her aching body.

Her jaw was sore and swollen, making it difficult to brush her teeth. But she was glad that at least he hadn't split her lip like the last time he hit her. She didn't dare leave the house for a week until it healed, afraid of the looks she'd get or the excuses she'd have to make up. Excuses she was running out of.

Letting the steaming water envelop her in a comforting cocoon, she leaned back and tried to relax, float away, to escape the hell her life had become.

Leave! her good sense told her. *Get away from him!* her head screamed. *You deserve better!* her heart reasoned.

Why didn't she leave? What on earth was holding her back?

Fear.

Pure, unexplainable terror.

James had told her time and time again that she was his. That if she ever did leave, he would track her down and find her, because they belonged together.

He said he loved her. But she didn't know what to make of this dual personality of his, the Jekyll and Hyde syndrome that turned him into a raging monster one minute, beating her senseless, and into a tender lover the next, caressing her intimately, whispering how passionately he loved her. It created such a confusion inside her that she didn't know where to turn for help or what to do.

She did know one thing.

She couldn't live like this any longer.

It didn't matter how many times James was sweet and thoughtful, romantic or loving. No amount of kindness could erase his blows that left her bruised and bleeding.

She didn't know how he could hit her, over and over, then turn around and tell her he loved her and needed her, expecting her to enjoy his touch and kisses. Even now as she replayed the events of last night in her head, her stomach curdled. His rage had seemed to come out of nowhere. Perhaps something had happened at work or on the way home and he'd merely taken it out on her. She didn't know. All she did know was that she didn't want to see his face again. Or feel his touch. Or smell that familiar aftershave she'd come to hate. Or hear the tone of his voice threatening her or confessing his love for her.

Tears she thought had long since been cried out reappeared and ran down her cheeks. She couldn't bear living like this for another day. And, she realized honestly, she had an even deeper fear. What if next time he hit her too hard, or too much, and he killed her?

In some ways death would be a blessing. Death would be a release from this torturous prison.

Her stomach grumbled. She'd barely had any dinner the night before, and only one of Mrs. Twitchell's cookies for lunch yesterday.

Climbing out of the bathtub, she wrapped herself in her fleecy robe and went downstairs to the kitchen. But after she looked in the refrigerator and cupboard, her stomach turned. The thought of food made her sick.

She jumped when the phone on the wall rang.

She didn't want to talk to anyone, but she didn't dare not answer. Especially if it were James. She remembered the last time she didn't answer the phone. He'd driven home from work to find out what she was doing and who she was with. That was the time he'd split her lip.

"Hello," she said. It was James. He'd gone golfing with colleagues, then had to go to the office.

"What have you been doing today?" he asked.

"Well, I slept in, then took a long bath," she told him, trying to stay calm and unemotional.

"Ahh, that's good. I like to hear that my princess is pampering herself," he said. "I just wanted to tell you that there will be a delivery coming this afternoon. Go ahead and accept it." He paused. "And I have some bad news."

She couldn't even begin to imagine what his bad news could be.

"I have to go out of town for a few days," he said.

A feeling of pure relief and joy filled Isabelle. The thought of having James gone for even a few days was too much to even hope for.

She infused her tone with as much disappointment as she muster. "When do you have to go?"

"Tomorrow. I have to fly to Chicago. I'll be gone two days. Maybe three."

Three days without James! She could almost believe she had died and gone to heaven. But she'd played her cards wrong once before and knew she had to handle the situation carefully, or she'd find herself confined to his hotel room for three days.

His law firm did a lot of business around the country. They even had accounts abroad, mostly in Europe and Asia, but occasionally James traveled to South Africa for the firm. She'd wanted to go with him to Africa, intrigued and interested in such a foreign place. But James had made it plain that she wasn't welcome on those trips. He'd reacted so suddenly and with such ferocity when she asked, that for a moment she wondered if perhaps there were more to his trips than just business. Seeing his reaction, however, she wasn't about to voice her suspicions.

If it wasn't for the fact that James asked his mother to come to their house or told Isabelle to go to the Dalton manor, rather than leave her alone while he was gone, Isabelle's greatest moments of peace were when James was gone.

"You'll be home for my birthday on Friday, won't you?" she tried to speak as if she couldn't bear the thought of him missing her birthday, when in reality, that would be the best present he could give her.

"Of course I will," he assured her. "I have something very special planned for you."

She shut her eyes, feeling herself beginning to crumble. In past years she used to hang onto the "special" moments he planned. To be sure, he still knew how to wine and dine her and be romantic and adoring. But she wasn't as forgiving of his dark, violent side as she used to be. She couldn't forget those terrifying moments as she used to. She didn't hope anymore that things would get better, that things would change. She knew they wouldn't. She also knew she couldn't carry on this charade much longer.

"I have another phone call to make, so I've got to go. I'll talk to you more about it tonight," he said.

She told him good-bye and hung up the phone, feeling a conviction grow inside of her. She couldn't take it any longer. He would never seek help for his problem, he would never change. It was up to her to do something.

And, she knew, it would have to be something drastic.

Isabelle reread the letter from her Aunt Sophie several times that afternoon. She wondered how serious her aunt was about her invitation. Was it possible that the heavens had sent her a lifeline, a way out? She couldn't help but wonder, even hope, that it was a sign for her to take the risk and leave, leave without telling James where she was going.

It was a risk she was willing to take because she knew she was at the point where she would rather die trying than live like this any longer.

The best time to leave would be while James was gone. That would buy her some time. Time to get to the airport and get away without him following her or knowing she had left.

It was now or never.

But how could she get to the airport without leaving a trail? She couldn't drive her own car and leave it. Then he'd know she'd left him. She could call a taxi, but that would also leave a record. She had to think. Somehow she had to get to the airport without leaving any trace of where she was going or what she was doing.

She thought about calling her aunt, but knew that too would leave a trail. She could only call her from a pay phone. Somehow she had to get away to make the call.

Reading the note one last time before putting it away, Isabelle felt an increase of courage and faith. She had to believe her aunt truly meant for her to come and visit. It was her only hope.

Her aunt wouldn't recognize Isabelle when she saw her, though. James had wanted her to dye her hair blonde and wear it long and straight. Her hair was naturally deep copper-red and wavy, like her mother's.

Red and wavy. She thought for a moment and realized what she had to do. But she'd have to wait until tomorrow, when she knew James was in Chicago, a far, safe distance from her.

The doorbell rang, interrupting her thoughts. Throwing the letter in the shoebox and stuffing everything into her suitcase, she hurried downstairs and answered the door.

"Oh, Mrs. Twitchell," she said, instinctively covering the side of her jaw with her hand.

"Hello, dear," the woman said, holding out a bucket toward her. "These are starts from my garden, violets and daisies. I thought you might like them for your flower bed."

Isabelle took the bucket from her, thinking that she wouldn't be around when they bloomed. "Thank you," she answered, keeping her head turned so her swollen jaw wouldn't show.

"Isabelle, dear," Mrs. Twitchell said hesitantly. "Is everything all right?"

Isabelle looked at her, puzzled. How did Mrs. Twitchell know?

"I'm going to be fine," Isabelle answered with conviction and a soft smile.

"You know, I always wanted a daughter of my own," Mrs. Twitchell told her. "Don't get me wrong, I love my two sons with all my heart, as I love my daughter-in-law. But, well . . ." She smiled at Isabelle. "I'd like to offer you some motherly advice, if you'd let me."

Isabelle looked at her with interest.

"I know I may be out of line for what I might say, but I can't help but worry about you dear. I see that look of terror in your eyes when your husband comes home. I've seen what he does to you and it breaks my heart. I guess I'm saying that if you were my daughter, I'd tell you to get away from him. You deserve better. You deserve someone who is loving and tender and takes care of you and treats you like a queen. Someone to treasure you and protect you. Not someone you need protection from."

Isabelle didn't answer.

"I know you have the courage and strength inside of you, Isabelle. Dig deep. It's there. I know it is. You're a fighter and a survivor."

Blinking quickly so the moisture in her eyes wouldn't collect, Isabelle braved a smile and said, "I appreciate your concern and your kindness. It's meant more to me than you'll ever know."

Mrs. Twitchell reached up and stroked her swollen cheek gently. Isabelle looked away, embarrassed. "I'd hate to see something worse than this happen to you," she said. "Not that this isn't bad enough," she added. "You be strong, my dear. And God bless you."

Isabelle could have sworn that Mrs. Twitchell's voice had quivered and that her eyes too had filled with tears.

Closing the door, Isabelle carried the bucket to the utility room and set it down.

Was this another sign from heaven? After all these years was God finally paying attention to her and helping her? Answering prayers that had grown less frequent? Helping her find the strength and the way to get away from James and the emotional and physical abuse she had been subjected to?

Her mother had taught her about God as a young girl. They'd even gone to church, but since her marriage to James, Isabelle had begun to wonder what good it did to believe in a Supreme Being who let families fall apart and husbands beat their wives.

The doorbell rang again and Isabelle debated whether to answer it or not. She appreciated Mrs. Twitchell's concern, but she wasn't sure she was up to more advice. She had too much on her mind as it was.

Another persistent ring forced her to answer. But it wasn't Mrs. Twitchell; it was the florist making a delivery.

"Are you Mrs. Dalton?" the woman at the door asked.

"Yes," Isabelle answered, staring at the huge box in the woman's arms.

"These are for you. Have a nice day." The woman hurried back to the delivery van.

Isabelle brought the box inside and set it on the counter in the kitchen. Untying the bow, she opened the lid and found a dozen beautiful, fragrant, long-stemmed white roses.

She admired their beauty for a moment, but the fact that they were from James seemed to dull their sweet fragrance and tarnish their pure whiteness.

James called Isabelle later that afternoon and told her not to make dinner. He'd stop at her favorite Chinese restaurant and bring dinner home.

This seemed to be the pattern for James. After one of his violent episodes, he'd swing the other direction and shower her with gifts and attention.

She used to fall for it, thinking that the worst was over. She'd try harder to please him and make him happy and, for a while, things would be good. James would buy her beautiful clothes and jewelry, then take her out to dinner, dancing, and glamorous social functions. Telling her to dress in her best, James would then parade her around like a prized possession. At first she enjoyed all the attention, knowing how proud James was to show her off. But she quickly tired of putting on a show each time they went out in public.

Still, she had no choice. It was what James wanted, what he expected, what he demanded.

She'd learned to stay aloof. To greet people, especially men, with a certain amount of indifference so James couldn't accuse her of flirting or being "too friendly" with someone. The first time he'd ever laid a hand on her was because of that. He'd left her side at a party while he'd visited with one of the other partners about a legal matter. A charming young man, one of the newest members of James's law firm, had engaged her in a friendly conversation.

The moment James found them talking, he'd escorted her from the building. Taking her home, he'd shown his displeasure in a painful and unforgettable fashion. He'd been furious that she'd behaved that way, especially in front of his colleagues.

The young man was fired the next day.

That evening as James arrived home from work, Isabelle greeted him with a kiss and a smile. As they ate their Chinese takeout, Isabelle thought of those first wonderful months right after they'd gotten married. Everything had seemed so wonderful, so perfect. But it had all been a facade.

As Isabelle rose to clear the table, James stopped her.

"I found out that I will have to stay in Chicago until Friday. But I'll be home by six; then we can celebrate your birthday," he told her.

She forced herself to smile, "I'm so glad."

"I do worry about leaving you for two nights, though. All alone."

"I'll be fine, James," she assured him. "I feel perfectly safe with the alarm system."

He took her hands in his, squeezing them so tightly it almost hurt.

"I couldn't bear it if something happened to you while I was gone. You are everything to me, Isabelle. You are my life."

She looked in his eyes, sensing the sincerity of his words. Words he thought she wanted to hear, but which only convinced her further that a love like his would continue to destroy and suffocate her, until she could no longer stand to exist. She was merely the object of his obsession, not a person with needs, feelings, and dreams of her own. His love was one-sided, completely selfish. There was no room in their relationship for what she wanted in life.

And in that moment, as he confessed his love and devotion for her, she made the decision.

She was leaving.

"Who were you talking to?" she asked James as he came to bed. He'd spent Tuesday evening packing for his trip. She'd spent it trying to formulate a flawless escape plan. She could leave no trace.

"I called Mother," he said. "I don't want you to be alone."

"James—"

"She's going to come and stay with you," he told her firmly.

Her heart stopped. Her breath froze in her throat. His mother couldn't come here.

"I don't need a baby-sitter," she said calmly, but inside, her mind was screaming. This was her only chance. If she was going to go, she had to go now.

"I'd feel much better leaving knowing that she'll be here with you," he said matter-of-factly. "It's decided. She'll be here tomorrow afternoon."

Chapter 4

The news blared from the television the next morning as James finished packing for his trip.

"Looks like we're in for a bad storm while I'm gone," he said, closing the lid on his suitcase.

Isabelle heard him but didn't answer. She hadn't slept all night, tossing and turning, her thoughts racing. Now that she'd made the decision to leave, everything was different. The thought of waiting on James hand and foot was unbearable. To spend the rest of her life pleasing him, enduring his punishments, and existing as an empty shell of a person—she knew she would rather die.

Additionally, being with his mother for three days would be a torturous hell. Her constant lecturing, nitpicking, and nonstop praise for her wonderful son were more than Isabelle could bear.

"Isabelle?" James's voice broke her thoughts.

"I'm sorry, what did you say?" she answered.

"I said it looks like there's a storm system heading this way. We could have some bad weather. I'm glad Mother's coming so you won't be alone."

Isabelle didn't answer. Her stomach churned, causing bile to rise in her throat. The only thing that kept her going was the thought of escaping from her prison. But how? How?

"We'll be fine," Isabelle managed to say.

She sat in a chair, watching him pack, wishing those were her suitcases and her plane ticket to anywhere but here.

He stopped tying his tie and turned to look at her. "Are you all right? You don't look well." He walked over and felt her forehead. "Maybe you should go back to bed."

"I will," she told him. "I am feeling sick."

"Too much Kung Pau Pork?" he said lightly.

She gave him half a smile. "Probably." She knew the last thing to do was alert him that anything was wrong. She didn't want him to cancel his trip. She could always tell his mother she was sick and spend the next three days in bed. At least that would be better than enduring her presence.

He finished dressing, checking his reflection in the mirror several times, then approached her.

"I'll call you tonight when I get to the hotel. I'll be in meetings all day, but if you need me, just call," he said, kneeling down beside her.

She smiled and nodded.

"Are you going to miss me?" he asked, leaning in closer.

"Of course," she replied, not wanting to endure a kiss from him.

"I'll make it up to you when I get home. I have something very special planned for you," he said, nuzzling his nose against her chin.

She flinched since it was her bruised side, and fought the urge to tell him she had something planned for him as well. She didn't know how, but she wasn't about to let this window of opportunity close on her. If God had truly given her this chance to leave, then she prayed He would help her find a way to do it, with or without James's mother around.

"What time does your plane leave?" she asked.

He glanced at the clock on the bed stand. "At nine. I'd better get going." He kissed her again. Isabelle prayed it would be the last time she would ever have to endure his kiss.

"Have a nice trip," she said, smiling dutifully.

He was just about to leave when he exclaimed, "I almost forgot." He opened his briefcase, pulled out a sack, and handed it to her. "Give this to Mother when you see her. She's been wanting one of these for her collection."

Isabelle nodded, knowing he expected her to take the assignment seriously. She, on the other hand, thought the whole Beanie Baby collection fad was tiresome, and was glad it had finally fizzled. Still, it was apparent that Marlene wasn't going to quit until she had a complete collection.

"I'll make sure she gets it," Isabelle assured him.

"Tell her to lock it up with the others," he insisted with a piercing gaze.

Not understanding what was so important about a ridiculous toy animal, Isabelle promised that she would give it to Marlene the first moment she saw her. Only then did he seem convinced enough to finally leave.

A sense of relief filled her as she heard his footsteps travel down the stairs, through the kitchen, then out to the garage. The creak of the garage door opening and the sound of his car engine brought her to her feet.

Peeking out the bedroom window, she watched him drive away. One last look, she told herself. One final glimpse of the man who had controlled everything about her except her thoughts and her heart.

But not anymore. It was up to her now. No one else would save her. If she wanted out, she had to do it herself.

She thought of her father and mother. Were they looking down at her from heaven? Were they trying to send her the message that it was time for her to get out?

She liked to think they were. That maybe they had a hand in creating this chance for her to escape.

She whispered a plea heavenward. "Mother, Father, if you're there, please help me. I'm scared and I'm not sure how I'm going to do this, but I know I need to leave. If I don't I will die, by his hand or by my own. Please, she begged, help me."

Isabelle's mind operated on overload the rest of the day. How could she pull this off? How could she not only leave, but have the assurance that James wouldn't come after her?

She paced around the house like a caged lion. Her heart jumped every time she heard a car drive by, afraid that James had changed his plans and come home instead. Looking out the window, she saw black clouds filling the sky. Just as the weatherman had predicted, the storm front was moving in, bringing with it a strong wind that tossed the delicate red and yellow tulips in her flower garden to and fro.

She hadn't yet heard from James's mother but expected to any minute. If she knew her mother-in-law, she'd come storming in, barking orders and insulting Isabelle in that subtle way only she could do. It was no secret that Marlene felt her son had married beneath him when he married Isabelle. She never let Isabelle forget it, either.

Isabelle had never met James's father. He had died when James was just a young boy. Marlene had come from a wealthy family, and money wasn't a problem for her. She lived a life of luxury and raised her son on her own. The Dalton family had an incredible art collection which hung in the family manor where Marlene lived alone with her three Pekinese and her staff of ten. Her work at a local art gallery was merely a way to keep her involved in Boston's "high society" crowd.

Along with the Dalton art collection, Marlene had myriads of other collections: nativity scenes from other countries, Lladró porcelain pieces, and, of course, her extensive collection of Beanie Babies, which James had lavishly contributed to. In fact, Isabelle had a hunch that many of the Federal Express packages that arrived at their home were rare Beanie collectibles. They arrived from all over the world, many, she was surprised, from Africa. Who knew that there was such a network of Beanie Baby collectors in Africa?

Isabelle found it odd that Marlene bothered to collect the stuffed animals and even stranger that James had become so impassioned with helping Marlene complete her collection, but Isabelle had learned long ago that if they wanted her to know something, they'd tell her. Otherwise, she kept her mouth shut and stayed out of their business.

Rain pelted the glass as the clouds began to release their hold. Even though it was only three in the afternoon, it was nearly dark outside.

The phone rang, startling Isabelle. She answered it, dismayed to hear her mother-in-law's voice on the other end.

"I won't be able to get away as early as I'd planned," Marlene told her. "We've had a bit of trouble here at the gallery and I can't leave until we've got it taken care of."

"That's fine," Isabelle told her. "I'm not going anywhere."

"How's the weather out your way?" Marlene asked.

"It's pretty stormy. I think we're supposed to get quite a bit of rain tonight."

"I hate driving that road to your house in bad weather. I probably won't even get out of here until seven or eight," Marlene complained.

The window of opportunity had just opened itself a little wider, but Isabelle knew not to appear too eager.

"I haven't been feeling well today," Isabelle told her mother-in-law. "I'm just planning on going to bed early. You're welcome to wait until morning, if that helps. Oh, and James left something for you," she remembered to tell her mother-in-law. The last thing she wanted was to suffer James's wrath because she'd forgotten to follow his orders.

Maybe Marlene was just in one of her moods, but Isabelle was surprised to hear what the woman said next. "I hope it's not another one of those wretched Beanie Babies. James has given me more of those ridiculous things than I know what to do with."

Isabelle didn't know how to answer. James acted as though his mother expected him to find every Beanie Baby issued, no matter where in the world he had to search, no matter what the price. But his mother had just said that she didn't want anymore of the "wretched" things. It didn't make sense, but Isabelle knew better than to say anything about it.

Marlene released an annoyed sigh as if it were an imposition for her to come out and stay with her in the first place.

"James won't be very happy with either of us if I don't come out," Marlene stated.

"He wouldn't want you to drive in bad weather, either," Isabelle suggested.

"I suppose not," Marlene said.

A voice in the background broke into the conversation. "Tell him I'll be right there," Marlene snapped at the person. "Isabelle, I have to run. I'll be there first thing in the morning."

"Okay—"

Click. The line went dead.

Isabelle looked at the receiver in her hand. Her mother-in-law wasn't coming.

She was alone. Alone for one entire evening. It was now or never. In a split second she had decided.

Finding the number for the airline, she called to make a reservation. Without a credit card they would hold her seat for twenty-four hours, which was plenty of time to get on the 12:40 red-eye flight to London.

Next she had to do something about her appearance. The less she looked like herself, the less chance she had of being spotted.

She crossed her fingers, hoping that James wouldn't call until after his meeting, and decided to hurry to the store.

With her stomach in knots, she drove quickly to the nearest drugstore. The light rain from earlier had turned into a torrential downpour. Negotiating the wet roads carefully, she pulled into the parking lot. Keeping a scarf on her head and wearing her sunglasses to disguise her appearance, Isabelle ran inside and found what she needed.

With her purchase in her hands, she ran back to the car. She didn't have any time to waste. Pulling onto the busy road, she headed home with a constant prayer in her heart. She knew if she stopped to think about what she was doing, she would probably talk herself out of it. Instead she let her instincts guide her and propel her ahead with her plan.

Without realizing that she'd increased her speed, Isabelle felt the back wheels of the car slip as she took a turn too fast. Her heart lurched into her throat. The back wheels grabbed onto the slick surface of the road, and Isabelle slowed down, berating herself for not being more careful. The last thing she needed tonight was to have an accident or slide off the road into the river.

Slide off the road into the river. The thought stuck in her head.

No, she reasoned, *it's too crazy. It won't work.* Her plan was bizarre enough without doing something like that. And yet . . .

She thought it through carefully and realized that it would solve the problem of what to do with her car. And it would look like an accident.

Could she actually go through with it?

She measured her courage against her options. If she didn't do it, she might never get another chance. Besides, James always told her to drive slower on the winding river road. It would be especially dangerous on wet roads.

She didn't have a choice. She had to do it.

Arriving home, she threw her coat and purse on the counter and ran upstairs to her bathroom. Taking a pair of scissors, she looked in the mirror and grabbed a handful of hair. Just as she was ready to snip, the doorbell rang.

Fear froze the blood in her veins. Her heart stopped beating. For a moment, she wondered who could possibly be at her door, then her hopes crashed at her feet. Marlene. She'd gotten away after all.

Knowing she had to answer the door, Isabelle forced her legs to move. Tears stung her eyes as she descended the stairs. She'd almost made it. She'd actually gotten the guts to escape, to finally flee this prison, and her mother-in-law arrived, blocking her path to freedom.

Yanking the door open, expecting to find the pinched, proper face of her mother-in-law, Isabelle was surprised to find the doorstep empty.

She stepped outside and looked in every direction, but saw no one. The downpour of rain continued. Shivering with cold and nerves, Isabelle headed back inside.

Taking the steps to her bedroom slowly, she listened for noises outside. Why would someone just ring the doorbell and leave? Her mother-in-law wouldn't; in fact, she wouldn't even ring the bell, she'd just come in. She had her own key to their house.

Trying to shake off concern that something was going to go wrong with her plan, Isabelle returned to her bathroom.

Am I really doing this? she asked the reflection in the mirror, the bruise on her cheek faint underneath the layer of makeup, still painful to touch.

Yes, she told herself. *You have to do this.*

Before anything else could happen, or she could change her mind, she grabbed a handful of hair and chopped it off to her shoulder. Carefully she put the locks of blonde hair in a garbage bag. She continued cutting until her hair was as even as she could get it, making sure to put every strand in the garbage sack.

Next she read the instructions on the hair dye and proceeded to turn her hair from light honey blonde to a deep copper-red. The processing seemed to take forever, and with every tick of the clock she grew more anxious. What if Marlene's meeting ended early and she decided to come tonight? What if James's plans changed and he came home? It was enough to drive her crazy.

Finally she was able to rinse out the dye.

The stranger's face in the mirror stared back at her. In her emerald green eyes, Isabelle saw sparks of fear and panic. But she also recognized something deeper. With the help of the shoulder-length copper waves framing her face, Isabelle recognized the emergence of her former self. The person inside who had been hidden and secreted away for so many years. Someone who was finally given permission to come out into the light, to live again.

A tremulous smile crept onto her lips, and she blinked as tears stung her eyes. There was no turning back now.

Stuffing the hair dye supplies, the towel, and any remaining traces of her transformation into the garbage bag, Isabelle checked the bathroom for any sign that would give her away. Even one stray hair, one drop of dye, would be enough.

Convinced that nothing was left, she turned out the light and went to her closet. Bypassing the designer clothes, the expensive shoes, and the dazzling jewels, she pulled out her suitcase and removed the shoe box. This was all she could take with her. It had to look like she wasn't planning on going anywhere, like she wasn't leaving. It had to look like she'd met her misfortune during an innocent trip to town.

Replacing everything just the way it was, Isabelle took one last look at her belongings and turned out the light. Carrying her shoe box and garbage bag with her, she went to the kitchen. It was nearly nine o'clock. Her plane left at 12:40. She needed to wait just a little longer so there would be less traffic on the road. She'd thought everything through carefully. It would work; she knew it would.

She removed the contents of the shoe box and placed them inside her purse. Then she put the shoe box inside the garbage bag. Suddenly hungry, she opened the fridge to find something to eat. This would be her last meal in this house. From now on she wasn't sure where her meals would come from, but it didn't matter. Hunger was a welcome alternative to being in this house.

There were still cartons of Chinese food left over from dinner the night before. She bypassed those and took an apple and an orange, shoving them into her purse for later. Then she grabbed a bagel. Her nervous stomach couldn't handle much more to eat than that.

Taking a drink from a bottle of Evian, she nearly spit a mouthful of water across the room when the phone rang.

"Hello?" she answered, knowing exactly who was on the other end.

"Isabelle, it's me," James said.

Breathing deeply to calm her racing heart, Isabelle spoke as evenly as she could. "I'm so glad you called. How was your flight and your meeting?"

"Everything's gone really well. I'm glad I came. It made a big difference to be here in person."

"That's great," Isabelle told him.

"How are you feeling?" he asked, actually sounding concerned.

"My stomach's been upset most of the day," she told him. "I was thinking of turning in early tonight, you know, trying to sleep it off," she lied.

"Good idea. How's Mother?"

She knew she had to be honest about this. Everything had to appear normal. There had to be no indication whatsoever that anything out of the ordinary was happening.

"You're not going to like this," she said. "But she's not coming until in the morning."

"What!" he exclaimed. "You're there all alone?"

"Everything's fine, James. She got hung up at a meeting and we're having quite a storm. The roads are terrible. It wouldn't be safe for her to travel," she explained.

"I don't like you being there all alone. Especially with you not feeling well." His voice was strained.

Isabelle knew he couldn't do anything about it from where he was, and she liked that, for once, he had no control over the situation.

"I'll be fine until she gets here. I'm a grown woman, James. I can take care of myself for one evening," she said.

He sighed. "I guess so. But I want you to stay right there. Don't go out for anything."

"The way I'm feeling," she said, "you don't need to worry."

"Alright then. If our meeting in the morning goes well, I'll try and come home tomorrow night," he said.

"That would be wonderful," she answered, anxiety coursing through her veins.

"Well," he hesitated, "I guess I'd better go. I have some work to do tonight."

"And I think I'll go take a long, hot shower and go to bed," she told him, hoping that would deter him from calling back.

"Take good care of yourself until I get home," he instructed her.

"I will," she told him. She couldn't help adding, "Good-bye, James."

They hung up and Isabelle realized happily that was the final good-bye. There was nothing left to do but turn and walk away, and not look back.

Leaving the light on to make her disappearance look even less intentional, Isabelle put on her jacket, gathered her purse, and went to her car. As she pulled out of the driveway, she looked at the front door to make sure she had left the porch light on, and noticed something on the front step.

Stopping the car, she ran up the walk to see what it was.

Federal Express. *So that's who rang the doorbell and left.*

She picked up the package, noting its familiar letter-sized shape and squishy lump in the middle. The return address was somewhere in Africa, like so many of the others they'd received. Hurrying back to the car, she tossed the package into her bag and without thinking, buckled her seat belt. Then she put the car in gear and drove off without a backward glance.

Chapter 5

There were only a few cars on the road as she drove toward town. Approaching the prearranged spot, she reviewed her plan one last time. Rain fell heavily, which she couldn't have planned any better. It would only help it look more like an accident.

Pulling off to the side of the road, Isabelle sat in her car for a moment, gathering her strength, courage, and belongings. This was it, the place where she parted ways with her old life. The moment of truth.

Knowing she had to leave the car running, the wipers and the lights on, she opened the door. Setting her things on the wet ground outside, she kept one foot on the brake while she watched and waited for just the right moment. With no cars coming in either direction, she quickly stepped outside, grabbed her belongings, and ran for the cover of some trees.

From her hiding spot, she watched as her pearl-white Lexus rolled down the embankment, bouncing over rocks and undergrowth, then plunged into the swift, icy waters of the river below. The current quickly flipped the car on its side, its headlights flashing wildly across the churning waters. Isabelle held her breath, hoping the lights wouldn't attract attention. She noticed the car door stayed open, which was what she'd hoped. That would help explain why her body wasn't inside.

The car began to glide downstream as it sunk lower and lower in the water, the headlights finally dipping under the choppy surface. A shiver ran through Isabelle's body as she thought about being inside that car, the freezing water swirling about her. Several cars passed just then, but were traveling too quickly to notice the Lexus in the river. Feeling safe enough to leave her hiding spot, Isabelle opened her umbrella and headed for the gas station a quarter of a mile down the road.

She managed to stay off the highway, thrashing along the grassy shoulder of the road. Her garbage bag was large and cumbersome, but she knew it was safer to put it in the dumpster at the gas station than anywhere else.

Soon the lights of the gas station came into view and Isabelle picked up her pace. It was after ten and she didn't want to waste another minute.

When she reached the gas station, she went directly to the pay phone and called a cab to pick her up. Next she located the dumpster at the back of the station and deposited her garbage bag of evidence.

Afraid to show her face inside, she waited by the phone for what seemed like an eternity. She couldn't help glancing back from where she came to see if her car in the river had caught anyone's attention.

Her nerves were strung tight and her adrenaline level climbed even higher. Just when she felt as if she would explode, the yellow cab turned into the gas station. She lifted her hand and the cab pulled up in front of her.

"The airport, please," she said as she climbed in the back. With no questions asked, the driver pulled onto the main road.

Isabelle sat rigidly on her seat. She was almost there.

"Are you comfortable, miss?" the airline attendant asked Isabelle as she settled into her seat.

"I'm fine, thank you," Isabelle replied.

Glancing around at the other passengers on the plane, Isabelle didn't see a familiar face among them. And for once, she was grateful to be alone among strangers. She didn't know them, they didn't know her. That was the way she wanted it.

But she knew she wouldn't feel better until they were in the air, leaving Boston, and James, behind. Forever.

She couldn't believe she'd actually gone through with it. But it was true. Here she was, on a plane to England, by herself. James and his mother, and her life of abuse, were over.

She pulled a mirror from her purse to touch up her lipstick. The reflection in the mirror showed the drastic change in her appearance:

her shorter haircut, the deep copper color of her curls, the anticipation in her eyes as she now looked toward the future. It also reflected the last remaining bruises on her cheek, bruises representing a life she hoped to put in the past.

A slow smile grew on her face as a feeling of pride welled up inside of her. "You did it!" she said to her reflection. "You got away!"

Over the loudspeaker the announcement was made that the pilot was ready for takeoff.

Isabelle was ready, but she couldn't shake the horrible image of James charging through the door of the airplane, finding her, and dragging her off the plane. She knew she was being paranoid, that there was a good chance no one even knew she was missing yet, but still, until they were up in the air, she wouldn't relax.

The sound of the engines and the movement of the plane generated a new feeling inside of her. A feeling of anticipation. What lay ahead for her, she wondered? Where was this new path going to lead her?

She knew she should be frightened, but she wasn't. As unsure of her future as she was, nothing could be worse than what she'd left behind. And that was enough. The freedom she felt already confirmed her decision.

Gripping the armrests of her seat, she braced herself as the plane taxied into position. Then, with a sudden burst of speed, the plane shot forward. First its front, then back wheels, lifted off the ground. Then they were airborne. Isabelle's new life had begun.

Chapter 6

Isabelle was surprised she slept for so long on the plane. Luckily, no one occupied the seat next to her, so she was able to stretch out and get comfortable. When she woke up, she lifted the screen on the window and was blinded by the morning sunshine.

The smells of breakfast filled the cabin and Isabelle eagerly accepted her meal when the airline attendant offered it to her. Never in her life had scrambled eggs, toast, and oatmeal tasted so good. She ate every morsel.

Once the dishes were cleared away, Isabelle opened her purse and removed the letter from her aunt. Looking at the address, she wondered how difficult it would be to get to Westmoor once she reached London. She decided to call her aunt as soon as she arrived at the airport.

Rereading the contents of the letter again, Isabelle prayed that her aunt had been sincere when she'd invited her niece to come visit her in England. If not, Isabelle wasn't sure what she would do. But she wasn't going to worry about that now. Somehow, some way, she would figure things out. If she had to, she could pawn her wedding ring. It was probably worth ten or twelve thousand dollars. Surely she could get a substantial amount from it.

Gazing out the window as the plane descended, Isabelle saw a patchwork of green fields below. The countryside was every shade of green, and breathtakingly lush and beautiful. Soon the fields gave way to scattered homes and farms, then the homes grew closer together until all she could see were homes and apartment buildings.

The airline attendant reminded everyone to return their seats to an upright position and lock in their tray tables. Isabelle couldn't help the buzz of excitement she felt in her stomach. She was arriving in London!

Heathrow Airport proved to be a daunting place for Isabelle. She passed swarms of people as she made the long walk, which seemed like miles, from the international gate to the central building. With each passing moment Isabelle felt smaller and smaller. She had no idea how to get to where she needed to go or who to ask to find out.

Standing in the midst of the thronging crowd, Isabelle stood on tiptoe to see over people's heads, trying to locate an information booth. Turning slowly, she drank in her surroundings as the constant motion of moving bodies bumped and collided with her. Finally, her gaze landed on the word, "INFORMATION."

Relief filled her and she pushed her way through the masses until she found the booth.

"Queue's over there," a brusque man in a rumpled coat and scruffy beard growled at her.

Isabelle looked to where he pointed and noticed a line of people waiting to talk to someone behind the counter. She tried to smile, but with her nerves all on edge she only succeeded in making her lips tremble. The man flashed a crooked, rotten-toothed grin at her, the look in his eye making Isabelle uneasy.

A hollow pit in her stomach flashed a warning sign of caution. She held her purse closer to her body and clutched the straps tightly, turning her attention to the line ahead of her.

Even though the people around her spoke English, she couldn't understand a word they said. The words were spoken so quickly and so slurred together that even when she strained she only made out a word or two.

"Next," the person at the booth called.

Already it was Isabelle's turn, and she hurried to the counter.

"Hello," she said. "I need to get to Westmoor, England, please."

"Come again?" the man said, leaning toward her.

"Westmoor." She enunciated each syllable.

"Westmoor you say?" the man asked with his clipped accent. He punched some information into his computer and waited. "Come on," he encouraged the computer with a swift smack on the monitor. "Ah, good, here it is."

Tearing a printout of information off the printer, he handed the paper to her.

"Follow these instructions," he said. "Next?" he called to the person behind her.

"But—" Isabelle wanted to make sure she understood what to do and where to go.

"Next?" the man called again, and Isabelle was pushed aside.

She looked down at the paper and the words blurred through the sudden onset of tears that stung her eyes. Exhausted and surrounded by unwelcoming strangers, she felt her knees begin to wobble. Suddenly, without warning, doubt flooded in like a tidal wave.

What had she done? Had she completely lost her mind to take off for the unknown like this? Had James discovered that she was missing yet? James . . .

The thought of his name brought forth no pleasant memories, no feelings of fondness or longing. If anything, a shudder of fear crawled up her spine.

She swallowed hard. Even though she was consumed with fear of being alone and uncertain of what the future held, it was nothing compared to her fear of James. Yes, the man ten feet away from her, leering at her, was frightening, but she knew he could truly do nothing to her. With James, her very life was in danger.

And if this was what it took to be free from him, then so be it.

With a deep, refreshing breath, Isabelle wiped the moisture from her eyes and straightened her spine. She could do this. She just had to calm down and think clearly.

James had always done everything for her; he had purchased the kind of clothes he liked her to wear, told her how to wear her hair, took care of any arrangements when they traveled, even made up the grocery list for her. He'd almost brainwashed her into thinking she could do nothing without him. But here she was, in the middle of Heathrow Airport, and she was determined to prove him wrong.

The paper told her to take the Heathrow Express train to Paddington station, which cost approximately twelve pounds. The ride would take anywhere between forty-five and sixty minutes. Once she was there she needed to locate the train departure board and take a train westbound to Bath. From Bath she would take a bus to Wells. Westmoor was just outside of Wells.

It took some searching, but she finally found another booth where she could change her money from American dollars to British pounds. She knew that the airport wouldn't offer the best exchange rate, but she couldn't board the train without money.

With the strange currency—mostly bills and a few coins—deposited into her purse, she followed the signs to the Heathrow Express.

Finally, she was on her way.

With two hours to kill before her train left for Bath, Isabelle decided it was time to call her aunt and tell her she was on her way. She bought a phone card to use with the public telephones, and could barely dial the number, her fingers were trembling so badly.

The ring of her aunt's phone was a flat, toneless buzz. *Buzz-buzz.* She waited. *Buzz- buzz.*

After four or five signals, an answering machine came on. Isabelle hung up the phone without leaving a message. It would be better to talk to her aunt directly.

Fighting off the fear that she might have the wrong number or that her aunt was gone on vacation somewhere or had moved, Isabelle decided she needed a few things to get by. All she had were the clothes on her back and what was in her purse.

Venturing around the station, then finally stepping outside, Isabelle took in a breath of London air. The smell of exhaust lingered with a hint of a recent rain shower. Steam rose from the pavement as a warm afternoon sun shone brightly. Car engines and honking horns, voices young and old, and the faraway sound of a siren filled the air. It was all strange, but somehow exciting.

Near the station she found a souvenir shop that had every possible tourist item needed, at prices, she was sure, were completely unreasonable. She bought undergarments, a toothbrush and toothpaste, hair items, deodorant, and a light blue cotton blouse. Everything else she'd have to buy when she got settled.

She also bought a bag of "crisps," which appeared to be the equivalent of American potato chips, and a bottle of Evian. Hurrying back to the station, she found a bench where she could wait for her train and have something to eat.

She watched the passengers swarm around the bustling station until her train finally pulled up with a screech and a hiss. Streams of people poured from the train, and once the dock was cleared the conductor blew a whistle, signaling that passengers could board.

Holding tightly to her meager belongings, Isabelle climbed aboard and found an empty compartment where two bench seats faced each other. Not wanting to face backward, Isabelle took a seat and waited anxiously for the next leg of her journey to begin.

From the train window, Isabelle gazed at the lovely English landscape of pasture and dale, working farms and beautifully manicured stone villages, with stretches of wild heather moorland and dense wood blanketing the slopes and swells of rolling hills.

The view went on like this for several hours. Occasionally Isabelle spotted the majestic ruins of a medieval castle or the lofty spires of a Gothic cathedral. Stone walls stretched out across the hills, crisscrossing like delicate latticework on a lush green blanket. The splendor of the hills and the tranquility of the misty clouds transformed the view to a land of fairy tales and magic. Before her lay Camelot, where knights in shining armor proved their love in battle, and damsels in distress might hope that their true love would rescue them from fates worse than death.

Such had been her life with James, a fate worse than death. It had been so bad, in fact, that she was willing to risk her life for something better. And anything was better than how her existence with James had been.

A feeling of peace she hadn't known for months, even years, settled in, calming her fears of the unknown. She didn't know what to expect, but she felt an optimism grow inside of her. A hope that here, in all this beauty, surrounded by history and legends, she would find a new life. A better life.

A grinding sound and the drag of the slowing train caused Isabelle's heartbeat to race. She wasn't there yet, but the longest stretch of her journey was over. She was in the city of Bath.

To her relief the bus terminal was near the train station, and she easily found her connection to the city of Wells, a forty-minute bus ride away. With time to kill she read a plaque that briefly told the history of the city. She was fascinated to learn that in 1702 Queen Anne had made the first royal trek from London to the old Roman city named Bath because of the natural hot springs located there.

This trek launched a fad, making Bath the most celebrated spa in England. Unfortunately, the city had suffered great destruction in 1942 at the hand of the Luftwaffe pilots, who had seemed more intent on bombing historical buildings than hitting military targets.

As far as Isabelle was concerned, the English had done a remarkable job restoring the city. As she gazed down the cobbled roads and gingerbread buildings, with window boxes overflowing with bright pink and vivid red ivy geranium, the city looked more like a picture out of a storybook than a real-life scene before her eyes. The streets thronged with tourists. Shops, pubs, and restaurants were filled with people. Delicious aromas filled the air, mingling with the delicate fragrance of flowers and a soft breeze. The sky was still overcast, but the dove-gray clouds held no threat of rain.

Before her bus left, Isabelle took the opportunity to use the "loo," a term she heard used by most of the English travelers around her. Then she attempted once more to reach her aunt, but again the telephone rang without answer. A hollow feeling grew in the pit of her stomach, but she was determined to stay optimistic; her aunt's invitation to come and visit remained in her memory.

Within minutes she was on board a bus, bound for the city of Wells, her last stop before Westmoor.

Twenty-one miles later the bus pulled up to a small white stucco building with a wooden bench in front.

From a tourist pamphlet she'd picked up at the bus station in Bath, Isabelle read that Wells was considered the smallest city in England. It was also considered a "medieval gem" because of its famous twelfth-century cathedral. Anxious to continue on to Westmoor to find her aunt, Isabelle made a mental note to come back and visit the city and its famous cathedral.

She stepped inside the small building to ask for directions and try to telephone her aunt one more time. Finding a public telephone just inside, she made the call, praying fervently that someone would be home. But still, there was no answer. Disappointed and concerned about dropping in unannounced, Isabelle asked the gentleman behind the counter for directions to Westmoor.

"Westmoor, you say?" his reply came quickly, his words slurred together so that Isabelle had difficulty understanding him.

"You're American, are you?" he asked, peering at her closely through the lenses in his glasses, then sliding them down the bridge of his nose and studying her again without his glasses.

"Yes, I'm American."

"I like Americans," he said, his eyes shifting from side to side. "But you just missed the bus to Westmoor and we haven't another one for two hours."

"Two hours?" She didn't particularly want to wait around for the next two hours.

"If you're up to walking, it's a quick jaunt to Westmoor. Only five, six kilometers westward if you take the footpath." He looked at her over the tiny glasses perched on the end of his nose. "Take you a little over an hour."

Weighing her options, Isabelle made her decision. "I guess I'll walk then."

"It's a pleasant walk," he said with a nod. "Just follow New Street until you reach a narrow cobbled passageway with a sign that says 'West Mendip Way'."

Isabelle paid close attention to his words, trying to memorize the directions exactly as he said them.

"The footpath takes you past the Cathedral School, over a bridge, and near the radio tower. Once past the bridge you'll see St. Cuthbert's church. Follow the path there through the fields and last bit of farmhouses, and you'll arrive in Westmoor."

Isabelle repeated his directions to make sure she had them right.

"Might want to refill your water flask before you go." He pointed to a water cooler in the corner.

Isabelle gave him an appreciative smile and did as he said. With a full water bottle and a deep breath, she set off down the road called New Street, watching carefully for the cobbled passageway.

Fluffy white clouds floated lazily overhead. The day had grown considerably warmer, and Isabelle removed her cotton sweater and tied it around her waist. To her delight the sign announcing *West Mendip Way* appeared before the passageway, and she turned up the cobbled path through a thickly wooded area offering a short reprieve from the sun.

Following the footpath that led up a hill, she noticed a grassy flatland below where a young boy flew a kite in the breeze. As the slope of the land curved upward, a cluster of cows grazed lazily off rich green grass.

The climb grew strenuous as the steep path ran along a ridge overlooking an imposing group of buildings that she determined was the Cathedral School. She crossed the bridge and caught a glimpse of the beautiful St. Cuthbert's church.

Needle-nosed spires and intricate craftsmanship created a breathtaking edifice that towered above clusters of trees, looking down upon the smattering of farms and homes in the valley below.

Standing in front of the church, Isabelle looked upward, where the spires carried her gaze to the heavens. A cool breeze stirred the trees and cooled her sweat-dampened shirt and brow.

In the shadow of the church she felt a moment of peace and tranquility pass over her. A smile played on her lips, and a feeling of freedom and joy filled her heart. She couldn't remember the last time she felt this way. She was all alone in a strange new land, with no plans for her future, yet she felt genuine peace inside.

Filling her lungs with fresh air, which seemed to energize her tired limbs and erase the jet lag that threatened to slow her progress, Isabelle gave the church one last admiring gaze and continued onward.

With each forward step Isabelle felt that much further away from her old life, from the torment and pain she'd lived with for so long. Away from James.

Pushing his memory and name from her mind, she focused on the lush green beauty ahead of her and listened to the twittering of birds in the trees, enjoying the solitude that was finally hers.

As the path began a downward slope, Isabelle felt a rush of anticipation. She prayed that her Aunt Sophie would be home and that she would be happy to see her. Even if her visit proved short and she had to move on, Isabelle was still glad she'd come. This trip signified a change of course for her. It signified her taking control of her life. From now on she would never, ever let someone control her and her happiness again.

The bleating of sheep drifted on the air, growing louder as she followed the path downward to the flat land below. She followed the dirt trail past the band of fluffy white sheep until the path ended abruptly at a narrow, paved road.

Searching for street signs and finding none, Isabelle stood in the middle of the road and wondered which way to go.

"This is just great," she muttered as she dug her water bottle out of her bag. She was hot and tired and hungry, and beginning to feel a bit queasy as well.

From out of nowhere, the growl of an engine filled the air. Roaring out of the field onto the road like a charging bull came a tractor at full speed. Isabelle screamed, dropped her water bottle, and jumped out of the way just in time.

As the driver whizzed by, he looked at Isabelle with alarm. He slowed the tractor immediately, then brought it to a complete stop.

Looking at the flattened water bottle on the spot where she'd been standing, Isabelle covered her racing heart with her hand and took in several ragged breaths. He'd nearly run her down.

"Flippin' heck! What are you doing in the middle of the road!" the man yelled as he hurried toward her. "I could've killed you."

"I'm sorry." Isabelle took several steps back, frightened by the raging tractor driver. "I didn't hear you coming."

"Are you okay?" he asked, his expression softening.

"Yes," she assured him, straightening up. "I'm fine."

He lifted his cap, scratched his head, then positioned the cap again. "This road is for cars, not people."

"I said I'm sorry," she tried again. "I'm not familiar with this area."

"Any bloke could tell that," he answered. "Who are you anyway?"

She wasn't about to tell this "English chap" who she was.

"What are you doing here?" he demanded, not waiting for an answer to his first question.

Again, she didn't answer.

"Well then, where are you going?" he insisted, wiping a trickle of sweat off his brow with the back of his hand.

Isabelle rolled her eyes with annoyance. Even though she'd taken an immediate dislike for the man, she had to admit she needed his help.

"I'm going to Westmoor," she announced.

"Westmoor!" he exclaimed. "By way of the old sheep trail?"

"The man at the bus station in Wells gave me directions," she returned with an obstinate tilt to her chin.

The tractor driver shook his head. "Old Nigel there is convinced we're still at war with the Germans. Any time an airplane goes overhead, he dives for cover. A bit senile, he is. You should've waited for the bus."

She didn't tell him she agreed. "Are you telling me this isn't the way to Westmoor?" she asked, more than a little concerned.

"Not directly, but you can get there from here. That is, if you're willing to swim through the river a bit. It would've been easier to follow the post road, though."

"How do I get to the post road?" she asked with a sigh.

"It's another five kilometers back that way." He pointed past his tractor to the right. "Then you meet up with the post road and it will take you right into town."

Isabelle's shoulders slumped. How long was five kilometers? With blisters on her feet and a pounding headache, Isabelle didn't know how much longer she could go.

"Listen," the man said, his voice growing kind, his eyes showing sympathy, "if you don't mind riding on the tractor, I can give you a lift into town."

Isabelle looked at the tractor without enthusiasm until her aching feet reminded her of what five kilometers might feel like.

"Thank you," she said. "I would appreciate it."

Chapter 7

With both of them sharing the tractor seat, the ride was bumpy, hot, and a little too cozy for Isabelle's liking, but every time she thought about her painful blisters, she told herself to be grateful for the ride, even if it was on a dusty, old tractor.

"So, who do you know in Westmoor?" the man asked.

Isabelle's protective wall grew immediately higher, and she pretended not to hear. There was a chance that James would learn the truth and try to find her. Having complete strangers nosing about her business sent up red flags of caution all around her.

The road, probably as ancient as some of the cathedrals and castles in the area, left a lot to be desired. As Isabelle was thinking how she might answer his question, the tractor hit a giant pot hole. She nearly fell off the seat, but the driver grabbed hold of her before she tumbled to the ground.

Clutching his arm tightly, she thanked him and continued to keep hold of his arm as the farm road finally joined the post road, which wound downward into the village, where a sign welcomed her to the city of Westmoor, population 15,000. A small river ran through the center of town, where a three-arched stone bridge spanned its width. On either side of the cobbled street were quaint storybook buildings. She made out some shops and pubs along the main street, which was also lined with rows of gabled homes. There were more homes along streets that wound along wooded hills, giving way to stretches of farm land with cow-filled pastures and lovely farm houses. A majestic old church with lofty spires stood sentinel over the village.

Isabelle felt like she'd stepped back in time. She could easily see King Arthur or Sir Lancelot riding through town, and peasants selling their wares in the village square.

The driver stopped before the bridge and turned onto a dirt road running parallel to the river. "Hope you don't mind if I drop you here. I'm expected over at McDougal's farm shortly."

Doubting she had much of a choice in the matter, she shook her head.

"So, who is it you said you know in Westmoor?"

Realizing that she'd probably bring more attention to herself by refusing to answer, she said casually, "Sophie MacGregor."

"You know Sophie?" he asked with some surprise.

Isabelle couldn't say she knew her aunt. She'd been four years old when her family moved to America.

"She's my grandmother's sister," Isabelle explained, sharing more information than she wanted to.

"Well, well," he said, nodding his head. "She never mentioned anything about you coming to visit."

"You know my aunt?" Isabelle asked, changing the subject.

"Very well. Well enough that I'm certain she would have mentioned you were coming," he persisted.

"Could you please tell me how to get to her house?" Isabelle asked, avoiding his comment.

His gaze narrowed. He studied her, as if trying to figure her out, making Isabelle uncomfortable. She slid off the tractor seat and gave him a questioning glare.

"Oh, right, you want directions." He snapped out of his trance. "Follow the street through town until you get to the Pig and Fiddle Pub at the end of the row. Turn left there and follow the lane. It will twist and turn about, but Swan Cottage is at the very end of the lane. You can't miss it."

"Swan Cottage?" Isabelle asked.

"Where she lives," he said, surprised at her question.

"Oh, yes, of course," she said with an embarrassed laugh, as if she'd just remembered the name of the cottage.

"You'll see the ruins of Dunsbury Castle on the ridge above," he told her.

Isabelle smiled her thanks.

"See you 'round, then," he said with a wave of his hand.

Isabelle turned to head up the road.

"By the way," he called.

She stopped and looked at him.

"The name is Ethan. Ethan Wilde."

Isabelle smiled and waved. "Thanks for the ride, Ethan Wilde." Then she turned and started walking. Behind her the tractor engine idled several moments longer before she heard Mr. Wilde grind it into gear and start moving.

Somehow she knew this wouldn't be the last she saw of Mr. Ethan Wilde.

Mr. Wilde's directions had proved exact and Isabelle soon found herself walking down a shady lane, where the branches on the over grown trees from both sides of the road touched in the middle, creating a leafy canopy cover.

Anticipation built inside of Isabelle until she felt her stomach bunch up in knots. How was her aunt going to react to her showing up out of the blue? But even more bothersome was her next question . . . What was going on back home? Had James discovered she was missing yet?

Her mind whirled at the possible scenario back in Boston: James calling to check on her and getting no answer; James calling his mother to have her go to the house and check on her; James flipping out when Isabelle and her car were missing.

The mere thought of James in a frenzy brought panic to her heart. He was capable of anything when pushed to the limit. And while she might give him more credit than he deserved, she knew that if she left even a shred of evidence that she wasn't in that car when it went into the river, he would find it. And he would also find her.

Pushing the terrifying thought from her mind, Isabelle came to the end of the road. An arch led to the pathway to the front door. Flanking either side of the flagstone walkway leading to the cottage were brightly colored flowers and a beautifully manicured lawn.

Isabelle stepped through the vine-covered arch and looked for the first time at Swan Cottage.

The cottage was brilliant white plaster crowned with a thatched roof. Large picture windows flanked either side of the front door, which was painted a glorious shade of geranium red. Beneath each window, wooden planter boxes held fragrant and colorful blooms.

Windows on the second floor peeked out underneath the graceful overhang of the thatched roof; they too were decorated with planter boxes overflowing with colorful flowers.

Standing before the front door, Isabelle looked at the doorbell, feeling her stomach flutter and tense. This was it, the moment of truth. Either her aunt would welcome her or send her packing. Her heart yearned for the unconditional and sincere love of family. A love that was kind and nurturing.

She pushed the button and held her breath as she waited for someone to answer. In the distance birds chirped happily in the trees, a bee buzzed busily from flower to flower, and a soft breeze tingled the wind chime hanging on the porch.

No answer. Her aunt still wasn't home.

Turning from the door, she decided to wait a while in hopes that her aunt would return home soon.

Following a path of stepping-stones around the side of the house, Isabelle walked to the backyard, marveling at her aunt's well-tended and lovely yard. A large sweeping lawn stretched out like a lush, green carpet. In one corner a weeping willow draped its long, graceful branches to the ground like a leafy curtain, while beds of flowering bushes and wild flowers framed the perimeter. A white, wrought-iron table and chairs sat on a patio in the shade, and rows of a neatly tended garden showed the promise of a bounteous harvest in the fall. But the feature that took her breath away was the lovely pond, with lily pads and banks of pussy willows and reeds, and a cheerful, bright red rowboat tucked away against the wooden dock.

It wasn't until Isabelle walked to the farthest corner of the property and looked past the trees at the ridge beyond that she saw the ruins of a magnificent castle.

What had Mr. Wilde called it? Dunsbury Castle?

The gray stone towers and majestic turrets stood proud amid crumbling walls which most likely had once been a commanding presence in the land.

Goose bumps tingled her arms, sending chills up her spine. How many people had a castle practically in their backyard? It seemed to be a fairy-tale land, a place where dreams came true. Could this be where she could finally realize *her* dreams of peace and solitude?

As if being summoned by her thoughts, a voice in the distance called, "Romeo. Romeo. Where in the world are you, Romeo?"

She wondered if it was her imagination, but the voice called for Romeo again.

Isabelle stiffened. The person, a woman, was coming her way. *Was it Juliet?* she thought sardonically.

"Rome—" the woman came around the corner and saw Isabelle. She froze in midstride.

"Hello," Isabelle said quickly, knowing she'd startled the woman. "I'm looking for Sophie MacGregor. Do you know—"

The woman gasped, her hands covering her mouth.

"I'm sorry, I didn't mean to—"

"Is . . . Is . . . Isabelle?" the woman finally said, reaching out her hand toward Isabelle. "Is it you? Is it really you?"

Surprised that the woman recognized her, Isabelle nodded her head. "Yes. Are you my Aunt Sophie?"

The woman walked toward Isabelle with a look of disbelief on her face. "You're here. You came."

Isabelle walked toward her aunt. "I'm sorry I didn't call first."

Sophie took Isabelle's hands in hers and looked at her with tear filled eyes. "You're so beautiful, just like your mother. Oh, my dear . . ." She pulled Isabelle into a hug as she dissolved into tears. "I can't believe you're really here."

Isabelle hugged her great-aunt as waves of emotion filled her. It had been such a long, long time since anyone had shown any warmth or affection towards her. She'd forgotten how it felt to be wanted or loved. Immediately she felt that from her aunt.

Sophie held her tightly, sobbing on Isabelle's shoulder. "I never thought I'd see you again. I sent so many letters, and I never heard from you."

"I know. I'm so sorry," Isabelle apologized. Her aunt's tears surprised her. Her aunt continued to hold her, crying. Isabelle wasn't prepared for such a response. She'd hoped her aunt would be happy to see her, but Sophie seemed completely overwhelmed with emotion.

At last Sophie stepped back to look in Isabelle's face. "You have no idea how happy I am to see you, to have you here finally. After all these years."

"It's wonderful to see you, too," Isabelle told her, grateful that her aunt was glad to see her.

"Looking into your face is like looking into your mother's face," Aunt Sophie said.

Isabelle recalled that Sophie had never had any children, so she'd treated her niece, Isabelle's mother, Jacqueline, as her own. And when Jacqueline's own mother died, Jacqueline had gone to live with her Aunt Sophie while her father worked on the railroad. She'd come to love Sophie as much as her own mother.

"You must be exhausted and hungry," Aunt Sophie observed. "Let's go inside and I'll get you something to eat and you can freshen up. We have so much to catch up on." She looked around for a moment, "Where are your bags?"

Isabelle indicated her purse and the plastic bag from the store containing her earlier purchases. "That's all I have."

Aunt Sophie raised her eyebrows with curiosity, then hooked one arm around her grandnieces's waist. "A light packer. I like that."

Together they went inside the cottage which, despite its ancient air, was not only well kept, but appeared to have every modern convenience possible.

"If I'd known you were coming, I would have readied the guest room. We can open the windows and change the sheets on the bed so everything's fresh and clean," Aunt Sophie told Isabelle as she guided her to an upstairs bedroom.

The room was narrow and long, located directly beneath the eaves of the thatched roof. At one end of the room, a window overlooked the front of the house; at the other end of the room, a window overlooked the backyard and pond. With both windows cracked open, a cool breeze swept through, filling the room with sweet, refreshing country air.

The room held a large bed with a lovely mahogany carved head and footboard and matching wardrobe, in addition to a cushioned chair, an end table, and a lamp.

"You can put your things in here and freshen up if you'd like. I'll go down and make us a bite to eat. I'm a bit hungry myself. Spent the morning in town, and I've been out looking for my dog, Romeo, this afternoon," Aunt Sophie said. "He doesn't run off like this very often."

"Would you like me to help you look for him?" Isabelle offered.

"Heavens no," her aunt said. "He'll find his way home. He quite likes female dogs, you know, even though I had him fixed years ago. Needless to say, his name fits him quite appropriately."

Isabelle smiled. Her aunt's warmth and genuine friendliness had helped Isabelle to feel welcome almost immediately. Even though she hadn't seen her for many, many years, there was a feeling of familiarity that Isabelle liked about the woman.

"Come down when you're ready, my dear," Aunt Sophie told her. "I'll be in the kitchen."

After changing into her only other shirt and washing the miles she'd traveled off her face and hands, Isabelle crept down the old wooden staircase to the main floor. Her aunt was at the counter arranging slices of lunch meat and various cheeses on a platter.

"There you are," she exclaimed when her grandniece entered the room. "You look a might weary, dear. I think that long trip took all the starch out of you. Are you sure you don't want to take a nap?" She carried the platter to the table, where sliced bread and glasses of cold apple juice waited.

"I'll be fine," Isabelle told her. "I slept quite a bit on the plane."

They took their seats at the table and, following her aunt's lead, Isabelle took a slice of bread, several different slices of meat, and a piece of cheese to make an open-faced sandwich. Her stomach was hollow and aching, and her mouth watered at the sight of the food.

"Now," her aunt said after a bite of her sandwich. "You must tell me all about your life in America and what finally brought you to England."

Isabelle didn't want to burden her aunt with the sad details of her life, nor was she ready to share information about her situation back in Boston. She kept her answer vague, leaving out specifics or details.

"There's not much to tell really," she said. "I've lived in Boston ever since I got married. I didn't have a career or a job, although I studied early childhood education in college and hoped to work in a preschool someday. Things between my husband and me haven't gone well for some time, and I finally decided it was time to leave. I mean," she corrected quickly, "move on with my life."

"So, you're getting divorced?" her aunt asked.

Isabelle wasn't sure how to answer. She didn't want to have any further contact with James. She hoped he thought she was dead and that would be the end of it. She couldn't think of any reason she'd need to formally divorce him.

Before she could answer, a strange buzzer sounded from the front room.

"Excuse me, dear. Someone's at the front door." Aunt Sophie got up from the table and went to the other room. Isabelle heard the front door creak open and her aunt's exclamation of joy. "Romeo, you little devil, where've you been?"

A small, whirling dervish of an animal darted into the room, yapping and jumping excitedly. It was her Aunt Sophie's prized Pomeranian dog.

"Found him down by the river, Sophie," a male voice answered. "I knew you'd be wondering where he was off to, so I thought I'd bring him home."

"Thank you, Ethan," Aunt Sophie said. "I looked for him this afternoon without any luck. I didn't make it as far as the river, though. Come in, Ethan. There's someone here I'd like you to meet."

Isabelle turned as her aunt and her guest approached the kitchen. When Sophie stepped inside she had a huge smile on her face. "Isabelle, I'd like you to meet my good friend and neighbor, Ethan Wilde," she said. Mr. Wilde stood beside Aunt Sophie, meeting Isabelle's surprised expression with a delighted one of his own.

Chapter 8

"Mr. Wilde." Isabelle stood and extended her hand. "Nice to see you again."

"Again?" Aunt Sophie exclaimed. "You two have met?"

While Ethan explained to her aunt how they'd "bumped" into each other earlier, Isabelle looked at Mr. Wilde, who looked nothing like he had on the tractor.

This Mr. Wilde wore a pair of light tan slacks and a pale blue oxford shirt, which matched his blue eyes. He had a thick head of dark blonde hair that he wore neatly trimmed in the back but longer on top, where it lay in tousled strands as if he'd just run his fingers through it.

There was nothing of the scruffy farmer she'd met earlier.

"So," Ethan addressed Isabelle, "how are you getting along?"

"Fine," Isabelle answered. "Just fine."

A clatter of footsteps broke their conversation, and into the kitchen ran a young boy, around five or six years old. "Papa, you took too long. I got tired of waiting for you."

Sophie and Ethan chuckled. Isabelle smiled at the adorable little boy in front of her. He had his father's smile and beautiful blue eyes, but his hair was much more blonde, almost white.

"Have you two lads had any supper?" Sophie asked. "I've got plenty to eat here."

"We don't want to impose," Ethan said quickly.

"But Papa, I'm hungry," the boy said.

"Ian Scott, you can wait until we get home." Ethan's voice was firm.

"But Sophie's food tastes better than yours," Ian Scott said.

Sophie looked at Ethan helplessly and shrugged. "It's nothing fancy, but it tastes good," she said, motioning to the empty chairs around the table.

"Who's that, Sophie?" Ian Scott asked, pointing to Isabelle when he sat down.

"That's my grandniece, Isabelle," Sophie introduced them. "Isabelle, this is Ethan's son, Ian Scott."

"It's nice to meet you, Ian Scott," Isabelle told the boy.

"You're pretty," the boy said.

His comment took Isabelle by surprise, and she couldn't help laughing. "Well, thank you. You're pretty handsome yourself."

While the four ate dinner, Isabelle uncomfortably found herself the focus of the conversation. Luckily most of the questions they asked her were about life in America, and she somehow managed to sidestep any questions that grew too personal or uncomfortable.

"So, how long are you planning on staying?" Ethan asked as he started on his second sandwich.

Isabelle swallowed. It was a harmless question for him to ask, but a dangerous one for her to answer. "I have no plans right now. I suppose as long as Aunt Sophie will have me," she said.

"You're welcome to stay as long as you'd like," Aunt Sophie told her. "I've hoped for years that you would come and visit me. I'm not anxious to let you leave anytime soon."

Isabelle was relieved to hear her aunt's words. For now she had a home. A home she felt welcome and loved in. A home she felt safe in.

Ian Scott had finished his meal and was fidgeting with his silverware, obviously having a difficult time sitting still.

"Ian Scott," Sophie said, "I've got a bag of crisps in the cupboard. Would you like to take them and see what's on the telly for a bit?"

The boy's eyes lit up. He flashed a glance at his father, who looked at his son appraisingly, then nodded his permission.

Ian Scott let out an excited whoop of excitement and raced to the cupboard. It was obvious that the boy had done this before, since he knew exactly where the snacks were located.

"The lad's got more energy than's good for him," his father said, shaking his head.

Aunt Sophie nodded. "I'd certainly like some of that energy."

"You'd think he'd play hard enough at day care to use up some of that energy, but some days he comes home even more wound up than when I drop him off," Ethan explained.

"Are things going any better at the day care?"

Ethan shook his head. "Pretty much the same. The children run unsupervised most of the time. Too many children and not enough teachers," Ethan said to Isabelle. "The place gets a little crazy sometimes."

Just then Ian Scott came back into the room. "Nothing good is on," he complained. He put the potato chip bag back in the cupboard.

Ethan pushed himself away from the table and carried his plate to the sink. "That's just as well." He ruffled his son's hair. "We need to get home anyway."

"Ahh, Dad," the boy complained. "But I haven't had one of Sophie's biscuits yet."

"Ian Scott," Ethan said sternly. "Didn't you eat your dinner?"

"I did. I'm still hungry though," the boy told his father.

"He's a growing boy," Sophie said with a chuckle. She retrieved the cookie jar off the counter. "Tell you what," she said, offering the open jar to Ian Scott, "why don't you take one for now and one for later?"

"Wow, thanks," Ian Scott said as his hand dove into the jar and he pulled out several cookies. He took a giant bite of one and with his mouth still full said, "These are the best biscuits ever."

"I don't know why you put up with us," Ethan apologized to the older woman. "Thanks for feeding us, Sophie," Ethan said, giving the woman a quick peck on the cheek. "You're very good to us."

"Same goes for you," Sophie answered.

"Can I come back later and take Romeo for a walk?" Ian Scott asked anxiously.

"I think he's had his walk for the day. How about tomorrow when you get home from day care?" Sophie offered.

"Alright." The boy seemed pleased with the arrangement.

Sophie and Isabelle walked them to the front door and watched as they walked hand in hand down the front path to the graveled road out front. From there, father and son walked up the road.

"They just live down the lane a piece," Sophie told her. "Such a handsome pair, wouldn't you say?"

Isabelle agreed with her. "Where's Ian Scott's mother?"

"Oh dear, now that's a sad story. Why don't we go sit in the garden where it's nice and cool and I'll tell you all about it."

While Aunt Sophie put plastic wrap over the plates of uneaten food, Isabelle put the dishes in the dishwasher. Outside the sun had dropped below the tall trees and the yard was filled with shade.

"It's so beautiful out here. How do you keep up with all the work?" Isabelle asked.

"Ethan helps tend the garden. He does the mowing and edging for me. I'm able to keep up the flower beds and the vegetable garden, but I couldn't do it without his help."

They sat in the chairs near the weeping willow and enjoyed the quiet of the evening.

"So, tell me about Ethan's wife," Isabelle asked curiously.

"Dear Ethan," her aunt said, her voice suddenly sad. "It breaks my heart to think about how hard his life has been. His greatest joy comes from his son. I don't know what he'd do without Ian Scott."

Isabelle listened as she watched a pair of birds pick in the grass for worms.

"His story, in a way, is somewhat like your own parents. Except your father was the American and your mother was from England. Ethan married a girl from America. He was living in London for a while—that's where he met Jennifer. He called her Jenn. She came to London to study for six months at the university. They fell in love and he ended up going over to America and marrying her. They settled down in New York, where he became a policeman."

"A policeman," Isabelle remarked. He seemed much too mild and gentle to go around arresting thugs and criminals, Isabelle thought to herself.

"He worked a lot with youth programs, trying to keep youngsters off the streets and out of gangs," Aunt Sophie told her. "He and Jenny were very happy there, and that was where Ian Scott was born. I guess they'd just bought a little home in the suburbs when the tragedy struck."

"What happened?" Isabelle was captivated by the story.

"They'd gone out for the evening, left the baby home with a sitter. If I remember right they were in the city, went to a play or something like that, and were on their way to their car when they were attacked by some muggers. They gave them all their money and valuables, but one of the men grabbed Jenny, and when Ethan tried to get her away . . . Well, the man had a knife and stabbed her. Jenny died in Ethan's arms."

Isabelle was horrified.

Aunt Sophie dabbed at her eyes with a handkerchief. "He couldn't stay in America after she died. It was just too hard for him. He came back home to be around the rest of his family so they could help him with Ian Scott. He blames himself for her death, you know."

The shadows grew longer, the air taking on a slight chill. Isabelle hugged her arms around her for warmth.

Sophie went on. "Ethan is as fine a man as they come. He works in his father's fields and does cabinetry work as well. Builds beautiful pieces of furniture, he does." Aunt Sophie paused and sighed. "But it's as if he lost part of his soul when his wife died. He's still grieving, he is."

Isabelle thought of how much she missed her parents, how empty her life was without them. She knew of grief. She knew how hollow a person could feel inside after the death of a loved one.

"I've tried to tell him many times that he needs to let go, to forgive himself and move on, but he doesn't seem to believe he deserves to. I don't quite understand his thinking, but it breaks my heart to see him so lonely." Aunt Sophie looked off into the distance, as if drawing upon her own feelings of loneliness to understand how Ethan felt. Isabelle remembered that her aunt had lost her husband to cancer at an early age. She'd been alone ever since.

Isabelle looked at the lines of age and worry etched upon her aunt's face and thought how lovely her aunt still was. She was petite and trim, and wore her soft, gray hair in a short, easy style that flattered her clear blue eyes. It wasn't hard to tell that her aunt was active and conscientious of her health; her cheeks were vibrant, her eyes sparkling.

Isabelle admired her aunt's strength. She'd overcome such great tribulation and still managed to have a healthy, optimistic outlook on life. Isabelle knew she could learn a great deal from this woman and was grateful that the heavens had provided a way for her to come to her aunt. She wondered if she could ever be as independent and strong as Aunt Sophie. Would she ever be able to let go of the last five years and build a future for herself?

"Look," Aunt Sophie said, pointing to the darkening sky.

Isabelle scanned the cloudless sky and saw a giant swoop of white wings. Then, as gentle and graceful as a ballerina, a swan glided down, landing softly on the surface of the pond. There it folded its wings and rested calmly upon the water, where it floated with poise and dignity.

"Swans have been protected by law for many, many years," Aunt Sophie said. "When Dunsbury Castle was occupied by the Earl of Rothsbury, this pond was dedicated to the preservation and protection of swans. We don't get as many now, of course, but we still get a few now and then."

Isabelle was fascinated by this bit of history and couldn't wait to learn more. "I still can't get over your having a castle in your backyard. Who owns it?"

"The Devon family owns the land from the lane out front to the land on the far side of the castle. My father, William Devon, your great-grandfather, was a direct descendent of the Earl of Rothsbury."

"Does that mean we have royal blood in our family?"

"It most certainly does," Aunt Sophie announced proudly. "Being the last surviving child, I am the sole heir to the property. And since my own husband is gone and I have no children of my own, I've often wondered what would happen to the castle and my home." She looked directly at Isabelle. "Swan Cottage is as much your home as it is mine, my dear. I'm so glad that you finally responded to my letters. This legacy you've been left, this land, it's in your blood," she said. "You'll see. The longer you're here, the more it will become a part of you."

Isabelle sat up taller in her chair. She'd never known much about her ancestors, her heritage. Knowing she was of royal descent, that she was somehow a part of this great history, gave her a feeling of belonging she hadn't felt before. A feeling of being anchored, rooted, part of a family. As often as she'd felt alone, she realized now, she wasn't.

"Because your mother was English and your father was American, and you were born in England, you are a citizen of both countries." Aunt Sophie leaned over and took Isabelle's hand in hers. "You belong here, my dear. Welcome home."

That night as Isabelle got ready for bed, she thought about the day she'd had: her arrival in London, her train ride to Bath, her aunt's warm welcome, the story of her ancestors—it was a lot to digest, yet it was all so wonderful. Already she'd lived more in the last two days than she'd lived the entire time she was married to James.

She'd lived the last five years in complete fear and caution, watching every movement she made and checking every word she said. She hoped that somehow, some way, she would be able to put that all behind her and be able to love, accept, and trust again. Her personal feelings, her own needs and hopes, had been pushed down so far that she wondered if she'd ever be whole again.

Placing her few belongings into the wardrobe, Isabelle emptied the contents of her bag and purse. She had nothing with her to remind her of her past, from the life she'd walked away from the day before, except the faint tenderness of a bruise on her cheek. Then she pulled a package from her purse and stared in shock. It was the Federal Express envelope she'd unthinkingly put in her purse the day before. She held the package up to read the address. The sight of her husband's name sent chills through her, as if his name alone would conjure up his presence out of thin air. Quickly opening the bottom drawer of the wardrobe, she shoved the package inside, covered it with a hand-crocheted afghan, and closed the drawer hastily, wanting to get it out of sight.

A sudden breeze wafted through the window, making her shiver. She hurried to the open window and reached up to close it, then paused to look out onto the darkened lane in front of the cottage. For a moment her imagination got the best of her as she thought about James again. Would he believe she was dead? Would he finally let her go? She had to believe that she was safe now, but in the back of her mind remained the haunting fear that he would find her.

Was that how she was to live out the rest of her life? Looking over her shoulder? Wondering if James was around every corner?

She shivered again and slammed the window shut with a loud bang, then closed the blind. Her good sense told her there was no reason to fear, but her insecurities wouldn't subside so easily.

Isabelle slept with the light on that night.

* * *

The loud crowing of a rooster woke her with a start. She'd fallen asleep last night the minute her head hit the pillow, and had slept like a petrified log. She closed her eyes, trying to shut out the faint light filtering into her room, but it was too late. She was awake.

Pulling on her jeans, shirt, shoes, and jacket, Isabelle walked to the window at the back of the room and looked out. The sun hadn't crept over the horizon, yet its glorious light illuminated the landscape in a soft pink glow. A low mist clung to the woods and pond, creating a mystical, magical fairyland, made complete by the commanding presence of the castle on the hill. Isabelle imagined the days gone by when the castle bustled with royalty and servants, grand balls, and knights in shining armor. Then she had an idea. Creeping quietly downstairs so she wouldn't disturb her aunt, she headed out the back door. It seemed like the perfect time to see the castle.

The trail wasn't difficult to find as it wound through the misty, grass-covered hillside. The clean, fresh air tingled Isabelle's lungs, clearing the jet lag from her head. For a while, as she climbed, the castle escaped her view, but when she finally climbed to the top of the trail, its sudden appearance stole her breath.

Surrounded by low, gray mist, the remains of Dunsbury Castle towered majestically in front of her, its rounded twin towers and crumbling walls whispering of the past, where bits of history were tucked between mortar and stone.

Even though the structure was a mere skeleton of its former self, it took little imagination to add billowing flags, guards and sentries, jousting knights, royalty in fine apparel, and gilded coaches.

Smaller squared towers flanked what was left of the main gate. In places, there was still the jagged edge of the battlement surrounding the upper walls. Tiny windows, barely more than slits, were strategically placed in the towers, perhaps used for defense or to simply provide some light inside.

As she drew closer, she had a clearer view of the decrepit state of the castle and felt saddened by its appearance. She wondered what it had been like to live during the days of queens and kings, knights and round tables, magicians and wizards, myths and legends.

Its rays creeping through the doorway, the sun rose higher on the horizon, burning off the mist. A rose-colored light descended upon the ancient stone walls as Isabelle entered the courtyard.

A flutter of wings startled her as several robins took flight at her presence. Her racing heart slowed down as she explored the crumbling interior of the castle. Wasn't there anything they could do to preserve it? It seemed like a shame and an act of disrespect to her ancestors to do nothing but stand by and watch the place deteriorate year after year.

A spiral staircase, made out of stone, remained in one of the rounded towers. Isabelle dared herself to climb up the staircase to get a look from the tower above. Part of the stone wall had fallen away, leaving a large opening in the wall. The rocks seemed to be suspended by magic, as if one big breath of wind could send them crashing down.

Knowing it probably wasn't wise or safe to be up there, Isabelle still couldn't stop herself. She had to go to the top, just once.

The view from above was as grand and picturesque as she'd imagined. Most of the landscape before her was farmland and low, rolling hills. The small, cozy town still slumbered in shadows. The sun's rays hadn't stretched far enough yet to burn the fog that clung to the river banks and dense forests surrounding the area. With the lush green of the landscape and the vivid blue of the cloudless sky, Isabelle felt like a princess, overlooking her kingdom from her tower on the hill. And for a moment a feeling of déjà vu washed over her. Had she stood in this spot before? Seen this view before?

The feeling left as suddenly as it came.

Half-expecting a knight on a white horse to charge out of the trees and present himself before her, she smiled, realizing that it had been many years since she'd thought of fairy tales and magic. Her life had been too full of a harsh reality to allow for daydreams and whims of imagination.

Without warning a chill ran up her spine. She stared for a moment at the shadows below, where the thick trees separated the castle from Swan Cottage. All was silent and still.

Just your imagination, she told herself.

The sun came into full view, and with the lateness of the hour Isabelle realized that her aunt might be looking for her. Telling herself she was being silly, she shook the fear from her and left her perch on high.

She carefully negotiated the stairs and hurried through the courtyard out the castle gate, then, following the path to the cottage, she walked through knee-high grass to the stand of tall trees and listened as birds sang in the trees. A sudden loud thrashing behind her made her stop in her tracks.

She froze in midstride, crouching and listening. Someone was following her.

Immediately her thoughts and fears conjured up the image of James coming after her. She knew, logically, that it just wasn't possible. But she also knew that if he did somehow know where she was, he could conceivably be here. And even if that was a one-in-a-million chance, she still didn't want to wait around and see.

Darting through the trees like a scared rabbit, she ran for the cottage.

Chapter 9

Bursting into the her aunt's backyard, Isabelle streaked across the lawn to the back door. Within minutes, her aunt's Pomeranian came flying across the lawn from the pathway behind her, barking like crazy.

Isabelle turned. "Romeo, you scared me to death!" she exclaimed at the dog who was crazily jumping and running about her feet.

She knelt down and the dog calmed a little, licking her hand and her cheek. After giving him one final pat, she slipped inside and closed the door.

"Isabelle, is that you?" her aunt called from the other room.

"It's me," she replied.

"I was beginning to wonder where you'd wandered off to." Aunt Sophie came into the kitchen dressed and ready for the day.

"I woke up early and thought I'd walk up and see the castle," Isabelle told her. "It's really wonderful."

"You don't remember the castle from when you were young?" her aunt asked, popping two slices of bread into the toaster.

Isabelle looked at her aunt, amazed at her question. "Actually, for a moment while I was up there, it seemed familiar to me. But that's silly, isn't it?"

"Why is that silly?" Aunt Sophie replied, pouring two glasses of orange juice for them. "You and your mother lived with me for several months before you went to America."

"We did?" Isabelle exclaimed, not remembering.

"While your father was in the States working and locating a place for you to live. You used to drag me or your mother up there

constantly. You were convinced you were a princess and told everyone
so. You had these sparkly dress-up shoes, and this purple—"

"—sequined gown with a feather boa!" Isabelle exclaimed. "I
remember. Aunt Sophie, I remember!" Isabelle collapsed against her
chair in amazement. "I'd forgotten all about that. I've forgotten so
much of my childhood," she said with sadness. "Even the memories
of my parents and brother have faded."

Aunt Sophie buttered the toast and brought it to the table, sat
down, and placed her hand tenderly over Isabelle's. "Don't worry
about it, my dear. It will come back to you. Bit by bit. You've been
gone a long time and so have they. The memories are still there; you
just have to stir them up a bit to bring them to the surface."

Her aunt's warm smile and loving expression touched Isabelle's
heart. *Yes,* she thought hopefully, *the memories are still there.* She just
hoped they would come back. It seemed as though her life for the
past five years had sealed her feelings and hardened her soul. It had
been the only way to survive.

Tears stung Isabelle's eyes as she realized she'd finally found a
haven of safety, a place of refuge where she could heal and become
whole once again. "Thank you," she barely managed to say.

"No thanks necessary," Aunt Sophie answered. Then, her brow
furrowed, a look of concern crossed her eyes. "Is everything okay,
dear?"

Isabelle shifted her gaze away from her aunt's face. There was so
much she could tell her aunt, but she just couldn't right now. She
didn't know if she'd ever be able to tell anyone about her past.

"Everything is fine," Isabelle replied, hoping her answer would
satisfy her aunt for now.

Thankfully, Aunt Sophie didn't press her further. But somehow
Isabelle knew her aunt understood that she needed space and time.
Her aunt had suffered great pain and heartbreak in her own life, and
Isabelle felt her compassion and strength.

After the moment of understanding passed, Aunt Sophie asked,
"So, is there anything special you'd like to do today?"

"If it's not too much trouble, I could use a few things. Do you
think we could do some shopping?" Isabelle asked, glad they'd
changed subjects.

"Of course!" Aunt Sophie exclaimed with delight. "I can't think of anything I'd rather do. We have a couple of nice shops right here in Westmoor. And we could stop and have lunch while we're in town."

"That sounds wonderful. I just need a few minutes to get cleaned up," Isabelle said.

She carried her empty glass and half-eaten piece of toast to the sink. She hadn't had much of an appetite, still feeling a bit queasy from the emotionally packed last three days.

"Here, now," Aunt Sophie said, standing up. "I'll get these. You go ahead and get cleaned up. There are clean towels in the cupboard by the bath."

The main street of Westmoor was busy with shoppers and tourists. Aunt Sophie explained that many of the tourists who traveled to the nearby city of Wells to see the famous cathedral and other sites stayed in hotels and bed and breakfast inns in Westmoor.

Aunt Sophie introduced Isabelle to each of the shop owners and townspeople they met on the street. Many were older women stopping at the outdoor market for fresh fruit and vegetables. Isabelle knew she'd never remember all their names but appreciated their warm welcome.

Her aunt didn't ask questions about Isabelle's lack of clothing or necessities, which Isabelle appreciated. Perhaps there would come a time that she would tell her aunt about her situation, but for now she was grateful to push it aside in her mind and forget about it. Still, her eyes searched every face in the crowd and she glanced over her shoulder constantly. She hated that James still had any power or control over her, even across an ocean, and she hoped that in time she would break free of the ties that bound her to him.

After purchasing pajamas, several pairs of pants, shirts, a skirt and top, a casual dress, another pair of shoes, and some makeup and hair items, Isabelle finally felt that she had enough to hold her over until she could find work and start making some money of her own. She was careful not to spend all of her cash, just in case she needed it for anything.

By the time they were finished, Isabelle felt as though her shoes were made of lead, each step took such effort.

"You look like you could use a rest, my dear," Aunt Sophie remarked. "Let's go into this pub and grab a bite to eat."

Grateful for her aunt's suggestion, Isabelle followed her into Merlin's Hideaway, where a lively crowd had gathered for a noonday meal. Aunt Sophie led them to a table in the corner and waved to a young girl behind the bar who was serving lager to a group of men watching a soccer game on a television mounted on the ceiling.

"Good to see you, Sophie," the girl called out when she neared their table. "And who've you got here?"

"This is my grandniece, Isabelle Dalton. She's here from America," Aunt Sophie explained.

"Nice to meet you, Isabelle. I'd have guessed you were Irish with that gorgeous head of red hair," the girl remarked.

"She's got a bit o' Irish in her blood," Aunt Sophie told her. "She was lucky enough to get her mother's hair."

The girl nodded. Isabelle guessed her to be in her early twenties, though the gruffness in her voice made her sound years older. "What can I get you ladies today?"

"They have wonderful fish and chips here," Aunt Sophie told Isabelle. "Their steak and kidney pie is a favorite, too."

"I'd love some fish and chips," Isabelle answered.

"Good choice," Aunt Sophie said. "Make that two."

"How about some tea with that?" the girl offered.

"None for me, thanks," Aunt Sophie said. "I'll take lemonade. How about you, Isabelle?"

"Lemonade for me also," Isabelle answered. Something cold and refreshing sounded wonderful to her.

"By the way," Aunt Sophie caught the waitress just as she was about to leave and pulled the girl down gently so she could whisper something to her. The girl looked at Isabelle, then nodded at Aunt Sophie. Isabelle wondered what was going on but didn't ask.

"So," Aunt Sophie said, "what do you think of our little town?"

"It's charming," Isabelle answered. She loved the cobbled walks and the lack of traffic. "I especially liked that first little shop we went to."

"The one with that light blue dress with the flowers on it?" Aunt Sophie asked.

Isabelle nodded. There had been a lovely rayon dress, nothing fancy, but soft and feminine. It seemed to complement her hair color and hang on her frame just right, almost as if it was made for her. But the price had been a little steep for her. She'd opted for a less expensive cotton dress instead.

"I noticed you had your eye on it," Aunt Sophie said. "That's why—" She lifted a bag onto the table and pushed it toward Isabelle.

Isabelle gasped. "Aunt Sophie, you didn't."

"Go ahead, open it." Aunt Sophie's eyes gleamed with satisfaction.

Isabelle opened the bag, hesitantly at first, then, forcing herself to look, she peered inside. There, folded neatly, was the soft, blue dress. "Really, Aunt Sophie, you shouldn't have done this."

"But it would look so lovely on you and after all, it is your birthday," her aunt said with a giant smile.

Isabelle's mouth dropped open. "How did you—"

"Remember?" Aunt Sophie finished her sentence for her. "How could I forget? You stole my heart as a youngster, with that mischief in your eyes and that curly head of red hair. You were an adorable poppet and I loved you as my own. That's why it means so much to me to have you come back. I've missed you so much."

Isabelle wished she remembered her aunt more. "Thank you," Isabelle told her, feeling a rush of emotion clog her throat. She didn't know how to react to such kindness. She wasn't used to it. "This means so much to me," she managed to say, hoping her aunt wouldn't ask her why she was so emotional.

"Here we are," the waitress interrupted as she approached their table carrying two large platters of steaming, deep-fried fish and thick-sliced French fries, or chips, as Aunt Sophie called them.

Isabelle was surprised to see a single burning candle lit her plate.

"What's this?" Isabelle exclaimed.

"It's your birthday, isn't it?" the waitress asked.

"Yes, but—"

"You're the guest of honor," the waitress told her. "Everybody," she called to the patrons in the establishment. "We have a birthday here. Let's all sing to Isabelle and wish her a happy birthday." Not everyone heard her. "Jasper," she hollered louder, "turn the telly down so we can sing."

The man at the bar reached up and turned down the sound, and to Isabelle's delight and complete embarrassment, everyone in the place sang "Happy Birthday" to her. Then, when the rousing rendition of the song ended, they held up their pints of lager and toasted her heartily.

Even though she was bright red and wanted to hide under the table, Isabelle couldn't deny that she'd never felt more welcomed or a part of a place in her life.

She was completely worn-out by the time they got back to the cottage. The day had grown warm, and coupled with the effects of jet lag that still lingered, Isabelle was only too happy to go to her room and fall asleep on the bed. It was several hours before she awoke.

The sun had dropped lower on the horizon and the trees blocked its intense rays, allowing a cool breeze to drift in through her window. For a moment she leaned against the window frame and watched several swans and a group of mallard ducks float on the pond.

As she descended the stairs she marveled at how immaculate her aunt's house was. Not a speck of dust was allowed to rest for long in the cottage.

She heard her aunt's voice coming from the kitchen and realized she was talking on the phone.

"Yes," her aunt said. "She's here with me now. You could come tonight."

Terror struck Isabelle's heart. Who was her aunt talking to? Had James tracked her down? Had he called looking for her? Her aunt didn't know the situation with James. She wouldn't know that Isabelle needed protection from him.

Now it was too late. He'd found her.

She wanted to run and hide, but her feet were glued to their spot. The edges of her vision grew fuzzy. She had to leave, had to get out of there.

Weak-kneed, she took a step toward the front door, not knowing where she would go. Her legs buckled. She reached for a chair, and that was the last thing she remembered.

"Isabelle, honey, please wake up." Aunt Sophie's voice came through the thick fog in Isabelle's head.

"No," Isabelle strained, forcing her eyes to open. "I . . . must . . . go."

"Where, honey? Where do you need to go?" Aunt Sophie asked.

"Away," Isabelle said as tears formed in her eyes, collected and trickled down the sides of her face. She was lying on her aunt's couch in the living room. "Away . . ." she said again, hopelessly.

"Honey, you need to rest. Dr. Holmes is here," her aunt said.

"Isabelle?" a man's voice followed. "I'd like to ask you some questions if you feel up to it."

Isabelle turned her head to the side. "No . . . please."

"Isabelle." Her aunt took her hand. Isabelle tried to pull it away. "Honey, you scared me to death when you fainted. Please, let the doctor take a look at you."

Her aunt didn't understand. If James found her, he wouldn't just beat her. This time he would kill her. She knew it.

Weakened by an overwhelming feeling of defeat, she let the doctor take her pulse and blood pressure. It was over. But she knew one thing, she would die by her own hand first. She would never give James the pleasure of taking her life.

"Blood pressure's a little low," the doctor said. Isabelle took a look at the man; he was older, probably late sixties, bald on top, with furry white hair around the sides of his head. A bushy white mustache and plenty of wrinkles adorned his kind face. He had a nose that was rounded on the end and round cheeks. He looked like Santa Claus without a beard.

"How are you feeling?" he asked with sincere concern.

"I'm fine," Isabelle answered, trying to sit up. She had to get away—now!

"Any headache? Nausea? Aches or pains?" he asked.

"No, yes . . . I don't know," Isabelle answered with exasperation. "Please, I have to go." She managed to sit up, against his gentle restraints.

"Isabelle, honey," her aunt spoke in soothing tones. "Everything is okay. You're safe here. No one is going to hurt you."

Isabelle looked at her aunt as fresh tears filled her eyes. If she only knew. The woman didn't, couldn't understand.

"Would you like something to drink?" her aunt asked. "Or maybe a bite of something for your stomach?"

"No," Isabelle answered. "I'm fine. Please . . ."

"You're in no condition to go anywhere," the doctor said firmly. "You need to have something to eat. I think you'd feel stronger if you did."

Isabelle realized that not only was she weak, she was also outnumbered. Perhaps if she ate something to appease them, she could finally convince them she had to leave.

Aunt Sophie brought her a small bowl of soup and several crackers. The cracker tasted like sawdust in her mouth. Taking a drink of water, she was aware of the cool liquid moistening her tongue and sliding down her throat. She was famished, yet her desire to get away was stronger.

As she sipped several of spoonfuls of broth, the concerned expressions on her aunt's face and the doctor's face softened.

"There now," her aunt said. "Isn't that a little better?"

Isabelle nodded as sadness filled her. She thought she'd found a place of safety and security. But she realized now that as long as she was alive, or James was alive, she would never feel peace.

Dr. Holmes and Aunt Sophie watched as Isabelle pushed herself to her feet, then stood.

"I'm fine now," Isabelle told them. "I think I'll go lay down and rest for a while."

"Capital idea," Dr. Holmes agreed. "That will help you get your strength back. Then I'd like to see you in my office first thing Monday morning. We'll run a few tests on you."

"I'll be up to check on you, my dear," Aunt Sophie said.

Isabelle knew she wouldn't be around for any tests, but she smiled and thanked him, then made her way up the stairs to her bedroom, where she began gathering some necessities together.

She berated herself for spending so much money on clothes earlier. Right now she needed that money to survive.

Devising a quick plan as she threw items into a grocery bag, she decided to go back to London and try to lose herself in the swarms of people there. She could figure out the rest later when she got there.

As if a warning siren went off in her mind, sending shivers of terror through her body, she froze when she heard the crunch of tires on the gravel road out in front as a car pulled up to the house.

"No!" she cried, clutching her bag to her chest.

The sound of footsteps came up the path.

Her mind flitted around, trying to identify her options. The only way out was down the stairs or through the window.

The front door squeaked open.

She strained to hear what was being said, but the voices were low and muffled.

Then, when she thought she was going to pass out again from pure fear, she heard footsteps coming up the stairs. She huddled back into the corner by the wardrobe and waited. Waited to see the fury in those eyes she'd grown to fear and hate. But instead her aunt came into the room.

"Isabelle, what's the matter dear? You look like a deer caught in headlights." Aunt Sophie took a step closer and Isabelle squeezed her eyes shut. A soft whimper escaped her lips.

"Look at you, you're shaking like a leaf. Why are you so frightened?" her aunt asked. "Isabelle, tell me. What is going on?"

"Please," Isabelle whispered in desperation. "Don't tell him I'm here. He'll kill me if he finds me."

Aunt Sophie's brow wrinkled in confusion. "Kill you? Who will?"

"James," Isabelle answered in a sob of emotion.

"James? Who's James?" Aunt Sophie asked.

Now it was Isabelle's turn to be confused. "Isn't he here? Isn't he downstairs?"

"James? What are you talking about?" her aunt demanded.

"Who's downstairs?" Isabelle asked. "I heard someone come in."

A tender smile grew on her aunt's face. "There's someone here I think you'll be very happy to see."

Isabelle's brows furrowed with distrust.

"I promise you, Isabelle. You are completely safe." Her aunt took her hand and pulled her gently from the corner.

Isabelle resisted, but her aunt drew her forward.

"You have to trust me," she said.

When Isabelle looked into her aunt's eyes, she knew her aunt was sincere. But trust wasn't something she was familiar with anymore.

Still, she knew that it was impossible to get away now.

Feeling a new level of fear rise inside of her, she allowed herself to be guided from the room.

Once they got downstairs, it was all Isabelle could do to not bolt out the front door. She forced her breathing to remain calm, but felt on the verge of a nervous breakdown.

Looking across the large room, she saw a man. He had light brown hair, nicely cut and styled, and looked like he was around thirty years old. He was trim, tan, and well dressed.

She breathed a little easier. At least it wasn't James.

"Isabelle," Aunt Sophie said, "this is your brother, Ryan."

Isabelle's mouth dropped open. Had she heard her aunt correctly? Was this man in the room, this person who seemed vaguely familiar, truly her brother? Tears filled her eyes.

"Ryan," she said, her voice trembling, "is it really you?"

The man smiled, then nodded. "Yes, Isabelle. It's me."

He took several slow steps toward her, reaching out his arms. Isabelle took a tentative step, then another, then in a rush of emotion, they embraced and quietly wept.

* * *

"I wrote you. I even went to Boston to find you, but when I went to the address I had for you, no one was home. I asked your neighbors about you, but it was as if no one had ever seen you or heard of you."

Isabelle guessed he'd come when she and James were out of town. As for her neighbors not knowing her, that didn't surprise her. She'd never met any of them, except for Mrs. Twitchell.

"I didn't know what had happened to you," Ryan said, blinking at the film of moisture in his eyes. The two siblings sat next to each other on the couch, holding hands. "I still can't believe you're here. After all these years."

"What happened, Ryan?" she asked. The question had haunted her for as long as she could remember. "Why did you run away from home?"

A pained expression crossed his face. He swallowed hard and looked away for a moment, then looked at her. "You will never know the regrets I have for doing what I did. I never even got a chance to say good-bye to Dad or Mom. And then when I couldn't find you . . . It's been hard to live with myself. I've asked myself that question hundreds of times, but there's just no excuse for what I did."

Ryan took another breath then told his story. "It all started when our family moved to Harrisburg, Pennsylvania."

Isabelle's memories of them living in Pennsylvania weren't happy ones, mostly because that was when her father had died and Ryan had run away. Her mother had completely withdrawn after that.

"I didn't fit in with any of the kids at school. Then, in my senior year, I hooked up with John Keetch."

Isabelle remembered John well. He'd always given her the creeps, the way he dressed in black. He had worn his hair long and stringy, and always smelled of cigarettes.

"John and his friends took me in. After a while, hanging out with them, I started getting into some of the stuff they were doing. Drinking mostly, but drugs too. Mom and Dad tried to help me, but I was mad at them for making us move and for the way my life was, and I guess, in a way, I was punishing them. Then Dad died."

He looked down at his lap and Isabelle felt her heart go out to him.

"Anyway," he finally continued, "things just kept getting worse and worse and I got pretty messed up. By that time, we were stealing stuff to pay for the alcohol and drugs. The others were into stealing cars, and I knew it was only a matter of time before we got caught, but for some reason I just didn't care. That is, until one night when we were driving around, stoned out of our minds, and my friend who was driving hit a pedestrian. I was afraid we'd all go to jail, especially when the pedestrian died."

Isabelle had known nothing about this.

"I couldn't bear Mom's disappointment when she found out, so Keetch and I took off. We went to New York thinking we'd get our acts together and make something of ourselves, then come home when we were rich and famous and everyone would forgive us." Ryan shook his head. "Boy were we young and stupid. John ended up getting some bad drugs and overdosed about a year later. With him gone, I was on my own with nothing—no money, no place to stay, just the clothes on my back."

"What did you do?" Isabelle asked. She was having a hard time believing that this was her brother talking and that he'd been through all of this.

"I don't think I could've sunk much lower than I was then. I pretty much lived on the streets, picking up odd jobs whenever I could. I slept in shelters and tried to get my act together a few times. By the time I was in my early twenties I figured that was pretty much how my life was going to be. My dreams of becoming rich and famous were gone. One day I sat next to an army recruiter on the subway. He told me about all the opportunities the army offers and that it makes men out of boys. Well, I considered myself a man, but I knew I wasn't the kind of man I wanted to be or even the kind my parents had wanted me to be. I saw the army as my way out, the opportunity to make something out of my life."

"Did you join?" Isabelle asked anxiously.

Ryan nodded. "I did. And when I got to boot camp I thought I'd landed straight in hell with the devil himself as my drill sergeant."

Isabelle, Aunt Sophie, and Dr. Holmes all laughed at his description of life at boot camp.

"But as hard as it was, I found that I liked the structure and the discipline of army life. And everything started falling into place. Kicking my drug habit was the hardest thing of all."

Isabelle shook her head, still in disbelief. "That's an incredible story, Ryan. You went through so much."

"Yeah," he said with disgust. "It was all my own fault, too. Mom and Dad did everything they could, but I just wouldn't listen."

"I'm sure they're proud of you now," Isabelle told him sincerely.

He looked at her, their eyes connecting, and a half smile turned the corners of his lips. "I hope so. Nothing would mean more to me than to know that for sure," he said.

"What happened after that?" Isabelle asked.

"I was stationed in Germany for a while, in Heidelberg. There I was assigned to work in the communications department, and eventually got into broadcasting and reporting. I loved my assignment and had some really great experiences while I was there. When the opportunity came to take a job working in London for the BBC, as hard as it was to leave the army, I knew I couldn't turn down the opportunity. I work for CNN in their London office now. It's great. I do a lot of traveling and cover some fascinating stories. I do some investigative reporting, you know, always looking for that one story that will make all the headlines, but I haven't been quite that lucky. Still, I've come a long way."

"I'll say you have," Aunt Sophie entered the conversation.

"Aunt Sophie's been a lifesaver for me," Ryan said fondly of his aunt. "I looked her up when I got to London, and she's been a second mother to me."

Aunt Sophie smiled at him. "You two are the only children I've got. And I'm so happy to finally have both of you, together." Tears brimmed in her eyes.

"So," Ryan turned to Isabelle. "Enough about me. What about you? Tell me about your life."

Isabelle looked at the eager, interested faces in front of her. Faces of people who sincerely cared for her. The only two people she had in the world.

She just couldn't bring herself to tell them, to share with them the private, personal information of her life. Information that could get her killed, and perhaps harm them as well.

Chapter 10

"Isabelle?" Ryan inquired. "What have you've been doing with your life all these years?"

"Well," she stalled, "I, uh—well." She cleared her throat and looked at her brother's face, then her aunt's.

"Maybe I should leave," the doctor said, finding his black medical bag on the floor next to the couch. "It's getting late as it is."

"Thank you, Dr. Holmes." Aunt Sophie reached out and shook his hand. "I appreciate you coming on a moment's notice."

"Happy to oblige," he answered. "I'll see you Monday morning," he told Isabelle.

Isabelle smiled, already deciding that she didn't need any "tests" run. She was worn out and stressed. She just needed to rest and relax, which she was hoping to do after the scare she'd just had.

After the doctor left, Aunt Sophie and Ryan cornered her again.

She looked at the two faces in front of her. She knew she should trust them; they were her family. But after five years of living so carefully, weighing every move she made and word she said, it just wasn't that easy.

"There's not much to tell," she said at last. "After college I moved to Boston to work for a friend who was opening a preschool. She ended up getting married and moving away instead, leaving me high and dry. I took a job as a nanny for a young boy whose parents were both attorneys. They were the ones who introduced me to my husband. We dated for six months or so, and got married. Soon after we were married, Mom had her heart attack and died." She swallowed hard, looking down at her hands. Her heart still ached when she thought about how much she missed her mother.

"As for my husband, well, things just haven't worked out, so I . . . um . . ." She paused, trying to find the right words. "I left," she finally said.

"I'm sorry, dear," Aunt Sophie said. "It must be awfully hard for you."

"Actually, the hard part is behind me. Coming here was the best thing I could have done," Isabelle told her.

"This is your home now," Aunt Sophie told her.

"And we're finally together as a family," Ryan added. He reached over and gave her a hug. "By the way, Aunt Sophie told me today is your birthday."

Isabelle nodded. "I guess it is. I kind of forgot."

"I'm sorry I don't have a gift for you," he said.

"Are you kidding?" she said. "Having my brother back is the best birthday gift I could ever hope for."

"This really is amazing. Now, after all these years, we're together again," he said. "We'll never let anything separate us again," he said with conviction. "Ever."

Tears stung Isabelle's eyes with the realization that she didn't know what the future held for her. But she hoped with all her heart that his words would hold true.

Ryan spent the night at the cottage. He'd been in Bath visiting friends when his aunt called him on his cell phone, which was the only way to reach him since he traveled so much and was never in his office. Fortunately, he didn't have to be back in London until Monday, so they had the entire weekend together.

The next morning after breakfast, Ryan suggested they drive over to Wells and show Isabelle the famous cathedral, then go on to the city of Glastonbury to see more ancient sites.

The drive through the countryside was glorious. The morning had started out with a misty rain, but by midday it had cleared away, leaving the land a fresh, vivid green. Most of the buildings were centuries old. Many of the homes were made of stone with thatched roofs. Again, it was like seeing a storybook come alive, and Isabelle realized that in a way, coming here was like being rescued from a horrible monster. Her own story very well could start with the words, *"Once upon a time. . ."* She just prayed that her story would end with, *"And she lived happily ever after."*

The tiny city of Wells owed its celebrity to its cathedral, and Isabelle found that it was indeed a charming, medieval gem. Together the threesome walked with crowds of tourists down narrow streets from the marketplace, and emerged into a clearing. The sight literally took Isabelle's breath away. The building was a majestic spectacle of English Gothic architecture. Work on it had begun in the twelfth century, and the broad lawn stretching out in front of the cathedral was a remnant of a former graveyard, which added to the mystical quality of the cathedral.

The west front, flanked by solid towers, held multiple tiers and levels containing over three hundred statues gilded in gold that had aged to a honey hue. Touring the inside, they marveled at the beautiful stained-glass windows and intricate woodwork of its early English architecture.

Isabelle found herself enjoying the company of her brother and aunt immensely. Ryan had a wealth of knowledge about the history of the area, which was interspersed with his quick wit and dry humor. Even though many years had passed since they were together, there was still a connection between them, and she hoped that with time they would strengthen the bond they shared as brother and sister and restore the sense of family between them.

"You know, you've picked up an accent since you moved to England," Isabelle told her brother.

"You think so?" he asked. "Well, I say old chap, that's a first-rate compliment if I've ever heard one."

Isabelle giggled at his exaggerated accent and the way he carried on about his "mates" and his "flat" back in London, and every other English phrase he could come up with off the top of his head.

They piled back into the car and took the motorway—the British equivalent of a highway—to the city of Glastonbury, six miles south of Wells.

"Glastonbury is my favorite place in all of England," Ryan told her.

Isabelle could easily understand why, seeing the lovely hills and dales with thickets of trees, shimmering ponds and lakes, all crowned by church steeples and castle towers.

"Have you ever seen the movie *Camelot?*" he asked Isabelle.

She thought back, remembering the tale of King Arthur and Guinevere. She had seen the movie with her mother, which made the memory even more touching.

"Back when I was a teenager," Isabelle replied.

"This is where the legend takes place, about the eleventh century. But the history of the city goes back even further. According to local folklore, it's believed Christ came to this area. The Romans came here to mine lead in the Mendip Mountains. One of the mines was owned by Joseph of Arimathea, a wealthy merchant. Some believe he was related to Mary, Jesus' mother. There is a great deal of time during Christ's life that isn't recorded in the scriptures, and it's commonly believed that Christ accompanied this man Joseph on one of his many visits to his mine."

Isabelle didn't recall much of what she'd learned about Christ when she was a young girl, but the thought of Christ leaving Jerusalem and traveling to England was intriguing.

"Now, mind you," Aunt Sophie said. "These are all just legends, but there is proof that the Romans were here long before the time of Christ."

The trio visited the Glastonbury Abbey next, where the two bodies of Arthur and Guinevere were supposedly buried. Then they hiked to the Glastonbury Tor, a 521-foot landmark that could be seen for miles around.

Isabelle marveled again at the feeling of freedom that prevailed as she strolled along the wildflower-lined trails. She truly felt as if she had been released from prison—emotionally, spiritually, and even physically. Still, she wasn't used to being able to think for herself, to explore her own feelings or give voice to her thoughts, so she kept to herself, unless Aunt Sophie or Ryan asked her a question.

After a day of sightseeing and climbing, everyone was starving. Stopping at a pub called Porter's, they each ordered mouthwatering helpings of steak and kidney pie. Isabelle wasn't sure about the dish at first, but she was determined to embrace the culture, since she had every intention of making this her permanent home.

"Tell me about Dr. Holmes," Isabelle ventured after draining the last bit of juice from her glass.

"He's about as old as some of these castles," Ryan said with a laugh.

"But they don't come any finer," Aunt Sophie declared. "He's a wonderful doctor. Has a real gift for healing, he does."

"He's a bit extreme though, if you ask me," Ryan stated. "I mean, the man thinks he's a direct descendant of Sherlock Holmes."

"But Sherlock Holmes is a fictitious character!" Isabelle exclaimed.

"My point exactly. Still, he says just having the name gives him a natural ability to sort out mysteries and crimes," Ryan said.

Isabelle covered her mouth with her hand to hide her smile.

"Now Ryan, the man can't help it if he likes a bit of intrigue. It's in his blood," Aunt Sophie said in the doctor's defense. "We'd better get on home. I've got to stop at the market before it closes, since tomorrow is Sunday."

"Are the shops closed on Sunday?" Isabelle asked, thinking that nothing in America closed on Sunday. In fact, if anything, Sunday was probably the busiest day for most stores.

"In the cities you can still find a few places open," Ryan explained, "but for the most part, businesses close on Sunday. You can find a pub or two open, but that's about all."

"It's just as well," Aunt Sophie added as they made their way back to Ryan's car, a sleek Peugot in shiny black. "We shouldn't be shopping on the Sabbath. If people were in church like they're supposed to be, we wouldn't have all the problems in the world that we do."

The ride back to Westmoor went quickly as Isabelle and her brother compared memories of their childhood. As they talked of the past, of days when they were young and innocent and life was good, she felt herself opening up. It felt good to remember family vacations, Christmases, and simple, day-to-day memories. Even Aunt Sophie exclaimed how wonderful it was to hear about their lives as children, since she'd missed seeing them grow up in America.

Back at Swan Cottage, Ryan needed to make some phone calls, and Aunt Sophie went to the market. Isabelle took the opportunity to take a much-needed rest. She'd felt like a wilting flower as the day had worn on, and was grateful to get some sleep.

An hour later she awoke, feeling refreshed and energized. Ryan was nowhere to be found inside the house, so she went outside to find him. She looked around the front yard, then went to the backyard. Still, no Ryan.

Filling her lungs with fresh air, Isabelle looked at the dozens of varieties of flowers edging the yard and decided to pick a bouquet for her aunt's dining room table. With a pair of garden scissors, she carefully cut an assortment of blooms until she could hold no more.

Carrying the bundle of blossoms across the lawn, she looked around, hearing the roar of a lawn mower. Suddenly, it came charging around the side of the house. She jumped out of the way of the machine, manned by no other than Mr. Ethan Wilde.

He waved when he saw her and brought the mower to a stop. "I about got you again, sorry."

"No problem," she answered. "I heard you coming this time."

He smiled warmly. "The day was so nice I thought I'd mow and do a bit of weeding."

She glanced around the yard. "That's a big job," she said. "Aunt Sophie's got a lot of flower beds."

"That she does," he said. "I usually bring Ian Scott with me, but he went swimming with a friend. Weeding doesn't compete well with that."

"I can imagine." Isabelle chuckled, placing the bouquet of flowers on her aunt's shaded workbench. "I'm pretty good at pulling weeds," she offered.

"You don't need to," he told her. "Ian Scott can come over another time."

"I really wouldn't mind," she said. "I enjoy working in the yard." For a moment their eyes connected, and then Isabelle, feeling uncomfortable, looked away. "I'll go see if Aunt Sophie has some gardening gloves."

"In the shed," Ethan told her.

Isabelle found the gloves and, after perusing the various flower beds, found the one with the most weeds and launched into it.

The warm sun beat down on her back as she worked in the hot, steaming soil. She loved the fragrance of the flowers mixed with the heady fragrance of the earth. It was therapeutic to her soul, and even though the outside temperature was making her perspire, it felt good to do something familiar.

Her mind returned to her flower beds back in Boston. She'd coddled and pampered her bulbs and bushes, producing beautiful flower beds every year. Gardening was the one pleasure James allowed, since their beautiful yard brought such praise from visitors to their home. Every winter she'd nearly gone mad waiting for warm weather so she could get outside and do something productive, something that brought some sort of fulfillment to her life. Without a nurturing relationship with her husband, and not having any children to love and take care of, the only way she filled that need in her life was to see the plants she so lovingly cared for blossom and thrive.

Lost in thought, she jumped when Ethan asked, "Would you like some help?"

Catching her breath, she accepted his offer and he knelt down beside her and began pulling at the weeds.

"So, you're getting settled in?" he asked casually as he worked.

"Yes," she answered. "Aunt Sophie's been wonderful."

"She certainly seems to love having you here," he said, adding weeds to the pile they'd created between them.

"I hope so. I hated to impose, but I had nowhere—" she stopped herself and quickly said, "I mean, I hadn't seen her in such a long time, and she'd sent an invitation to come and visit."

"So you're just visiting?" He looked over at her for a moment.

"I'm actually considering living here permanently. Aunt Sophie and my brother, Ryan, are all the family I've got. I'd like to be with them."

He nodded. "Sophie's a wonderful woman. She treats me and my son like her own. I know she gets lonely."

The thought of Aunt Sophie being alone all these years made Isabelle sad.

"So, tell me about yourself," Ethan said. "Where did you live in America? What did you do there?"

She answered his questions in general terms, leaving out the details of her life in Boston. She felt that the less anyone knew, the safer she'd be. She told him about her college education and living in Boston, leaving out any mention of her marriage or James.

"You wouldn't happen to be looking for work, would you?" he asked.

"I haven't started looking, but I will need to get a job soon," she answered, not wanting to be a financial burden on her aunt any longer than she had to be. "Why?"

"It's just that with your degree in early childhood education, I thought you might be interested in working with children. I know that my son's day care is sorely in need of help. They're awfully short-handed right now."

As if a light switch suddenly went on inside of her, Isabelle immediately took to the idea. She didn't want to get her hopes up, but she couldn't think of anything she'd enjoy more than using her education and working with children. Children were loving and accepting. With children she felt safe.

"I appreciate the suggestion. I'll think about it," she replied. She needed to sit down and plan her future. She wasn't used to having control of her life, being able to make decisions and choose her own path.

"I know one little boy who would be very happy to have you work there," Ethan said.

"Really? Who?" she asked.

"My son. He's taken quite a fancy to you," Ethan told her.

"Me!" she exclaimed.

Ethan laughed. "He thinks you're quite lovely."

Isabelle felt her cheeks flush. Even though she was embarrassed, Isabelle couldn't help but smile. Still, she didn't know what to say.

Gratefully she didn't have to grope for words, as Ethan went on to say, "You have to understand, our town is small and we know most of the people here. Even though we have some attractive women here, I have to agree with my son, you're like a rose among dandelions."

Isabelle wasn't sure how to answer. His words were kind, but because of James she had learned to quell her reactions to any compliment—especially from men—not only for her safety, but for theirs. Instead of answering, she changed the subject. "Tell me about yourself, Ethan."

Ethan looked at her appraisingly, his eyes connecting with hers for one brief moment. Isabelle avoided his gaze by plunging her trowel into the dirt and loosening a stubborn weed.

Once Ethan began talking, however, he spoke openly and freely about his life growing up in Westmoor, then going away to school in London and meeting his wife, Jennifer. He talked about living in America and how much he missed pizza, hamburgers, and the Yankees. He somberly shared the tragedy of losing his wife, of holding her in his arms as her life slipped through his fingers.

"Not a day goes by that I don't miss her, that I don't think of her. I see her in Ian Scott's eyes and the way he smiles." His voice was filled with pain, his eyes distant with the past.

"I'm so sorry," Isabelle said, wishing she had something more to offer, something more profound and comforting to say.

"Thanks," he said, shaking his head as if to clear the memories. "I certainly didn't mean to unload all of that on you. Sorry."

"It's okay." She wanted to tell him she knew of heartache and pain, of dreams dashed to pieces and expectations thrown away.

They continued to weed together, in silence. The smudges of dirt on his face made him look boyish and youthful, yet the creases around his eyes and lines of worry on his forehead revealed the tragedy he'd endured. For a brief moment, Isabelle wondered how different her life would be if she had met and married someone like Ethan. But it was too late for those kinds of dreams now.

The next morning Isabelle awoke feeling queasy. She could barely get out of bed. Her aunt came looking for her around nine o'clock.

"Good morning, dear. Would you like some breakfast? Ryan's downstairs hoping you'll join him."

The thought of food turned her stomach.

"I don't think so. I'm not feeling well," Isabelle answered.

"Oh dear. We've definitely got to get you into Dr. Holmes in the morning."

"I must've picked up a flu bug or something," Isabelle answered, feeling deep down that maybe there was another explanation. One she couldn't bear facing.

"It might help to get a little something inside your tummy. Why don't I bring up some toast and see if that helps."

Isabelle wasn't up to any food but didn't want to offend her aunt.

"I guess you won't be joining us for church at eleven, then," Aunt Sophie said. "I'd wanted to show you off. Oh well . . . perhaps next week."

Isabelle highly doubted that she'd even get out of bed that day, let alone go to church. Besides, she wasn't in the mood to listen to a sermon about God's love and concern for mankind when her life had reflected anything but that.

To her surprise, the toast Aunt Sophie brought her actually did calm her nausea. She still didn't feel well enough to go to church, but while Ryan and Aunt Sophie were gone, she got up and showered, and put on her new skirt and blouse.

The day was overcast and cool, with a hint of rain floating in the air. Isabelle found herself in the backyard admiring the neat flower beds and lovely blooms full of fragrance and color. She drew in several breaths as she looked around the garden, her gaze taking in the castle as well.

Against the backdrop of low, gray clouds, the castle looked dark and foreboding, and she felt a shiver up her back as a sudden breeze kicked up and droplets of rain fell. She looked around for her aunt's dog. Romeo had come outside with her and had disappeared into the trees.

"Romeo," she called. "Come on, boy."

She waited for the dog to return, but got no answer.

"Romeo?" she called again, walking in the direction she'd last seen him.

She thrashed through the brush and ferns along the path leading through the trees toward the castle, calling for the dog.

"Romeo!"

From the distance she heard barking. Relief filled her as she followed the sound.

She found the dog down by a stream, where several cows were drinking their fill. Romeo seemed to delight in trying to rile the large, docile creatures, but he wasn't having much luck.

"Come on, boy, it's time to go home," Isabelle said in a commanding tone. To her delight, the dog turned from his antics and fell in at her side.

She was grateful to have the company of the little pooch even though he wasn't exactly her idea of a guard dog. What he lacked in size, however, he made up for in noise.

He sniffed and frolicked on his way back to the cottage while Isabelle noticed sprinkles of rain coming faster.

"We'd better hurry," she said to the dog, "or we're going to get a good drenching."

Not realizing she'd walked so far, she picked up her pace. Suddenly Romeo came to an abrupt halt and began barking wildly.

The sudden onset of yapping startled Isabelle and sent a bolt of fear through her.

Crouching down beside the dog, she patted his side and tried to calm him. "What is it?" she said, "What's wrong boy?"

The spattering of rain drops grew heavier, and Isabelle shivered as her blouse grew damp.

The dog continued barking and crouching low, working himself into a frenzy, until out of the trees stepped a large figure of a man in a black rain slicker and hat.

It was James!

Isabelle screamed and bolted in the opposite direction.

"Isabelle!" he hollered.

At the creek she hesitated. It was wide and at least two feet deep, the water traveling its course rapidly.

"Isabelle!" He shouted her name again over the noise of the creek. Fear propelled her onward.

Stepping gingerly into the icy water, she attempted to cross, feeling the slippery rocks beneath her feet. Just as she was about to reach the other side, she lost her footing in the rapid rush of water and felt herself go under.

The water carried her downstream as she fought to get her feet back under her, bumping and colliding into boulders along the way. Taking in great gulps of water and gasping for air, Isabelle fought with a vengeance, but the water's rush was too much.

An excruciating pain raked across her right side as she was caught in a tangle of tree limbs. Unable to stifle a groan, she clung to the limbs, trying to decide if drowning was a better alternative to facing James. She didn't have long to decide as a pair of hands reached down and grasped her shoulders, pulling her to the safety of the shore.

Chapter 11

Keeping her eyes tightly shut, Isabelle waited for hands to circle her throat and choke the life out of her. He would kill her. She knew he would.

"Isabelle!" He shook her until she thought her neck would snap. "Say something, please."

The voice wasn't angry and threatening, but desperate and terrified. "C'mon," he said. "Please talk to me."

Isabelle recognized the voice and knew she'd made a terrible mistake. Her eyes flew open. "Ryan!"

Ryan crushed her to his chest, holding her and rocking her. "Why did you run from me? You nearly drowned."

What a dolt she'd been, thinking it was James coming after her. But with every strange sound, unexpected phone call, or visit, she was overcome with fear that James had found her. Then to have Ryan jump out at her on the path like he did, dressed like Jack the Ripper, scaring her into a panic . . .

"Are you okay?" Ryan asked, cradling her protectively in his arms.

Isabelle drew in several more long breaths as she shivered and shook from the cold.

"I didn't mean to scare you," Ryan said. "But why did you take off running like that?"

Her teeth were chattering so much she couldn't answer.

"Here," he scooped her up in his arms, "I'd better get you home; then we can talk."

Wrapped in several warm quilts, Isabelle managed to calm down as she rested on the couch in the living room.

"We got home from church and you weren't in the house," Ryan explained to her. "Aunt Sophie was afraid you might have gone up to the castle and would get caught in the storm, so I came to find you."

"It's just not very safe up there," Aunt Sophie said. "I didn't want you up there alone, especially in a downpour."

Isabelle appreciated her aunt's concern. It had been a long time since someone was truly concerned about her well being.

"Why did you take off running?" Ryan asked. "Who did you think I was?"

Isabelle avoided Ryan's and Aunt Sophie's questioning stares. She knew she owed it to them to come clean, but she was so afraid of getting them involved in her problems. Yet she also knew they were already involved, whether they wanted to be or not.

Praying she was doing the right thing, Isabelle began to tell them about James.

"You had to get away," Aunt Sophie said patting her hand. "The man drove you to do something desperate like that. It must have taken a lot of courage for you to finally leave."

Isabelle wiped at her eyes. It had been an emotional purging to finally open her heart and tell them about her life with James. And for her, it was a quantum leap of faith to trust someone that much. But she could trust them, couldn't she?

She swallowed her fears and her concerns. She had no choice. She had to trust them. And if she couldn't trust her own family, who could she trust?

"It certainly explains why you never received any of our letters," Ryan said. "I tried to call so many times, but your number was unlisted."

"I'm positive now that James intercepted all of my letters. He didn't allow me to get the mail."

Aunt Sophie shook her head. "You poor thing."

"I know it sounds paranoid, but I think he might have had the phones wired," Isabelle told her brother.

"It's possible," Ryan agreed. "I've heard of bizarre situations like this before. People like James feel like they own you. Like you're their property."

"The man has you scared of your own shadow," Aunt Sophie said, stroking Isabelle's brow gently. "No wonder you're constantly looking over your shoulder."

"I am?" Isabelle asked.

"I noticed it when we were in town. You flinched every time someone bumped up against you or made any sudden move. I wanted to ask you what was wrong, but I didn't want to pry," her aunt said. "I had a hunch something had happened to you, especially when you arrived without any luggage or belongings."

Isabelle sighed. "I should have known you would wonder about that. You know, having your letter delivered to my neighbor by mistake was my lifeline," she said. "When I read your note I felt as if God had given me one small window of opportunity. If I was going to get away, it had to be then or never."

"I believe with all my heart that God helped you have the courage to do what you needed to do," Aunt Sophie said with conviction. "And I believe you're safe here with me. If you covered your tracks as completely as you said you did, there's no way this man could ever find you."

"I wish I knew for certain," Isabelle said. "But you don't know James. He's got ways to find out things. He has connections."

Aunt Sophie and Ryan both looked confused at her comment.

"On the outside he's charming and charismatic and irresistible," she explained. "But I know what's inside of him, and what he's capable of frightens me. I can't really put my finger on it, and I couldn't even prove it, but I know that he's involved in many things that aren't . . ." she searched for the right word, "above board, I guess."

"What do you mean, Isabelle?" Ryan asked. "I thought you said he was an attorney. But you think he's involved in illegal activity?"

She lifted her hands helplessly. "I know it doesn't make sense, but so much of what he did, how he operated, was behind closed doors and done in secret. Letters, deliveries, conversations, meetings."

Ryan's brows narrowed. "And you have no idea what he was up to?"

"He didn't involved me in anything," she said. Then she shrugged. "I guess it doesn't really matter now anyway. It's over. I'm gone and I don't ever want to see him again. Still . . ."

". . . you'd like to be certain he's not after you," her aunt finished her sentence for her.

Ryan took her hand, and Isabelle's first impulse was to pull it away. But she didn't. She forced herself to accept his touch, his support.

"I'll check the Boston papers to see what kind of write-ups there have been since you've disappeared," Ryan offered. "I'll find out if there've been any questions about your 'death.'"

"Would you, Ryan?" Isabelle exclaimed. "I would feel so much better."

"Anything for you, sis," Ryan said, leaning over to give her a peck on the cheek.

Tears filled Isabelle's eyes. The urges to withdraw, to cope with and deal with her trials by herself, were so strong. It was what she'd done for the last five years. It was the only way she could survive. But she also felt the tugging in her heart to reach out to these wonderful people, to let them into her life. To let them help her.

She hadn't seen them in years, yet she was beginning to realize that the bonds of family went far beyond the span of time or distance. They were linked together by invisible ties. They had the same blood in their veins, the same essence in their souls. Knowing she was surrounded by family gave her the courage to try, and the desire to flee was replaced by the desire to fight.

"Thank you," she whispered, not only to them, but as a prayer of gratitude to whatever heavenly hand had a divine role in her escape.

"Listen, sis," Ryan said, "I have to get back to London, but I'll give you a call tomorrow and tell you what I find out. And I'll come back next weekend. There's still so much to catch up on, and there are so many wonderful places to take you and show you. How would you like to visit Stonehenge?" he asked.

"Is that around here?" Isabelle asked with growing excitement. "I'd love to go to it."

"It's a date," Ryan said firmly. He made a move to stand, then stopped. He turned toward her, meeting her eyes with a confident gaze. "Don't you worry about James," he told her. "I won't let anything happen to you. I promise."

Ryan pulled her into a fierce hug, warming her with the conviction of his words. Isabelle felt stiff and awkward in his embrace but she resisted the urge to push away, knowing that it wasn't a crime to hug another person. It had just been so long since anyone other than

James had touched her.

"I love you, Isabelle," he said.

The words felt strange in her mouth, the feeling foreign in her heart, but it was there nonetheless. "I love you too, Ryan," she replied, realizing that even though she'd come so far by seizing control of her life and feelings, she still had a long way to go.

Aunt Sophie dabbed at her eyes and Ryan reached an arm out, pulling her into their hug. "We're all we've got," he said. "We have to watch out for each other."

By late afternoon Isabelle was feeling much better after her "swim" in the icy creek. She relaxed on a chaise lounge in the garden, looking at a magazine and sipping on lemonade. Though she hadn't received any severe injuries, she had a few scrapes and several bruised ribs from the ordeal.

Her nerves flinched when she heard the doorbell ring, a reflex she hoped would fade with time. Several minutes later the back door opened and Aunt Sophie walked outside with two middle-aged women. Isabelle sat up and smiled at them.

"Isabelle," her aunt said, "I'd like you to meet two of my dearest friends—Margaret Crompton." She pointed to a rotund woman, with sparkling, friendly eyes and pixie-like features.

"Hello, Isabelle, it's nice to meet you," she said.

"And this is Naomi Langley," Sophie motioned to the other woman, a trim middle-aged woman with a stylish bob, an attractive face, and beautifully tailored clothes. "They're my visiting teachers."

Isabelle raised her eyebrows curiously. "Excuse me? They're your—"

"My visiting teachers. From church. They visit me every month, just to see how I'm doing," Aunt Sophie explained.

Isabelle's memory recalled a time when her mother had visiting teachers. But it had been many, many years ago. Isabelle smiled politely. "It's nice to meet both of you."

Aunt Sophie and the two women sat down in the semicircle of chairs close by. They asked Isabelle a few questions about America, both sharing accounts of trips they'd taken to the States.

"Your aunt tells me you studied early childhood education in college," Margaret Crompton said.

Isabelle nodded.

"You may not be looking for work yet, but I thought I'd ask if you'd be interested in helping out at the day-care center I own here in town. I'm shorthanded at the moment, and have had an awful time trying to fill the position."

"Work? At your day-care center?" Isabelle asked, recalling her conversation with Ethan. She thought about how it would be to feel the energy and excitement that came from working with children again. A chance like this didn't come along every day. And maybe, once again, the Lord's hand was guiding her path. She liked to think it was.

"I know you just barely got to town," the woman said quickly, "but I'm quite desperate for help."

"I would love to work with the children again," Isabelle replied. "But do you really think I could do it?" It had been so long since she'd had any kind of job, she wasn't sure she could do anything.

"Of course you could do it!" Mrs. Crompton exclaimed. "An education is helpful, but a desire and a bit of energy is going to get you further with our little brood."

The decision made Isabelle feel warm and tingly inside. "I can't think of anything I'd rather do," she told the woman.

Mrs. Crompton clapped her hand over her ample chest and laughed with relief. "This is wonderful," she said breathlessly. "You're an answer to prayers. I'm so happy you said yes. When can you start?"

"When do you need me?" Isabelle answered.

"Tomorrow?" the woman said with some hesitation.

"That would be perf—"

"Don't forget your doctor's appointment in the morning, Isabelle," her aunt reminded her.

"Oh, that's right," Isabelle said. "I have an appointment with Dr. Holmes, but I could come in after that."

Mrs. Crompton beamed, looking even more like a pixie.

"I'm so glad this worked out," Aunt Sophie said, clasping her hands together with excitement. "And since Isabelle has dual citizenship, it shouldn't be difficult to get her working papers in order."

After visiting a few minutes longer, the women bid farewell. Aunt Sophie and Isabelle waved from the front door as they watched the two women walk to their car.

"That certainly worked out well," Aunt Sophie said. "But are you sure you're up to it? Taking care of children is a lot of work."

Isabelle appreciated Aunt Sophie's concern. "Ever since I graduated from college I've wanted to work in a preschool or a day care, somewhere where I could be with children. I never got that chance until now. I would never pass up an opportunity like this."

She looked at her aunt, who was smiling proudly at her.

"What?" Isabelle asked her.

"You reminded me of your mother just then," Aunt Sophie said. "She was such a dear, special person. Very strong and independent. I felt as though given the chance, she could have moved a mountain. Your mother never let anything stand in her way. She always said, 'If you want something badly enough and are willing to work for it, you can do anything.' She believed that with all her heart. She lived her life with that philosophy."

Isabelle loved hearing about her mother.

"There's a lot of her inside of you. You just have to believe in yourself, my dear. This is a chance for you to have a whole new beginning in your life. To leave the past behind. We can't change the past, we can't control the future. But we can do our best to make the most of what we have here and now."

"Is that how you've survived the losses in your life, Aunt Sophie?" Isabelle asked, knowing how devastating her aunt must have been after losing her husband to cancer at such an early age.

"That and faith in the Lord that I would be with him again when I pass beyond the veil," Aunt Sophie answered.

"The veil?" Isabelle asked.

Aunt Sophie looked at her with sadness in her eyes. "Don't you remember?"

"Remember what?" Isabelle asked as they sat down at the kitchen table, nibbling at a plate of sugary sweet biscuits one of the visiting teachers had brought.

"Things you were taught in church," Aunt Sophie answered.

Her family had gone to church when she was little, she knew. But they'd moved around a lot and it was difficult to grow any roots in one spot. Then, when Ryan had left, her mother completely fell away from the Church and consequently, Isabelle did too. After she married James, she often had urges to go back to church, to rediscover her religion. She often wondered if that was what was missing in her life, but James wouldn't even hear of it.

"I remember. It's just been years since I thought about it," Isabelle explained.

Aunt Sophie shook her head, a look of sadness in her eyes. "After your father died your mother stopped going to church, didn't she?"

Isabelle wished her memories of her father were more clear. "It all seems blurry to me. Between Dad's death and Ryan taking off, Mom kind of withdrew from life, you know?" Isabelle was quiet a moment, remembering. "I did most of the grocery shopping and cooking. Mom worked as a secretary at the bank, then spent the rest of the day in her room, watching television. It was hard."

"I wish I could've been there to help her. To help both of you," Aunt Sophie said.

"Well," Isabelle stiffened her spine and brushed it away, the pain still just too hard to bear. "We managed the best we could."

"I want you to know something about this church you belong to," her aunt spoke with conviction in her voice. "Many of your ancestors paid a very high price so you could be a member. They suffered ridicule, even beatings, and were often shunned by their own families when they joined the Church. Some of them even paid the price with their own lives."

Isabelle stared at her aunt. She hadn't heard this tone of voice from Sophie before.

"Any trial, any challenge, any pain that weighs you down can be lifted if you put your trust in God and your life in His hands."

Isabelle's face must have reflected the skepticism she felt inside because her aunt quickly said, "How do you think I've been able to cope with the death of my family? It is not humanly possible to suffer such loss, to endure such pain. The only way I've been able to carry on is to rely completely upon the Lord. He's been there for me every time I've needed Him. He's helped me carry on."

Aunt Sophie's words were sobering but her voice was loving and gentle.

"Dear child. Your Heavenly Father is aware of you and everything you go through. He loves you more than you can comprehend. Let

Him help you. Don't try and do it alone anymore. All you have to do is ask. He'll help you. I know He will."

Even though doubts still filled her mind, Isabelle couldn't control the warmth filling her heart. And with that warmth came unbidden tears.

Dinner was a quiet meal. Isabelle digested her aunt's words along with her food. Were the things her aunt told her actually things she'd been taught at one time in her life? And if so, why couldn't she remember them? It was as if a dark curtain had been drawn across that part of her life. But her survival had depended upon her ability to block out the pain. It was the only way she knew how to cope, the only way she could handle it. Apparently she had blocked out everything.

As Isabelle helped her aunt put away the dishes, the sound of voices and laughter floated in on the evening breeze.

"Sounds like Ian Scott and his father. I'll bet they're in the boat."

The two women walked outdoors and across the lawn, passing through a small lattice archway dripping with soft, lavender-colored wisteria. Sure enough, there in the boat, rowing like a little sailor, was Ian Scott with his father relaxing in the bow.

"Ahoy there!" Aunt Sophie called when they got closer.

Ian Scott turned about and hollered, "Ahoy, Aunt Sophie!" He jumped up with excitement, tipping the boat side to side. This brought some quick action from his father.

"Ian Scott, sit down!" he commanded. Water sloshed over the sides of the boat, getting them both wet, which made Ian Scott squeal with delight. Ethan grabbed the oars and began rowing them to shore.

Aunt Sophie and Isabelle laughed when Ethan stepped out of the boat with splashes of water covering his pants and shoes. Ian Scott was in shorts, so he didn't mind the dousing.

"Would you like a towel?" Aunt Sophie asked Ethan.

"I'll be alright. It'll dry in a hurry. I think I should install some seat belts in that boat, though."

"At least you didn't tip over this time," Aunt Sophie replied. She turned to Isabelle. "Last time they were out they took a spill," she explained.

Isabelle pressed her lips together to hide her smile. Ian Scott was a little rascal, but the fact that he was so charming and adorable would make it difficult to get upset with him.

"Dad said we could walk up to the castle," Ian Scott announced. "Do you want to come with us?"

Isabelle smiled at the boy. His clipped accent sounded so cute coming from someone so young.

"Sure," Isabelle answered. "I'm game. What about you, Aunt Sophie?"

"You go on ahead. I'll wait for you in the garden," she answered.

"Are you sure?" Isabelle persisted. She still wasn't comfortable being alone with men, even though Ian Scott would be there.

"Quite sure, dear," Aunt Sophie declined.

"Can Romeo come, too?" Ian Scott begged.

"Of course he can," Aunt Sophie answered. She called for the dog, and Romeo came running out of nowhere. The first person he went to was Ian Scott, who was nearly bowled over by the dog's greeting. Ian Scott laughed as Romeo jumped up and licked his face, panting excitedly, his tail wagging so fast Isabelle thought for certain it would fly loose or lift him airborne.

"Be careful up there," Aunt Sophie cautioned as they followed the footpath leading to the castle. "Don't climb the stairs. They're liable to crumble beneath you."

Isabelle looked back at her aunt as the small procession left the yard. She knew it was silly, but she wasn't sure she'd even know what to say to a man.

"Come on, Isabelle," Ian Scott hollered back as he raced up the path. "We're almost there."

They followed the winding trail through the forested patch of trees and up the steep slope leading to the castle. As they hiked, Ian Scott filled Isabelle in on each of his friends and how their soccer team had gone undefeated last season. Since Isabelle didn't know much about soccer, she asked all kinds of questions about the game, amazed at the young boy's knowledge of the sport.

Approaching the castle, Ethan gave his son a stern warning about climbing on any of the crumbling stone walls or stairs. With an annoyed, "I know, Dad," Ian Scott ran off with Romeo to explore and no doubt imagine great battles and daring sword fights.

"What is it about this place that's so intriguing?" Isabelle said to Ethan as they stood in the shadow of the castle and looked out over the dale below.

"There's a certain magic about this place, isn't there?" Ethan agreed. "Perhaps it's all the myths and legends that surround it. I've heard tell that this is where St. George slew the famous dragon."

"Really? A dragon?" Isabelle asked.

"Actually, St. George was probably drunk on ale and slaughtered a poor, innocent cow, but that doesn't make much of a fairy tale, now does it? St. George and the cow." He shook his head. "Just isn't the same."

Isabelle laughed, her voice echoing in the distance. It felt good to laugh freely. And she was surprised at how comfortable she felt with Ethan. Being able to walk wherever she wanted to, to talk to anyone she wanted to talk to, would take some getting used to. But she was eager to try. She wanted to be like normal people. She wanted to finally have a life.

"But even with its mystical presence," Ethan said as he gazed across the broad expanse of farmland, meadows, and moors, "I also find it quite tranquil here. There's a certain peace within these crumbling walls."

Isabelle felt it, too. It was as if the castle was worn out, tired from having to be strong for so many decades, but it still possessed a quiet dignity, an air of reverence.

She nodded slowly, feeling the brush of wind on her cheek.

"Sometimes I come here when I need to sort things out," Ethan told her, still looking out at the sweeping view before them. "I seem to think a little clearer when I'm up here."

"I've felt drawn here myself," Isabelle confided. "And believe me, I have plenty of my own sorting to do," she assured him.

"If you're looking for answers, then you've come to the right place," he told her.

"I hope so. I have a lot of questions. I could use some answers."

Their gazes connected, and for a moment, their souls did too. And Isabelle wasn't sure how, but she knew Ethan was a good man. A man whom she could trust as a friend.

A movement over Ethan's shoulder, at the top of the castle wall, caught Isabelle's gaze.

"What?" Ethan asked when her expression changed to one of concern.

"It's Ian Scott. He's up on the castle wall," she said.

"Ian Scott!" Ethan hollered as he turned to see his son ducking behind the craggy edge of the crumbling parapet. "Don't move," he ordered. "I'm coming to get you."

Isabelle followed Ethan as he ran for the staircase.

"You'd better stay here," Ethan told her at the bottom of the stairs. "I'd hate for you to get hurt."

"Be careful," Isabelle called after him, watching him anxiously.

"I told you not to go up the stairs," Ethan lectured his son as their voices echoed in the empty chambers of the inner walls of the castle.

"But Dad," Ian Scott replied, "it was Romeo's fault. He ran up the stairs and I had to get him."

"Wait, son," Ethan warned him. "Pay attention to where you're stepping. The stones are loose right—"

A scattering of pebbles sprinkled off the stairway followed by a loud thud.

"Ethan!" Isabelle hollered, "Are you okay?"

"We're fine," Ethan answered. "I stepped too close to the edge right here by the window and bumped one of the stones."

A few moments later they came into view, with Romeo right beside them, and Isabelle heaved a sigh of relief.

"You two scared me to death," she told them. "Are you sure you're okay?"

"We're fine," Ethan assured her. "I think we'd better gate off this stairway, though, or someone could get killed. I'll try to get up here sometime and reinforce it somehow. Until then," he gave his son a warning glare, "no one goes up there. Understand?"

"I understand," Ian Scott echoed.

Chapter 12

"We'll do a work up on your blood and call you with the results in the next day or two," Dr. Holmes told Isabelle the next morning at her appointment. "I'm going to give you a prescription for some vitamins with extra iron. That should help with your lack of energy. As you adjust to the time change and your new surroundings, the nausea should also subside. Eat a lot of small meals; don't let your stomach get empty, and that should help a little."

"Thank you, Dr. Holmes," Isabelle said gratefully. If she'd known either of her grandfathers, she thought, she would have wanted them both to be just like Dr. Holmes.

"One more question," he asked taking out his prescription pad. "Have you had an increase of stress in your life? Stress can make us feel worn-out and run-down; it can even mimic flu symptoms sometimes." He looked at her, his eyebrows lifted in an appraising arch.

Isabelle wasn't sure how to answer the question. Yes, she'd had an increase of stress in her life in the form of a physically abusive husband, a demeaning and condescending mother-in-law, and fear for her life; add to that staging her own death and running away from the life she'd known for too long. "I guess you could say that," she answered.

He nodded as he wrote something on her chart. "Well, hopefully that will change now that you're getting settled in at your aunt's house."

"I hope so," Isabelle replied.

"And what are your plans now?" he asked as he filled out her vitamin prescription.

"I met Margaret Crompton yesterday," Isabelle said. "She's offered me a job at her day care." Isabelle smiled at him shyly.

"Capital idea!" he declared, handing her the prescription slip. "You'll do a splendid job, I'm certain."

"I hope so," Isabelle said, wishing she had as much confidence in herself as others seemed to have.

"She wouldn't ask you if she didn't think you could do it," Dr. Holmes explained. "Work hard and do your best. That's all she asks."

"I can do that," Isabelle said, trying to match his enthusiasm.

"Of course you can," he escorted her to the door of his office. "I'll give you a call when I get these lab results back. Don't worry, we'll figure this out. Until then, get plenty of sleep and drink plenty of water, and go outside and get a little exercise. Have your aunt throw on a pair of sneakers and go with you. She likes to get out and walk, too."

"I'll do that," Isabelle said. "Thanks for squeezing me in."

Aunt Sophie sprang to her feet when Isabelle came out of the doctor's office. "What did Dr. Holmes say?" she asked. "Are you okay? Is that a prescription?"

"It's just for vitamins," Isabelle reassured her aunt, who was worried enough for both of them. Giving her aunt a tender squeeze, Isabelle went on. "Dr. Holmes said I check out fine; there's no need for concern."

"You can be certain if there was something to find, he'd find it," Aunt Sophie said, then sighed. "I'm so glad that's over."

"Me too," Isabelle echoed. "I guess I'd better head over to the day-care center. I'm sure Mrs. Crompton is wondering if I forgot."

"She called this morning to check, and I assured her you'd be there," Aunt Sophie said as she pulled car keys from her bag. "We'll be there in no time at all."

Isabelle was surprised to feel so nervous as they approached the day-care building. It was an old farm house that had been converted into a center for children called "Over the Rainbow." It was painted a traditional barn-red color, but had a giant rainbow painted on one side that went up, over, and down the other side. The windows were decorated with drawings and artwork from the children.

"Are you ready?" Aunt Sophie asked as she reached to open the door.

Isabelle blew out a nervous breath. "Actually, no, I'm terrified."

Aunt Sophie patted her shoulder. "You're going to be fantastic," she said.

Inside, the rainbow motif ran everywhere, from colorful curtains to rainbow-shaped throw rugs. The check-in desk was unattended, so they ventured further inside, following the sound of children laughing and yelling.

They followed the noise up a staircase to a giant loft room, where toys were strewn everywhere and kids were climbing, crawling, running, and one was even swinging from a climbing rope like a monkey, which was exactly how Isabelle felt—like she was in the monkey cage at the zoo.

Standing in the corner, looking as though she wanted to tear out her hair, was Mrs. Crompton. Her face lit up like a Christmas tree when she saw Aunt Sophie and Isabelle enter the room. She rushed over to greet them, and Isabelle could see that she was near her wits' end.

"Thank you for coming," the woman said. "My other teacher went home sick. I'm alone with twenty-two children. Please tell me you can stay."

Isabelle's fears were replaced by the desire to help the poor woman. "Of course," Isabelle assured her. "Have they been like this all day?"

"Like what?" Mrs. Crompton asked. She looked around at the children. "Oh, you mean a little rambunctious?"

A little? Isabelle wanted to ask. "They seem very energetic," she said instead.

"We like to let them have their free time, where they can express themselves and discover who they are inside," Mrs. Crompton explained.

A loud crash in the corner of the room sent Mrs. Crompton running.

"Tiny little devils inside, that's what they are," Aunt Sophie said. "They all look like they could use a swat in the britches if you ask me."

"Aunt Sophie!" Isabelle exclaimed, not admitting that she'd had the same thought. She'd never seen such lack of control or rowdy behavior in her life. Then she spied a piano in another corner of the room. "I've got an idea," Isabelle said. All that time she'd spent playing the piano was about to pay off. It took some internal convincing for her to make herself do it, but forcing herself outside of her comfort zone, she strode over to the piano, sat down on the bench, and began to play a song. Pretty soon, like the Pied Piper's rats, the children began to gather around the piano.

Thrilled that the children had responded, Isabelle kept playing, wondering what to perform next. It had been ages since she'd played songs that children could sing.

Praying for strength, she gave the children a tremulous smile and, feeling like Maria Von Trapp, began to sing some songs from *The Sound of Music* along with the accompaniment. Some of the children who knew the words began to sing along with her. The other children stared in confusion at the strange lady sitting at the piano, as if trying to figure out what was going on.

When each song ended, Isabelle launched right into the next one, trying to find songs that would be familiar to the children. She ran the gamut of nursery rhymes and familiar Disney songs. With each song the children's enthusiasm grew along with her confidence. They were eating out of the palm of her hand and the thought thrilled her and set her knees to knocking so badly she could barely press the pedals.

Aunt Sophie and Margaret Crompton followed Isabelle's lead and stood on either side of the piano, leading the children in singing the songs, making up actions whenever they could.

Isabelle wasn't sure how long they'd been singing, but she finally ran out of songs and finished with "Somewhere Over the Rainbow," from *The Wizard of Oz.*

It had been years since she'd sung like that. She'd had a piano at her home in Boston and had spent many hours playing classical tunes and some of the more popular songs from movies, but her favorite were the cheerful children's songs. It felt wonderful to sing and play again, and to see the children's faces light up when they knew the words.

"Let's give a hand for Miss Isabelle," Mrs. Crompton announced when the last note sounded. The children clapped wildly. Mrs. Crompton went on, "She's a new teacher here at Over the Rainbow, so I hope you'll be on your best behavior and show her what good children you can be." She checked her watch. "Now, it's time to wash hands and get ready for lunch."

"Yayyyyy!" the kids shouted and began running.

To everyone's surprise, even her own, Isabelle stuck her two little fingers into her mouth and gave a loud whistle, stopping the children in their tracks. They turned and looked at Isabelle as if she'd just turned into an alien life-form.

Again, with her heart racing and knees trembling, she forced herself to remain calm as she asked in a quiet voice, "Raise your hand if you heard Mrs. Crompton—"

"Miss Maggie," Mrs. Crompton told her.

"—Miss Maggie," Isabelle corrected. "Raise your hand if you heard her excuse you," Isabelle said, looking at each of the children, giving a wink to Ian Scott when she located him in the crowd. Not one of the children raised their hands. "I didn't think so," she said. "I want everyone to come and sit on their pockets in a semicircle on the floor. We're going to play a game while we take turns washing our hands."

The children quickly took seats on the floor, anxious to see what kind of game their new teacher had for them to play. Isabelle looked to Aunt Sophie and Miss Maggie for help, but they both nodded their approval to continue with what she was doing. With a deep breath and a nervous smile, Isabelle addressed the children.

"I want everyone who's wearing yellow to stand up, spin around in a circle three times, then go and wash their hands. AND—" she said loudly as three of the children jumped to their feet "—after you finish washing your hands, I want you to get your lunch bags and take a seat quietly at the table and wait for the others."

She gave everyone a questioning look, making sure they all understood her.

"Ready?" she asked the three children. "Go!"

The children in yellow completed the exercise and were off to wash their hands. She next chose children who had long tails and pointy ears. That brought a giggle from the group. She then invited children who had any teeth missing. They were told to quack like a duck all the way to the washbasin. This continued until all of the children were washed and sitting quietly at the table.

"Amazing," Mrs. Crompton told Isabelle. "You had them eating out of your hands."

"Better that than eating me alive," Isabelle joked. "I hope it was okay for me to start singing with them. It seemed like they needed a distraction. I don't know what came over me."

Mrs. Crompton clasped her hands together and said, "You're an answer to my prayers, Isabelle. I'm so glad you came to Westmoor." To Isabelle's surprise, Mrs. Crompton gave her an enormous hug. "I was about ready to close my doors. I'm just getting too old for this, but having you here makes me want to give it one last try. I hope you're not planning on going anywhere soon."

"Not if I can help it," Aunt Sophie interjected.

Isabelle smiled at her aunt. "I'm hoping to make Westmoor my home," Isabelle told her.

Mrs. Crompton hugged her again. "While the children are eating, I'd like to go over our daily routine with you. I'm hoping you can help me make some changes that will put a little more structure in our day. I'd like to have more of a preschool atmosphere than just a day care."

"I'd be happy to," Isabelle answered, amazed at how good it felt to have someone actually ask her opinion, to feel that someone valued what she had to say.

"I'll stay here with the children while you two talk," Aunt Sophie volunteered.

"Thank you, Sophie," Mrs. Crompton said. "Thanks to both of you."

By five o'clock when the day care closed, Isabelle was worn out but very fulfilled. The best part of the day was when Ian Scott came up to her and gave her a picture he'd drawn during art time. In the background was the castle. Standing in front of it were three stick figures holding hands.

"This one in the middle is you," he said. "That one's Daddy." He pointed to the taller one on the side. "And that one is me." He pointed to the smaller one on the other side.

Tears came unbidden to Isabelle's eyes. "Thank you, Ian Scott," she told him. "It's a beautiful picture."

He wrapped his arms around her neck and gave her a hug. "I'm glad you're going to be my teacher. You're lots prettier than our other teacher, Miss Alice. She has a mustache."

Isabelle clamped her lips tightly shut as she stifled her laughter. It took a moment before she could answer.

"I'm glad I could be your teacher too. I know we're going to have a lot of fun together. I'll see you tomorrow, okay?" she told him as he slid his arms into the straps of his book bag.

"Okay," he answered, then was gone down the stairs.

Isabelle looked around the activity room with satisfaction. Before excusing the children, she made a game out of cleaning up and putting things away. She sang a song about cleaning up that used the word "stop" in each line. Every time the children heard the word "stop" they were supposed to freeze like statues. They had so much fun that they wanted to pull out more toys and sing it again.

Aunt Sophie and Isabelle arrived home exhausted but very happy.

* * *

"Are you sitting down?" Ryan asked over the phone. Aunt Sophie and Isabelle had just finished dinner and were cleaning up the dishes when he called from London.

"No," Isabelle answered. "Why?" She clutched the phone tightly to her ear. What had he found out about James?

"I've got some news for you," he answered. Feeling weak-kneed, she took his advice and sat in the nearest chair.

"What did you find out?" she asked. Aunt Sophie stopped drying dishes to listen to Isabelle's side of the conversation.

"You did a convincing job of staging your own death," he told her. "It was all over the weekend paper. Apparently your mother-in-law called your house several times the night you left. When she couldn't reach you, she had the police go to your home to find out what was wrong. Of course, you weren't there, and before they even had a chance to let her know, they received a call about a car being spotted in the river."

Isabelle closed her eyes, remembering the image of her car in the water. She'd left the door open, hoping the water would go inside and sink it. Had someone seen her climb out of the car before it went into the river?

"The report doesn't go into a lot of detail, but it says the car was retrieved and the owner's identity discovered. At first they didn't disclose your name, but it was assumed that the driver of the automobile lost control of the car on the slick road. A search for the body of the driver was launched, but they believe the driver tried to get out of the car and was swept away by the strong current."

She wondered how much trouble with the law she'd be in if it was ever discovered that she was alive.

"The paper says James returned on Friday, cutting his business trip short after he was notified of the accident. He immediately hired a special team of divers to search the river, to aid the efforts of the police. The paper says, 'He's distraught over the situation but isn't giving up hope. Mr. Dalton says he will never give up the search until he finds his wife.'"

"What does that mean?" Isabelle asked, wondering if James suspected anything.

"There was an update on the progress of the search effort in today's paper," Ryan went on. "According to the report on the local news station, authorities are convinced you didn't survive. Even if the impact in the water didn't injure you or knock you unconscious, the near-freezing temperature of the rushing water would make it nearly impossible for you to swim to shore. But again, they report that your husband isn't giving up. Which of course is making him out to be a devoted, loving husband who can't accept the fact of his wife's death. In fact, he's claiming that he believes foul play was involved. He says he won't rest until he knows what's happened to you."

Isabelle shut her eyes and pinched the bridge of her nose. She had been afraid James would respond like this. He would search until he was absolutely convinced she was dead. But that would never happen until he had found actual proof—her dead body.

"His mother is by his side, helping him through this whole ordeal. The family is in shock, the news report says, claiming that you were 'the love of James's life, and like a daughter to his mother.'"

"Ha!" Isabelle scoffed. "If they only knew the truth. The Dalton family is a pillar of the community, a model family that has suffered great loss, but still gives so much to the people of Boston. I'd give anything to show people what James is really like."

"Well, you might just get your wish," Ryan said.

"What do you mean?" Isabelle didn't understand.

"There was something else in the article. It talked about the unfortunate timing for James to be named as a possible suspect in connection with an illicit diamond trading organization."

"What!" Isabelle exclaimed. "Illicit diamond what?"

"Illicit diamond trading. Have you heard the controversy over what are called 'conflict diamonds'?"

"No, I've never heard of them," Isabelle told him.

"Sure you have. They're diamonds that are sold and the money is used to fund wars. It's not just a small problem anymore. The United Nations has gotten involved and issued an embargo on the sale of conflict diamonds. I did a report on this several months ago. It's a huge problem."

"But James wouldn't be involved in anything like that," Isabelle said, thinking back and trying to remember anything he might have said or done to link him to diamond smuggling. She was the first one to admit there had been some strange phone calls and deliveries to their house, but she couldn't imagine James involved in anything downright illegal. "I've never seen any indication of diamond smuggling," she told her brother. "Not even a diamond chip."

"The paper didn't say he was accused of any crime, just that his name has somehow been connected, which makes him a suspect. Of course, he's getting a lot of sympathy with the disappearance and likely death of his beloved wife."

Isabelle rolled her eyes, feeling no sympathy for James. "Is there anything else?" she asked.

"It only says that the FBI is involved."

"The FBI!" Isabelle exclaimed.

"The paper wouldn't mention his name if they didn't have something substantial to go by. Somehow he's been connected with diamonds coming out of Africa. And with all the civil wars breaking out—"

"Did you say Africa?" Isabelle was stunned.

"That's right," Ryan said. "The conflict diamonds are coming out of Angola and Sierra Leone. The money from the sale of these diamonds funds rebel groups like the National Union for the Total Independence of Angola and the Revolutionary United Front. Both groups are opposed to the government's efforts to restore peace in those two countries. It's a bloody mess down there, and a lot of innocent people are getting killed."

"Ryan." Isabelle felt her heart rate speed up. "James has been to Africa several times in the last year. He said it was part of the international business their firm conducts. Of course, I didn't question him. I was just glad to have him leave town for any reason. But I have to wonder what kind of business his law firm would have there."

"Isabelle, if what you're telling me is true and you can help prove that James is, in fact, involved in the illegal trafficking of conflict diamonds, he could go to prison."

"But I don't have access to any of that information, except I just know he went on those trips," she told him. "Besides, it would mean having to come back from the dead, and I'm not ready to do that."

Ryan sighed. "You're right. We'll just have to watch the situation and see what develops. But do you realize just how big this could be?"

"Sounds like it could be huge," Isabelle replied, still not quite believing that her husband could be involved—not that she wouldn't love to see him in prison. "Let me think about this for a few days, and see what I can remember," she said. "I'll call you."

"And I'll keep an eye on the reports and keep you posted," Ryan said.

Isabelle was suddenly grateful for her brother, even if it was difficult to receive affection and accept help from someone else. She'd been on her own for so long she'd forgotten what it was like to have someone care, someone who really wanted to help, someone with no ulterior motive. But she was slowly growing more trusting, more open. It gave her hope that one day she would be whole again, able to give love and receive love.

So many times in her life she'd wondered about her brother, had wanted to see him, to be with him again. She couldn't think of a better time for him to come back into her life than now. More than ever she needed the strength, support, and unconditional love of family. Not only that, but for the first time in many, many years, she finally felt the desire to pray, to offer some sort of thanks to the Lord for bringing her brother back into her life.

When she hung up the phone, Aunt Sophie bombarded her with questions. As Isabelle explained her telephone conversation to her aunt, she found herself thinking about James. Nearly every morning he'd left the house by seven, and usually didn't get home until about that same time every night. She assumed he went to the law office and did his job, but she knew it was possible that he could be involved in many other things. She never asked questions and never kept tabs on him. But she wasn't blind or stupid. She'd seen things, heard things, noticed things. But always, always, she kept everything inside and put on a front of disinterest. What James did was his business and not hers. He'd made that perfectly clear on many occasions.

But deep in her heart she'd often wondered if he wasn't involved in something illegal. Was it really possible that her husband, a respected lawyer from a prestigious Boston family, was involved in diamond smuggling?

Chapter 13

After an exhausting day at Over the Rainbow, Maggie Crompton gave Isabelle a ride home.

"Thanks again for your help today," Maggie said. "The children just adore you."

"I hope they like me," Isabelle replied. "I certainly enjoy being with them."

"They love you!" Maggie exclaimed.

"And I love working with them," Isabelle replied. "They are so accepting, so honest."

"Sometimes painfully honest," Maggie said with a chuckle. "Today little Ronan Toggleby asked me if it hurt my skin to be fat."

"He didn't!" Isabelle exclaimed, completely mortified for the woman.

"He most certainly did, the little scamp. I'm not saying his question was meant to be cruel; he was just curious. But sometimes you don't want to hear what you already know." Maggie pulled her car up in front of Swan Cottage. "Will I see you tomorrow, then?"

"Bright and early," Isabelle answered with enthusiasm. She hadn't felt this tremendous sense of satisfaction and fulfillment in years. Freedom, happiness, and peace—these were emotions and feelings she hadn't felt since before her marriage to James. She still had reservations, a protective wall around her heart, but with time she hoped that would fade. Aunt Sophie had affirmed several times that the Lord was guiding her path. He'd led Isabelle to Westmoor. In fact, Aunt Sophie had told Isabelle this so many times, she was beginning to believe it herself.

Thanking Maggie for the ride, Isabelle hopped out of the car, skirted her way past two beat-up bicycles parked next to the gated entrance to the cottage, and followed the path to the front door, where she was greeted by her aunt.

"Come in. How was your day?" Aunt Sophie ushered her inside.

"It was wonderful, but I'm very tired," Isabelle told her.

"I hope you don't mind, dear, but we have company for dinner," Aunt Sophie said.

Isabelle felt like relaxing in a hot bath, but didn't want to disappoint her aunt, especially after all she'd done for her. "No, of course not," Isabelle answered, following her aunt into the kitchen.

At the table sat two young men in dark suits and white ties. She knew right off who they were. Jehovah's Witnesses. What in the world was her aunt doing with them?

"Isabelle, I'd like to you meet Elder Schildmeyer and Elder Miller." Aunt Sophie carried two bowls of soup over to the table and placed one in front of each of the young men.

Isabelle thought about their names for a moment, and then it dawned on her they weren't Jehovah's Witnesses—they were Mormon missionaries.

"Hi," Isabelle gave each of them a halfhearted handshake.

"Your aunt's been telling us about you," Elder Schildmeyer said, in a distinctly German accent. "You are from America?"

Isabelle nodded. "Where are you from?" she asked them.

Elder Schildmeyer told her he was from Dusseldorf, Germany; Elder Miller was from Las Vegas, Nevada.

After the blessing was said on the food, Isabelle kept the conversation steered away from herself, asking the elders everything about themselves she could think of. She found out that Elder Miller only had a few months left on his mission. She also learned that Aunt Sophie had the missionaries over every couple of weeks for dinner. The news didn't surprise her. Aunt Sophie seemed to be the type to take everyone under her wing, especially those who needed a little extra love and care—like the missionaries, Ethan and Ian Scott Wilde, and herself.

Aunt Sophie invited everyone out on the patio for some of her famous trifle, a delicious sponge cake coated with plum jam and topped with vanilla cream custard. The elders raved about the dessert and not only had seconds, but thirds.

"I sure do love your trifle, Sister MacGregor," Elder Miller said. "And if I didn't feel like I was going to pop, I'd have some more." He leaned back in his chair and patted his stomach. "My family isn't going to recognize me when I come home with as much weight as I've gained over here."

A familiar voice came from around the side of the house. Moments later Ian Scott and his father appeared around the corner. "Aunt Sophie, Miss Isabelle," Ian Scott exclaimed when he saw them. He dropped his soccer ball on the ground and ran over and gave each of them a hug. "We brought you a surprise," he announced proudly.

Ethan held out a clear glass bowl full of nothing other than trifle.

"We made it ourselves," the boy said, beaming with pride.

Isabelle and Aunt Sophie looked at each other, trying to suppress their smiles of surprise, but the look on Elder Miller's face did them in. They burst out laughing, along with Elder Schildmeyer. Ethan and his son looked at the others in confusion. Finally Aunt Sophie gathered herself together and explained that they'd already eaten trifle, Elder Miller to the point of making himself sick.

Since there wasn't any more of her own dessert left, Aunt Sophie dished up helpings of new trifle for Ethan and Ian Scott, and as the sun began to sink they enjoyed the elders' visit a while longer.

Since Ian Scott brought his ball, he and Elder Schildmeyer engaged in a rigorous game of soccer. Elder Schildmeyer had amazing skill and gave Ian Scott some pointers on how to improve his game. They tried to coax Elder Miller and Ethan to join them, but Elder Miller just groaned and held his stomach. Ethan got up and kicked the ball around for a minute, but they needed one more person to make the teams even.

Giving into the pleading and begging, Isabelle reluctantly joined them, teaming up with Ethan against the German elder and Ian Scott, who ran circles around them.

Even though Isabelle wasn't sure of all the rules, she knew enough about the game to know she was going to hurt Ethan's chances of winning more than help him. It didn't help that she was terrified of getting kicked in the shins, nor that no matter how hard she aimed, the ball never seemed to go in the direction she kicked it. But Ethan was a good sport about it and encouraged her to keep trying.

By this time it had grown so dark Aunt Sophie had turned on the porch lights. The elders decided it was time to get back to their flat, and Elder Schildmeyer demonstrated one last passing technique to Ian Scott before he left. Isabelle took the opportunity to put the remaining trifle away and dirty dishes in the dishwasher for her aunt. She was just rinsing the last dish when Ethan came inside carrying the glasses of water she hadn't been able to bring inside.

"Thank you," she said as he put the glasses in the sink. "Would you care for anything else to drink? You worked pretty hard out there, making up for all my mistakes."

"You weren't bad for a first-timer," he said, giving her a warm smile.

She liked how disheveled his hair was and how rosy his cheeks were from running around outside. No wonder all the little girls at day care had a crush on Ian Scott; he was just like his father.

"My son is quite a fan of yours," he said. "It was all I could do to get him to bed last night, he was so excited to go to day care today. I don't know what you've been doing there, but whatever it is, it's working."

Isabelle couldn't help the rush of warmth to her cheeks. She blushed and smiled at the same time, but his words meant so much to her. "That's wonderful to hear," she told him. "I've loved every minute with those children."

"I think they can tell. I've heard several other parents say how much their children have enjoyed you coming to the center."

"Thank you for mentioning it," Isabelle replied, meeting his gaze shyly. For a moment they both stood without speaking, then the opening of the back door broke the moment. "Dad," Ian Scott announced his arrival, "Elder Schildmeyer's bike tire is flat. Can we give the elders a ride home?"

"Of course," Ethan said. "I'll be right there."

"Okay," Ian Scott answered. "See you tomorrow, Miss Isabelle."

"Remember to bring your picture from home," she reminded him.

"Oh yeah," Ian Scott exclaimed. "We have to get home, Dad. I have to find a picture of our family to take to school."

"Guess we're off then," Ethan said to her.

"We'll see you tomorrow evening for more?" she asked before she realized what was coming out of her mouth. She sounded like she hoped they would return again. And even though she enjoyed Ethan and his son's company, she certainly didn't want to give the wrong impression.

"I think we can pop in for a bit tomorrow evening, *Miss Isabelle*," he said with a teasing lilt to his voice. "That is, if you're certain you want us to come over again."

"Aunt Sophie invited you; I think she's expecting you to come," Isabelle said, hoping that would help dilute her remark.

It obviously did the trick, since Ethan's expression quickly changed. "Yes, of course she did," he answered. "Tomorrow then." He took off out the back door without another glance, and for some reason Isabelle couldn't help feeling just a bit troubled. She hadn't wanted to hurt his feelings, but she knew she certainly wasn't about to foster a relationship with another man. Her life was a mess, and whether she liked it or not, she was still a married woman. To involve anyone else at this point would be selfish on her part and unfair to him. Ethan had said that Westmoor was a good place to sort out one's life. She hoped he was right.

The next morning Isabelle awoke to a drizzle of rain. She remained in bed, feeling as sleepy as she had when she'd retired the night before. She'd thought that maybe her vitamin prescription was beginning to help her lack of energy, but this morning she lacked the strength or ambition to even get up.

Isabelle heard Aunt Sophie downstairs in the kitchen fixing breakfast. Within minutes the strong aroma of frying bacon drifted up the stairs to her room. The aroma sent a wave of nausea over her.

She pulled the covers over her head to block out the odor of the bacon.

She knew it was time to be honest with herself and quit dodging the truth. But she just couldn't face the reality of the situation. She just couldn't bear the possibility that . . .

"Isabelle?" Aunt Sophie's persistent tap on the door broke her thoughts. "Dear, it's time to get up. Breakfast is ready."

"I can't," Isabelle's muffled voice came from under the down comforter. She felt a knot of emotion choke her. "Please God," she prayed, "please let it be anything else but this."

"You're not feeling well again?" she asked. "I better call Dr. Holmes."

"No, please," Isabelle pulled the covers off her head. "I'll be fine. I just need to rest," she said, trying to convince herself as much as her aunt.

"Would you like some toast? That seems to settle your stomach," her aunt suggested.

The last thing Isabelle felt like doing was eating, but her aunt was probably right.

"I'll be back in a jiffy," Aunt Sophie said, then hurried from the room.

Tears slid out of the corners of her eyes. Hadn't she been through enough already? Was it really necessary for her to have more trials? More challenges?

Her aunt quickly returned, and Isabelle took a bite of the toast to appease her. She had to chew a dozen times before she could make herself swallow the bread.

After another bite she asked her aunt to leave it by her bedside, and she'd try and eat more later.

"Could you please call Maggie and tell her I can't come in today?" Isabelle asked.

"Right away, dear," Aunt Sophie answered with a worried expression.

Grateful for the peace and quiet, Isabelle forced her fears to the back of her mind as she fell back asleep. Her troubled stomach and overwhelming exhaustion pulled her into a deep slumber, where dreams and hidden fears mingled together.

As her deep sleep took her away, Isabelle felt herself riding on the back of a horse, plunging through sweeping moors and forests thick with trees. Her hair flew in the wind, her lungs filled with the fragrances of countryside; the warmth of the sun caressed her back.

Her horse seemed to read her thoughts and know exactly where she wanted to go. Up the hillside he climbed, as she rode bareback, her heels digging into the horse's side, her fingers buried in the tangle of his mane.

Freedom—a feeling so empowering, so unshackling, that it filled her soul until she felt as if she truly could fly. Faster and swifter, the horse's hooves traveled as they neared Dunsbury Castle, where colorful banners waved in the summer breeze. The castle now stood solid and strong, not old and crumbling.

They neared the top and crested the hill where, on a beautiful white horse, wearing shining armor, was the knight of her dreams— her protector, her guardian, the man who would deliver her from the many evils and dangers surrounding her.

As if drawn together, the two horses trotted toward each other. And as the distance between them narrowed, Isabelle's heart beat wildly.

Then, without warning, her horse's hoof slipped and, as if in slow motion, he went down, taking her with him.

Isabelle felt no pain as she was thrown to the ground. Instead, she lay on the ground, looking up at the blue sky overhead until she heard the pounding of hooves close by.

Her knight. Surely he was coming to rescue her.

Pushing herself onto one elbow, she turned and watched as the rider dismounted before the horse came to a complete stop. The knight dashed to her side, kneeling down next to her, then scooping her up in his arms.

I'm safe, the thought came to her. *He will protect me. He will take care of me.*

The knight carried her to his steed and effortlessly mounted the horse, still carrying Isabelle in his arms. Then she heard laughing. Not gentle laughter like water in a brook, but an evil, insidious laugh that made her skin crawl.

Reaching up, Isabelle lifted the flap on the knight's helmet, and screamed . . .

Drenched in sweat, Isabelle sat straight up in bed, her breath coming in ragged gasps.

James!

She saw his face, his eyes full of hatred, staring back at her from inside the knight's helmet.

Tears oozed from her eyes, creeping down her cheeks. Was this how her life was to be? Living in fear? Would she ever feel safe again? Free of the constant worry that James was around every corner, hidden in every shadow?

She decided to get up and take a long, relaxing shower. The warm spray would soothe her nerves and relax her muscles. Maybe she was wrong about why she was sick. Maybe it was just the stress she'd been going through. Certainly she'd been through enough to make a person physically ill. Did she dare hope? Could it be possible?

Her eyes shut, she basked in the streams of water, washing the suds of shampoo from her red hair.

A sudden movement outside the shower curtain turned her stomach to stone.

"Aunt Sophie?" she said, but received no reply.

Glancing around the shower for something to protect herself with, Isabelle grabbed the bottle of shampoo, not sure what good it would do, but feeling slightly braver.

"Aunt Sophie?" she said again. Still no answer.

Taking a deep breath and steeling herself for whatever was to come, she threw the shower curtain open and screamed, causing poor Romeo to practically jump out of his fur.

The dog had merely been getting a drink from the toilet.

"You scared me to death!" she scolded the dog as her chest heaved with deep breaths of relief. Giving the dog a gentle push, she closed the bathroom door and dried herself off.

She had to believe that James knew nothing of her existence, had no idea she was still alive. But James was a powerful man. No distance, no fortress, no army could keep him away. She was afraid that death was the only way she could be truly safe from him

After getting dressed, Isabelle went downstairs to find her aunt. Instead she found a note saying that Aunt Sophie had gone to the market and would be back later, and that Maggie's other part-time assistant, Miss Alice, was able to cover for Isabelle at the day-care center.

Relieved that the children were taken care of and feeling much better than she had earlier that morning, Isabelle found a blueberry muffin to eat and sat down in front of the television while she enjoyed her breakfast.

She watched the news program for a while and was about to turn off the television when footage from the Sierra Leone coastline was shown. The reporter explained how millions of years ago, diamonds had tumbled down from the rivers into the sea; when the ocean receded, the diamonds remained on the beach, and others were left on the ocean floor.

Now beach miners combed the shore, stripping away sand and gravel, sweeping the bedrock for gems. Some miners used vacuum machines to clear away the sand and gravel. The diamonds were so plentiful in some places, workers could literally scoop up diamonds from the sand with their hands.

The scene then changed from diamond mines to show the brutal wars that had resulted from the diamonds. The reporter claimed that the price of peace for these areas of Africa was just too high. Thousands of innocent people had been brutalized, mutilated, and killed because of the rebel groups being funded by the sale of these "conflict diamonds."

Isabelle watched in horror as orphans begged for food, and youth without arms, hands, or legs hobbled around on crutches. Did James really have a part in this atrocity? Couldn't anything be done to stop what was going on?

Disturbed after listening to the program, Isabelle watched out the window as the clouds overhead broke apart, allowing columns of sunlight to shine through.

Thinking that a walk outside might be invigorating, Isabelle called for Romeo to accompany her, but he didn't respond. *He's probably already outside,* she thought. A small flap in the back door allowed the dog to come and go as he pleased. He was prone to wander, but he always seemed to find his way home when it was time to eat.

Pulling on her aunt's sweater, Isabelle stepped into the fresh air that followed the morning rain shower. Everything seemed greener, the colors of the flowers more vibrant, their fragrance full and rich.

The fresh air did wonders, and as Isabelle strolled up the lane to the cobbled back streets of Westmoor she felt her energy return and strength return to her limbs. It was a wonderful day and the lanes were filled with the intoxicating fragrance of window boxes overflowing with flowers and the hearty aromas drifting from pubs and cafes.

Greeted with smiles from the women and gentlemen tipping their caps, saying, "Mornin'" to her, Isabelle was enchanted with this wonderful city of Westmoor. Filled with joy and confidence, she drank in the essence of history and culture, marveling at the aged stone and brick homes, the solid timbers of the roofs, the cobbled walkways, and the occasional marble statues or facade carvings.

The main street of the village was thronged with tourists enjoying the town as a stopover, and to some, as a destination. The friendly townspeople and wonderful shops gave the village a warm, welcoming flavor that was intriguing and inviting. Rare was the automobile that traveled these streets, which were mostly populated with pedestrians and bicycles.

Isabelle wound her way up High Street toward the town square, where lovely, well-manicured grounds and a beautiful fountain with statues spilling water adorned the center of town.

A shaded bench beckoned to her and Isabelle took a seat, enjoying a quiet moment, watching as people bustled and scurried, occasionally stopping to snap a photograph or glance at a map or travel agenda.

"Playing truant today?" a voice from behind asked.

Startled, Isabelle jumped at the voice, but knew immediately who it was.

"Ethan!" She turned to find him with a questioning grin on his face.

She found herself returning his smile. He was so warm and genuine, it would be impossible not to like him. And even though she kept a wall of caution around her feelings and gave her complete trust to very few, Isabelle found herself slowly warming toward this man. Whether or not she admitted it to anyone else, she couldn't lie to herself. She liked this man, Ethan Wilde.

Chapter 14

"Mind if I sit down?" he asked.

"No, of course not." She scooted over, giving him a wide berth on the bench.

"So, does this mean you've had enough of all those little scoundrels at the day care?" He stretched out his legs and crossed one ankle casually over the other one.

"Oh no," Isabelle answered with a start. "Not at all. The kids are great. I didn't feel well this morning when I woke up, so I wasn't able to go in."

"You look great now," he said, then quickly he reworded his last comment. "I mean, you look like you feel better."

Isabelle hid her smile. She couldn't help noticing that he was definitely cute when he got embarrassed. "Thanks. I feel much better."

"Well enough to get a bite to eat?" he offered.

She was, in truth, starving. The muffin hadn't satisfied her for long. With a quick shrug, she answered, "Sure, I'd love to."

"I'll take you over to Adelaide's. She makes the best Cornish pasties in the U.K.," he bragged.

They'd missed the lunchtime rush and managed to snag a table at the front of the pub where they could watch tourists and feel the refreshing afternoon breeze coming in through the open windows.

Just as Ethan promised, Adelaide served up a delicious meal. First, as a starter, they enjoyed a delicious soup called "cock-a-leekie," made of chicken stock and leeks, followed by the Cornish pasty, which was nothing more than seasoned vegetables and meat enclosed in a light pastry envelope. Isabelle didn't realize how hungry she was until she tasted the savory morsels, and then accepted Ethan's offer of dessert, a serving of warm gooseberry fool, similar to a cobbler.

While they ate, Ethan and Isabelle talked about Ian Scott, life in Westmoor, and Ethan's work as a cabinetmaker and part-time farmer. Isabelle wasn't ordinarily comfortable around men, but being with Ethan didn't feel like being with just some man; it felt like being with a friend. Maybe that was the difference.

"Do you ever miss law enforcement?" she asked, taking a final bite of her half-eaten dessert and admitting that she was stuffed.

"I struggled at first, when I came back to England," he said. "I really loved my job as a policeman. I believed I was making a difference, that somehow I was contributing to society." He polished the inside of his spoon with his thumb. "But when Jennifer died, it was like the one person whose life I cared about the very most was the one person I failed. I became very disillusioned after that."

Isabelle searched for something to say, something to soothe his broken heart, to let him know he couldn't blame himself.

"I'm so sorry," she finally said, for lack of something better.

"Yeah." He shoved the spoon out of the way, sending it clinking against his water glass. "Me too."

Isabelle wished he hadn't brought up the subject of his wife's death. They had been having a perfectly enjoyable time.

Ethan glanced down at his watch.

"It's probably getting late," she said apologetically. "I should let you get back to what you were doing."

"No, no," he answered without pause, "I was just checking to see how much time I had before Ian Scott finished at day care. I was wondering if you had plans for the rest of the afternoon.

"I'm driving to Salisbury," he continued when she didn't answer right off. "I thought you could come along and we could stop at Stonehenge. That is, if you'd like to see it."

Isabelle's first thought was to turn him down. Her life with James was over, yet she wasn't sure about spending time with another man. Still, it wasn't like they were going on a date.

But she wondered, what would Ethan think if he knew what she'd done? She was almost ashamed of herself for taking the coward's way out of her marriage, running away instead of facing the problem. But she'd felt she had no other choice. She knew if she had to do it again, she'd probably do the same thing. Still, Ethan wouldn't understand if he'd known how she'd left her husband.

"Stonehenge," she murmured, remembering that Ryan had talked about going there but it just hadn't worked out. "I've always wanted to see Stonehenge. Is it close by?"

"It's not far," he assured her, "and it's a beautiful drive through some of the prettiest country in England."

Her desire to go to the famous site overrode her concerns about spending time with Ethan. He was a friend and obviously someone trustworthy, since her aunt spoke so highly of him. Deciding to ignore her fears and concerns, she said only, "I should let my aunt know first."

"Here," he took a small cell phone out of his shirt pocket. "You can use this."

She accepted the phone, then realized she didn't know her aunt's number. Before she could mention it he offered to dial the number for her.

Getting no answer at the cottage, Isabelle left a message on the machine, knowing her aunt would check it throughout the day.

"You can try again later," Ethan said. "We won't be too long."

Remembering the last time she'd gone on a ride with Ethan, she half-expected some kind of farm equipment or rusty old truck to be their transportation, but to her amazement he drove a gorgeous, light silver Saab—very sporty, and very classy.

He laughed when he noticed her expression. "You weren't expecting the tractor again, were you?"

She raised her shoulders sheepishly. "Sort of."

"I may be a farm boy at heart, but I have big city taste," he confessed. "I don't allow myself many pleasures, but my car is one allowance I make. With as much driving as I do for bids and measuring for cabinet jobs, I figured I deserve something to make the trips more enjoyable."

"You didn't hear me complaining or asking for excuses. Frankly, I prefer this over a tractor any day," she told him.

Ethan wasn't kidding when he claimed to be showing her some of the most beautiful scenery in England. Grassy uplands and rolling plains spread out as far as she could see. Much of the Wiltshire area was agricultural, but most of it was green pastureland, dotted with small villages, complete with tall-towered parish churches, thatched cottages surrounded by orchards, and ornate cathedrals that attracted tourists from all over the world.

They stopped at a lovely home being renovated, which was located on a quaint street on the outskirts of Salisbury. On the outside, the home looked ancient, even though it boasted a fresh coat of paint and newly thatched roof. Inside, Isabelle was surprised to see lovely hardwood floors, modern Scandinavian-designed furniture in soft neutral tones, and a kitchen full of state-of-the-art appliances and beautiful maple cabinets.

The owners of the home, a lovely middle-aged woman and her husband, had been so pleased with Ethan's work that they decided to have him design a built-in hutch and bookshelves at the end of the kitchen where the dining room table was situated. Ethan needed to take some detailed measurements before he began work on the pieces. While Ethan and the woman discussed last-minute adjustments, Isabelle studied the craftsmanship of the cabinets, impressed at the attention to detail, quality construction, and beautiful design.

After getting what he needed, they climbed back into the car and headed through the center of town until they came to a roundabout, where they drove around in a circle with dozens of other cars until Ethan darted off on an exit toward Amesbury. He drove another ten miles and pulled up to a large parking lot with no less than five buses and dozens of cars parked in it. Opening her door, Ethan offered Isabelle his hand, and together they followed a pathway leading to the world-famous stone circle known as Stonehenge.

Isabelle's breath caught in her throat as she caught her first glimpse of the prehistoric monument.

"Five thousand years old," Ethan said. "It's difficult to comprehend something that old, isn't it?"

They could only get within fifty feet of the megalithic pillars, but nevertheless, Isabelle was completely mesmerized by the sight before her. Pushing their way in front of the crowds of tourists, Ethan and Isabelle gazed at the huge concentric circle of stones, asking themselves the same question everyone who came to see Stonehenge asked: "What is it?"

Ethan told her that some believed Stonehenge was an astronomical observatory, capable of predicting eclipses. Other theories surrounding the amazing structure stretched from a connection to the pyramids of Egypt, to the people of Atlantis, to King Arthur, and more extreme, to beings from outer space.

Isabelle was mesmerized by the immense and mysterious circle of stones. Side by side, they followed the walkway that completely circled the stones, stopping occasionally for lingering gazes at the structure.

"I guess we'll never really know why it was built," Ethan said. "But something this amazing causes you to think that it was of great significance to whoever built it. Some of the stones weigh several tons, and were carried clear from Wales."

Isabelle nodded, wondering about the methods used to transport stones of this size and weight.

"It seems that people from the very beginning of time have tried to make sense of the universe, don't you think?" Isabelle wondered out loud. "Maybe they were trying to unlock its secrets."

"And who knows," Ethan took it a step further. "Maybe they did and that's why they aren't around to tell us about it."

After they'd finally absorbed as much of the site as they could, they made the drive back to Westmoor. They continued their discussion in the car.

"Even though I have a hard time accepting Jennifer's death, I don't think I could go on without faith in the fact that I'll be with her again," Ethan said. "I know we don't have all the 'secrets of the universe' like we were talking about earlier, but we know everything we need to know, don't we," he added, his statement requiring her validation one way or the other.

"Actually, I didn't know we had any of the 'secrets of the universe,'" she answered. "Are they located in some ancient Celtic writings somewhere?"

His eyebrows narrowed with confusion. "You're kidding, right?"

"Aren't you?" she asked, feeling confused herself.

"May I ask you a personal question?" Ethan requested as he put the car into a higher gear to accommodate the faster speed of the motorway.

"You can ask," Isabelle replied. "I can't promise that I'll answer."

Ethan smiled, keeping his eyes on the road.

"You're LDS, like your aunt, aren't you?" he asked.

"Yes, I guess," she answered. "I mean, sort of."

"Sort of?" This time he did look away from the road at her for a moment.

"Well, I was baptized and I went to church when I was young, but I quit going when I was a teenager," she explained.

"Oh." He nodded, prodding no further, for which she was grateful.

"Does that mean you're LDS, too?" Isabelle asked. He didn't seem overly religious to her.

"I joined the Church in New York with my wife," he told her. "The sister missionaries came to our door and Jennifer let them in. It was a good thing I didn't answer the door that day, because I would have sent them on their way, but not Jenn." He shook his head with the memory. "She was like that, you know. Feeding stray animals, feeling sorry for the homeless; she was always giving money to someone for something. So naturally, when the missionaries came by, she invited them in because she felt sorry for them. It was a hot day and she said they looked like they needed something cold to drink, so she took pity on them."

Isabelle had a feeling she would have liked Ethan's wife.

"Anyway, one thing led to another and she got really interested in their message. I figured it was some emotional woman's thing, and that she'd eventually get over it, but she was very serious about it. Read the Book of Mormon in two weeks, went to church, the whole bit. I started to get nervous, wondering what my wife was getting into, so I decided to sit in on some of their discussions. Everything sounded pretty much like other religions until they came to the part about the Plan of Salvation."

"The Plan of Salvation?" she repeated, the words triggering her memory. "If I remember right, that's what tells us that we lived before we came to earth and that after we die we'll go back to heaven?"

"Right," Ethan said. "But returning to heaven wasn't the part that got to me as much as the fact that we can be with our families and live together forever. That knowledge has given me a lot of strength when many times I've wanted to give up."

Isabelle knew that Ethan truly believed that what he said was true. And for a moment, the concept crystallized and she considered the possibility of seeing her parents again. As she searched her soul for her own feelings on what she thought happened after death, a tingling warmth touched her heart, spreading throughout her body with each beat. She didn't know how she knew, or how to explain what she was feeling, but somewhere inside of her, not in her brain, she knew that Ethan had told her the truth.

The sensation grew until tears formed in her eyes, somehow releasing the billowing feeling inside of her.

She would see her parents again.

He steered the car onto the country road Isabelle recognized as the post road to Westmoor. The landscape and layout of the town was finally becoming familiar to her.

"I didn't realize there were so many members of the Church here in England," she said.

"There's quite a few, although not too many in Westmoor. Many of the townspeople think we're an odd bunch, you know—no tea, no alcohol . . . But they're getting used to us and to having missionaries around. Some are still antagonistic toward the Church. Keep in mind, our culture and history date back thousands of years; most people aren't very open to having strangers from an American church come in and try to change their religious traditions."

Isabelle nodded as she tried to understand how difficult it would be.

"But the Church is strong here in England. Our membership is growing every year. It's exciting to be a part of it," he said, his face glowing with enthusiasm.

"I think I'd like to meet a prophet," Isabelle said. "I'd like to meet a person who actually talks to God. In fact, I have a few questions I'd like him to ask God next time they talk."

Ethan raised his eyebrows with amusement, then turned to her. "You can talk to God too, you know."

"I'm no prophet," Isabelle replied.

"You don't have to be. Anyone can. It's called prayer."

Isabelle already knew about prayer. She just hadn't thought of it as a direct link to heaven. She viewed it more as an act of faith, like an affirmation of a person's will for something to happen. She'd certainly never thought of it as a way to communicate with the Almighty.

"Don't you pray, Isabelle?" he asked pointedly.

"In my own way, I guess," she answered. "I don't know if I'm doing it right or not, though."

"There's not really a right or wrong way," he said. "You just say what's in your heart. He'll listen."

"How do you know that, Ethan?" she asked.

"I just do." He pulled up to a stop sign and let the car idle for a moment. "I've had prayers answered. I've felt the warm, tingling feeling of the Spirit, giving me strength and comfort."

She noted that he'd just described the feeling she'd had earlier.

"Heavenly Father loves you," Ethan told her with conviction. "You're His daughter. He wants you to talk to Him. Often. You should pray," he instructed. "You'd be surprised how much it can help you."

"How often do you pray?" she asked, looking him square in the eye.

"At least once a day. Usually twice. Some days, constantly."

The frank truthfulness of his answer wasn't lost on Isabelle. She appreciated his candor. He wasn't ashamed of his beliefs; in fact, he seemed proud of them and she respected him for that.

"I'm amazed," she told him as he finally drove on.

"Really? About what?" He negotiated several pot holes in the road.

"You are so open, so honest, with your feelings and your life. I feel as if I could ask you anything about yourself and you'd tell me," she said.

"I tried it the other way and it nearly killed me," he said with a bluntness that surprised her.

"What do you mean?"

"After Jenn died, I couldn't deal with her death. I was so empty, so lonely, I didn't know what to do. I couldn't face people, I couldn't see anything that reminded me of her. That's when I moved back to England. I think I was trying to escape her memory. I had to escape it because remembering was just. . . too. . . painful. . ." He spoke slowly, deliberately, as if keeping his emotions in check.

"One day I found myself actually contemplating suicide, to the point—" he swallowed before he continued, "to the point that I began considering ways to end my life. It scared me, and I knew if I didn't do something drastic, I'd go through with it."

Isabelle listened, feeling her heart go out to him. She knew the exact feeling he meant—the feeling of hopelessness, of desperation—the feeling of almost choosing the last resort.

"I needed help. I had a son who needed me. I couldn't abandon him. I couldn't be that selfish. He'd already lost his mother; he didn't deserve to lose his father, too. So," he slowed the car to a stop after he turned onto the lane to Swan Cottage, "one day your Aunt Sophie was tending Ian Scott while I helped install some cabinets. When I went to pick him up, she made the mistake of asking me how I was doing."

Ethan had to clear his throat before he could go on.

"Ian Scott ended up sleeping on her couch, and your aunt and I stayed up most of the night talking. Actually, I should say that she listened, and I talked. Did you know your aunt's a wonderful listener?"

"Yes," Isabelle nodded. "I did."

"She's also very wise, and by the time the sun came up, I felt like the first day of a new life was dawning for me. I hadn't solved any of my problems really, but I felt so cleansed, so free, because I'd finally unloaded all that heavy baggage. So now, even though I still have a tendency to want to hold something in, I don't do it. I know it only leads to trouble. I just get it off my chest."

Easier said than done, Isabelle thought. Sure, in theory, it was much more emotionally healthy to talk about problems and concerns, but Isabelle didn't think her problems and concerns were the run-of-the-mill kind. Hers involved danger and death, and the fewer people who knew about it, the safer she would be, and probably the safer they'd be too. She worried for her aunt and her brother now that they knew about James. Would they get caught in her tangled past as well?

Chapter 15

Sitting in front of the telly that night, Isabelle and her aunt relaxed watching some outrageous British comedy that Isabelle found completely hilarious. The husband had a deadpan humor that played off the wife's straightforward honesty, and the one-liners were delivered with perfect timing.

A knock on the door caught them off guard. As always when she was startled, the hair rose on the back of Isabelle's neck.

"I wonder who that could be this time of night," Aunt Sophie said, getting up off the couch.

Isabelle tensed as she waited with a racing heart, wondering who would be stopping by so late in the evening.

"Dr. Holmes," Aunt Sophie announced when she opened the door. "Come in."

Isabelle felt herself relax and take in a great breath of relief.

"Sorry to come by so late. I was at the pub down the street for some late supper and I took a chance you'd still be up." The doctor looked quite distinguished in brown twill slacks, a pale blue oxford shirt, and an argyle vest that buttoned down the front. He smiled at Isabelle, and kindness radiated from his face.

"Could I get you something to drink or something sweet, perhaps?" Aunt Sophie fussed over him.

"Thank you, but I can't stay long," he replied, taking the seat Aunt Sophie offered. "How are you feeling?" he greeted Isabelle.

Isabelle wondered if he'd come to tell her some news. Some bad news about her blood test.

Or maybe he was just pretending to take time out of his busy schedule to check on her so he could come and see Aunt Sophie? Isabelle could have sworn by the look in both of their eyes that they liked each other.

Before she could answer, his cell phone rang. "Excuse me, ladies," the doctor said before answering the call.

Isabelle and her aunt slipped into the kitchen so he could talk in private.

Taking advantage of the opportunity, Isabelle inquired as nonchalantly as she could. "Dr. Holmes certainly is a handsome man, don't you think?"

Aunt Sophie was busy arranging assorted biscuits onto a tray. Isabelle reached for one of the shortbread kind that had quickly become a favorite. She nibbled the cookie as she studied her aunt, trying to decide if a pair of seventy-year-olds could get romantically involved.

"Oh, yes. Dr. Holmes has always been a dapper fellow and a smart dresser. As long as I've known him he's been this way," Aunt Sophie explained.

"Does he have a wife?" Isabelle asked. There hadn't been any mention of a wife, and the way the doctor spent so much time attending to the townspeople she highly doubted it.

"His wife died, oh, . . . about ten years ago," Aunt Sophie answered thoughtfully. "She was a lovely woman. Such a lady, very well bred. She didn't care much for Westmoor. She would have preferred to live in London. But Dr. Holmes wouldn't leave. He thinks of the people of this town as family."

"How did she die?" Isabelle asked.

"Cancer," Aunt Sophie replied. "She didn't suffer long. Diagnosed one week, a month later, she passed away. He's very lonely, but he stays busy. That's the key, staying busy."

"Like you?"

Her aunt got a handful of cloth napkins from the linen cupboard. "I suppose so. I don't know; I don't really think about it. I do enjoy staying busy, though. I'm not one to sit around watching the telly all day or sleeping all morning. I'd rather be productive and tired than lazy and rested."

Admiring her aunt's courage and strength, Isabelle helped her carry in the tray of biscuits and three glasses of refreshing blackberry juice.

The doctor was just finishing his conversation when they entered the room.

"Is everything all right, doctor?" Aunt Sophie asked.

"It appears as though one of the missionaries hit a famous Westmoor pothole and fell off his bike. He's at the hospital now, where they're x-raying his arm. It sounds like a fracture."

"Oh dear," Aunt Sophie exclaimed, holding one hand beside her face. "Which elder was it?"

"The German boy—Schildmeyer is it?" Dr. Holmes answered.

"Is he going to be okay?" Isabelle asked.

"He'll be fine. I'll stop in and take a look at him on my way home. I don't think it's an emergency."

The doctor accepted the refreshments without hesitation. Isabelle watched the eye contact between the two adults and decided that they were a perfect match. These two were made for each other.

The conversation was mostly small talk—town happenings, community events, and such. Isabelle had begun to feel like an outsider and was about to excuse herself when his cell phone rang again.

"It's the hospital," Dr. Holmes said as he checked the phone before answering.

He said a few, "uh-huhs," a couple of, "I sees," and one, "It's that bad, is it?" and Isabelle immediately became concerned. Were they talking about the missionary?

He hung up and got to his feet. "The elder's bleeding internally," he told them. "I have to go. I'll try and talk to you later."

He was off in a flash but Isabelle wondered what the purpose of his visit had been—to socialize with her aunt? Or was there something more? Had the doctor come to confirm her worst fear?

Elder Schildmeyer ended up getting transported to a London hospital where he could receive more extensive care. It was clear to Isabelle that her aunt was very protective of the elders and sad to see the one elder leave.

When she got home from the day care on Friday, Isabelle found Elder Miller and his new companion at the cottage. Aunt Sophie had invited them over for dinner.

"Isabelle," Aunt Sophie sprang from her chair when Isabelle walked into the kitchen. "You're just in time." Aunt Sophie always greeted her with a hug when she came home. "Did you have a good day?"

Isabelle laughed. "You know how we were going on a field trip? Well, that little redheaded boy, Tommy—"

"The McCracken lad," Aunt Sophie said.

"Right," Isabelle said. "He fell in the river. Maggie had to go in after him and got herself drenched in the process."

"Oh, mercy." Aunt Sophie shook her head. "Those youngsters are such a handful."

"They sure are," Isabelle agreed, taking a seat at the table. "Hi, Elder Miller. Is this your new companion?"

Elder Miller nodded. "He's not new though; he goes home in a few weeks. I won't get a regular companion until the next transfer."

The other elder gave a wave of his hand. "Hi. I'm Elder Twitchell."

"Nice to meet you," Isabelle replied, realizing that she was starving and her aunt's leek-and-potato soup smelled heavenly.

A prayer was said and the meal began. The elders gave an update on Elder Schildmeyer's condition, which had improved enough for him to leave the hospital to recover at the mission president's home.

Aunt Sophie left to answer a phone call, so Isabelle dished up more for the elders to eat and asked them about themselves. "So, Elder Twitchell," she said as she placed a bowl of soup in front of him, "where have you served?"

The elder gave her a list of cities he'd worked in. "I've been working in the mission office up until now. I'm kind of glad to finish my mission back out in the field. I've missed working with investigators and teaching. I even miss tracting," he said.

"What's that?" Isabelle asked.

The elder explained that tracting was the act of going door to door and meeting people and telling them about the Church.

"And you like doing this?" she asked.

"I love it," the elder answered enthusiastically. "Some of my best contacts have been made tracting. It's not the most effective way to do missionary work, but I really like talking to the people."

From the brightness in his eyes, the animated expression on his face and the sincere tone of his voice, Isabelle could see that this elder truly loved what he was doing.

"Is it going to be hard for you to go home?" Isabelle asked him.

"I'm dreading it," he admitted, then added, "Oh, not that I don't want to see my family again. But I love the people here so much. I love serving them and sharing the gospel with them. I don't want it to end."

Her heart went out to him. Even though she couldn't understand what being a missionary was like, it was obvious he was truly torn.

"Where is home anyway?" she asked.

"Boston," he answered.

The blood froze in Isabelle's veins. She checked his name tag again. Twitchell. From Boston.

"Excuse me for just a minute—" She stood so fast she nearly knocked over her chair. "I'll go see what's keeping Aunt Sophie."

She raced from the dining room, through the kitchen into the living room, and up the stairs to her room, all the time searching her memory. Hadn't her neighbor in Boston, Cynthia Twitchell, said her son was in the United Kingdom? Was it possible that they were one and the same?

"Isabelle," her aunt called up the stairs. "I have good news. That was Ryan on the phone. He's driving down for the weekend. He'll be here first thing in the morning."

"That's great," Isabelle replied.

"Are you coming back down?" she asked.

"In just a minute," Isabelle answered, trying to settle her nerves. If this Elder Twitchell was her neighbor, he could never find out who she was. If he did, and told his mother, and the truth came out—

She couldn't even think about it. Taking several deep breaths, she forced herself to calm down. She needed to tell her aunt before she accidentally said something.

"Aunt Sophie," Isabelle called. "Can you come here for just a minute please?"

Aunt Sophie's footsteps tapped across the floor and up the stairs.

"What is it, dear? Is something wrong?" Aunt Sophie was breathless when she got to Isabelle's room.

"You know that new elder?"

"Elder Twitchell?"

Isabelle nodded. "He's from Boston."

"Yes, I know. I asked him earlier."

"You didn't happen to tell him I'm from Boston, did you?" Isabelle held her breath, waiting for her aunt's answer.

"No, of course not. Why?"

"It may be just a strange coincidence but my next door neighbor's name was Twitchell and she has a son living in Great Britain."

Aunt Sophie pondered Isabelle's words. "You're worried about him discovering who you are?"

Isabelle nodded.

"We just have to be extra cautious then, that's all. Don't worry, he won't find out. Besides, it may not even be him."

"You're right," Isabelle said with a sigh of relief. "We'd better go join them before they begin to wonder what's going on."

After dessert the elders left for a teaching appointment. Before leaving, Elder Twitchell asked if the two ladies would be at church on Sunday. Since Ryan would be in town, Isabelle had already decided to go to church with him and Aunt Sophie. "Yes," Isabelle answered to her aunt's surprise. "We'll be there."

The elders gave a hearty handshake in parting and rode off on their bikes. Isabelle fairly collapsed onto the couch, weak with relief, glad that they were finally gone.

Getting up early to get the housecleaning done before Ryan arrived, Isabelle and her Aunt Sophie worked together changing sheets, dusting, sweeping out the cottage, and hanging laundry outside on the clothesline to dry in the sweet-smelling country air. The day was overcast but warm. If it did rain, Isabelle hoped it wouldn't be until after they brought the clothes in from the line.

Aunt Sophie took a shower first, leaving Isabelle to trim several rosebushes in the front. The aroma of all the different flowers in the garden blended to one intoxicating fragrance. Just as she finished the chore and gathered up the clippings of wilted roses, Ryan's car pulled up in front.

Isabelle met him at the gate. Their hug was awkward but not unpleasant. It still took a moment for her to digest the fact that this really was her brother standing in front of her. They walked the stone path to the front door together.

"How are you doing, sis?" he asked.

Isabelle smiled, liking the way he called her "sis."

"I'm good," she answered, "but I'm sorry you have to see me looking like this." After cleaning and gardening, she looked anything but presentable.

"It's great seeing you, no matter what. And you know—" he stopped walking and took her by the shoulders and studied her at arm's length, "My memory's not that great, but you remind me a lot of Mom," he said.

"I do?" she replied, fingering a strand of hair, knowing she needed to go in for a trim and color by a professional.

"I don't mean just your hair. Your eyes remind me of hers, too. Mom had eyes that could look right through you. I always felt like she knew when I was lying to her." He sighed wearily. The memory of his mother was tinged by memories of his past actions and attitudes. "There's so much I wish I could go back and change. If only I'd listened to her."

Isabelle certainly understood those feelings; she felt the same way. If only she'd listened to her mother too, she wouldn't have married James. "I know what you mean," she said.

"But we can't change the past, can we?" he said.

Isabelle shook her head.

"But if it weren't for our past mistakes and experiences, we wouldn't be who we are today," Ryan said.

And who is that? Isabelle wondered. *Who am I today?*

"Hey," Ryan said, brightening his tone and slipping an arm around her shoulders, "I didn't mean to make you sad. Come on, now," he coaxed. "Let's just forget about all of that and have some fun."

Aunt Sophie was dressed and ready when they walked inside. Refusing to take no for an answer, she made Ryan sit down in the kitchen and tell her about his week while she whipped him up some breakfast. Isabelle ran for a quick shower.

In no time they were out for a drive in the country and a late lunch at a quaint little pub in the town of Cheddar, famous for, as Isabelle guessed, cheddar cheese, first made in the twelfth century. While in the area they drove through Cheddar Gorge, where gently rolling hills, perforated with limestone caverns and gorges, gave way to massive gray cliffs. Isabelle's neck ached from looking upward at their beautiful formations.

It was late afternoon by the time they returned home. Isabelle was amazed to find that each moment she spent with her brother brought them closer and closer together. They had been separated by years, but shared the eternal ties of family, and no amount of time apart could erase that.

As painful as some of their past regrets were, they still had many fond memories to share and laughed themselves silly as they recalled Christmases, birthdays, and family vacations.

They were surprised as they pulled up to the cottage to find Dr. Holmes just getting back into his car. Ryan greeted the doctor as he hurried around to the other side of the car to help his aunt out.

"Dr. Holmes," Aunt Sophie said, pushing a few errant strands of hair back into place. "How lovely to see you. What brings you by on a Saturday evening?"

"Hi, Dr. Holmes," Isabelle said, feeling a seed of worry plant itself at the bottom of her stomach.

"Isabelle, I wondered if you had a moment we could talk."

"Of course." Isabelle led the way into the cottage as the seed of worry began to sprout and grow.

"We'll be in the back garden if you need anything," Aunt Sophie told her.

"No!" Isabelle reached for her aunt. "Please, I want both of you to stay."

Aunt Sophie and Ryan both looked at the doctor, who nodded, and they all sat down on the couch. Aunt Sophie held Isabelle's hand tucked safely inside of hers.

Vines of worry wrapped around Isabelle's heart and lungs. She could barely breathe, feeling as though she would pass out at any moment.

"Doctor?" Ryan asked. "What is it?"

"I'm not certain if this is good news or bad news." he said. "But . . ." he paused, "I might as well come right out with it. Isabelle, your test results came back and . . ."

Isabelle felt lightheaded and had to remind herself to breathe.

"You're pregnant."

Chapter 16

Isabelle closed her eyes, and for a moment, she felt as if her soul had left her body and been replaced by an empty numbness. In the back of her mind she'd wondered, she might have even known she was pregnant, but part of her wouldn't accept it. As if she never admitted it, it wouldn't be true.

"Isabelle," her aunt squeezed her hand. "Are you okay? Talk to us."

Her aunt's words sounded as if they echoed through a long, black tunnel.

"Come on, sis," Ryan said, his voice full of anxiety. "It's going to be okay. We're here for you."

Isabelle knew her brother was talking, but it was as if she lacked the ability to respond.

"I think she's just trying to process all this," Doctor Holmes said.

Aunt Sophie stroked her forehead and cheek with her finger and spoke soft, soothing words to her.

Isabelle finally opened her eyes, drew in a long, shaky breath, then collapsed in tears. Covering her face with her hands, she sobbed.

"There, there," Aunt Sophie said, pulling her into a hug. "We'll get through this, dear heart."

Isabelle didn't understand. Her entire married life she'd wanted a child, but James had never allowed it. She'd felt unfulfilled and lonely, her longing for a child growing with each passing year. Until recently.

Before leaving James, she'd come to the conclusion that it was fortunate they didn't have children. As good of a mother as she wanted to be, she couldn't bear to see what James might have done to an innocent child of his own. No, she'd finally faced facts, and after all that time wanting a baby, she'd understood what he was capable of. And it wasn't fatherhood.

Now this. A baby of all things. The last thing she wanted was a reminder of James. She'd been able to leave with no loose ends, with nothing to connect her to James. Except this.

"Isabelle." Ryan knelt down beside her and took one of her hands. "It's going to be okay," he assured her again. "And who knows, maybe this child will be a blessing in disguise."

Isabelle couldn't stop crying and she couldn't stop asking herself why. Why now?

Finally, exhausted, she looked at the faces of her brother and aunt, people she was just getting reacquainted with, yet who had nonetheless shown her love without conditions or demands. Even Dr. Holmes had shown her more compassion and kindness than James or his mother had the entire time they'd been married.

The silence grew awkward and finally Ryan spoke. "Isabelle," his tone was firm, almost fatherly, "this was the last thing you expected to hear, but it's not the end of the world. We will get through this. If I have to commute from here to London for a while so I can help out, I will."

"And I'd be lying if I told you that the thought of having a wee one around the house again didn't excite me," Aunt Sophie told her. "Just like your brother said, we'll help you through this."

Doctor Holmes smiled at them. "Even flowers can bloom in winter, my dear. I know that this news seems very bleak to you, but I agree with Ryan, this baby could be one of the greatest blessings in your life."

As much as Isabelle doubted, she had to admit that their words brought her a small measure of comfort.

"Thank you," she told them, her voice barely above a whisper. "I just need some time."

Aunt Sophie pressed a tender kiss on her forehead and hugged her again. "Can I get you something, dear? Are you thirsty, hungry?"

"If you don't mind, I think I'd just like to go to bed," Isabelle said. She was completely drained—physically, mentally, and emotionally. There was nothing left inside of her.

They all made movements to help her but she held up her hand and stopped them. "I'll see you in the morning."

"Let me know if you need anything?" Aunt Sophie called after her.

Isabelle said she would and plodded up the stairs feeling as if the weight of the universe rested on her shoulders. Pregnant. She wondered just how much more complicated life could get.

* * *

Just before dawn Isabelle woke up. She'd gone to bed so early she'd slept nearly ten hours. Trying to go back to sleep was useless; she was wide awake.

The house was quiet as she crept from her bed and looked out the back window. The view, dreamlike and surreal, took her breath. The sky was overcast with low hanging clouds, like fluffy batting, blanketing the sky. The tops of the trees peeked above a sea of soft, gray mist. And perched just above the mist and tree line, as if suspended in the clouds, was the magnificent outline of Dunsbury Castle. Feeling the beckoning call of the ancient stone structure, Isabelle dressed quickly and slipped out of the cottage unnoticed.

The cold mist enveloped her as she followed the path through the thick woods and up the side of the hill. Emerging from the dreamlike fog, she crested the top of the hill and stood in full view of the castle. It never ceased to amaze her.

As she turned, she saw that the sun was just about to peek over the horizon. Without a second thought, she hurried through the castle gate, into the courtyard, and found the staircase leading to the upper level. Knowing which steps to avoid, Isabelle carefully climbed the stone steps and safely arrived on top.

Then, with anticipation, she waited, wondering if through the clouds, she'd be able to see the sunrise.

No sound, no movement, not even a breath of air, stirred the stillness. It was as if time had somehow been suspended. Then slowly, the clouds went from gray to blue, then to a soft, glowing pink. The glowing orb of the sun peeked over the rim of the earth, sending a blaze of glory to the sky. Streaks of crimson, pink, and orange lit up the heavens in an amazing show of light and color.

Isabelle watched as the rays of sunlight reached farther and farther across the valley, until she felt the warmth of the sun upon her own face. The clouds that had seemed so thick and heavy seemed to magically become light and fluffy as they began to drift apart.

It was a magnificent sight, and there were no words to truly describe the beauty she'd just witnessed. And even though she was full of questions, longing for answers and explanations, she was somehow filled with a sense of tranquility, and an even more profound sense of peace. As if the words were spoken deep within her heart and mind, she knew undeniably, everything would be all right.

She blinked at the tears that stung her eyes.

She wasn't a spiritual person. She wasn't even sure how she felt about God, but she knew, uncertain of *how* she knew, that these feelings had come from Him. And more than the feelings of peace, a feeling of love.

"Are You up there?" she whispered. "Do You really care?"

Shutting her eyes she let her mind absorb her feelings and impressions. There was nothing audible, tangible, or noticeable, but something deep within her knew He was aware of her.

"Please," she spoke softly, "take my life into Your hands."

The feeling of surrender, not of defeat, brought relief to her soul. Her burdens were heavy, the challenges in her life, almost unbearable, and she knew she had to hand them over. It was the only way she could survive.

She bowed her head and lowered herself to her knees. Resting her face in her hands, she wept. God had heard her. She knew it.

The crack of a twig below brought her head up sharply. Rising enough to look over the edge of the castle wall, she scanned the area with haste, saw nothing, and ducked back down.

Something had made that noise, something or someone heavy enough to snap a twig. She wasn't going to wait and around and find out who, or what. Bolting to her feet she rushed to the landing, then took the stairs as swiftly as she dared.

Safely at the bottom, she breathed a sigh of relief. Rubbing the morning chill from her arms, she exited the stairwell, stepped into the courtyard, and froze. There, in the shadows, was a man.

In a split second, she turned the other direction and started running, hoping that there was a back way out of the castle.

"Isabelle," the man called. "Wait. It's me, Ethan."

Ethan? Why would he be up at the castle at the crack of dawn?

Slowing her pace, she turned and looked back. It was indeed

Ethan. But what was he doing here?

She'd been running into him a lot lately, in some of the strangest places. Was he following her?

She stopped and turned.

Ethan approached her, breathlessly. "Hello," he said, leaning forward and resting his hands on his thighs, drawing in a few deep breaths. "I seem to keep startling you. I'm sorry."

"What are you doing?" she asked, not trying to hide the suspicious tone in her voice.

"I had a rough night," he told her. "I needed to clear my head."

Sure, she thought with sarcasm. Most normal, reasonable people get up before the sun and climb to a nearby castle to clear their minds.

"Looks like you had the same idea," he said.

"Um," she cleared her throat. Well . . . after all, she was up there, clearing her mind too. "Yeah," she had to admit, "I guess I did."

"So, are you all right?" he asked with such sincerity and kindness that she was ashamed to admit that for a moment she thought he was actually stalking her. Criminy, she was paranoid. Pregnant and paranoid. That couldn't be a good combination.

"I think so," she answered. "How about you?" They walked together toward the front gate facing the southeast.

"Today is mine and Jennifer's anniversary," he told her. "I couldn't sleep, and for some reason, I feel close to her when I'm up here. I don't know why."

"I'm sorry," Isabelle said, wishing she had something helpful to say.

"Yeah." He nodded. "Me too. How about you? What brings you up here so early?"

"Couldn't sleep, either," she told him. "And . . ." she shrugged, "I don't know why I came up here. I felt drawn or something." She chuckled, knowing it sounded silly.

"I understand," he told her, his eyes communicating more with a look than a thousand words could.

A bird in flight soared at her eye level, flapping its wings as it climbed higher into the sky.

"Do you think a person ever feels truly content in life?" Ethan asked her.

Isabelle wasn't quite sure what to say.

"I mean," Ethan rephrased his question, "is it just human nature to always want something more, or something better?"

Isabelle pondered his words thoughtfully. "I think it's normal for us to always be wanting and searching for something better. But I think a truly content person is the one who is grateful for what he has, not for what he hasn't."

Ethan nodded thoughtfully as he looked out over the miles of rolling green hills. "I think you're right. I'm happiest when I focus on all the things I have, and not so much on what I don't have."

"Me too," Isabelle echoed.

"Sometimes when I dwell on the fact that Jennifer is gone, I forget how grateful I am to have Ian Scott. Without her, he wouldn't be here. He's a real blessing to me," Ethan said, looking over at her. "I don't know what I'd do without him."

"It must be difficult raising him alone." She couldn't imagine how hard it had been for him to be a single father.

"Yes, of course," he said. "But mostly I remember what a joy he's been and what an empty spot in my life he's helped to fill."

Empty spot. Isabelle certainly had that. Lack of fulfillment and purpose, questions about why she'd had to go through everything she'd been through, then to end up pregnant on top of it all.

Would this child fill that empty spot? Would she actually be able to love this child for who he or she was? Or would she resent this baby because of James? And what if the baby looked like him? Would she forever see James in this child's face and have a constant reminder of the pain and hell her life with him had been?

"Isabelle?" Ethan said with alarm in his voice. "Are you okay?"

Snapping out of her thoughts, Isabelle looked at him, her eyes welling up in tears. The future was going to be hard, of that she had no doubt.

She tried to say "yes," but the word wouldn't come out.

"You look like you could use a hug," Ethan said, pulling her into his arms.

Her first reaction was to resist. She didn't know of hugs that provided tenderness and understanding, but his was exactly that. His warm, gentle touch enveloped her in a cocoon of strength and protection. There was no underlying threat. She found that it felt good to lean on someone else for a change, someone who was truly kind and caring.

After a few moments, she relaxed, feeling stronger to face her challenges.

"Thanks," she said shyly, unfamiliar with sincere affection, with hugs that gave instead of demanded.

"I've been behind that expression before," he told her. "Any time you feel like talking about it, I'm here. Deal?"

"Deal," she said with a brave smile.

He glanced at his watch. "I'd better get home. Ian Scott will be wondering where I am."

"Aunt Sophie and my brother are probably up by now too," she said.

"Ryan's in town again?" he asked as they started on the path.

"He came yesterday morning," Isabelle replied.

"I'll be seeing him in church, then," Ethan said. "And you too, I hope."

"I didn't know you went to my aunt's church. Of course, it's not *her* church. I mean . . ." She got flustered. "You know what I mean."

Ethan chuckled. "I know what you mean. I go to the same church your aunt goes to. There aren't many members around here, and most people think we're a pretty strange bunch, so I count myself lucky to live so close to another member."

They got to the bottom of the hill where their paths parted.

"I'm glad I ran into you this morning," he told Isabelle. "You helped brighten my day."

She smiled, knowing she hadn't done much, if anything, for him. "You brightened my day too," she told him.

They both stood, looking at each other, as if they were hesitant to say good-bye. Finally Isabelle said, "I'll see you later then?"

"Oh, right," Ethan answered. "Later."

He turned and headed through the trees toward his house. Isabelle watched him for a moment, then hurried back to the cottage.

Guess I'm going to church, she thought.

On the way home from their Sunday meetings, Isabelle marveled at how familiar attending church had felt. It wasn't so much that she remembered words to hymns or answers to questions in the classes, but it seemed as if something spiritual inside of her had reawakened and remembered. But even more amazing was how good it felt to be there.

It seemed as if every person in the entire congregation had introduced themselves to her and shaken her hand. The bishop had even asked if he could come by some time that week and visit. She'd never received such an outpouring of friendliness and fellowship in her life. Those people were truly happy to meet her and learn that she was going to be a part of their ward family.

She saw Maggie, who was excited to see her in church, and Sister Langley, who introduced Isabelle to her distinguished husband, Harold. He owned a car dealership and offered to help her out whenever she decided she was ready for an automobile.

"I don't know if I could ever get used to driving on the wrong—I mean, the *other*—side of the road," she told Brother Langley. "I'll have to get a lot braver before I give that a try."

The missionaries also made a point of saying hello. The sparkle of enthusiasm in their eyes was contagious, and before she knew it, she found herself accepting their offer to come to the cottage and go through the missionary lessons with her.

She couldn't put her finger on why she'd enjoyed herself so much at church, but she had, and she looked forward to going again.

"I hope you don't mind, but I invited Ethan and Ian Scott over to eat," Aunt Sophie announced when Ryan pulled the car up in front of the cottage. "I feel like they deserve a home-cooked meal now and then, and I can just add a little more water to the soup."

Isabelle didn't say so, but as she set the table, she found herself looking forward to their visit. She enjoyed Ethan's company, and Ian Scott brought with him enough energy and life to brighten up any room.

Even though the meal planned was simple, it smelled heavenly and Isabelle was thankful she was feeling well that day. She didn't want to ruin Ryan's visit, nor their guests' nice Sunday meal, with her nausea.

"Isabelle, you've done enough now, dear." Aunt Sophie shooed her from the kitchen. "Go sit down with your brother and chat until our other guests arrive. I've almost finished anyway."

Isabelle sat on the couch next to her brother, who had been reading the local newspaper. He complained that the paper didn't cover enough of national and international news and that his aunt ought to subscribe to some of the bigger London daily papers.

In truth, Isabelle couldn't complain. She liked the snugness and security of the small village. And if it meant not hearing about some of the tragedies, murders, and other depressing events in the world, that was fine with her.

"You know, speaking of news, you haven't really said much about what's going on in Boston," Isabelle inquired. More than anything, she wanted the whole ordeal to blow over and be forgotten. Somehow she knew it wasn't going to happen quite that way.

"I was going to talk to you yesterday about it, but after the news you received, I didn't think the timing was right," he said.

Isabelle groaned inwardly. Judging by what he said, whatever Ryan had found out must have been pretty bad. She knew she had to hear it; she just wasn't sure if she was up to it.

She decided it was best to get it over with quickly. "What did you find out?"

"You're certain you want to know?" Ryan asked.

Nodding, Isabelle steeled herself for the news.

"Unless there's a breakthrough in the search, your funeral is scheduled for this coming Wednesday." He spoke calmly, watching her to gauge her reaction.

"My funeral." The words sounded foreign to her. Then, for some reason, they struck her as funny. She laughed out loud. "My funeral," she said again.

Ryan lifted an eyebrow and looked at her warily.

"I'm sorry," she chuckled. "It's just so bizarre. What I'd give to go to it, just to see how much James is mourning my death."

"According to the news reports, he's devastated and is driven to keep looking until he finds your body. But the authorities claim that given the height of the river and swift current from the storm that night, it would be like looking for a needle in a haystack. With the authorities searching and all the private divers James hired looking day and night, they feel like they've exhausted all their options."

"So," Isabelle nodded. "I'm dead."

"I guess so." He looked at her sympathetically. "Are you okay?"

She nodded. "I'm fine. It might take some getting used to, but my life is here now." She took a deep breath. "I have no reason to go back. Ever."

Chapter 17

Dining on Aunt Sophie's delicious beef stew and homemade rolls, the family and their guests enjoyed the wonderful meal.

Ryan put some of the meat from his soup inside one of the rolls, telling everyone the story about the fourth Earl of Sandwich, an infamous gambler, who had such a good card hand one night back in 1762 that he couldn't leave the gaming table to eat. Instead he asked his manservant to rustle up a slice of beef and put it between two slices of bread.

"And voila!" Ryan held up his own version. "The sandwich was born."

"It's a good thing, too," Ian Scott proclaimed, "Or what would I have for dinner every day?"

Isabelle laughed at the boy, still not used to lunch being called dinner and dinner being called supper. Not to mention tea at four o'clock.

"The lad's right," Aunt Sophie agreed. "We should have a national Earl of Sandwich day."

Isabelle found herself enjoying the meal greatly; the food was delicious, and she wouldn't trade the company for anything in the world.

She looked at the people around her, and already felt a bond with them as she realized something very important: family was family, no matter what. And that one fact brought with it a sense of loyalty, trust, support, and love. The things she'd missed in her life, the things she hadn't had in her marriage. Things she had to learn and get used to slowly, step by step, all over again.

She felt a bond of friendship with Ethan and Ian Scott as well. Ian Scott with his immediate acceptance of her and Ethan with his kindness and genuine caring.

When she thought about it, she had gained more friends in two weeks than she had in five years of marriage. And whatever sacrifices she had to make, whatever she'd gone through to get to this point in her life, was worth it. Because she was happier now than she'd been in a very long time.

"I want you and Aunt Sophie to come to London some weekend," Ryan told Isabelle before he left to go home.

"London, why?" Isabelle asked. She wasn't sure that she was ready to go back to the crowds and masses of the big city. There was something daunting and frightening about traveling that far away from this place that had provided her safety and shelter.

"I want to take you to the Royal Opera or to a ballet. Or the symphony—you would love the London Philharmonic." He spoke with such enthusiasm that Isabelle found herself thinking perhaps someday she would enjoy going to London. "There are so many sights to see. I want to show you everything. London's a wonderful city."

"We will," she assured him. "Someday, I promise."

Giving her a hug before he left, Ryan said, "You ring me if you need anything, even if you just need to talk, okay?" Ryan held her eyes, forcing her to respond.

"Okay," she answered, liking how it felt to have someone to watch over her and protect her. To care about her.

Ryan gave his aunt a kiss and a hug and was off.

The two women stood arm in arm, watching him leave until his taillights disappeared in the distance. It was a lonely feeling having him gone, but Isabelle knew he would return soon.

The next few days fell into a comfortable routine. Isabelle felt queasy each morning as she awoke, but with the help of a lot of dry biscuits and continual nibbling throughout the day, she found she felt better and had more energy.

Her job at the day care kept her busy and gave her a sense of fulfillment that she'd longed to have for many years. Knowing that she was contributing and making a difference boosted her confidence and lifted her spirits.

Except for the occasional queasiness and fatigue she struggled with throughout the day, she didn't think much of her pregnancy. She realized she was still in denial, or perhaps it was just an unwillingness to accept her fate. Or, she considered, maybe she was just plain scared to bring a child into her world which was full of uncertainty, riddled with trials, and tangled with secrets.

At night she often had nightmares, terrifying dreams that the baby she delivered was a miniature James, with mocking, laughing eyes. A child she couldn't bear to look at, a child she couldn't love. The dreams usually woke her up in a cold sweat, shaking and haunted by the look in those eyes.

So for now, she pushed the pregnancy into the furthest recesses of her mind, not allowing herself to think about or acknowledge it. The day would come when she would have to face it, but for now, she needed to concentrate on building a future and slowly digest the reality of having a baby, of becoming . . . a mother.

On Wednesday, Isabelle caught herself thinking about what her funeral had been like, but she didn't dwell on it. She knew she could count on one hand all the friends she had in Boston; the others who showed up for her funeral would be friends and acquaintances of her husband. As much as she thought it might bother her, it didn't. Because in a way, Isabelle Dalton, the wife of James Dalton, really was dead.

That night, the elders dropped by and taught two of the missionary lessons. The first one was about Joseph Smith. Isabelle was surprised at how much she remembered from her childhood and youth. She knew the story, she just hadn't thought about it for all these years.

The second lesson was about the Savior and the Atonement. The elders told her where she lived before she came to earth, why she was here, and what happened after a person died. She hoped that somehow the Lord would forgive her for having to deceive James the way she did. Her aunt and brother seemed supportive and understanding of her choice, but sometimes she wondered if there could have been a less drastic way out. If there had, certainly she would have taken it. But she had known he would never let her leave him. He'd made that plain and clear in more ways than one. No, she knew deep inside, she'd made the right choice. Leaving James the way she did was the only chance she had. She'd been given a small moment in time, a rare opportunity, and she was amazed at herself for having the courage to go through with it.

By the end of the week Isabelle was exhausted and looking forward to Ryan's weekend visit. They talked about driving to the coast, and she couldn't think of anything she would enjoy more than seeing the ocean, walking along the beach, and tasting some of the local seafood dishes.

But instead of Ryan showing up the next morning, he called them from London.

"What are you doing in London?" Isabelle asked him. "Did something come up?"

"You could say that," Ryan answered, his voice full of disgust.

"What's happened?"

"I had a break-in," he said.

"A what!" Isabelle exclaimed.

"Somebody broke into my flat last night. I had to work late, then I went out with some mates afterward and didn't get home until late. The place was destroyed. My whole flat is in shambles."

"How awful," Isabelle cried. "What did they take?"

"That's the really strange part," Ryan said. "I can't find anything missing. It's almost as if the person was looking for something. I mean, I had a laptop computer sitting out, CDs, all sorts of electronic gadgets, and everything is still here. I'm completely baffled. And it's going to take the entire weekend to get the place put back together. So it doesn't look like you'll be seeing me until next week."

"I understand," Isabelle said. "I just wish there was something we could do. Did you call the police? Do they have any clues?"

"They don't know what to make of it either. They did get some fingerprints and took a lot of pictures but that's about it."

"I'm so sorry," Isabelle sympathized. "Are you okay?"

"I'm fine. I'm just mad. This isn't what I wanted to do all weekend," he complained.

"We could come and help you," Isabelle offered.

"No, really. It probably looks worse than it really is. I need to run, but I'll give you a call tomorrow then."

Isabelle wished him luck and hung up the phone. Why would anyone break into his apartment and not take anything? It didn't make sense, but it was possible he'd find a few things missing as he cleaned up the mess. Still, she couldn't help worrying about her brother.

* * *

"So . . ." The girl at the beauty salon wrapped a cape around Isabelle and fastened it snugly around her neck. "What are we doing for you today?"

"Could you just trim the bottom of my hair and fix the color? My natural color is a little darker than this." Isabelle spoke to the girl, who sported a short, spiky hairdo that made her look even younger than she probably was.

"Sure," the girl said as she chomped on a wad of bright green chewing gum. She brushed through Isabelle's copper-colored waves, then pinned most of it on top of Isabelle's head and got out her scissors. "I'm going to have to cut off an inch in places to get it even."

Isabelle was embarrassed the cut was so bad. But she'd done the best she could.

"That's okay," Isabelle told her. "The person who cut it didn't really know what she was doing," Isabelle told her in all honesty.

"She should have her license taken away. This is really awful." The girl blew a bubble, popped it, and sucked it back into her mouth. "But we'll get you fixed up. And I think instead of dying your hair just one color, we should weave in three different shades of red. It'll look more natural that way."

Two hours later Isabelle walked out of the beauty salon, not believing how much money she'd just spent on her hair, but loving the results. The neatly trimmed ends and rich vibrant colors made her thick, wavy hair glisten in the sunlight. Isabelle loved it.

And so did her aunt.

"My dear, you look ravishing," Aunt Sophie exclaimed when she pulled up in front of the salon to pick up Isabelle.

"Thanks," Isabelle flipped her hair to show off the radiance of the color. "Samantha really knows her stuff. She's leaving after the summer though, to take a job in London."

"That's the trouble with these young ones," Aunt Sophie sighed. "They aren't content with our small town; they think they have to experience the big city. So many of them never come back home."

"It must be hard for their parents to have them leave, knowing their children probably won't return," Isabelle said.

"I imagine so," Aunt Sophie replied. "Of course, jobs are scarce around here; the bigger cities provide more opportunity to work."

"Well, I know I'm content with being in a smaller community," Isabelle told her aunt. "I guess I'm a small town girl at heart, because I never really enjoyed the traffic and stress of the bigger cities."

"You sound like my dear Ambrose," Aunt Sophie said.

"Ambrose? Was that your husband?"

"He was born and raised just outside of London and couldn't wait to move to the country. He wanted plenty of open space and fresh air. He loved the out-of-doors."

"I think I would've liked Uncle Ambrose," Isabelle said.

"And he would've loved you and Ryan," Aunt Sophie told her. "We wanted children desperately, but it didn't work out that way. The Lord had other plans for us, I suppose."

Isabelle noticed the sad, drawn expression on her aunt's face. It was one thing to lose a husband so early in life, it was another to not have children or family to help fill the emptiness. She knew how that felt herself, all the years she'd longed for a child. Her heart ached for her aunt.

"I've learned that there are much worse things than death. And for me, that was living." Aunt Sophie said, her voice soft and underscored with longing. "For many years after Ambrose died, I felt there was no purpose to my life, no reason for living."

"How have you done it?" Isabelle asked. "You seem so happy now, so at peace."

"It all came down to faith, for me," Aunt Sophie answered matter-of-factly. "Faith in my Savior, faith in God. I realized that I had no control over what happened. It was in the Lord's hands. Once I accepted that, I began praying for the strength to accept the Lord's will and the courage not only to live, but to live meaningfully. To make a contribution."

"And . . ." Isabelle prompted.

"And I found the answer. You look outside yourself for happiness, not inside. No one is going to make you happy. It's up to you to do it. And the only way to be truly happy is to give and serve and love and help others. It's the only way."

"And it works?"

"What do you think?" Aunt Sophie asked her point-blank.

"To see you now, after all you've suffered. . ." Isabelle gave her aunt a smile. "Yes, I think it does work."

"You have a mighty burden to bear, my dear," Aunt Sophie counseled. "Your life has been hard. Don't look at it as if the Lord has forgotten you or that He has given you more than your share of pain and trials. Inside you there is a strong, determined spirit. The Lord knows that. He's giving you opportunities to prove that to yourself. Once you do, you will be free. The pain, the heartache, the fear, will be gone. Giving your life to the Lord is the only way you can find your life."

They sat in the car in silence as Aunt Sophie's words drifted away on the gentle breeze that blew through the open car windows. They rang true in Isabelle's heart and mind. She'd already given her life to the Lord. It was her only choice. Now it was time for her to find that strong, determined person inside of her. She didn't know how, but with the help of her amazing aunt and her Savior, she felt like she had a fighting chance.

Sunday afternoon Ryan called to tell them he'd managed to get his flat cleaned up. He also wanted to see how Isabelle was doing.

"I hated leaving you after getting the news about the baby. How are you?"

Isabelle wasn't sure how to answer. How did she explain the strange emotions and sense of apathy she felt? For a person who'd wanted a child as badly and for as long as she had, even she was confused by her feelings. "It hasn't really sunk in yet. I'm fine, though. Aunt Sophie's been wonderful."

"She's a rock. I don't know what I'd have done without her all these years," Ryan told her. "She's been like a second mother to me."

"I know what you mean." Aunt Sophie was the closest thing she'd felt to having a mother in years.

"I've got some more information about what's going on in Boston," Ryan said. "Are you up to it?"

"I think I have to be," Isabelle said, bracing herself, but vowing to be strong.

"The article on the funeral was short, but it basically said the funeral was well attended and that the grieving widower refused to give any comments. There was a picture of James and his mother at the cemetery looking very much bereaved."

"I'll bet." Isabelle couldn't hide her sarcasm. If anyone could put on a facade for the public, it was James and his mother.

"The press didn't give him long to mourn though," Ryan went on. "The very next day there was an article about his possible involvement with the diamonds. I guess things have really heated up in Sierra Leone and it's getting a lot of international attention. I'd hate to be him if he's got anything to do with it. He could see the inside of a prison cell for a long time if they can find hard evidence on him and convict him."

"I doubt it will ever happen," Isabelle murmured. "People like him are just too sly. They never get caught. I have no love or respect for that man, but I also can't deny that he's brilliant. I'm not saying he's not involved; I'm just saying if he is, he's too smart to leave any evidence around."

"Maybe so," Ryan said. "But you never know. There's a chance he's missed something. And if he has, maybe the FBI will find it during the investigation."

"Either way, just the fact that the press has mentioned a possible connection can't be helping his career any," Isabelle said with some satisfaction. She didn't seek revenge for herself, but if he was up to something illegal, she hoped he got caught. She also hoped that with him involved in an FBI investigation, he wouldn't be free to travel about, especially out of the country. But she still didn't rest easy. James had his ways; he was a powerful man. A man of influence. If he had any reason to come looking for her, he would. Nothing would stop him.

And that thought was enough to curdle her stomach. Was he onto her trail? Was it possible that he had anything to do with Ryan's break-in? Had he gone there looking for her?

"Isabelle?" Ryan said, his voice growing louder.

"Yes?" she answered with a start, not realizing that he'd been talking to her. She didn't like being paranoid about everything, but couldn't help it.

"You know," he continued, "if you and Aunt Sophie had a computer there, you could access all of this on the Internet."

"I don't know much about computers and I don't think Aunt Sophie does either," she confessed. "I'm willing to try, though."

"Tell you what—we've got a few older PCs kicking around the newsroom. If I can pick one up pretty cheap, I'll bring one with me next time and hook it up," he said.

"Thanks," Isabelle replied. "You know, I kind of like having a big brother around again. Even though you teased me mercilessly when we were kids."

"Hey, that's not nice to say," he said defensively. "It's true," he admitted, "but you don't have to remind me."

"Well, you're making up for all of it now," she told him sincerely. "I don't know what I'd do without you."

"Same here, sis. I'll see you this weekend."

She hung up the phone feeling more blessed than she had in years.

Wednesday after day care, as the children waited for their parents to pick them up at the front door, Isabelle busied herself wiping finger paints off the tables and vacuumed the carpet. It was amazing how much more paint the kids could get on themselves and on the table than they could get on their pictures.

She pulled the chairs out around the table and vacuumed underneath them, wondering how it was going to be to have a child of her own—wiping fingerprints off the windows, cleaning crayon off the walls, getting gum out of hair. Was this really going to happen? Lost in thought, she nearly jumped out of her shoes when Ethan and Ian Scott appeared behind her.

She turned off the vacuum and tried to catch her breath. "Hi," she said breathlessly, "You startled me."

"I'm sorry," Ethan said sincerely. "I was afraid we might."

"We tried to be noisy so you'd hear us," Ian Scott said. "But the vacuum was too loud."

"That's okay," she told them as she wound the cord onto the machine.

"I know where that goes," Ian Scott said. "You want me to put it away for you?"

"If you don't mind." Isabelle gave him a grateful smile. "Thanks."

She looked at Ethan, who seemed a bit nervous.

"So," she looked at him. "Can I help you with something?"

"Oh, right!" he exclaimed. "You're probably wondering why we were sneaking up on you in the first place."

Eyebrows raised with interest, she waited for him to continue.

"Well, Ian Scott and I were wondering . . ." he paused.

"Yes?" she prompted.

"We were wondering if you and your aunt had plans for dinner tonight."

Isabelle smiled. The expression on Ethan's face, right that very minute, looked just like Ian Scott's—so charming, fresh, and honest.

Ian Scott came running back just then. "Dad, did you ask her yet?" he said anxiously.

"I just did," Ethan told him.

"What'd she say?" Ian Scott asked, his eyes wide with excitement.

"Nothing yet," Ethan answered.

Both of them looked at her, their similar hopeful expressions melting her heart. As skittish as she was around strangers and men, she was surprised that she didn't feel that with Ethan. She was glad that her ability to trust others hadn't been completely destroyed by James. Maybe this was one of the ways the Lord was helping her in her life.

"We don't have any plans that I know of," Isabelle answered. "Why?"

"We want to take you on a picnic by the pond. And we can take you in the boat and feed the ducks and the swans," Ian Scott said, fairly jumping up and down with excitement.

"Well, that's an offer we can't refuse," Isabelle said. "We would love to go on a picnic with you and your dad," she told Ian Scott, then looked up at Ethan. Their gazes met and locked for a brief moment. She wasn't sure what she saw in his eyes, but it set her heart pumping and made her feel warm and tingly all over.

On a large flannel quilt near the shimmering pond, Ethan and Ian Scott hosted a lovely dinner for Aunt Sophie and Isabelle. They had several different assortments of breads, meats and cheeses, a delicious potato salad, several varieties of crisps, delicious sweet grapes, and ice-cold bottles of soda.

For some reason the food tasted especially delicious to Isabelle. Maybe it was the calm surroundings, the fun of eating outside, or . . . the company. A little of everything, she decided. But no matter what the cause of it was, the meal was tasty and delightful.

After eating, Ian Scott was anxious to take Isabelle out on the rowboat. Isabelle told him in no uncertain terms that she didn't want to end up *in* the pond.

Since there was only room for two in the boat, Isabelle and Ian Scott climbed aboard, with Ethan shouting orders from the shore as they pushed off into the open water.

Manning the oars, Ian Scott rowed like a pro to the center of the pond, where he let the boat drift gently to a stop.

"I'm going to be the captain of a boat when I grow up," he announced to Isabelle. "And I'm going to sail around the world."

"What about your dad? Don't you think he'll miss you?"

"Probably, but I won't be gone that long, and besides, you and Aunt Sophie can baby-sit him for me," he said confidently.

Isabelle chuckled and nodded. "Oh, right. Okay."

"And we can stay in touch by e-mail, and maybe by then we'll have computers that show our faces and we can talk in person." He had it all figured out.

"You're probably right," Isabelle agreed, realizing that if Ryan did indeed bring them a computer, Ian Scott could probably teach them how to run it.

"I wonder where Genevieve is today," he said, looking over the pond. In one of the corners isolated by a bank of reeds and tall willows, several swans and a half dozen ducks bobbed and rested on the water.

"Who's Genevieve?" Isabelle asked.

"One of the swans. She's been coming here for a long time. Since I was a little boy," Ian Scott told her.

Isabelle smiled. He wasn't even six.

"Maybe she found another pond to go to today. I'm sure she'll be back," Isabelle assured him.

"Yeah, probably," Ian Scott answered.

"Ian Scott!" Ethan called from across the pond. "Everything okay?"

Ian Scott lifted his hand, then almost stood.

"Don't stand!" Isabelle exclaimed, putting her hands on his knees. "Your father can hear you just fine."

"We're okay," Ian Scott hollered back and waved his hand, the motion sending the boat rocking.

"I think I'm ready to go back to shore now," Isabelle told him.

"Okay, me too. Dad brought some sweets along," Ian Scott told her as he began rowing.

Steadily the boat trolled along the smooth water, then, safe and sound, they arrived at the small wooden dock.

Ethan was there to meet them.

"How was your ride?" Ethan asked her.

"It was wonderful," Isabelle praised. "Ian Scott is quite a sailor."

Ian Scott puffed his chest out with pride.

"Dad, can we have some sweets now?"

"Of course, son. See what's inside the basket."

Grateful to be back on shore, Isabelle found herself tempted with some of the wonderful shortbread cookies she'd grown so fond of. Except these were dipped in a creamy milk chocolate that was delectable.

"Can I feed the ducks, Dad?" Ian Scott asked, holding up several pieces of uneaten bread.

"Of course," Ethan answered. "We'll join you in just a minute."

Ian Scott skipped off happily while the other three sat on the blanket, enjoying the cool, clear evening. It was very relaxing and Isabelle found herself marveling at how calm and peaceful it was here—the charming Swan Cottage, the beautiful pond that Aunt Sophie lovingly referred to as Swan Lake, and the mesmerizing presence of Dunsbury Castle. It truly was a place out of a fairy tale.

"DAD!" Ian Scott's scream split the silence and sent a tremor of fear through them. "Dad, hurry!"

Ethan bounded to his feet and took off running, with Isabelle and Aunt Sophie close behind.

They found Ian Scott with a tear-stained face, his eyes wide with horror as he stood looking over the limp body of a large, white swan hidden in the thick grass.

Chapter 18

Ethan pulled Ian Scott into a hug and held him as the boy cried. Isabelle felt her stomach lurch at the sight of the dead animal. It was obvious that the swan's long, lovely neck had been snapped in two.

Terror struck her heart. James.

He was there, somewhere. He had to be. First Ryan's flat, now this. It was too much together to consider this a coincidence.

Aunt Sophie gasped out loud, one hand over her mouth, then looked quickly away. "That poor thing," she whispered.

They joined Ethan and his son a distance away from the limp bird. Ian Scott continued crying, and accepted a soothing hug from Aunt Sophie.

"I'm going back to take another look," Ethan said.

Isabelle straightened her back bravely. "I want to come with you." She stepped up to his side and accompanied him over to the swan's lifeless form. She studied the odd angle of the swan's broken neck.

"This was no accident," he said, picking up the swan's head, then letting it fall back to the ground.

"Are you sure?" she asked, trying to convince herself that she was being ridiculous, thinking that James would come all the way to England. That he had actually found her.

"But who would break a swan's neck? And why?" Ethan mused, a worried expression clouding his eyes. "It doesn't make sense. I'd hate to think of any more swans ending up like this one." He looked at her, his face showing deeper concern. "Isabelle, what is it?"

She couldn't tell him what she suspected. He didn't know about James, and the whole idea seemed preposterous. Yet, deep inside, her instinct told her to be on guard. To gather her strength and be prepared.

"It's nothing," she replied. "I'm just worried about Ian Scott and Aunt Sophie. They're both very upset."

"Ian Scott loves these birds." He glanced toward the edge of the pond at the cluster of ducks and swans huddled together. "I don't want him to find any more like this," he nodded toward the swan.

"What should we do with the bird?" she asked.

"I'll bury it," he told her. "I might give Doc Holmes a call. He's a good one for finding clues and figuring out mysteries."

"Yes," she said anxiously. "And you'll let us know what you find out?"

He studied her expression. "Are you sure you're all right?"

Isabelle shuddered at the mental picture of someone actually snapping the swan's neck.

"Isabelle?" he said again.

"I'm fine," she answered, turning away quickly, wishing she could shake the image from her mind. "I'm fine," she said again in a whisper.

By the time the weekend rolled around, life at the cottage had become routine again. It helped that nothing else peculiar had happened. Isabelle had almost convinced herself that her fears were unfounded and that there was just no way James could have found her. She'd left nothing behind in Boston to raise suspicion or doubt. Yet the possibility nagged at the back of her mind. She was grateful for her job at the day care, which was fun and also very busy.

After a day with the children she came home from work exhausted, but didn't mind. Staying busy kept her mind off her worries and fears. And working with the children was very fulfilling. She'd quickly grown to love the children and was touched by their instant acceptance of her. And she knew that was why she enjoyed being with children so much. They didn't judge her, and they didn't care about all the skeletons in her closet or the life she'd left behind. They just loved her.

She'd particularly developed a special place in her heart for Ian Scott. His frequent hugs and tendency to seek her out during the day just to see what she was doing told Isabelle that the boy was hungry for the attention of a mother figure. Not that Isabelle thought she could ever replace his real mother. But if a little tender affection could help the youngster, Isabelle was happy to give him all she could. He was easy to love, and gave her a dose of affection she needed in her own life.

That weekend Ryan showed up earlier than usual on Saturday morning. Luckily, Aunt Sophie and Isabelle were dressed and ready for the day when he arrived. Isabelle ran out to his car when she saw it pull up out in front of the cottage.

Ryan got out of the car just in time to greet her with a hug.

"We didn't think you'd be here until later," she told him happily.

"I woke up early this morning and couldn't get back to sleep, so I figured I might as well get an early start. The motorway out of London is usually crowded even on Saturday, but I was able to miss most of the traffic."

"I'm glad you're here," she said, putting her arm around his waist as they walked together to the cottage. "Anything new on your flat? Did you figure out why your place got broken into?"

"No," he answered. "Nothing. Probably just some random, senseless act, with no real motivation."

Isabelle stopped walking, and Ryan looked back at her. "Isabelle? What is it?"

"Ryan." She swallowed, trying to find the right words. "I know this sounds crazy to you, but part of me wonders if James had something to do with this."

"James!" he exclaimed. "Your husband?"

Isabelle pulled a face. "Don't remind me," she said.

"He's in Boston. There's no way he could be over here doing this sort of thing."

"You don't know him," Isabelle insisted. "He would get a great deal of satisfaction trying to scare me. He has this need to control, and for him to know where I am, but know that I'm not aware of him, would give him exactly that . . . control."

"Isabelle." Ryan took her hands in his. "You are safe here. If he were around, someone would have spotted him by now. We would know about it."

Isabelle shook her head.

"Isabelle," he said, his voice growing stronger. "James cannot get to you here. This place is so small he would stand out like a sore thumb. Word would get around. I guarantee it."

Licking her lips, Isabelle tried to believe her brother's words. The reasonable part of her agreed with him; the fearful part of her remembered how manipulative and possessive James was. Her brother's promises were no match for James's obsession.

"I promise, Isabelle. I won't go back to London until I'm convinced you are safe. I'm not about to put your life in danger, or Aunt Sophie's."

"What about you?" Isabelle asked. "Are you being careful? Did you add that deadbolt to your front door like you said you were going to do?" She couldn't bear the thought of anything happening to her brother.

Ryan nodded. "I even went as far as getting a security system installed. I've got a motion sensor and all the windows and doors are wired."

Isabelle drew some relief knowing her brother's flat was secure.

"The problem is," he added with a grin, "I don't even dare get up in the middle of the night to go to the bathroom for fear of setting it off."

Isabelle laughed, but her nerves were still on edge. Ryan gave her an affectionate squeeze.

"Please trust me, Isabelle. You are safe and I'm going to protect you."

Isabelle realized that Ryan didn't know what he was asking. Trust and love were things she didn't give away easily. She wanted to trust him, though. And she knew she really had no other choice.

Their trip to the coast was postponed because of a heavy rain that settled in later that morning, and they decided to save the outing for a warm, sunny day another time. Instead they went to Adelaide's for a delicious lunch, then browsed through several antique shops and used-book stores.

They enjoyed the day in spite of the foggy weather, and the more Isabelle got to know the people of Westmoor the more she appreciated them. They were good, hardworking people who cared about others and were proud of their little village.

Back at home, Ryan built a fire in the old stone fireplace. Its warm, cozy glow took the chill out of the damp air and chased away the gray dreariness of the rain.

It was the perfect time for Aunt Sophie to bring out family photo albums. Isabelle sat in awe and fascination as she saw the pages of her past unfold. There were a few pictures of her aunt, a lovely, young Sophia Williams, and sisters, Elena and Isabelle's grandmother, Maria.

It was wonderful seeing the three sisters on family vacations at the beach, or dressed in their Sunday best for Easter, or in their pajamas around the Christmas tree. There weren't a lot of pictures, but the ones there said volumes.

Then came the pictures of Aunt Sophie with her beau, Ambrose MacGregor, during their courtship. Following these were pictures of their wedding, with Sophia in her lovely, satin wedding gown, simple yet very elegant, and her handsome groom, standing tall and regal next to her in a black tuxedo.

"You two made a beautiful couple," Isabelle said breathlessly.

Aunt Sophie smiled broadly, her eyelashes glistening with tears. "My Ambrose was very handsome. He had girls from all over England after him. But he only had eyes for me," she told them, dabbing at the corners of her eyes with her handkerchief.

They'd gone to Paris on their honeymoon and had pictures of them standing in front of the Eiffel Tower and other famous sights.

"I have a picture of your mother when she was just a baby," Aunt Sophie said, turning the page. "Maria and I were pregnant at the same time. Here it is." She pointed to a picture of Maria holding a baby with lots of dark, curly hair and big, round eyes. "Your mother was by far the most beautiful baby I had ever seen," she said, her voice wistful and distant.

"And what's this?" Isabelle asked, pointing to a picture of Aunt Sophie.

Aunt Sophie closed her eyes for a long moment. Then she finally explained. "That's the only picture I have of me pregnant. I lost my baby," Aunt Sophie said. "It was a girl." Aunt Sophie touched the picture of Isabelle's mother. "I think that's why I had such a very special place in my heart for your mother. Jacqueline helped fill that empty spot in my soul. I loved her as my own."

Ryan gave his aunt a hug, who was wiping at tears as fast as they fell.

With a shaky laugh, she said, "You can see why I don't get these books out very often."

To Ryan and Isabelle's delight, there were dozens of pictures of their mother as she grew into a young girl, then into a young woman.

"Look at that," Ryan said, pointing to a photograph of their mother, standing out by the pond. "Isabelle, you look so much like her."

"My goodness," Aunt Sophie exclaimed. "The resemblance is amazing."

Isabelle studied the picture, her mother's wavy, shoulder-length hair, petite nose, round eyes, and generous smile. She was as lovely as a movie star.

"You really think so?" Isabelle asked.

"Your mother's hair wasn't as red as yours," Aunt Sophie said. "But I'd say you are the spitting image of your sweet mother."

"Aunt Sophie," Isabelle couldn't help asking. "Do you think I could frame this picture and hang it in my room?"

"Of course, my dear, you're welcome to any of the pictures of your mother."

Isabelle looked at the picture with longing in her heart. How she missed her mother and father. What she would give to see them again.

Her eyes misted over as she looked at the picture. She'd forgotten so much. It was as if the years with James had erased her memory. But each reminder, each representation of her loved ones and her past helped her recall, bit by bit, those special, precious moments with her parents. And she was grateful, for memories were all she had.

That evening, just before sunset, the clouds cleared. Since most of the village, except for a few pubs, closed down on Sunday, Aunt Sophie ran to the grocery store to get a few things for dinner the next day.

"You feel like going for a walk?" Ryan asked his sister. They'd been watching television but nothing interested them.

"I'd love to," Isabelle answered, eager to get some fresh air. She loved going outside after a rain shower. Everything smelled so fresh and clean, almost as if the earth was new again.

They donned windbreakers and hats, and Isabelle borrowed a pair of her aunt's rubber galoshes so she wouldn't get her shoes wet and muddy.

Heading out the front door, they stopped at the cottage gate. "Let's go up to the castle," Ryan suggested. "I haven't been up there for years."

Isabelle agreed without hesitation. The castle was by far her favorite place to spend time.

Wet grass brushed against their legs as they made their way along the muddy path. Above them, the remains of Dunsbury Castle lay as a silent reminder of an area steeped in history, legend, and folklore. It was the kind of place that spurred the imagination and set it free. Where the fog and haze that blocked the mind's eye could clear away, giving way to clarity and focus.

Ryan reached for her hand and helped her as together they crested the hill and came in full view of the castle.

"It looks bigger to me," Ryan said.

"The castle?" Isabelle asked

He nodded. "Maybe it's just because I haven't been here for a while."

They walked the perimeter of the imposing structure, exchanging few words. The place demanded respect and reverence, as if the knights and ladies of the court, the royalty and social elite, still existed.

They found several large stones that had crumbled from the building and took a seat. Isabelle had been wondering about her brother and had something she wanted to ask him.

"Tell me about your girlfriend," she questioned directly.

"Girlfriend!" he exclaimed. "I don't have a girlfriend." His face registered surprise. "Why do you ask?"

"You've just never mentioned anything about a girl back in London," she answered.

"That's because there isn't one. I'm not much for commitment," he said. "Too much traveling, too many hours at work." He shrugged. "I'd like to have a relationship; I guess I just require too much maintenance."

Isabelle smiled with encouragement and patted his knee. "Don't worry. You'll find someone."

"I'm afraid if there is someone out there, she'll have to find me. Because I'm just not looking."

"Me neither," Isabelle said.

"You don't think you'll want to get married again?" Ryan asked, somewhat surprised.

Isabelle shook her head, "Once is definitely enough for me. I'm never getting married again."

"But you don't know what it's like to have a healthy relationship with a man. You should never say never."

"Let me put it this way. I *can't* get married again," she said.

"Why is that?"

"For me to get married, it would mean I have to get divorced first. And to get divorced means I would have to disclose not only where I am, but the fact that I am alive. I can't let James ever know that."

Ryan pondered her words for a minute. He lifted his finger and opened his mouth to say something, then thought a moment longer. Finally he looked at her and said, "I guess you're right."

"As far as the law is concerned I'm still married to him. He doesn't have to seek for divorce to remarry because my death certificate takes care of that for him," she said. "I don't know much about the legal system here in the United Kingdom, but I would think it's about the same here."

"I have a friend who's a barrister in London. I could ask him if you want," Ryan offered.

"It's okay," she said. "Maybe someday there will be a need, but for right now, I'm happy just the way I am. In fact, I can't remember when I've ever been happier."

Ryan leaned over and gave her a hug. "You deserve to be happy after all you've been through," he said.

"I don't know about that," she answered. "But I'm certainly going to enjoy it while I have it. I will never take happiness for granted again."

Chapter 19

The next few days settled into a predictable routine, and Isabelle found herself becoming more relaxed and feeling less like hunted game. But she still glanced over her shoulder when she walked around the village, and she still felt uncomfortable when she caught someone's eyes looking at her.

One day after school Ethan came to pick up his son as usual, but this time, instead of a brief chat and a friendly wave of good-bye, he lingered around the check-in desk while Ian Scott gathered his belongings and put them in his book bag.

"So, how have you been?" he asked Isabelle. She was busy checking off the name of each child as they were picked up, just to make sure each child was accounted for. They didn't want to lock anyone in the building by mistake.

"Really good, thanks,"she replied, putting a check by Ian Scott's name. "How about you?"

"Fine," he nodded, as if at a loss for words. When Ian Scott appeared with his backpack on, ready to go home, Ethan finally spoke up. "Isabelle," he said, looking boyishly handsome as his cheeks flushed red, "Ian Scott and I, . . . well, . . . we were wondering if . . ."

Ian Scott nudged his dad on the thigh with his elbow.

". . . if you would like to go to the cinema with us sometime. Maybe Friday, if you're not busy."

Isabelle smiled at the handsome father-son duo standing before her, their faces both full of anticipation.

"That sounds great," she responded. "I would love to go to the cinema."

Ian Scott's face brightened like a switch had just turned on. "Brilliant!" he said, nudging his father. "We're going out with a real girl, Dad!"

Ethan and Isabelle looked at each other and laughed.

"We thought we could leave right after you're finished here on Friday and grab a bite to eat, then catch a film over in Wells," Ethan told her. "What do you think?"

"I think it's perfect. Thank you for asking." She reached over and tousled Ian Scott's mop of hair. "How could I turn down an offer from two handsome men?"

Ian Scott beamed like a lighthouse on a foggy day.

"Well, then." Ethan reached for Ian Scott's hand. "We're all set for Friday."

"Yes," Isabelle smiled. "Friday."

* * *

"I'm such an idiot," Isabelle said through gritted teeth. With balled-up fists she pounded the couch cushions on either side of her. "Why did I say yes?"

"Isabelle, dear," Aunt Sophie tried to soothe her. "You're making too much of this. It's just a night out with friends. It's nothing serious. You're doing nothing wrong."

Isabelle pulled in a deep breath. "I just don't want to mislead them. I don't want to sound presumptuous—heaven knows why Ethan would be attracted to me—but if, by chance, he is, it's not fair to him. There's no future with me for him, or for any man."

"Things can change," Aunt Sophie told her.

Isabelle shook her head. "Not for me, I'm afraid. I can never marry again. That's the price I had to pay for my freedom," she said.

Aunt Sophie sighed. "I hate the thought of someone as young and beautiful as you are being alone for the rest of her life."

"But I'm not alone," Isabelle told her. "I have you and Ryan . . ."

Aunt Sophie opened her mouth to reply but Isabelle continued speaking before she had a chance to speak.

". . . and even if I was free to marry, I don't think I ever would again. I never want to feel that way again," Isabelle said. "Like I . . ." she searched for the right words, "Like I'm somebody's property. Like they own me." Isabelle shook her head slowly. "No. I gave someone control over my life once, and I will never do it again. Never."

* * *

Isabelle knew she needed to tell Ethan and Ian Scott that she couldn't go out with them. She tried to come up with valid reasons not to go, but she knew they were just excuses, and lame ones at that.

Ian Scott was his regular precocious and energetic self, but whatever mischief he managed to get himself into he made up for with his magnanimous charm and thoughtfulness. Whenever something spilled, he was the first to grab paper towels to help clean it up. Whenever they went outside for field trips or nature walks, Isabelle always received a bouquet of wild flowers from him. She didn't want to love him like she did, but she couldn't help it. The adorable child had already won her heart, and she found herself looking forward to his cheerful smile and daily shenanigans.

By the time Friday arrived, Isabelle was cross with herself because she hadn't canceled her date with Ethan Wilde and his son.

Her dark mood at breakfast didn't escape Aunt Sophie. "Cheer up, dear. It's not that bad now, is it?"

"I'm a fake, I'm a basket case, and I'm pregnant," Isabelle declared, "I doubt it could get much worse."

"It's dinner and a film. That's all," Aunt Sophie told her. "You're doing nothing wrong. They are dear friends. You're allowed to have friends, aren't you?"

Isabelle pushed her fork through the yolk of her egg and grimaced. It didn't help matters or her disposition that her stomach was unsettled. "Yes," she mumbled.

"You just go and enjoy yourself this evening. I can't think of anyone who deserves a little fun more than you." Aunt Sophie gave her a warm smile.

Isabelle felt a tug at the corners of her mouth. "Okay, I'll try. I just feel so guilty."

"That's rubbish!" Aunt Sophie said in a scolding tone. "You have nothing to feel guilty about. Now, go on, finish your breakfast and it's off to work with you."

"You'll be all right tonight?"

"My visiting teachers are dropping by for tea, and we might even go for a little walk later on. Naomi's husband is out of town, so it's just us girls." Aunt Sophie gave her a wink.

"I'll probably be home around ten or so," Isabelle told her.

"Don't worry about me, I've plenty to do." Aunt Sophie got up from the table to gather the breakfast dishes. But Isabelle stopped her and gave her a peck on the cheek and a warm hug.

"Well now, what was that for?" Aunt Sophie asked.

"For everything," Isabelle said, as her voice began to crack. "I will never be able to thank you enough for all you've done for me."

"Don't go thinking you haven't done anything for me, dear," Aunt Sophie replied, her own voice growing foggy with emotion. "I've been alone in this house for many years. I can't tell you how much I enjoy having you here with me."

The two women smiled at each other, realizing that both of them needed each other. Isabelle felt good knowing that she could do something for her aunt, especially since her aunt had done so much for her.

"I love you, Aunt Sophie," Isabelle said.

"I love you too, dear," her aunt said with affection.

"What was your favorite part of the movie, Ian Scott?" Isabelle asked as they pulled off the main road and headed down the lane. A light rain had begun to fall, and the wipers streaked against the windshield.

"I liked the part where the little brother hides under his sister's bed and waits for her, then grabs her ankles when she goes to bed!" He dissolved into giggles as he recalled the scene in the movie.

"I liked that part, too," Isabelle said. "The sister deserved it. She was mean to her little brother. I felt bad for him when she ran over his bike."

"If I had a little brother or sister, I wouldn't ever be mean to them," Ian Scott said as a yawn crept up on him.

Ethan pulled the car up to the front of the cottage. The place looked dark. Even the porch light was off.

"Aunt Sophie must've already gone to bed," Isabelle said.

"I'll walk you up to the door," Ethan put the car in park.

"No, it's okay." she told him.

"I want to make certain you get inside safely," he told her, not taking "no" for an answer.

Isabelle gave him a grateful smile, then turned to Ian Scott.

"Good night, Ian Scott," she said. "I had fun tonight. Thanks for inviting me along."

"You're welcome," the boy replied with another yawn. "I had fun too."

Ethan opened the door for her and they hurried through the rain up the walk to the front door, then stood under the protection of the thatched overhang above the front porch.

"Thanks, Ethan," Isabelle said. "It really was fun."

"I'm glad you had a good time. I hope we can do it again some-time," he said.

She didn't reply. She didn't think going out with them again was a good idea. The more attached they all got, the harder it would be to keep the relationship on a "friends only" basis. And if she were completely honest with herself, she had to admit she could easily get attached to these two.

She looked up into his face and smiled. "It's late. I'd better go in. Thanks again."

She opened the cottage door and flipped on the living room light.

Ethan stood for a moment, looking at her as if he had something he wanted to say, and she paused a moment before shutting the door to give him a chance to speak. But he said nothing, so she gave him a wave and closed the door as he turned away.

Isabelle watched out the window as Ethan's car turned around and headed the other way. There was an unmistakable connection between them; Isabelle felt it and she knew Ethan felt it. Maybe it was just that they had both suffered heartache and could relate to each other on many levels. Or maybe it was that they were both trying to figure out how to carry on with their lives under their own circumstances. But sometimes when she looked in his eyes . . .

For a moment she was lost in thought as she thought about Ethan's eyes and the way he looked at her. There was kindness and caring in those eyes, but there was something more. Something deeper. And she was afraid that what she saw was the one reason she needed to be careful with him.

He liked her.

It didn't take a rocket scientist to see it. And if she weren't so mixed up about her life, she would be flattered. But she knew there could never be anything but friendship between them. The thought saddened her. Ethan couldn't be more wonderful than he already was—handsome, kind, witty, caring. He was nothing short of perfect.

She drew in a slow, thoughtful breath. She took in several quick breaths. That smell. She froze as goose bumps prickled her arms. The faintest hint of the odor struck terror in her heart. But it couldn't be!

She forced herself to laugh at her silliness. There was obviously a flower in bloom in the garden that had a similar fragrance. A fragrance that reminded her of James's cologne. A fragrance she'd grown to despise and that brought bile to her throat.

Still, the hair stood up at the on the back of her neck.

With sudden urgency, she raced up the steps to her aunt's room. It was dark and quiet. Isabelle crept closer to the bed and whispered, "Aunt Sophie?"

There was no answer. And as her eyes adjusted to the darkness, she saw that her aunt's bed was empty.

"Aunt Sophie!" she cried, flipping on the bedroom light.

She searched but there was no sign of her aunt. Like a fist slamming her in the stomach, fear hit her. It was after ten; where was her aunt? Her next question made her knees tremble.

Was she alone in that house?

She sniffed, unable to detect the smell again. But the thought of the impossible suddenly seem real. Was James in that house? Had he done something to her aunt?

Filled with panic, she stood, her feet frozen to the spot with terror. She thought through her options, knowing that if her aunt were in danger, she had to help her.

In the corner of the room was Aunt Sophie's sewing basket. Spying a pair of scissors, Isabelle grabbed them and held them tightly in her hand. Then, searching for any measure of courage she could find, she went to the doorway and peered down the hallway.

Creeping toward the bathroom, Isabelle flipped on the light and lunged inside, wielding her sharp weapon.

Nothing.

She listened cautiously for any noise, tried to sense any movement, but detected nothing.

The next room she checked was the small front bedroom, used mostly for storage. With a flick of the light switch, Isabelle scanned the room quickly. Seeing nothing out of order, she moved on to her room. Her stomach muscles tensed as she reached for the light switch.

Gripping the scissors tightly in her other hand, she flicked the switch, ready to fight or flee.

Nothing.

She checked under the bed and found nothing. The wardrobe was undisturbed. As far as she could tell, nothing had been touched.

It didn't make sense.

Leaving all the upstairs lights on, she went back downstairs. The living room was clear, and so was the bathroom. She even checked the coat closet. Breathing a little easier, she tried to piece together what was going on. Where could her aunt be?

Outside, the rain fell faster. Flashes of light followed by low rumbles of thunder vibrated the windows.

Maybe her aunt had left her a note on the kitchen table or near the telephone.

Still on guard, Isabelle crept toward the kitchen. Just as she reached her hand up to turn on the light, a flash of lightening split the sky, illuminating the figure of a man at the back door.

James!

The doorknob rattled as he turned the knob to get inside. Stifling a scream, Isabelle turned and flew across the living room, bolting through the front door into the rain-filled night. Running for her life, she splashed through puddles, slipping on rocks and mud. Down the lane she ran, not knowing if James were behind her, not daring to look back and see.

Stumbling up the path to Ethan's house, Isabelle tripped, landing on her hands and knees. Scrambling to her feet, she shot for the front door and pounded on it with all the strength she had left.

Ethan yanked the door open and Isabelle rushed inside. Turning, she threw herself against the door and bolted it.

"Isabelle!" Ethan cried when he saw her. "What's wrong? What happened?"

"He's here!" she cried. "He's in the house. And Aunt Sophie. Oh, Ethan," she said, falling into his arms. "What has he done to Aunt Sophie?"

Ethan held her wet, trembling frame. "Isabelle, what are you talking about? Who's here? Why would he hurt your aunt?"

"James!" she cried. "James is here. I know he is."

"Who's James?" he asked, completely confused and panicked.

"My husband!"

"Your—" His eyes grew wide.

"We have to find Aunt Sophie," Isabelle said. "Ethan, please. You have to help me."

"Okay, okay. Sit down and tell me everything." He helped her to a chair. "Look at you. You're bleeding." She hadn't noticed her hands, cut by sharp rocks and bleeding, the knees of her pants torn and saturated with blood.

She told him about smelling the cologne, about searching the house, then seeing James at the back door.

"Didn't you say your aunt was going out with Maggie and Naomi Crompton?" he asked.

"They were coming over for tea. She thought they might go on a walk. But they wouldn't be gone this late. Not in the rain."

Ethan gently pressed a wet cloth onto her bleeding hands as he listened.

"The first thing we do is call the others and see if they know where she could be. Maybe she had something unexpected come up."

Isabelle nodded quickly. "We have to hurry!" she said, her voice full of urgency.

Ethan made the first call to the Cromptons but got no answer. Isabelle's heart sank lower into the pit of her stomach. *Please Father,* she pleaded, *don't let anything happen to my aunt.*

Next he tried Maggie's number. Just as he was about to hang up, he got an answer.

"Maggie!" he cried. "Have you seen Sophie MacGregor?"

He listened, saying, "yes" and "I see" several times. "No, no, everything's fine. Thank you."

He hung up the phone and started dialing again.

"Who are you calling?" Isabelle asked.

"Your aunt. Maggie said she should be there—Hello?" he said into the receiver. "Yes, she's right here with me. Is everything okay over there?" He listened for a moment. "Do you need some help?" Again, he listened. "I'll be over first thing in the morning to help then. I'll bring Isabelle over in a few minutes."

Isabelle felt tied in knots by the time he finished the conversation.

"Your aunt is fine. I just spoke to her," he told her.

Shutting her eyes, Isabelle felt her throat tighten as tears of relief threatened. "Thank you," she whispered before opening her eyes again.

"They've been looking for Romeo for over an hour, but it got dark and started raining so they had to come in. I think it was Brother Crompton you saw at the door. He was helping them."

"Brother Crompton? But he was supposed to be gone this evening," she said trying to picture the man she saw at the back door. "What does he look like?"

"Tall, thin, balding. Distinguished in a Sean Connery sort of way," he said.

Tall and thin? The man in the doorway was tall. He didn't seem noticeably thin, but then, it was dark and she was frightened.

"Does he sound like your man?" Ethan asked.

"I don't know," she answered, "I suppose it could be him." And she supposed it was possible that Brother Crompton's cologne smelled similar to the one James wore.

"Maybe we should go visit him and you can see for yourself. I can take you to their house if that would make you feel better," he offered.

"No." She shook her head, feeling foolish. "It was probably him." *But what if it wasn't?* she wondered.

"Isabelle." Ethan kneeled down in front of her. "You're still white as a sheet. And you're shivering. Let me get you something dry to put on and something warm to drink."

"I'm okay," she said as a tremor of shivers rippled up her spine.

He raised his eyebrows and gave her a stern look.

"Okay. Maybe just a dry shirt or something," she said.

He grabbed her a thick cotton shirt from his bedroom and handed it to her. "Here, put this on while I heat some water. You need something warm inside of you."

In the bathroom Isabelle examined her hands and knees. Along the heels of her hands were numerous scrapes and abrasions; they were sore and stung something fierce, but would be fine. Her knees were scrubbed raw, and she had to pick out tiny pebbles with her fingernail. Those scrapes would take awhile to heal.

The dry shirt felt warm and snug, and smelled fresh and clean, like the outdoors. Just like Ethan. A man who was the opposite of James. Ethan was strong, but not overbearing; secure, but not controlling. With him she felt safe and appreciated. He was giving and caring, and he didn't have his own agenda or interests in front of everyone else's.

Back in the front room, she stared out the window at the downpour of rain. Crossing her arms over her chest, she tried to shake the image of James in the doorway. She had been so convinced it was him. With all her heart she hoped that it was, in fact, Brother Crompton.

"Here we go," Ethan said, carrying two steaming mugs into the room. He handed one to her. "I hope hot chocolate is okay. It's all I had."

"It sounds wonderful." She accepted the cup and let the steam bathe her face. It was too hot to sip so she blew on the creamy froth to cool it.

"Ethan," she said, still looking at her cup. "Thank you." She didn't know what else to say. She was embarrassed by her overreaction and her display of panic. Her fears and paranoia were obviously at their height. But the circumstances had seemed so real in her mind.

His brow wrinkled, as if he wasn't sure what she meant.

"I'm glad you were here. I didn't know what to do or where to go." She took a tentative sip of the hot chocolate.

"I'm glad I could be here for you, Isabelle. I'll always be . . . I mean, I hope you know you can always . . . ." He put the mug on the coffee table. "Anytime you need help, just holler," he finally said.

Isabelle smiled. She liked how his cheeks were flushed red like they were now.

"So . . ." He crossed one ankle over the other knee, his expression becoming serious. "Are you going to tell me about it?"

Now it was her turn to furrow her brow. "About what?" she asked, knowing full well what he meant.

"About this James. About your husband." He picked up his mug again.

She didn't want anyone to know about James who didn't absolutely have to know, Ethan included. But she trusted him and even more surprising, she found she wanted to tell him about it. Something inside told her she should tell him.

Trying to leave out the unnecessary and private details, she began her story. She told him about her and James, their five-year marriage, and how he treated her, controlled her, and abused her.

"I couldn't take it anymore," she told him, feeling her voice grow shaky. "So I left."

"You just walked out on him? He doesn't know you're here?" Ethan asked in surprise.

"He doesn't know I'm alive." Isabelle took a drink of her hot chocolate.

"Why would he think you're dead?" Ethan asked.

"Because I staged my own death," Isabelle said softly, unable to look at him.

"It was that bad?" Ethan said.

She shook her head as unbidden tears slipped onto her cheeks.

The next thing she knew Ethan was at her side with his arms wrapped around her. "You poor thing," he said, holding her close.

She stiffened in his arms, but his kindness and his gentle touch relaxed her, unlocking floodgates of her emotions. Unable to stop the tears, she laid her head on his shoulder and cried.

"It's going to be okay," he told her. "You're safe here."

She wiped her eyes on the sleeve of his shirt she was wearing. "Sorry, I'll wash it before I give it back."

"It's okay," he said with a gentle smile.

"There's something else," she said, dreading what she had to tell him next, but knowing in a few months she wouldn't be able to hide her secret.

"There is?" he asked, as if he couldn't imagine there could possibly be more.

"You know how I said James didn't want children?" She couldn't look at him. Her throat suddenly went dry.

Ethan waited.

"I'm pregnant."

Chapter 20

Isabelle didn't know how long they talked, but the next thing she knew, sunlight was streaming in on her face. She lifted one lid and saw two eyes peering at her. Her breath caught in her throat and both eyelids flew open.

"Ian Scott!" she exclaimed.

"Hi, Isabelle," he said.

"Ian Scott!" Ethan's firm voice rebuked him and Ian Scott jumped back. "I thought I told you not to bother Isabelle."

"I wasn't," Ian Scott pouted. "I was just watching her nose doing a twitchy thing."

Isabelle looked down at her nose and her eyes crossed, which made Ian Scott giggle.

"What am I doing here?" Isabelle asked, sitting up on the couch. She pushed the thick quilt off of her.

"You fell asleep while we were talking and I didn't have the heart to wake you up. I called your aunt and she said you could stay here. I hope that's okay."

Isabelle covered a yawn with her hand.

"Wow!" Ian Scott exclaimed when he saw her hand. "What happened to you?"

"I fell down in the rain last night," she told him. "Pretty klutzy, huh?"

"You want a band-aid? I have some with Donald Duck on them," he offered.

"Thanks," Isabelle said, "but I think I'm fine now."

"You want some Frosty-Os cereal? It has little marshmallow race cars in it." He was so excited about the cereal Isabelle couldn't turn him down.

"That sounds yummy," she replied, casting a quick glance at Ethan, who shook his head.

But it was too late; Ian Scott was already in the kitchen, pouring cereal into a bowl.

"You didn't have to do that," Ethan told her.

"I know," she said as she pushed herself to her feet. "But I like marshmallow race cars."

Ethan chuckled and shook his head.

Her knees were stiff from last night's tumble, and it took her a minute to stand completely upright.

"Need a hand?" he offered.

"I think I can make it," she replied.

In the kitchen Ian Scott had bowls of cereal ready, but waited for his dad to pour the milk.

"You're not joining us?" Isabelle asked, taking her seat at the table.

"I've already eaten. I'm going over to your aunt's house to help look for the dog."

"He didn't turn up during the night?" Isabelle asked, feeling a streak of panic clutch her heart. That dog was part of the family, almost like a child to Aunt Sophie. If something happened to Romeo . . .

"I want to come and help," she said, pushing herself away from the table.

"Me too," Ian Scott piped up.

"Why don't you two walk over after you have something to eat first?" Ethan suggested.

They agreed and, grabbing a New York Yankees baseball cap, Ethan was gone.

By the time Ian Scott and Isabelle got over to her aunt's house, there were half a dozen people ready to help look for Romeo. The elders had been in the area and when they found out about the missing dog, offered to help. Dr. Holmes was also there. He'd heard about the missing dog from Brother Crompton, who was one of Dr. Holmes's golfing buddies. Since he loved a good mystery, he offered to help in the search, too. Even the Plimptons from down the lane and around the corner offered to join the effort.

The area was split into sections. The elders, the Plimptons, Dr. Holmes and Aunt Sophie, and Isabelle, Ethan, and Ian Scott all split up and headed in separate directions. With cell phones and water bottles in hand, they commenced the search.

Isabelle had changed into a cotton shirt and walking shorts, and gratefully so. After last night's soaking, the clouds had cleared and the glaring sun, combined with the humidity from the steaming, wet ground, made the air hot and muggy.

Two hours later the group returned to Swan Cottage without success. Romeo was nowhere to be found.

Aunt Sophie busied herself rustling up something cold for everyone to drink, and Isabelle made roast beef sandwiches for the hungry bunch. Keeping herself busy, Aunt Sophie did her best to keep her chin up, but Isabelle knew she was worried sick about her dog. Isabelle didn't share her concerns with her aunt, but visions of the dead swan kept popping into her head. Try as she might, she couldn't help wondering if Romeo had somehow met the same fate. He was known to wander, but always came home.

Before leaving, the Plimptons promised to keep a look out for the dog. The elders, too, were happy to mention it as they went door to door and traveled through the area. As they left, Elder Twitchell told Aunt Sophie and Isabelle good-bye. This was his last week as a missionary.

"I wish we could've known you longer," Aunt Sophie told him with a motherly hug. "You're a fine elder and I wish you the best of luck in your future."

"Thank you, Sister MacGregor. I'm glad I got to know you even if it was just for a few weeks."

He shook Isabelle's hand. "You're the lucky one," he told her.

"I am?" she asked.

"You get to stay here in England," he said.

She smiled. "But you'll get to come back and visit, won't you?"

"My folks are coming here to pick me up and we'll do some traveling for now. After that I plan on coming back often," he answered.

"Good. We'll see you again then," Isabelle told him.

He nodded. "You sure will." He turned to his companion. "We'd better get going."

The elders waved good-bye, then were off on their bikes, their shiny helmets reflecting the midday sun.

"Is there anything I can do?" Dr. Holmes asked.

"No, Kingsley," Aunt Sophie answered, addressing the doctor by his first name. "But thank you for helping. Especially on your day off."

"I was happy to help. And don't worry, he'll turn up. I have a notion Romeo is just out looking for his Juliet." He picked up his empty cup and plate.

"I'll get those for you," Aunt Sophie said, rushing to his side. "Did you get enough? I could make another sandwich."

"Thank you, but that first one was just plenty."

"Well, let me at least wrap some of the banana bread I made. You might enjoy it later." Aunt Sophie busied herself in the kitchen slicing and wrapping the bread for the doctor.

The doctor leaned toward Ethan and Isabelle and said in low tones, "I haven't said anything to Sophia, but I noticed footprints around the back of the house. A man's print, probably size eleven or twelve. A loafer is my guess. The rain washed most traces of the prints away, but there were enough that I was able to find several clear outlines."

"What are you saying?" Isabelle asked.

"It's just not beyond the scope of possibility that there could be some sort of foul play involved here," the doctor suggested. Although he seemed to be enjoying the drama, it was clear that he took all this very seriously.

"Foul play?" Ethan questioned.

"Concerning the dog. I noted, Ethan, that you wear size ten, ten and a half?" the doctor said, with a questioning lift of his brow.

Ethan nodded, "A ten. But what about—"

"Crompton is a nine and a half. I checked this morning."

Isabelle and Ethan looked at each other. Chills, like icy fingers, crawled up the back of Isabelle's neck.

"What?" the doctor asked, noticing their reaction.

Ethan cast a questioning gaze at Isabelle. He wasn't going to say anything if she didn't want him to. Realizing that her best protection was the awareness of her friends and family and their interest in her safety, Isabelle decided to tell Dr. Holmes. And, in a way, she would be glad to give him an explanation for her pregnancy.

After she gave him a brief explanation of her situation, the doctor had several questions.

"You say your husband may have wired the phones in your home in Boston?" the doctor asked.

"I don't know," Isabelle answered. "I mean, there were times when I could have sworn I heard some strange tones or faint electronic noises in the background, but I can't be sure."

"I don't want to alarm you," Dr. Holmes said, "because it sounds like you planned a flawless escape. But your husband sounds like the type of person who would notice even the slightest detail, anything out of the ordinary."

"Yes," Isabelle said with a nod. "He would. That's why I was so careful. I'm sure there was nothing to give it away. I covered every possible trace of evidence. There was no reason for him to think I did anything but take an innocent trip to the store."

"I just talked to Ryan." Aunt Sophie finally returned with a plate of bread wrapped in plastic for the doctor and one for Ethan and Ian Scott, who'd been in the living room the whole time watching Saturday morning children's programs.

"Is he okay?" Isabelle asked with alarm.

"He's fine. He's going to be here a little later this afternoon. He had to go into the office for a while this morning." Aunt Sophie's forehead was creased with lines of worry. Isabelle wished there was something she could do to ease her aunt's mind, but Isabelle wasn't so sure herself that Romeo was okay, or even . . . alive.

After everyone left, Aunt Sophie and Isabelle finally had a chance to talk about last night. Isabelle explained to her why she'd been so concerned to come home and find the house dark and empty. And then to smell the cologne Brother Crompton had been wearing had reminded Isabelle so much of James's cologne . . . it had all been too much.

"Look at your poor hands," Aunt Sophie said, taking Isabelle's hands in hers. "I've got some salve we could put on those to help take out the sting. But those knees—" Aunt Sophie's face bunched up with disgust. "They look like minced beef."

"I think I just need to soak in the tub," Isabelle said. Then she looked at her aunt in complete seriousness. "Do you think I'm crazy,

Aunt Sophie? Do you think it's possible James is responsible for any of this or do you think it's all coincidence?"

Aunt Sophie shook her head. "I'll admit, there have been a few strange things happening around here, but I think it's all coincidence. You're safe here, my dear. I, for one, am not about to let anything happen to you, and you've got many friends here now who care about you. They won't let anything happen either."

Isabelle felt a knot form in her throat. She desperately wanted to believe it was all coincidence, and that James had accepted her death and moved on, forgotten about her. She wished she could know for sure so she could move on with her own life.

She'd lived such a sequestered life, a life from a distance. It was overwhelming to feel such an outpouring of concern and caring from so many people, people from the community and people from the Church. Aunt Sophie had once made the comment that the members of her ward were like family to her, and Isabelle was beginning to realize just how true that statement was.

"We're going to find Romeo," Isabelle told her aunt before she left to take her bath.

"I hope so," Aunt Sophie said as her gaze shifted to look out the window. "I really hope so."

Feeling better after her bath, Isabelle went outside in the garden to clip some flowers for an arrangement for the living room while she waited for Ryan.

Aunt Sophie had spent the morning like a cleaning tornado. Every time Isabelle offered to help, Aunt Sophie had shooed her away, claiming she needed to stay busy to keep her mind off of "things."

No speck of dust was safe that day. Aunt Sophie vacuumed under furniture, dusted blinds, and cleaned baseboards.

The warm, clear day made it hard to believe everything that had happened the night before. Isabelle was grateful to have it behind her and more than ever, wanted to put the past where it belonged and focus on her future.

"Hello there," a voice called from behind. With her arms full of wild-flowers, Isabelle turned to find Ethan, standing and smiling at her. "Well, don't you look lovely? Those flowers are almost as pretty as you are."

Isabelle felt her cheeks blush.

"Any news on Romeo, yet?" he asked.

Grateful he changed the subject, Isabelle told him that the dog still hadn't turned up.

"How are you?" he asked, eyeing her closely.

"I'm fine." She showed him her bandaged knees. "I think I'll be saying my prayers standing up for the next few days."

He chuckled, then said, "I've been worrying about you."

"You have?" The way he looked at her, with such caring and concern in his eyes, with so much sincerity, made her heart pound inside her chest.

"I wondered if our discussion with Dr. Holmes this morning upset you. I think there could be a dozen explanations for those footprints he found."

"You know," she said, realizing it for the first time, "I haven't really thought about it." She laughed. "I must've fallen harder than I thought. That's not like me at all."

"I'm glad you're doing well." Their gazes met and held for a moment, until the growl of a car engine roared down the lane. It was Ryan.

They met him at the gate and filled him in on all of the excitement from the night before. Isabelle told him of the doctor's suspicions, but Ryan looked unconvinced. Even though the news coverage of her death had diminished, there was still a huge conflict-diamond investigation going on.

"I just don't think James would be allowed to leave the country if he's a suspect in their case," Ryan told her.

Isabelle breathed a little easier although she knew letting her guard down wouldn't be a wise move. She doubted there would ever be a time in her life that she'd feel completely safe.

"I'd better get to work on the lawn," Ethan said. "Good to see you, Ryan."

Ryan told him good-bye, then slipped an arm around his sister's waist. "How's Aunt Sophie doing?"

"I hope Romeo turns up soon. She can't lose that dog," Isabelle told him. "It just wouldn't be fair."

"We can go out looking again later," he said. "I have a three-day weekend, so we'll have a lot of time to find that crazy dog."

"I'd like both of you to sit down," Aunt Sophie said after dinner. "We need to talk."

The three of them had spent a relaxing afternoon in the village, getting ice cream and browsing through shops. Now Ryan and Isabelle sat on the couch while Aunt Sophie sat in a chair opposite of them.

She looked at both of them, her eyes brimming with tears. Still, with a smile, she said, "I just want both of you to know how much I love you and how grateful I am that we are together. I don't know what I'd do without you."

"We feel the same, Aunt Sophie," Ryan told her. Isabelle nodded her agreement.

"I want you to know that I believe the Lord brought us together for a reason." She dabbed at her eyes with her handkerchief. "I'm getting old and I won't be around forever."

Isabelle opened her mouth to speak, but Aunt Sophie stopped her. "No, it's a fact. And I'm fine with it. I have plenty of loved ones waiting for me on the other side, so when it does happen, please don't feel bad for me. Because I won't. Anyway, I want you both to know that you have a great legacy. Your forefathers were incredible men and women. They sacrificed a great deal for us to have all that we have. So I would like to keep that tradition going."

Ryan and Isabelle looked at each other, then at their aunt.

"This lovely cottage, and all the land around it, is yours to share after I die," she said.

"But Aunt Sophie—"

"No buts," she said. "There is no one else to leave it to. It is yours by right and I want you to know this. There are also some bank accounts that are yours as well. Like I said, your forefathers worked hard, and they have a lot to show for it. And last of all, the castle is yours, too."

"The castle!" Isabelle said excitedly. "We, . . . you mean, . . . the castle?"

"I thought you'd like that, my dear," Aunt Sophie said with a smile. "It's inside of you, it's in your blood. That's why you feel so drawn to the castle. Something inside of you recognizes that. It is rightfully yours and I can't think of better hands to leave it in than both of yours."

"But why are you telling us this?" Ryan asked. "Are you feeling well, Aunt Sophie?"

"Yes, I'm fine," she told them. "And I hope I have some good years left, but just in case something happens, I wanted to tell you these things."

Isabelle felt tingles inside. She knew it was juvenile and silly, but she couldn't believe it. She had a castle!

Chapter 21

Sunday at church Elder Miller showed up with a new companion. His name was Elder Bordeaux, from South Africa. He stood barely five-foot-five, weighed ninety-nine pounds soaking wet, and had beautiful ebony skin and dark eyes. He was as cute as a new puppy and very shy.

Isabelle found herself looking for Ethan and Ian Scott, but didn't see them sitting in the chapel during church.

"You're going to break your neck," Ryan whispered during the first talk.

"What?" Isabelle whispered, shifting her position on the hard bench seat.

"He's over by the back exit sign, behind the lady with the white straw hat."

"Who is?" Isabelle wasn't sure who he was talking about.

"Ethan." Ryan looked straight ahead as if completely mesmerized by the speaker's message, but a smile played on his lips.

Aunt Sophie leaned forward and gave both of them a stern look, making Isabelle feel six years old. A wave of memories flooded her mind as she recalled days from her youth when she'd gone to church with her family and gotten in trouble from her mother for talking with her brother during the meeting.

The memory brought a warmth to her soul. It surprised her how something small, like Aunt Sophie's warning look, could trigger a memory that had long been forgotten. Isabelle strained to remember every detail she could of the image: her white patent leather shoes, the lilac-colored dress sprigged with tiny, white daisies, a satin purse with a beaded handle.

She glanced sideways at Ryan, realizing that his profile reminded her of their father. Ryan's coloring wasn't quite the same, but the slant of his nose, the heavy brow and broad forehead, and the teasing look he got in his eyes took her back twenty years.

After the meeting they walked into the foyer to go to Sunday School, and to her delight, she ran straight into Ethan and Ian Scott. After giving her a crushing hug and nearly knocking her backwards, Ian Scott ran off to find his class.

"Sorry about that," Ethan said. "I've told him not to tackle you like he's playing rugby, but he gets so excited to see you."

"He's fine. I'm glad he likes me. I love his hugs," Isabelle told him.

"I'd hate to see one of his hugs accidentally break your arm or leg though," Ethan joked. "Hello, Ryan," Ethan said when he noticed Isabelle's brother standing behind her. "Did you have a quiet night last night?"

"Yes, thank goodness," Isabelle answered for him. "Having Ryan in the house helped me sleep a lot sounder."

"I'm planning on installing a security system in the house. That would give you some peace of mind when I'm not around," Ryan said.

"I've installed a couple of those," Ethan said. "I'd be glad to help if you need it."

"Thanks, Ethan. I'll check into it first thing in the morning. I'd like to get started on it tomorrow."

"I have a light day. I could come over after lunch," Ethan volunteered.

With a nod, Ryan thanked him for his offer to help.

"Miss Isabelle, can you help me?" Four-year-old Kelsey Morgan, with naturally curly, golden hair raised her hand that was covered with red finger paint. "I need to go to the toilet."

Isabelle gave her a smile and grabbed a wet cloth. Finger painting was one of the children's favorite activities to do at day care, but it was by far the messiest.

"Do you need help?" Isabelle asked her.

"No, I can do it," Kelsey said, "I'm a big girl."

Isabelle grinned. "You sure are. Wash your hands good after, because it's time for snack. Everyone," she told the rest of the class as

Kelsey skipped off to the bathroom, "it's time for your snack. Finish your pictures and wash your hands."

The bell on the front door jingled. "I'll get it," Isabelle told Miss Maggie, who was up to her elbows in finger paint.

Maggie has as much fun as the kids, Isabelle thought as she hurried down the stairs to find a delivery man at the check-in counter.

"Delivery for Isabelle Dalton," he said, lifting a long, narrow box tied with a white ribbon.

"That's me," Isabelle said, noticing the FTD logo on the box. Someone had sent her flowers.

He handed her the box. "Have a nice day," he said and was off in his delivery truck.

Untying the ribbon, Isabelle slowly lifted the lid on the box. Separating the tissue paper inside, she exposed the contents and drew in a sharp breath, staring at the flowers in fear. A dozen white roses.

The only kind of flowers James ever sent her were white roses. Twelve of them. Long-stemmed, without thorns.

Feeling weak in the knees and lightheaded, Isabelle braced herself against the counter, drawing in several deep breaths. After a moment, she felt steadier on her feet and searched the box for a card, but found nothing.

Telling herself to calm down, she tried to be rational. It was possible that Ryan or even Ethan had sent them. The card could have fallen out in the delivery truck. There was one way to find out. Picking up the phone, she called information and got the number for the florist in town.

"Camelot Floral," the woman answered.

"I just received a flower delivery and wondered if you could tell me who sent them," she asked.

"You didn't get a card?"

"No. Nothing," Isabelle told her.

"What's the name?"

Isabelle gave her name and address where the flowers were delivered.

"I'm sorry. I didn't take that order. It was paid for with cash and there's no name on the receipt," the woman told her.

"Is the person who took the order there?"

"No, she's gone to lunch. You can call back in an hour if you want to. Ask for Penelope."

Isabelle hung up the phone, telling herself to calm down. Ethan or Ryan must've sent them. But she still couldn't shake off the concern in the back of her mind. She couldn't rest until she knew everything at home was fine.

Calling her aunt, she let the phone ring four times until the answering machine picked up. She knew her aunt and brother were home because she'd talked to them earlier. Ryan had called to tell her he'd found a security system and was going to install it that afternoon, with Ethan's help. So why weren't they answering the phone?

Knowing she was acting on a paranoid impulse, she ran back upstairs.

"Maggie?" Isabelle pulled the woman aside while the children settled down for their snack. "Do you think you can manage without me for a little while? I need to run home for a bit."

"We're fine," Maggie told her. "Take your time. It's quiet time anyway."

They always had the children take an hour of quiet time after snack. The kids needed some time to wind down, and it gave the teachers a chance to catch their breath. The children read books or quietly colored pictures; some actually fell asleep.

"Thanks, I'll try and hurry back." Isabelle rushed from the building, hopped on her aunt's bicycle, and peddled toward the cottage. A stiff wind blew, and dark clouds rolled in from the south. The pungent smell of rain was in the air.

She usually enjoyed riding the bike. The exercise felt good and she loved the fresh air, but today she would have preferred a car. She was anxious to get home and check on everyone.

Several droplets of rain pelted her forehead and arms as she pumped harder and faster toward the house, hoping to get inside before the clouds let loose.

Jumping off the bike before it came to a complete stop, she ran for the front door and burst inside.

"Ryan! Aunt Sophie!" she called. When she received no answer she called again, then checked the backyard to see if they were outside, but the garden was quiet.

"Where are they?" she said out loud.

Then a note on the table caught her eye.

Isabelle,
Someone saw the dog up by the castle. We went up to find him. Come and join us when you get home.
   Aunt Sophie

Someone had seen Romeo? Isabelle was thrilled at the news and prayed that her aunt and brother had found him. Grabbing a weatherproof jacket out of the closet, she hurried out the back door and across the lawn to the path leading toward the castle.

She hurried along the path, pushing branches and bushes out of her way, and finally arrived at the top of the hill, out of breath and weak.

"Aunt Sophie! Ryan!" she yelled, but the wind diluted her cries to nothing.

Keeping up her anxious pace, she ran the perimeter of the castle, yelling and looking for any sign of her aunt and brother.

Where could they be? she wondered, thinking that maybe their search had led them away from the castle. Then a loud sound, like the dull thud of a rock hitting the ground, caught her attention. It sounded like it came from inside the castle.

"Aunt Sophie? Ryan?" she called as she walked through the crumbling entry inside the courtyard. "Where are you?"

She scanned her surroundings and saw no sign of them. Then, as she turned to leave, she detected a movement out of the corner of her eye. "Romeo, is that you?"

It had to be the dog. Maybe he was caught somewhere or injured.

"Romeo, Romeo," she called as she walked toward the staircase. "Wherefore art thou, Romeo?"

Smiling at her weak rendition of Shakespeare, she rounded the corner—

"Hello, Isabelle."

Isabelle gasped. A scream caught in her throat. Her gaze met James's gleaming eyes and mocking smile.

"James!" Taking a step back, she wavered. Then, without another thought, she turned and ran.

Within several yards James caught her by the arm, nearly jerking it from its socket. Spinning her around to face him, he pulled her to him in a bone-crushing, arm-breaking grip.

"You didn't thank me for the flowers," he hissed, backing her up against the wall.

Isabelle struggled to get free. A whiff of his cologne, the exact scent she'd smelled in the cottage that night, twisted her stomach into a knot.

"You honestly thought I wouldn't find you?" He twisted her arm up higher behind her back, sending hot streaks of pain down her arm and back.

"What do you want?"

"Want?" His tone was low and menacing, almost a whisper. "Why, Isabelle, I want you." Isabelle struggled against his hold, but he merely tightened his grip, causing her to wince in anguish.

"Leave me alone," she told him. "It's over between us."

"You're mine, Isabelle. You're my wife. You belong to me."

He pressed her back against the castle wall, and the sharp edges of the stones dug into her flesh.

"You're hurting me!" she cried.

"This is just the beginning. Do you realize what you've put me through?" His words seethed with anger.

"How did you—"

"Find you?" he finished the sentence for her.

She nodded as the pain in her twisted arm became a numb throbbing.

"I had all the letters. From your aunt. From your brother." He shook his head in mock regret.

So he had been keeping her family's letters from her, Isabelle thought, trying to ignore the pain James was causing her.

"You almost had me. I almost believed you'd really drowned. Then I got on the Internet, and saw the history."

What history? her brain screamed.

"Do you remember searching for plane fares to the United Kingdom?"

Closing her eyes, she swallowed hard.

"It wasn't hard to put two and two together," he said. "Too bad I didn't find out before your funeral." He pressed his entire body weight against her. She cried out in pain. "You made a laughingstock of me," he said through gritted teeth.

"James," she pleaded. "Please . . ."

"I gave you everything." His voice softened, his body relaxed. For a moment Isabelle could draw in several deep breaths. "Everything."

Knowing this was her only chance, she drew up her knee with a quick, sudden jerk. James swore and doubled over in anguish, and she tried to run past him, but he grabbed at her with one arm.

Wrestling free from his grip, she turned and bolted up the stairs. At the top she began screaming for help. Someone had to hear her. If her aunt and brother were out there, they'd hear her. They had to.

"It's no use," James yelled as he staggered up the stairs. "They're miles away from here."

"Who is?" she demanded, searching below for a sign of help.

"Your aunt and brother. They've gone to Bath to get their dog."

"How do you—"

His gaze mocked her. His laugh echoed through the empty ruins.

"You called them and told them Romeo was there?" Her thoughts began to swirl. "That means you wrote that note for me. You knew I'd come home after I got the flowers."

"Yes, Isabelle. I know you better than you know yourself." He closed the distance between them.

"Was it you who broke into Ryan's house?" she demanded.

"Of course not," he scoffed. "I would never stoop that low. But I have connections in London. I have people who will do things for me," he said with a menacing tone. "I had Ryan's apartment checked first. I thought you might be there."

"And the swan?" she asked, bravely meeting his narrowed gaze.

"Ah, yes, the swan." He nodded. "Once I knew where you were living, I thought it might be fun to make you wonder. Did you wonder, Isabelle? Did you think about me?"

Isabelle didn't even want to dignify his question with an answer. Instead, she scoured the area with her eyes to find some sort of weapon. *Be strong*, she told herself. She couldn't cave in now.

"By the way . . ." he said.

Isabelle prepared to run.

"I like you better as a blonde."

She didn't waste another second, but took off running, swinging out far around him.

James ran after her and tackled her to the ground, smacking her head hard against the stone floor, scraping the side of her face.

"You won't get away this time," he growled.

It wasn't fear that exploded inside of her, but anger. He'd kept her from her family and from being happy for their entire marriage. Finally, she had a life, and a brother and an aunt who loved her. She had a purpose in life. She wasn't going to let him take that away from her.

With all the strength she could muster, she balled up her fist and threw a punch backwards. Her knuckles connected with his left temple, a stunning blow that left Isabelle's knuckles split and bleeding and James momentarily dazed.

Isabelle scrambled to her feet, but James reached out and grabbed at her ankle, causing her to fall to the ground again. He lunged at her, his hands circling her throat.

A tornado of fury built inside of her as she realized that once again, she was under his control. "Go ahead," she said to him, barely able to whisper. "Kill me."

James blinked.

"I'd rather die than be married to you," she said.

James didn't move, but his grip around her neck loosened.

They stared into each other's eyes, then James removed his hands from her neck and pushed himself off of her. Drops of rain began to fall. A low rumble of thunder sounded in the distance.

"You're my wife," he told her, his tone even and calm. "It's time to come home."

She looked at him with amazement. Was he crazy? And did he think *she* was crazy?

"I will never come home with you. Never! It's over."

A heavy pause hung between them. The rain fell faster and harder. Then, in a sudden rage, he lunged at her, grabbing her by the shoulders, pulling her face within inches of his. "You've put me through hell. No more games. We're going home."

He dragged her to her feet, keeping a painful grip on her arm as he led her toward the stairwell.

She stumbled along while her mind searched for a plan. If only she could break away . . .

It took all the courage she had to drive her elbow into his ribs and break free, but she managed to catch him by surprise and before she knew it, she was flying down the stairs, with James close behind. Choosing her footing carefully Isabelle managed to dodge the decayed section of stairs, then slowed her pace.

Please let this work, she prayed.

"Isabelle!" James's voice bellowed down the stairwell as he followed in hot pursuit.

Isabelle turned just in time to see him hit the crumbling section of stairs with full force.

And just as she had hoped, underneath his weight, the stairs gave way. In an avalanche of stone, James was swept away, the roar of crumbling rock and debris drowning out his cries. The stairs and decayed section of wall collapsed in a deafening crash. Then, when the last stone clattered on top of the heap, everything grew quiet.

In shock, Isabelle listened for movement. Nothing. Was he dead? Unconscious?

She didn't wait to find out. Instead she ran across the courtyard and through the entry.

Frightened and soaked clear through, Isabelle ran through puddles and rain. Just as she was almost to the path, she glanced back. James was nowhere in sight.

Her next step landed in a slick patch of mud. Down she went, slamming hard against the ground. And everything went black.

Chapter 22

"Isabelle," the voice called. Someone shook her trying to wake her. "Isabelle!"

Startled into awareness, Isabelle woke up fighting. With arms flailing and legs kicking, she hollered, "Stay away from me!"

"Isabelle, it's Ryan. What happened? Are you okay?"

"Ryan?" she said weakly, as energy drained from her arms and legs. "Is it really you?"

"I'm here," he said, pulling her weak, trembling frame into his arms.

"He's here," Isabelle cried. "James is here."

"Shhh," Ryan tried to soothe her. "You're safe now."

She relaxed in his arms for less than a minute, then stiffened. "I think I killed him."

She looked at Ryan's startled expression, then saw Ethan, Aunt Sophie, and Dr. Holmes there with her.

"What do you mean?" Ryan asked.

"The stairs. They collapsed. He fell." She shuddered and buried her head in her brother's shoulders.

"We'd better go take a look," Ethan said to the doctor.

The men turned toward the castle, then stopped.

Stumbling towards them came James. Blood oozed from his forehead and chin. One eye was swollen shut. He held his left arm bent across his waist as he limped closer.

The four of them watched in silence as the man approached. When James was about ten feet from her he stopped, teetering on his feet.

Ryan motioned for Aunt Sophie to take his place. She quickly drew Isabelle protectively to her.

Stepping forward, with Ethan and Dr. Holmes flanking either side, Ryan faced his brother-in-law and said, "What do you want?"

James stared at Ryan with a level gaze. "She's my wife. I came to take her home."

"She's not going anywhere with you," Ryan spat the words with controlled anger.

James glared at Isabelle. But instead of cowering, Isabelle stared him in the eye.

"Isabelle?" James spoke her name.

"It's over, James. I never want to see you again," she told him.

His jaw clenched, and the veins in his neck throbbed, matching the fury in his eyes.

"You heard the lady," Ethan said, stepping up to Ryan's side. "She wants you out of her life."

James's face got red and sparks of anger ignited in his eyes.

"The police should be here any minute," Dr. Holmes said. "Just in case you decide not to cooperate."

The look of hatred in his eyes chilled Isabelle to the bone. "I'll leave, but it's not over," he threatened.

"It is over, James," she told him. "I'm suing you for divorce."

He took a step toward her, but Ethan and Ryan stood shoulder to shoulder, daring him to move another inch toward Isabelle.

"You'll have to kill all of us before you even get close to Isabelle, let alone touch her again," Ethan returned his threat.

Dr. Holmes stepped forward and added to the threat, "You even set foot in England and I'll have all of Scotland Yard after you."

James gave them a calculating glance, then shrugged. "You never know what the future might hold," he said enigmatically, giving Isabelle a long look before he turned away and started toward the path.

"We'll make sure he gets out of town," Ryan told Isabelle. "We'll meet you back at the cottage."

Relief flooded Isabelle's entire body, and she watched as her brother and Ethan escorted James down the path and hopefully out of her life.

And as soon as they were out of sight, Isabelle collapsed in tears and relief into her aunt's arms.

* * *

Even with James's threat hanging over her head, Isabelle managed to resume some semblance of normalcy in her life. In part it was because Ryan and Ethan installed a security system that was nothing short of a personal SWAT team. Or maybe it was the fact that Isabelle was rarely left alone. Every measure to ensure her safety was taken. And even though Isabelle still had nightmares about her encounter with James, there was a sense of relief inside knowing that the charade of her death and the initial confrontation with James was over. She had a feeling of strength inside of her knowing that she'd actually stood up to him. That for once, he hadn't walked away victorious and in control of her life.

Facing him as she had, fighting him and standing her ground, made her feel as though she had taken back her life. She still wondered and worried that he would return, but she didn't live in fear. She felt empowered and free. Free to live again and to trust again.

With each passing day, Isabelle's sense of security returned. She was amazed at the amount of love that surrounded her. Ryan came from London as often as he could, and it wasn't uncommon for Ethan and Ian Scott to drop by or call every day.

Even Dr. Holmes wrapped a wing around her, especially since he was concerned about her health and that of the baby. He'd worried about Isabelle's traumatic encounter with James, but there were no outward manifestations of any problems. Isabelle was filled with relief.

At first, she hadn't been sure about the baby and how she felt about it. But the longer she was pregnant and the more time she had to think about it, the more her insides filled with flutters of excitement. She wasn't the only one excited either. Aunt Sophie was either crocheting baby booties and working on a receiving blanket constantly or bringing home outfits or baby items every time she went to the store. The woman was beside herself at the thought of having a baby in the house.

Isabelle felt content for the first time in years. She loved her job with the children, she loved spending time with her family and friends, and she enjoyed spending her free time working in the garden.

"I've never had such lovely gladiolas before," Aunt Sophie said one Saturday afternoon as she and Isabelle took a lemonade break after weeding flower beds most of the day.

"I think anything could grow in this soil," Isabelle answered, admiring the tall, stately flowers, vibrant with color. "My garden back in Boston wasn't anywhere near as beautiful as yours," she said. "But I was working on it."

They both took a sip of their drinks and enjoyed a cool breeze that rustled the trees and danced with the flowers.

"Do you miss it, dear?" Aunt Sophie asked.

"Boston, or my home?" Isabelle replied.

"Both, I guess." Aunt Sophie stirred the ice in her glass with a straw.

"No," Isabelle answered without a moment's hesitation. "Not at all. I had nothing there. No friends, no purpose, no life." She turned and smiled at her aunt. "I've never been happier than I have been here with you."

Aunt Sophie smiled, then noticed a car coming down the lane toward the cottage.

"I wonder who that could be. I don't recognize the car," she said.

Isabelle watched with trepidation as the car pulled up in front of the cottage and stopped.

A moment later a young man stepped out of the driver's side of the car. It took a moment to recognize him in a pair of casual pants and a polo shirt, but there was no mistake, it was Elder Twitchell.

He called hello and gave them a wave, then turned and opened the door to the backseat. Out stepped a man and a woman. Isabelle nearly fainted when the woman turned around.

"Cynthia?" she said out loud. "I don't believe it!"

Aunt Sophie looked at her with surprise. "Isabelle, do you know that woman?"

Isabelle nodded, completely floored at the coincidence. She stood and began walking toward their visitors.

Cynthia Twitchell was going on and on about the garden and didn't notice Isabelle approach them.

"This is magnificent," she exclaimed as she admired all the types and varieties of flowers in full bloom.

"Hey, Mom," Elder Twitchell said, tapping his mother on the shoulder.

Cynthia stopped talking and turned. Her mouth dropped open, her eyes opened wide, and she blinked them several times before saying, "Isabelle, is that you?"

Isabelle nodded, swallowing a lump in her throat.

"Omigosh!" Cynthia cried as she rushed to her friend and smothered her in a joyful embrace. "I don't believe it," the older woman said. She stood back and held Isabelle at arm's length, then hugged her again. "You're alive." Tears filled her eyes and rolled down her cheeks. "I don't believe it!" she exclaimed again.

"What's going on, Mom?" Elder Twitchell asked.

Keeping one arm around Isabelle's waist, Cynthia turned to her husband and son and said, "This is Isabelle Dalton. She lived next door to us in Boston."

Mr. Twitchell and their son looked at Isabelle in amazement.

"Wait a minute," Mr. Twitchell said, "I thought you—didn't we go to her funeral?" he asked his wife in confusion.

"Yes," Cynthia said, suddenly remembering. "Isabelle, what's going on? And look at you." She touched Isabelle's copper-colored waves. "None of this makes sense."

Aunt Sophie came to the rescue and offered them all a chair in the shade and a glass of lemonade. They made themselves comfortable and Isabelle began her story.

When she finished her explanation, Cynthia immediately spoke. "I knew it. I knew that man was hurting you. Oh, Isabelle . . ." she reached over and grabbed Isabelle's hand. "Forgive me for not helping you more. You poor dear."

Isabelle couldn't help the tears that filled her eyes. "You don't understand," she told Cynthia. "You were the one who gave me the courage to leave. Do you remember our last conversation?"

Cynthia had tears in her own eyes. "Yes," she said with a nod. "Every time I saw you with a cut or a bruise I wanted to go after him myself. I've never hated a soul in my entire life. No one, that is, except your husband, for what he was doing to you."

"It's over now," Mr. Twitchell offered. "We're just glad you're safe and sound. And what a lovely place to call your new home."

"You seem very happy," Cynthia said. "It's wonderful to see a light in your eyes." She smiled warmly at Isabelle. "What about James? He doesn't know then, does he?"

"Actually, yes, he does. He paid me a visit just a little over a week ago."

"He did?" Cynthia exclaimed. "He came here? That must have been horrible."

"It was," Isabelle told her. "He had several people working for him, trying to find me."

"The man was trying to scare her to death," Aunt Sophie piped up. "He was stalking her."

"Stalking her?" Cynthia repeated, horrified.

Isabelle didn't go into detail about Ryan's apartment, the swan's death, or the roses, but said only, "It was just his way of playing with my head, of letting me know he knew where I was. He liked playing that type of game. It must have made him feel powerful."

"What an awful man," Cynthia said, shaking her head.

"You know, the house next door did seem empty for a while there," Mr. Twitchell said. "We can see your garage from our bedroom window. James usually leaves for work about the time I get up."

"I'm just glad he's back in Boston," Isabelle said.

"I'll bet he's not glad to be back," Cynthia said.

"Why?" Isabelle asked.

"This investigation that's going on. You'd think with all the Dalton money and power in Boston, James or his mother would find some way to clear James's name. But the papers say he's still a target for the investigation," Cynthia explained. "I'm sure his mother is fit to be tied."

Isabelle laughed. She could easily picture Marlene Dalton pitching a fit over the whole ordeal.

"Well, let's just hope justice is served," Cynthia said. "If he is involved, he deserves whatever he gets."

"Now Cynthia," Mr. Twitchell said.

"Well, he does. Especially after he treated Isabelle so horribly."

The conversation turned to their son, Justin, and his plans after his mission. The Twitchells ended up staying for dinner and enjoyed a walk up to the castle and around the pond.

When it was time to leave Cynthia and Isabelle had a difficult time saying good-bye.

"I don't suppose you'll come to Boston to visit, will you?" she asked.

Isabelle shook her head. "Probably not, but I'd love to have you come back anytime you can."

"Yes," Aunt Sophie added her invitation. "We have plenty of space and we can show you around the area. It's lovely any time of the year, but especially in the spring."

"You know I'll come with you anytime you want, Mom," Justin said.

"Then, this isn't good-bye," Cynthia said. "Because we'll see each other again. And we'll stay in touch."

Their parting was tearful, yet Isabelle knew she'd see her friend again.

That night she made a special effort in her prayers to thank her Heavenly Father for her wonderful friend and neighbor, Cynthia Twitchell. Looking back she could see the Lord's hand in her life, helping her along the way. This knowledge and understanding brought a greater appreciation for her blessings and a greater strength to deal with the challenges she would face down the road.

Placing her life in the Lord's hands, exercising faith that His will and purpose would be done, was the best thing she'd ever done. She knew He had been able to do more for her than she could do for herself.

The next time Ryan came, he brought a PC to hook up at their home. Isabelle was excited to have the Internet and e-mail so she could stay in touch with Cynthia, but Aunt Sophie didn't want anything to do with the "contraption" and said that she was much too old to learn anything as fancy as a computer. But when Ryan pulled up web site after web site of gardening tips, home decorating sites, and recipe ideas, she began to change her mind and with some help she managed to learn how to turn "the thing" on and log onto the Internet. Isabelle and Ryan laughed every time she said she was "surfing the Web."

"I think we've created a monster," Ryan told Isabelle one day when they were both starving and Aunt Sophie wouldn't pull herself away from the computer long enough to make dinner.

"Looks like it's grilled cheese tonight," Isabelle suggested.

Together Ryan and Isabelle worked in the kitchen, making sandwiches and a tossed salad for dinner. Ryan was telling her about a beautiful model he'd met while on assignment. They'd gone out to lunch one day and then to dinner and a movie.

"You really like her, don't you?" Isabelle said, noticing the sparkle in her brother's eyes when he talked about Gabrielle.

With a boyish smile, he nodded. "Yeah, I do."

"You'll have to bring her down sometime. We'd love to meet her," Isabelle said as she carried the salad bowl to the table.

"That's a great idea," Ryan exclaimed, scooping the last of the sandwiches out of the frying pan. "I know you'd—"

"Isabelle, Ryan, you need to come here!" Aunt Sophie's urgent call came from the other room. Leaving the food behind, they rushed from the kitchen to join their aunt at the computer.

"What is it, Aunt Sophie?" Isabelle asked.

"Look at this," Sophie pointed to the screen where a headline of a news release stated, "FBI Washes Hands of Conflict Diamond Scandal Investigation."

"What?" Ryan knelt down by the side of his aunt's chair to get a closer look. Out loud, he read the article to them, which reported that after an in-depth investigation, there just wasn't enough hard evidence against James to incriminate him. Several people who had originally come forward with information now denied having any knowledge of James's involvement with the diamonds. The FBI had turned the case over to the local authorities, who weren't sure at that point whether they would continue the investigation or not.

"He got to them," Ryan said. "James got to them and either paid them off or threatened them. I'd bet my life on it."

"So that's it?" Isabelle cried with disbelief. "He's off the hook."

"Now that it's up to the local authorities, there probably isn't enough manpower to continue the investigation," Ryan explained. "It happens. And it's a convenient way to handle cases like this, especially when you're dealing with high-powered individuals. People like James."

"It's not right!" Isabelle stomped her foot. "I know he had something going on in Africa."

"You're positive?" Ryan asked her.

"Well, not for sure, but, he made several trips there, claiming to have some international accounts for the law firm that he needed to visit. And there were phone calls. International calls. Of course, he never shared much about his work with me, but one time, while he was gone, I needed to get in touch with him. His mother had slipped on some icy stairs and was in the hospital with a fractured hip." She thought back for a moment to gather as many details as she could remember. "He usually left me an itinerary of his business trips, but now that I think about it, he never did for these trips to Africa." She remembered feeling frantic about getting in touch with him because Marlene had been asking constantly for her son from her hospital bed.

"Did you ever reach him?" Aunt Sophie asked.

"I tried to track him down, but when I called his assistant at work to get his number, she didn't have it. In fact, I remember thinking how odd it was that she didn't seem to have any knowledge of his trip, or where he was. She just said that James was out of the office and hadn't left a number where he could be reached. She said he did call in for messages, and she'd give him my message."

Ryan looked thoughtful. "We should write down everything you can remember about these trips. Dates, conversations, things he said, any information at all. You never know what would be helpful. Here," he grabbed a notepad off the desk, "I'll write while you talk."

"What's the use?" Isabelle asked.

"If you've got something solid, I promise you, we'll find someone who will listen."

Over dinner Isabelle recalled every shred of information she could remember about anything to do with his traveling to Africa, strange phone calls, and special delivery letters. The more she recalled details, the more other memories were triggered.

"Isabelle, I know that a lot of this just seems like useless information, but if some of these phone records can be accessed, some of these trips can be tracked, I think they could build a case on this. If we only had some hard, clear evidence—"

Hard, clear evidence. Isabelle thought about Ryan's words. Then suddenly she remembered something.

"The package!" she cried, startling her aunt.

"What package, dear?" Aunt Sophie asked, patting her chest to calm her racing heart.

"I completely forgot about it," Isabelle said.

"What is it?" Ryan asked. "What are you talking about?"

Isabelle thumped her hand on the table. "I knew he'd been in here that night we lost Romeo. He was looking for me. But I bet he was also looking for the package."

"Will you please tell us what you're talking about?" Ryan insisted. "What package?"

"He got deliveries at the house all the time. You know—Fed Ex, UPS, special delivery. I never really thought much of them, or even paid any attention to who or where they were from." She got up from the table. "Just before I left Boston, one of those packages was delivered. For some reason, I just shoved it in my purse."

"Are you saying what I think you're saying?" Ryan asked with excitement.

Isabelle nodded. "I still have the package. That is, unless he found it when he was here."

"Well, what are we waiting for?" Ryan bolted from the table. "Let's go see."

Rushing up the stairs to her room, Isabelle threw wide the wardrobe doors and yanked open the bottom drawer. Digging wildly through the contents, she held her breath, hoping with all her heart that it was still there.

"I found it!" she cried when she saw the envelope at the bottom of the drawer.

"Open it," Ryan told her. "This is incredible, Isabelle," he said as she peeled open the envelope. "I can't believe you thought to keep the package. You're brilliant!" he exclaimed. He turned to Aunt Sophie, "My sister's brilliant."

Aunt Sophie agreed and they watched with anticipation as Isabelle ripped open the envelope, reached inside, and pulled out the small, fist-sized, bubble-wrapped contents.

"What is it?" Aunt Sophie peered at it.

Peeling off the tape that held the bubble wrap in place, Isabelle slowly exposed the carefully wrapped item that might have the potential to change James's life.

"What is it?" Ryan asked.

Isabelle felt disappointment crash around her. For one, brief moment, she'd hoped that finally, James would get what he deserved, that justice truly would be served.

"It's a Beanie Baby," she said, holding it up for them to see.

"A Beanie Baby!" Ryan exclaimed. "Why in the world would he be getting a Beanie Baby sent to him?"

"His mother collects them. She's an art collector, and for some reason James helps her collect them. They think a complete collection will be worth a lot someday. This one's probably retired so he's had to search all over for it. Well, I'm glad I have it," she proclaimed, feeling anger well up inside of her. "He can search the entire universe for another one if he has to."

She looked at the smiling pink bear in her hand and felt a sudden rush of fury. "Darn him!" she cried, crushing the bear in her grip. "Just once I'd like to see him get caught, you know?" Angry tears stung her eyes. "Just once!"

She took one last look at the bear, then flung it with all her strength against the bedroom wall. Burying her face in her hands she burst into tears of frustration and anger. Aunt Sophie circled her with an understanding hug and held Isabelle as she cried.

"Hey," Ryan said. "Look at that."

Isabelle wiped at her eyes and looked at Ryan, then her gaze followed the direction he was pointing. On impact the bear had burst a seam and lay in a heap on the floor, with white styrofoam beans spilling out of it.

"Those Beanie Babies certainly aren't constructed very well, are they?" Aunt Sophie observed.

Ryan went over to the bear and bent down.

"I think you'd better come take a look at this," he said, his voice sounding suddenly strained.

Isabelle and her aunt shared a curious glance.

"Hurry!" Ryan exclaimed.

Isabelle and Aunt Sophie knelt down, and Isabelle had to blink her eyes several times before she could believe what she was seeing.

"Are these what I think they are?" From the scatter of styrofoam beans, Isabelle picked up one of the rough, cloudy rocks about the size of a gumball and examined it closely. There were dozens of the stones of various sizes mixed in with the styrofoam balls.

Ryan nodded. "Uncut diamonds," he said.

Wide-eyed, Isabelle looked at Ryan, whose face mirrored the same surprised shock as Aunt Sophie's and her own.

"He's smuggling the diamonds out of Africa in the Beanie Babies," Ryan said. Then he started laughing, a laugh that grew in intensity and volume. "He's smuggling diamonds!"

Ryan's contagious laugh got Aunt Sophie and Isabelle laughing, too. Disbelief, surprise, and sheer shock hit them with a giddy force.

"He's busted," Ryan said, finally getting his breath back. "We've got him."

"I can't believe it," Isabelle exclaimed, wiping at her eyes. "That's what all these stupid Beanie Babies were about." She thought for a moment. "I wonder if Marlene knows?"

"Probably," Ryan guessed.

"No," Isabelle said. "I'm not sure she does. Several times she complained about James and those 'ridiculous things.' I don't know. I think he was using her as an excuse to collect them. Maybe I'm wrong, though."

"Do you think she still has them? Could we get to them?" Ryan asked.

"Her house is as solid as the Pentagon and the collection is kept in a locked case. But . . ." she said with a gleam in her eye, "I'm guessing James isn't selling off the diamonds until the heat's off from the investigation. Which means . . ."

"What?" Ryan and Aunt Sophie asked together.

"I know where James keeps a stash of Beanies. He doesn't know I know about it. I just happened across it one day. That is, unless he's gotten rid of it because of the investigation."

"I wish there was some way to find out. When we expose him, it would be better if we had a few more of these guys to back us up," Ryan said, lifting the limp, beanless bear up for view.

"Cynthia!" Isabelle said. "She could get in the house and get them for us."

"You think she'd do it?" Aunt Sophie asked.

"The way she feels about James, I'm sure she would."

The phone call went even better than Isabelle expected. Assuring Isabelle a dozen times that she wouldn't get caught, Cynthia quickly agreed to do it.

"You don't even have to go into the house," Isabelle explained to her. "They're in the garage, in a box, on a shelf behind a bunch of paint cans."

"If I didn't want to see James behind bars so badly, I'd be petrified to do this," Cynthia told her.

"I know." Isabelle completely understood. "But if we don't do this, he'll get away with it."

"Just think of all those innocent people, especially children, who've died over these diamonds. And James is responsible for some of it." Cynthia spat the words with disgust.

"Some people will do just about anything for money and power, won't they?" Isabelle said, knowing how important both of those things were to James.

"It's scary to think just how far some people will go," Cynthia said.

"So, when do you think you can do it?" Isabelle asked.

"I'll wait until he leaves for work on Monday. I'll have to wait until Phil goes to work, too. He'll have a conniption if he knows I'm doing this," Cynthia told her.

"I don't want your husband to get upset at you," Isabelle said.

"Don't you worry about it. I'll have Justin stand guard for me. We won't get caught," Cynthia assured her.

"Be careful. We'll pray for you," Isabelle.

"Good idea," Cynthia said. "I'll call you as soon as I get back to the house. This is kind of exciting, isn't it?"

"Let's just hope there are some diamonds in those Beanie Babies," Isabelle said.

Waiting until Cynthia called nearly drove Isabelle insane. Ryan skipped work Monday so he could be around for the news. He told his supervisor he was working on a story and wouldn't be in for several days. Not only did he have a personal interest in the outcome of what Cynthia discovered, but he knew he would be the first to report the story to the news. This was a break he'd been waiting for his entire career.

Staying home from work that day, Isabelle did her best to keep busy. The hands on the clock seemed to pause for an eternity with each tick, and the only way to not to go crazy was to stay busy.

With Ryan doing some work on the Internet and Aunt Sophie cleaning like a supercharged robot, Isabelle went outside to work in the garden, hoping to find some peace and solace in being out of doors.

The smell of earth and fragrant flowers filled her lungs as she knelt beside a bed of columbine and smiling daisies. Keeping the weeds down was a never-ending job, but she didn't mind the work; it was therapeutic for her.

The sun beat down on her back, causing beads of perspiration to form on her forehead and trickle down between her shoulder blades. Sitting back on her heels she looked over the garden and smiled with pleasure. The fresh-turned soil was rich and black, contrasting vibrantly against the field of color. Looking out over the fence at the field beyond, she noticed cows grazing lazily in a deep green pasture. The bold, blue sky was broken up by streaks of feathery white clouds. It was heaven on earth, pure and simple.

Isabelle's heart filled with appreciation and gratitude for the beauty of the Lord's creation. The world was an amazing place, and she was grateful to be where she could enjoy it, surrounded by people she loved.

"Hey there," a voice called from the distance.

Isabelle recognized the voice immediately and pushed herself to her feet. "Ethan," she called back. "What are you doing here this time of day?"

"Playing truant," he told her. The smile on his face and the warm twinkle in his eye told Isabelle that he was as happy to see her as she was to see him. "You look hot."

"I am," she said. "I was just going inside for something cold to drink. Can you come in?"

"Of course." He accepted her invitation readily. "I have a surprise for you."

"For me?" Isabelle asked with delight, eyeing the cardboard box in his arms.

"It's something I made for you," he told her.

Isabelle could tell he was excited to give it to her.

"Bring it inside," she said, leading the way through the back door into the kitchen. She washed her hands in the sink, poured them cold glasses of blackberry juice, and brought a plate of shortbread biscuits over to the table for them.

"So," she said curiously. "What did I do to deserve a present?"

Ethan gave her a wide grin. "You didn't have to do anything. I just wanted to do something nice for you. You've come to mean a lot . . . to me," he said, looking away. "And to Ian Scott, too."

"You two mean a lot to me, too." Isabelle stumbled a bit with her words as color rushed to her cheeks.

Their gazes met and Isabelle knew their feelings went much deeper than their words. She wasn't an expert at reading other people's emotions, but she felt so close to Ethan, so comfortable and so connected, it was almost as if she knew what he was thinking.

"Well, hello, Ethan," Aunt Sophie said, coming around the corner in a whirlwind of feather dusters, glass cleaners, and latex gloves. "This is a surprise."

"He brought me a present," Isabelle announced. "Something he made."

"Really, now," Aunt Sophie plopped her supplies onto the counter and removed her gloves. "Mind if I watch the unveiling."

"Not at all," Ethan invited. He jumped from his chair and pulled one out for Aunt Sophie. "Would you like something to drink?" he offered.

"No, dear, I'm fine," she answered, but she did take one of the shortbread cookies.

"Now then," Isabelle placed the box directly in front of her. She pulled off the strapping tape holding the flaps down and opened them wide. Peering down inside the box, she gasped. "Oh, Ethan," she said breath-lessly. "Oh, my goodness." Carefully, with both hands she reached inside the box and pulled out a wooden chest about the size of a mailbox. It was a glossy chestnut brown, sanded and polished until it was as smooth as silk. There was a small latch on the front that could be locked, and on the top, beautifully carved with swirls and flowers, was her name, "Isabelle."

Tears quickly filled her eyes and trickled down her cheeks. It was the most beautiful and thoughtful thing anyone had ever given her.

Leaving her chair, she went to Ethan, who stood and accepted her embrace with open arms. "Thank you," she whispered.

Ethan held her tightly but gently. He stroked the back of her hair. "I'm glad you like it. You didn't look inside, though. There's more."

"More?" she asked, eyes wide with astonishment. "Ethan, the chest is more than enough."

"Just open it," he coaxed.

Lifting the lid slowly, Isabelle exposed the midnight blue velvet lining, where poised in a glittering array of light was a delicate, hand-blown, crystal castle.

"Ethan," Isabelle whispered. "It's beautiful." She lifted the castle, placing it in the palm of her hand. Prisms of light glinted off the diamond-cut towers, dancing in pin dots of color on the kitchen wall. "It's perfect," Isabelle said breathlessly.

Aunt Sophie was equally taken with the castle and marveled at the detail and workmanship of the piece as Ethan looked on with satisfaction. If he'd wanted to please Isabelle, he'd done a spectacular job of it.

"How can I ever thank you?" Isabelle asked, placing the delicate piece back in its container.

"The look on your face is thanks enough," Ethan told her as he looked into her eyes.

Once again, Isabelle rose from her chair and gave him another hug. She was beginning to like the feel of his arms around her and the fresh smell of his clothes that reminded her of a warm summer day. Their hug lingered a moment longer until the abrupt ringing of the telephone made Isabelle stiffen in his arms. She quickly pushed herself away and looked at her aunt with anticipation.

"Is something wrong?" Ethan asked, glancing at Isabelle, then at Aunt Sophie.

"We've been expecting an important phone call," Aunt Sophie said. "This might be it."

Isabelle wrung her hands and bit her bottom lip. *Please, Heavenly Father, let Cynthia have good news.*

Before Aunt Sophie could answer, Ryan hollered from the other room. "It's Cynthia," he called. "Come in here and we'll put her on speaker phone."

Ethan's face registered confusion, but he followed them into the living room to the corner where the computer was set up.

"Okay, Cynthia, go ahead. Everyone's here," Ryan said.

"Hi, everyone," Cynthia's voice came over the speaker. "I didn't have any trouble getting into the garage. It went just like you said it would, Isabelle," she said.

"Good," Isabelle exclaimed with relief. She'd worried that James might have changed the codes on their alarm system. "What did you find?"

There was a pause. "Nothing," Cynthia finally said. "The box is gone."

Disappointment filled Isabelle's heart. "Are you sure?" she cried. "Did you look around? Maybe James moved it."

"I looked everywhere. I could see where the box had been hidden behind the paint cans, but there was nothing. I searched all over. He's taken them."

"Now what are we going to do?" Isabelle worried out loud.

"We'll figure something out," Ryan assured her. "We're not giving up now."

"Are you sure you don't want me to go inside?" Cynthia offered.

"I wouldn't know where to tell you to look. He never kept any inside that I knew of," Isabelle told her.

Isabelle and Ryan looked at each other with frustration.

"Darn him!" Isabelle exclaimed, thumping her fist onto her thigh. "He must be worried about something or he wouldn't have moved that box."

"We need more proof," Ryan said. "Listen, Cynthia, we'll let you go and talk about what we want to do next. Then we'll give you a call later."

"Okay," Cynthia said. "Sorry it didn't work out."

"Thanks anyway," Isabelle told her. "I appreciate you being willing to try."

Ryan hung up the phone and released a frustrated sigh.

"So," Ethan said with raised eyebrows. "Would someone mind telling me what's going on?"

Isabelle spoke up. "We've found something on James," she said. "Something that might just help put him behind bars. My neighbor in Boston was trying to help us find it."

With Ryan's help, Isabelle recounted the discovery of the diamonds in the Beanie Baby to Ethan. But she didn't have a chance to finish before the telephone rang again.

Ryan grabbed the receiver before it rang again and said, "Hello."

"Cynthia!" he exclaimed. "Just a minute."

Again he put the call on speaker phone.

"Go ahead, Cynthia," Ryan instructed.

"You guys are never going to believe what I just did!" The excitement in Cynthia's voice carried over the phone line.

"What did you do?" Isabelle asked anxiously.

"I went outside to call the dog back into the house and saw the Federal Express man drive by . . ."

"And?" Isabelle prompted.

"He dropped a package off at your house—I mean, James's house."

"And?" Isabelle asked again.

"And I went over and took it."

"Cynthia, you're incredible!" Ryan cried.

"Was there something inside?" Isabelle asked with fingers crossed.

"Yes," she answered excitedly. "I found another Beanie."

"And?" Isabelle said, nearly dying with anticipation.

"It's full of diamonds!"

The crowd in England let loose a whoop of joy.

"Good job, Cynthia," Ryan told her. "You did a first-rate job of Beanie snatching."

"Thank you," Cynthia said. "There's just one problem."

"What's that?" Ryan asked.

"I'm not sure I'm willing to go to jail over this. I mean, isn't it illegal? You know, taking James's package and opening it?"

Ryan flashed a concerned glance at Isabelle before he answered. "Cynthia, I won't lie to you. You are now heavily involved by taking that Beanie Baby."

Cynthia sighed loudly. "That's what I was afraid of."

"But listen," Ryan replied quickly, "The worst that's going to happen is that you may have to testify. The state can give you immunity in exchange for your testimony. They won't prosecute."

"Are you positive, Ryan?" she asked.

"Ninety-nine percent," Ryan answered. "Just like Isabelle bringing the package with her to England. If and when this goes to court, the defense may try and get this evidence thrown out but it won't happen. I've studied the United States legal system for years and covered dozens of court cases, and it's actually quite difficult to get anything thrown out. Unless it was something like an unlawful search or seizing drugs or something without a warrant, the judge usually allows it."

"That's a relief," Cynthia said, voicing Isabelle's feelings exactly.

"Do you want me to overnight this bear and the diamonds to you?" Cynthia asked. "You should see these stones. Some of them are cut and I've never seen such brilliant, beautiful diamonds," she added.

"Yes, send them," Ryan said, then he corrected himself, "No, actually don't. I think it's time to contact the investigating officer and prosecuting attorney and tell them what we've got. They may just want you to bring it to them."

Isabelle broke out in goose bumps. She realized just how big this could get. Bringing down James, a Dalton no less, was huge. She felt like David going up against Goliath with the Beanie Babies as her slingshot.

"Have you got somewhere safe you can hide it for the next day or so?" Ryan asked.

"Of course. Don't you worry. It's safe with me," Cynthia assured them.

"We'll be in touch," Ryan said, then added, "You're a real sweetheart."

"That's what they all say," Cynthia joked. "You're my friends. I'd do anything for you."

Isabelle was touched. She didn't know what she'd done to deserve such wonderful blessings. Then she remembered something important, something she knew she couldn't deny. She had taken all her faith and courage and placed her life in the Lord's hands. And ever since that time, wonderful things had been happening in her life. Yes, there had been challenges. Confronting James had been the scariest thing she'd ever had to face in her life. But she had found the strength to do it and she had triumphed.

She knew that whatever lay ahead wouldn't be easy, but the Lord would be with her. He would help her. He would stand by her.

Chapter 23

The last place Isabelle ever thought she'd see again was Boston. But here she was, with Ryan, Aunt Sophie and . . . Ethan.

Isabelle had been surprised and thrilled when Ethan had offered to join them. She'd secretly hoped that somehow he could come to the United States with them. His physical presence and support would give her more strength to return to the place and the people that represented nothing but pain, heartache, and nightmares.

It was Ryan who had invited Ethan to join them, and she would be forever thankful to her brother for doing so. Even though Ian Scott was sad to stay behind, he was excited to stay with his grandma in London, and he made it absolutely clear that he expected a lot of great toys and surprises from America.

"We're here, Mr. Rakesh," Isabelle told the man on the phone. He was the U.S. District Attorney who was working on the case, now that the FBI had stepped aside. He'd been thrilled to have Isabelle come forth with damaging proof of James's involvement with the conflict diamonds.

In fact, Mr. Rakesh had been so ecstatic to have her involved in the case that he'd even offered to pay for her and the others to come to Boston and stay in one of the city's nicest hotels.

"Come directly to my office," he instructed. "I've arranged for a private meeting room on the third floor so you can keep a low profile." He told them to enter from the side door, where he would be waiting for them. Each time she'd spoken with the man, she'd detected his great passion and commitment to the case.

"Mr. Rakesh, do you get this involved with every case you work on?" she asked.

"No," he answered, "But I have a personal interest in this case. I'll explain when you get here."

They arrived at the appointed address and met Mr. Rakesh at the side door of the building. He was about the size of a refrigerator and wore an expensive suit by a designer label Isabelle recognized. Mr. Rakesh was also African-American.

"Welcome," he said. "Please, put your luggage in this corner and have a seat."

The room had a desk and chair and four chairs in a semicircle in front of the desk. The four guests took their seats and stared at the imposing figure of a man seated in front of them.

"I must say again, your original phone call was a very unexpected, but welcome surprise," Mr. Rakesh told Isabelle. "I have until Thursday to prove that Mr. Dalton is involved in the smuggling of diamonds from Africa. Your phone call was indeed timely."

"So James's name—I mean, Mr. Dalton's—name hasn't been cleared?" Isabelle asked.

"Far from it," Rakesh said. "When the FBI turned the case over to me, there wasn't enough evidence to implicate him. And I must be honest, it helped to lower the heat on this case when the FBI handed it over to me. Too much media attention can foul up an investigation. I wanted to get the story out of the news so I could conduct the investigation without the press breathing down my neck every step of the way. I was also hoping to draw any witnesses forward. You see," he said, with elbows resting on the desktop, his fingers forming a tepee, "two coworkers from Mr. Dalton's law office were willing to testify that Mr. Dalton did indeed go to Africa on business, but it wasn't for his firm. It was for himself."

"You say, 'were,'" Ryan asked, "What do you mean?"

"Someone got to them. Neither of them will testify and now they swear they were mistaken. But they were sure of it in the beginning." Mr. Rakesh nodded and tapped the tips of his fingers together. "They had no doubts of his involvement."

"You mentioned that you had a personal interest in this investigation," Isabelle reminded him.

"Yes, I do." Mr. Rakesh gave her a level look. "I came to America from Africa when I was a young man, in my early twenties. I came as a student, hoping to gain an education, then return to my country and help my people. My family is still there, but many of the cities in Africa are not safe places to live. Most of the members of my family have been victims of crime—they have been beaten, robbed, raped, and even murdered."

Isabelle felt her chest tighten. She thought she saw a glimmer of pain in his eyes behind his calm demeanor.

"Some of the crime is due to the poverty and desperation of the African people, but most of it is a result of brutal wars that exist in areas controlled by rebel groups opposed to the government. These wars are funded and backed by money that comes from the sale of these diamonds. I believe that Mr. James Dalton is helping to supply military arms, equipment, and even manpower, to these factions and rebel forces through his purchase of these diamonds."

"What about the embargo issued by the United Nations?" Ryan asked.

"It's all lip service," Rakesh told him. "There is no way to regulate it. The government leaders say they are complying, but many of them are corrupt themselves and stand to benefit from the sale of these diamonds."

Aunt Sophie shook her head. "All those poor innocent people, those children."

"Yes," Rakesh said. "And something has to be done. I am finally in a position to help my people. I feel God has led me here, to this particular place and time, to make a difference. I have to do this. But I can't do it without your help."

Knowing that it would take every ounce of courage and strength she possessed do to so, Isabelle looked at Mr. Rakesh and said, "We'll do everything we can."

"Good!" He nodded. "But I won't lie to you; this could get ugly. We're talking about the Dalton family here. Their lineage goes back to the founding fathers of this city."

Isabelle nodded. She knew full well the special privileges the Daltons received because of their names. What the Kennedys were to Martha's Vineyard, the Daltons were to Boston.

"But I want you to know something else," he said in a confident tone. "James Dalton is going down. We just have to prove that he was involved in the illegal smuggling of diamonds."

"What about giving funds to the rebel armies?" Ryan asked.

"That will be tried in a federal court. And if we prove that James is indeed smuggling diamonds, that will be right where he's headed." He looked directly at Isabelle. "I need you to help me."

Isabelle squirmed uncomfortably in her chair. "What more can I do?"

"I'm putting you on the stand," Rakesh told her.

Isabelle swallowed but still choked on her reply. "On the stand?"

"Yes. You're the only one who can do it."

As soon as they got to their hotel, Isabelle called Cynthia to tell her they were in town. Cynthia had been hoping to spend some time with Isabelle, but until after they met in court on Thursday, Rakesh wanted them to lay low and stay out of sight. He didn't want word to leak out that Isabelle was not only alive, but also back in town. Isabelle was Mr. Rakesh's ace in the hole, the trick up his sleeve, the key to winning the case. If the media caught wind of it, they would jump all over it.

Of course, the defense was aware that she was on the witness list, but Rakesh was willing to bet that they didn't expect her to show up. Not after what she told James back in Westmoor.

Isabelle was a nervous wreck inside. She didn't know if she had the guts to get up on that stand, in front of James and his mother, and get raked across the coals. But she'd promised she would help.

She barely slept that night.

Early the next morning the telephone rang in Isabelle and Aunt Sophie's hotel room.

"We need records," Mr. Rakesh said directly to her. "Phone calls, airline tickets, hotel stubs, credit card receipts. I need to prove that James actually went to Sierra Leone. I've been to his office, checked his records there. We found nothing out of order."

"They're probably in the file cabinet in the house," Isabelle told him. "I know exactly where it all is."

"Is there any way you can get it for me?"

"Me? Go back into that house?" She barely choked out the words.

"I need specific dates and times and places. I have to have these records," Mr. Rakesh told her. "It is still your home. You are not legally dead. You may have allowed Mr. Dalton to assume you were dead, but there was nothing illegal about you leaving your husband, especially an abusive husband. You didn't obtain an illegal death certificate, did you?"

"No."

"Then we need to get those records. Except . . ."

Isabelle waited for him to continue, somehow knowing she didn't want to hear what came next. "Yes?"

"I have a feeling James will have someone watching the house. He may expect or anticipate your return, and if they see you go in, it could complicate matters."

"You're right," Isabelle agreed, knowing that it wouldn't be beneath James to have someone on the lookout for her. Then she had an idea. Maybe she could talk Cynthia into going to the house. "Mr. Rakesh, I think I might have a solution. I'll call you right back."

Cynthia was more than thrilled to go back to the house, and even more excited that she actually got to go inside. Isabelle wondered if the woman had missed her calling in life. She would have made a wonderful spy.

"Call us on your cell phone as soon as he leaves for work," Isabelle said. "I'll walk you through the steps to get into the house."

"I feel like I should dress in black and put on a black ski mask," Cynthia joked.

"I'm sure that wouldn't draw anyone's attention," Isabelle replied. "But now that you mention it, if you carried over a plate of cookies or something, you could pretend you're just being neighborly. That would look a lot less suspicious."

"Great idea! I've got some brownies," Cynthia said.

"I don't know how I can ever thank you for all of—"

"Oh, pooh!" Cynthia blurted out. "You don't have to thank me for anything."

"Promise me you'll be careful," Isabelle worried out loud.

"Believe me I will," Cynthia answered. "Right down to wearing latex gloves so I don't leave fingerprints."

"We'll be waiting by the phone and praying for you," Isabelle told her.

As soon as the two friends got off the phone, Isabelle quickly dialed Mr. Rakesh. "It's all arranged," Isabelle told him. "I've a got a friend who's going to go into the house for me and—"

"Wait!" Mr. Rakesh interrupted. "Don't say anymore. If you yourself aren't going then I don't want to hear anymore about it. I don't care how you get the records, I just don't want to know the details."

"I understand," Isabelle answered. "We'll call you as soon as we have them."

"That's fine," Mr. Rakesh said in his booming voice. "Is there any way we can get some more of these Beanie Babies? I need some unopened to take to court."

"The only person I know who would have them is James's mother," Isabelle said.

"I see," Mr. Rakesh said. "We may have to get a search warrant then, but that will take time."

"I'll try and remember if there are any other places he kept the Beanie Babies. He might have some in his office," Isabelle offered.

"Call me then as soon as you—I mean, your friend . . ." a flustered Rakesh said, "as soon as *whoever* gets the records. It would be a good idea to make copies and get them back in his office so he doesn't miss them."

Things were starting to get complicated, Isabelle thought. But he was right. James was the type who would notice something missing, especially something that could incriminate him.

No sooner did she hang up the phone then Cynthia called back. "He's gone!" she said with nervous excitement. "I've got the brownies ready and I'm even wearing an apron. I couldn't look any less dangerous."

"Good, Cynthia. Let's get you in and out of there as fast as we can."

Aunt Sophie had summoned Ryan and Ethan to their room, and they listened to the conversation on the other extension.

"I'm at the code box on the garage. I think I remember the code," Cynthia said.

"It's 951JWD," Isabelle helped her.

"That's right, I wanted to ask you what the 'W' was for," Cynthia said.

"His mother's maiden name was Witherspoon," Isabelle told her. There was a silence. "Cynthia?" Isabelle asked.

"Right here. I was just waiting for the code to register." She paused. "There. I'm in."

"Enter the same code to close the door," Isabelle told her, feeling anxiety rush inside her chest.

"It's closed," Cynthia informed her.

"Good. Now you have to go to the door leading into the kitchen and you'll have exactly ten seconds to get to the security system box and enter that code. If you enter it too late, a silent alarm goes off."

Cynthia released a nervous breath. "I'm ready."

"As soon as you step inside, shut the door and turn to your left. There's a cabinet above a desk. Open the left cabinet door. The security box is right there inside."

Cynthia repeated the instructions back to her.

"That's right," Isabelle assured her. "Now, if for some reason you enter the wrong code, make sure you push clear and you'll have ten seconds to reenter the code; otherwise the alarm will go off."

"I think my deodorant just wore off," Cynthia said with a tight laugh.

"This is the worst part. Once you're in, you'll be back out in less than two minutes. I've been through this in my mind several times. It's a piece of cake," Isabelle said.

"Let's do it then," Cynthia said anxiously. "The sooner I'm in, the sooner I'm out. Wait!" she exclaimed. "You didn't tell me the code."

"They're the letters to my first name," Isabelle told her.

"Okay, good," Cynthia said. "I got it. Are you guys ready?"

The group answered her and wished her good luck.

There was a moment's pause before she spoke again. "I'm in, I'm closing the door, I'm opening the cupboard and there's the box."

"A green light will flash two times after you enter the code," Isabelle told her.

"Here I go," Cynthia said.

The others waited, praying and holding their breath.

"It flashed red!" Cynthia cried.

"Red!" Isabelle panicked. "Oh no! What if James changed the code?"

"Push clear," Ryan yelled into the phone. Then he said, "Cynthia, try it again. Maybe you accidentally pushed the wrong letter."

"Okay, okay, I'm trying again." There was a tiny pause, then, "It's flashing red again."

"He changed it," Isabelle said, devastated. "What are we going to do?"

"Push clear," Ryan said again.

"How are you spelling her name?" Ethan asked.

"What?" Cynthia cried.

"Her name," Ethan said.

"I-S-A-B-E-L-L," Cynthia answered.

"That's it," Isabelle nearly shouted into the phone. "I have an 'E' on the end of my name."

Cynthia didn't answer for a moment. "It's green!" she cried with joy. "It's green."

A collective sigh of relief filled the airwaves.

"Now what do I do?" Cynthia asked. "Besides have a heart attack."

Isabelle instructed her to go through the kitchen to the entry where James's office was located adjacent to the formal living room.

"The key to the file cabinet is inside the duck decoy on the bookshelf," Isabelle told her.

"Inside the duck?" Cynthia asked.

"It's a little storage box shaped like a mallard duck," Isabelle explained.

"I see it," Cynthia said. "Okay . . ." she paused, "and here's the key."

"Open the bottom drawer and check in the very back of all the files. It should say 'Work Receipts' on the file tab."

It took several seconds for Cynthia to perform the task, then her voice came on the line. "I have it," she said. "It's right here in my hand."

"That's great!" Ethan cried. "Now get out of there!"

"You have to reset the system before you leave," Isabelle told her. "This time put in James's name."

"And it's spelled 'J-E-R-K,' right?" Cynthia asked.

Everyone laughed.

"I'm putting in the code," Cynthia said. "The green light flashed."

"Good," Isabelle said. "Now get out of there. You remember the code for the garage, don't you?"

They waited while Cynthia got out of the garage safely.

"I'm out," she said. "Mission accomplished."

"Good job, Cynthia!" Isabelle cried. "We've got to make copies and get it back in his office before he gets home."

"I'll run home and make the copies, then call you back," Cynthia told her.

With relief, Isabelle hung up the phone. They were halfway there.

The others ate their room-service breakfast and watched the morning news programs for any information or further developments in the conflict diamond story.

Seeing nothing, Isabelle looked out the window from their fourteenth-floor hotel room as rain pounded the roof tops of buildings below.

"Hey," Ethan's voice came from behind her. "How are you doing?"

She turned and gave him a smile. "I'm fine."

"What are you doing?" He leaned against the other side of the window frame and looked at her face with concern in his eyes.

"Praying mostly," she said. "I don't want anything to happen to Cynthia. I'll feel much better once we get that file back in James's file cabinet."

Ethan nodded. "It's a bit unnerving, isn't it?"

"It's a lot different when you're watching it on TV than when you're actually living it. James Bond makes it look so easy," she said.

Ethan laughed. "That Cynthia, she's quite a lady," he observed.

"She's been like a guardian angel for me. If it weren't for her, I would've never had the courage to leave James," she said.

"Then remind me to give her an extra special thanks when we see her next," Ethan said with a smile.

Isabelle returned his smile, then sighed wearily. She hadn't slept well since the day they'd discovered the diamonds.

"Are you certain you feel well? You didn't eat much," he said.

The phone rang before she could answer. Ryan picked it up.

"Cynthia," he said. "You're done?"

Isabelle hurried and picked up the extension.

"I'm done. I noticed a lot of receipts while I was going through the file. He must've taken two or three trips to Africa," she said.

"The problem is, if he had any legitimate legal business in Africa, he could use it as a decoy for the real purpose of his trip," Ryan speculated.

"Hopefully Mr. Rakesh can find something in all of this," Cynthia replied. "I'm ready to put this file back. I'm getting a little skittish. I feel like I'm in the middle of a John Grisham novel."

This time Cynthia was able to get the file put away without a hitch. Aunt Sophie timed the entire task, and it took less than three minutes from Cynthia's backyard to James's office, and back to the safety of her yard again.

"I'll run them over to Rakesh's for you," Cynthia offered. "Since you guys are supposed to stay in hiding."

Isabelle didn't know what they'd do without Cynthia. She'd been invaluable to them and had, thankfully, been protected from any harm or danger.

Chapter 24

Two days before the trial, Isabelle began to feel like a caged animal. Pacing the floor, she barely slept or ate. How was she ever going to get up on that stand? The thought of being in the same room with James terrified her, but having to actually look him in the face again froze the blood in her veins. What if she couldn't do it?

Over and over again in her mind she reviewed her testimony. Rakesh had prepared her for her statement, they'd rehearsed it and gone over it a dozen times, but she still didn't feel ready. What if she got up on the stand and forgot what to say? Or what if she said something wrong and messed up the entire trial? The thought of getting up on the stand nearly stopped her heart, yet she knew she had no choice.

"Isabelle, dear, you haven't eaten a thing," Aunt Sophie called to her. "I'm worried about you. You have to eat. You have to keep up your strength."

Isabelle turned to her aunt and attempted a brave smile but failed miserably. "I know. I just don't have much of an appetite." In all honesty, she hadn't been feeling well at all. Her lower back ached and she felt occasional twinges in her stomach muscles.

"Still, you have to think of the little one," Aunt Sophie said. "You both need nourishment."

With a sigh, Isabelle went to the table, where her tray of food sat unappealingly in front of her. She knew her aunt was right. For the baby's sake, she had to take care of herself.

Forcing down several bites of chicken parmesan and a few forkfuls of salad, she took a long drink of ice water and pushed herself away from the table.

A knock came at their door, a special "code knock" to let them know it was either Ryan or Ethan. Aunt Sophie answered and invited both men into the room.

"We needed a change of scenery," Ryan said. He looked around their room, then joked, "I guess we came to the wrong place."

The others chuckled, since their rooms were identical.

"I think Isabelle needs a breath of fresh air," Aunt Sophie told them. "The poor girl's wasting away."

"Do you feel like going up to the roof?" Ethan offered. Their closest escape to the outside world was going to the roof, where there was a lovely garden.

Isabelle jumped at the chance. "Yes, thank you. That would be nice."

Sliding into her shoes and grabbing a light jacket, Isabelle was ready in a flash.

"Are you coming?" Isabelle asked her aunt and brother.

"We'll be up in a minute," Ryan said. "I want to catch this news program on CNBC."

"And I promised Kingsley I'd e-mail him and I haven't written yet," Aunt Sophie said.

Ethan and Isabelle took the elevator to the top floor and stepped outside into the oasis at the top of the hotel. A lit path led them toward the lovely fountain in the center of the garden and beyond. Flower pots overflowing with fragrant flowers, ivy and fern, and tall shimmering trees seemed suspended in time against the twilight sky.

At the edge of the roof was a clearing where they could look out over the city and see the skyline against the darkening heavens, watch as city lights and stars emerged and twinkled like glittering diamonds.

Diamonds!

Who would have thought that something so precious, so lovely, could cause so much trouble?

"Do you feel like sitting?" Ethan said, pointing to a marble bench seat.

Isabelle nodded and they sat next to each other and watched as the last rays of light faded from the sky.

They were alone on the roof. The few times they'd been there, they'd only run into one other couple, and were grateful for the privacy. Without others around, they could relax and enjoy the peace and quiet without worry.

"You'll be glad when all this is over, won't you?" Ethan asked.

Isabelle nodded. "I know that James is guilty, but he's a very brilliant man. I don't think he would take any chances or leave any clues around. I can't help worrying that he'll go free." Her voice was strained as she spoke.

"Are you afraid that your involvement will fuel his anger?"

"He came after me once, and I got away. Next time I might not get so lucky," she said.

Ethan took her in his arms and held her close. "Isabelle, nothing is going to happen to you. I won't let it. Ryan won't let it. And James will get convicted. The man's guilty as sin and Rakesh is determined to prove it. You have to have faith that it will happen."

Isabelle didn't know where it came from but instead of following her head, she followed her heart and found herself saying, "I'm really glad you came with us, Ethan."

"I wanted to be here for you," he answered softly.

"And I wanted you here with me," she said.

Ethan looked into her eyes. "After Jenny I never thought I would ever care about anyone again. Not like I cared about her. And then you came into my life," he chuckled. "Actually, I almost ran you over with a tractor."

"How could I forget?" she said with a laugh.

He reached out and cupped her cheek in his hand and looked at her for several moments. "I don't know what the future holds, but I will always be there for you. I will protect you with my life if I have to." Then he leaned forward and placed a tender kiss on her forehead and pulled her close.

Isabelle blinked at the tears stinging her eyes. Ethan's heartfelt embrace stirred her soul. He gave instead of demanded. He was sincere instead of controlling. He asked for nothing in return.

She reached up and circled her arms around his neck. "Thank you," she whispered. "I don't know what I'd do without you."

"I feel the same," he told her. "You've brought the light back into my life."

"And you've brought joy back into mine," she said.

He stroked her copper waves with his hand and spoke softly, "You've been through so much. You still have much more ahead of you,

I'm afraid. I don't want to complicate your life or make you feel trapped or scared," he said, "but I want you to know how much I care for you."

Isabelle pursed her lips together for a moment before she spoke. "I never thought I would ever feel the need to have a man in my life. I don't know what the future holds either," she said, "but I know I want you in it. I have to know that you'll be in it."

"I'll be there. We'll be there together. I promise."

"There's so much baggage, though," she said. "Are you sure you know what you're saying?" She couldn't help but think about the baby she carried. James's baby.

"I've got a whole room full of baggage. We'll just shove all of yours in there with it and close the door. We have our own lives to live now. We won't have time for baggage."

Isabelle smiled, feeling her heart grow even warmer towards this wonderful man. "I feel like I can do anything as long as you're beside me."

"You can," he said. "And that's where I'll always be. We'll get through this, then we'll go back home where we belong."

"Home," she said. "England really is my home. Everything I care about, everyone I love, is there." She paused for a moment. "I miss Ian Scott."

"I spoke to him earlier. He said to tell you hello. He's having the time of his life."

"We have to find something extra special to take back to him," Isabelle said.

"We will. After Thursday, we'll go shopping," Ethan replied.

Thursday seemed so far away. But knowing that Ethan cared about her as much as she cared about him helped give her the strength she needed to face the challenges the next few days would bring.

* * *

"I think I'm going to throw up!" Isabelle told her aunt Wednesday afternoon. She wasn't feeling well at all, and the closer the trial got, the worse she felt.

"What can I get you?" Aunt Sophie fussed. "Some crackers? Something to drink, perhaps some ginger ale?"

"No, I just need to sit down for a minute," Isabelle said, plopping onto her bed.

But a frantic banging on the door brought her back to her feet with a bound.

"Who in the world?" Aunt Sophie said, as she rushed to the door and opened it. "Mr. Rakesh!"

The big man rushed inside, barely making it through the door frame.

"Mr. Rakesh," Isabelle said. "I thought we wouldn't see you until morning."

"I need you to come with me," he told Isabelle tersely. "I need those Beanie Babies. I have to have some that haven't been opened."

"But I told you, my mother-in-law is the only one who has any," Isabelle said.

"That's where we're going." His voice boomed throughout the entire room.

"Me? You want me to go to Marlene's house?" Her knees went weak and she sat down on the bed again.

"She's been listed as a potential witness and she's been subpoenaed," Rakesh said. "I've also listed the Beanie Babies you said she has in possession as potential evidence, but we need both of them at the trial to prove our case."

"You're having Marlene testify?"

"I was hoping to, but she's resisted any form of contact and has been completely uncooperative, even though she's been subpoenaed. I have no assurance that she'll show up tomorrow to testify against her son. But the shock of seeing you alive, if James hasn't already told her, might just be enough to make her cooperate. You are my only hope in getting to her."

"But Mr. Rakesh . . ." Isabelle stalled, hoping to come up with some good reason she couldn't do it.

"We don't have any time to waste. I'm going to win this case or die trying. We have to go," he said firmly.

"Don't you need a search warrant or something?" Isabelle said with desperation. She did not want to see her mother-in-law.

"I don't plan on forcing my way in nor do I plan to take anything. I just want to reason with this woman and help her see her son for what he really is."

Isabelle knew it would never happen. James was Marlene's golden boy. She would never see what he was really like. Ever.

"We don't have much time."

"Okay, okay," Isabelle said, feeling the bottom drop out of her stomach.

They were at Marlene Dalton's house before Isabelle had a chance to even gather her thoughts. What in the world was she doing here? What would she say? How would Marlene react to seeing her?

The imposing structure made her feel small and insignificant. The sight of the Dalton mansion brought back unbidden memories, unwanted recollections of her past.

"Isabelle," Mr. Rakesh said before he rang the doorbell. "You have to be strong. I'll back you up, but you're the one who will get through to her."

The deep tones of the doorbell sounded and the doorbell was answered by Potter, Marlene's butler. She had an entire staff of people working for her, none of whom she treated with respect or dignity.

"We're here to see Ms. Dalton," Rakesh said to the man, who visibly cowered in the large man's shadow.

"Is she expecting you?" Potter asked, his eyes darting nervously to Isabelle, then back to Rakesh.

"No, she's not. But she will want to see us, I guarantee it," Rakesh told him in his deep, commanding voice.

"I'll see if she's up to accepting callers," Potter said, then closed the door. Several minutes later he opened the door again.

"Who's calling please?" he said, a bit breathlessly.

"Jonas Rakesh, District Attorney, and my assistant, Ms. Canfield," Rakesh answered, using Isabelle's maiden name.

"Please come in and I'll announce you."

Potter guided them toward the library, where, Isabelle remembered, Marlene did most of her business.

The familiar sights and smells of the house turned Isabelle's stomach. The home had always seemed stuffy and formal, not inviting and cozy. There was a constant strain of tension in the air, and Isabelle fell under its influence just standing there.

Sliding open the library doors, Potter announced their names, "District Attorney, Jonas Rakesh, and his assistant, Ms. Canfield." Then he stepped aside, and with a broad sweep of his arm, directed them into the room.

Leading the way, Rakesh walked inside. Dreading the confrontation, Isabelle followed behind, keeping on her dark glasses.

"Mr. Rakesh," Marlene said, her tone even and unwelcoming. "What could possibly bring you here? I told you I am not going to help you win this case against my son."

"You're an upstanding citizen and a valued member of the community," Rakesh told her. "After what I have to say, I think you will."

"Hmphf!" Marlene scoffed. "Talk to my lawyer."

"Mrs. Dalton, whether you like it or not, or are willing to face the truth or not, your son is involved in something not only very serious but also very illegal. I have proof that he's smuggling diamonds out of Africa and aiding in the sale and distribution of arms to rebel factions in Sierra Leone."

"What proof?" Marlene shot back.

Mr. Rakesh stepped aside, exposing Isabelle completely to Marlene's view.

Giving her a scathing glare, Marlene dared the woman to speak.

Removing her sunglasses slowly, Isabelle said, "Hello, Marlene."

The older woman's glare remained unchanged for several seconds, then her eyes narrowed. The strained muscles holding her expression tight and unyielding, softened in surprise.

"Yes," Isabelle said. "I am who you think I am."

"But you're dead!" the woman hissed.

"Not quite. Perhaps to you and your son. But I'm very much alive," Isabelle said, feeling strangely courageous and strong. It helped to have a giant of a man standing at her side.

"You . . ." Marlene pointed her finger and Isabelle. "You tricked my son and put him through hell. You nearly ruined him."

Isabelle couldn't believe her ears. If this woman knew what it had been like living with James all those years. He was the one who practically ruined her! "He experienced a small fraction of the hell he put me through for five years," Isabelle replied. "I'm sure he felt no grief for my death."

"What are you doing here? What do you want?" Marlene asked, the rigidity of her backbone seeming to slacken before their eyes.

"This isn't about the abuse, it's not about the beatings and the control, it's not about my marriage or revenge, Marlene, this is about the thousands of innocent women and children dying because of what your son is doing. This is about justice!" Isabelle spoke with conviction. "James has broken the law and he's tarnished your family name. The least you could do is salvage your own dignity and have the courage to admit that your son is a fraud. If you don't help us, he will make you look like a fool."

"Help you how?" The woman acted offended at the suggestion, but Isabelle knew something they'd said had hit the mark.

"We need to see your collection of Beanie Babies." Isabelle said to her.

The woman's eyebrows arched high with surprise.

"James has been smuggling the diamonds into the country inside of them," Isabelle told her.

Marlene gave a tight laugh. "That's preposterous. Almost as preposterous as you faking your own death."

Isabelle's defenses flew into place. "Faking my own death was the only way I could save my life and get away from your abusive, controlling son!" Isabelle spoke loudly, her voice shaking with anger. "And preposterous or not, those ridiculous Beanie Babies mean nothing to James except as a means to get his diamonds into this country. He's used you just like he's used everyone else!" Isabelle told her.

"Get out!" Marlene yelled. "Potter, call the police. Get my attorney on the phone. I want these two out of here."

"Check them yourself," Isabelle said. "Open one up and you'll see. They're full of diamonds."

"Potter!" Marlene yelled again and a scrambling of footsteps came their way. The butler appeared, breathless, at the door. "Call security, call the police, do something. Just get them out of here!" Marlene ordered.

"If I have to I can get a search warrant and tear this place apart to find them," Mr. Rakesh's voice boomed.

"I don't even have them in my home any longer," Marlene told them.

Isabelle didn't believe her and tried to reason with her. "For once in your life, look at your son as the man he really is. He's a horrible, manipulative person who uses people for his own gain. Because of him people are getting maimed and killed. He doesn't care. But you're not like that. You're a decent person, Marlene. Look past the fact that he's your son, Marlene—" A sharp pain gripped her lower abdomen and she stiffened.

"Security is on the way," Potter said, resuming his earlier position at the doorway.

Isabelle looked at Rakesh, who stood without flinching.

"Please, Marlene," Isabelle pleaded, a vise of pain squeezing her. "The only way . . ." she swallowed, forcing away the pain, "we can stop the killing is to find these diamonds. It's not a choice between you or your son, it's a choice," she took in a deep breath and felt the pain subside, "between right and wrong. Whether or not James is your son doesn't matter. He's breaking the law. He shouldn't be allowed to continue to do it. Not when people are dying because of it."

"Get out of my house!" Marlene cried, her voice a thin, strangled cry.

"You have to go," Potter said to them. "The security police are on the way. Please."

Rakesh looked at Marlene one last time, "My youngest brother was shot and killed on his way home from work. He left a wife and six small children who were already living in poverty. The rebel soldier who killed him was a fourteen-year-old boy carrying a rifle provided by James Dalton. It's no different than your own son going over there and killing people in cold blood."

"Stop it!" Marlene cried. "Potter, get them out of here. Now!"

Potter walked toward them, but Rakesh gave him a look that stopped the butler in his tracks. "Don't bother, we're leaving."

Rakesh stomped through the room. Isabelle followed. Just before she left, she turned, giving Marlene one last look. The woman's gaze connected with hers for just a moment, then Marlene looked away.

* * *

"Where is she?" Isabelle said, hanging up the phone. "Cynthia was supposed to be here over half an hour ago." Cynthia had volunteered to pick the group up and take them to the trial. But she hadn't arrived and she wasn't answering her home phone or her cell phone.

"I wonder where she could be," Aunt Sophie added her own concerns. "This isn't like her."

"Not at all," Isabelle agreed. "Even if something did come up, she would call and let us know."

"We don't have any more time to wait," Ryan said.

"He's right," Ethan said. "We better call a taxi."

They agreed as Ryan called the front desk. Isabelle wrung her hands nervously. "What if something awful has happened to her?"

"Her son or husband would have called to tell us," Aunt Sophie assured her. "Maybe she's caught in traffic and her cell phone is dead."

Isabelle wanted to believe the explanation but couldn't make herself do so.

"I'll tell you what," Ethan offered a suggestion. "I'll take a taxi over to her house and make sure everything's okay. I can come directly to the courthouse from there."

"Would you Ethan?" she asked him. She knew she'd feel better if he did.

"Of course, I'll call you from her house," he assured her. "No one knows me, so I shouldn't have any trouble going out in public."

"We have to go," Ryan announced. "Our taxi's waiting."

"Ethan," Isabelle caught his arm and gazed into his eyes. "Be careful."

"I will," he promised. "You go on now. I'll get Cynthia and be right over. Neither of us want to miss the show. I'm looking forward to seeing James's face when you walk into that courtroom," Ethan said.

"Then hurry," Isabelle said. "We barely have an hour before we're supposed to be there."

As they went their separate ways, Isabelle said a prayer in her heart. A prayer for Cynthia, a prayer for Ethan, a prayer for Mr. Rakesh, a prayer for her, and even a prayer for the judge. If they ever needed the blessings of heaven to shower down upon them, it was now.

Chapter 25

"Where are they?" Isabelle said, pacing back and forth. Aside from a small table with a water pitcher and a stack of paper cups and two lightly padded chairs, there was nothing else in the room.

Ryan and Aunt Sophie waited with her. Most of the morning had been spent weeding out potential jurors. Once the jury was finally selected they were ready to start the trial. But there was still no word from Ethan or Cynthia. Mr. Rakesh promised he would tell them as soon as he heard from them, but he hadn't yet.

"Sit down, Isabelle," Ryan told his sister. "You need to relax, take some deep breaths."

"I can't sit down," Isabelle told him. "I'm worried about Cynthia and Ethan, and I've got to face James any minute. How can I relax?"

"You're going to do fine. You've been through your testimony a hundred times with us and with Rakesh. You've got it down cold," Ryan assured her.

"But we don't know what James's attorney is going to ask me. He's going to try and trip me up and twist my words. I know he's going to bring up the whole thing about my death," she said, knowing that information could make her look like a psychological dingbat.

"Rakesh told you not to worry. He will object to any inference about your death and the state of your relationship to James," Ryan told her. "Just tell the truth and you'll be fine."

"He's right," Aunt Sophie said. "Stick to the truth. They can't twist that around."

Just then Rakesh's assistant, Miss Morgan, burst through the doors. "Your friend, Ethan, is here. He's brought your other friend, Cynthia, with him. Follow me."

They hurried after the young woman, who wore her stark black hair in a severe, angled, A-line bob. She wore no makeup and had on black-rimmed glasses. Her gray suit was trim cut and stylish, but it looked like she'd slept in it. Knowing Rakesh, the poor woman probably had.

Astonishment hit them when they walked into the room. There was Cynthia, looking disheveled and unkempt.

"Cynthia!" Isabelle cried when she saw her friend. "What in the world happened to you?"

"Oh, Isabelle," Cynthia bawled. "It was awful. Just awful."

Cynthia was so upset she could barely get the words out. So while Isabelle held her friend, Ethan explained what had happened.

"You remember the brownies Cynthia took over to the house that day?" Ethan reminded them. "She forgot to bring them home."

"Cynthia, you left the brownies inside the house?" Isabelle asked, feeling sick inside for her friend.

"This morning, after her husband and son both left for work, guess who showed up on Cynthia's doorstep with the brownies?"

"No!" Isabelle couldn't even bear to hear him say it.

"Yes," Ethan nodded. "James. He asked her if the brownies belonged to her, then before she could even reply, he grabbed her. He took her to the basement where he tied her up with duct tape."

Isabelle noticed the bright red streaks across Cynthia's face and wrists where the tape had pulled at her skin. "Did he hurt you?"

"Yes," Cynthia managed to say. "He wanted to know why I had been at his house, what I was looking for, and who had sent me."

Cynthia held up her chin but her lip quivered as she spoke. "He hit me several times, but I wasn't about to tell that dirty, rotten beast anything. He could have pulled off my fingernails and I wouldn't have said anything."

Isabelle shook her head, truly amazed at her friend. "Your left eye is swollen."

"Good!" Cynthia cried. "I want the press to get some good pictures of what he did to me. The worse I look, the better."

"How did you ever find her?" Aunt Sophie asked Ethan.

"It wasn't easy," Ethan said. "When she didn't answer the door, I didn't know what to think, but then I looked through the glass in the front door and saw her purse and keys on a chair in the hallway. I knew she wouldn't be too far without either of those, so I started walking around the yard, thinking she might be outside. I went around to the back of the house and found the back door unlocked."

Cynthia spoke again. "I had just finished watering the flowers in the backyard before I left to pick you up at the hotel when James came to the door. I didn't even have a chance to lock the back door," Cynthia added.

"It's a good thing, too," Ethan said. "I doubt I would've been able to get inside the house otherwise."

"What did you do?" Isabelle asked him.

"I began looking, from top to bottom. Nothing looked out of place or out of the ordinary," Ethan said. "By the way, Cynthia, you have a lovely home."

"Thank you," she said.

"I went through all the upstairs rooms, the main floor rooms, and found nothing. Then I happened onto the basement door. I looked downstairs at the unfinished basement and thought surely she wouldn't be down there, but just as I was about to shut the door, I heard something. It stopped me long enough to make me reconsider, and I decided to take a quick look."

"It was a good thing you did," Cynthia said.

"I'll say. I found her tied up and covered with some old burlap bags. At first glance you wouldn't have thought there was anything under those bags," Ethan said.

"What made you look?" Ryan asked.

"I sneezed," Cynthia said. "Nearly blew my brains out too, with my mouth taped shut like that."

Everyone couldn't help but laugh.

"James didn't expect my husband or son home until that evening," Cynthia said. "He said he'd be long gone before then."

"What did he mean?" Ryan asked.

"Who knows? I hope it means he's leaving for good. I never want to see that man again." Cynthia was fuming with anger.

Mr. Rakesh stepped into the room. "It's time to start," he said. "How are you, Mrs. Twitchell?" he asked Cynthia.

"I'm fine," she answered.

"You're sure? My assistant can get you anything you need."

"I'm fine. Just let me at the press. I want to talk to them," Cynthia sat up on the edge of her chair, wincing with the movement.

"Hold on a minute," Rakesh told her. "All in due time. Right now we have to make an appearance in court, and I have a feeling that when James sees you walk in," he spoke to Cynthia, "he's going to need more than legal counsel to pick him up off the floor."

"Let's hope," Isabelle said, hoping it would be enough.

"Alright then, let's go get him!" Rakesh bellowed.

The two men helped Cynthia down the hallway to the court-room, pausing while Mr. Rakesh opened the door and led the way. Behind Rakesh walked his assistant, followed by Ryan and Ethan, helping Cynthia, who limped her way down the aisle.

From the doorway Isabelle watched as James, sitting at one of the desks in front, stopped talking to his attorney, and turned to see who had entered the room. The expression on his face, the cold steel-like glare in his eyes, sent a chill up Isabelle's spine. He was out for blood.

It was going to be an ugly fight.

Isabelle fought to hold her composure and erase any reaction from her expression. Getting up on that stand was going to be one of the hardest things she'd ever done, but she now knew she'd walk through fire to get up there. It was time for the truth to be told.

"Ready, dear?" Aunt Sophie asked.

"I'm ready," Isabelle answered.

The soft clatter of shoes on the polished wooden floor made the audience once again turn to see Isabelle and Aunt Sophia enter the room. James and his attorney, who were engaged in conversation, stopped again. This time, when James turned and saw Isabelle, his expression went quickly to anger and then to red-faced rage. His eyes sparked with fury, his jaw clenched tightly shut.

Feeling composed and assured, Isabelle stared him straight in the eye, then smiled.

He looked so incensed that she thought smoke might come out of his ears and the top of his head would blow. The thought brought a smile to her lips.

Taking her seat, Isabelle relaxed back into her chair and avoided James's glare, which she felt boring into her.

Mr. Rakesh turned to her and the others and gave a knowing wink. Their first goal was accomplished. On the outside James and his attorney appeared collected and unshaken, but their constant whispering and frantic rustling of papers and files showed otherwise. Rakesh had warned her that they hadn't expected her to show up in court that day. No doubt James hadn't expected Cynthia either, but Isabelle doubted he'd mentioned it to his lawyer.

The proceedings began, and Isabelle became fascinated in the legal process: the eloquence of the language, the theatrics of the two opposing legal counsels, and the dissecting of the charges brought against the defendant, James Dalton.

Isabelle was anxious to get to the incriminating evidence. She watched out of the corner of her eye as James grew hot under the collar while the investigating officer was questioned by Mr. Rakesh. His testimony gave details on how the case came to be, how the evidence was gathered. He revealed nothing new, but presented the facts with solid conviction.

After the lead officer's testimony, Rakesh then requested that Marlene Dalton take the stand.

The room buzzed with an undercurrent of voices, but Isabelle didn't bother looking around the room. Marlene wasn't there.

"Mr. Rakesh?" the judge said.

"Your honor, I have sent a deputy to look for Mrs. Dalton and would like permission to preserve her as a witness," Mr. Rakesh answered.

"Granted," the judge said. "Call your next witness."

"The prosecution calls Isabelle Dalton to the stand."

Ethan gave her hand a quick squeeze and Aunt Sophie wished her luck. Isabelle swallowed hard. She was going to need it.

Taking the stand, Isabelle was sworn in and took her place in the hot seat. She purposely avoided James's glare and concentrated on breathing. Feeling lightheaded and sick to her stomach, she focused on Mr. Rakesh as he stood behind the lectern and addressed her.

Their line of questioning went just as they had planned. Her answers came easily and were sincere and honest. Yes, she had known of James's trips to Africa. He had told her that his firm had international clients there. No, she had no knowledge of his alleged involvement with the smuggling of illicit diamonds into the country. She admitted that James had kept most of his dealings at work to himself and that there had been several occasions he had gone out of town on business when she'd called his office in an effort to contact him only to find out that they had no knowledge of his travel plans. Of course, due to the nature of their volatile relationship, she'd never asked him about it.

Mr. Rakesh paid special attention to his wording and asked Isabelle to tell about the package she'd taken when she left for England.

Isabelle explained that it had come just as she was walking out the door and she wasn't exactly sure why she took it. She'd kept it for weeks before she finally opened it up to see what was inside.

"Exhibit B has been offered to the jury for their inspection," Mr. Rakesh stated.

The Beanie Baby that was admitted into evidence was presented to the jury and passed from person to person.

Isabelle told the judge and jury that after finding the diamonds, she knew it was time to get involved. Another Beanie Baby was found, containing even more diamonds, and she had no doubt that her husband was up to something.

Mr. Rakesh's main emphasis in the line of questioning was to establish the fact that James had indeed gone to Africa, that Isabelle had no knowledge of his associations or activities there, and that she had discovered the diamonds by accident.

Since Mrs. Dalton still hadn't shown up, the prosecution rested, and it was time for the defense to begin their line of questioning. Isabelle waited nervously for her name to be called next, but James's attorney, Mr. Dupré, had several witnesses lined up before her.

Just as she anticipated hearing her name, the judge decided to adjourn for the day and continue the trial first thing in the morning.

Isabelle was unprepared for the media that was waiting outside the courthouse. It was like walking into a fiery furnace of questions.

Ethan held tightly on one side of her and Ryan latched onto the other as they plowed their way through cameramen and a sea of microphones.

"Tell us, Mrs. Dalton," one reporter demanded, thrusting a

microphone in her face, "if your husband hadn't been brought to trial, would you have ever told him you were alive?"

"Mrs. Dalton," another reporter called loudly, "what did you do the day your husband was having your funeral?"

Isabelle felt her knees buckling, afraid she was going to pass out at any minute. Her head swirled with the shouting and tug-of-war for her attention. But Rakesh had warned her not to say a word to anyone. So she remained silent and stoic all the way to the taxi.

But once inside she dissolved into tears, wondering if it was all worth it.

* * *

"Isabelle, dear, you're as white as a sheet," Aunt Sophie said first thing the next morning. "You don't look well at all."

Isabelle didn't tell her that she'd been feeling abdominal pains and nausea for the last hour. She was worried that if she complained, they might make her go to the doctor and the last thing she wanted was to prolong the trial. She could go to the doctor after it was all over if she still needed to. But right now, all she wanted was to get this case over and get on with her life.

"I'm fine." Isabelle tried to speak as though nothing was wrong. "I'm just worried about taking the stand this morning." Which was true. She did not want to face James's attorney and his barrage of questions.

"The taxi will be here in ten minutes," Aunt Sophie reminded her.

Isabelle forced herself to go into the bathroom and finish putting on her makeup. She needed to look as polished and calm on the outside as she could, but she doubted she was anywhere near that good of an actress. Inside her stomach was twisting, her heart was racing, and her nerves were near the breaking point. She didn't know how much more she could take.

With her personal support group at her side, Isabelle braced herself for the obstacle course through the media into the courthouse. She looked straight ahead and kept walking, trying to ignore the reporters, but it wasn't easy. They attacked her character, they asked about her claims of abuse, then they reminded her of her husband's status in the community and the life of luxury she'd had. Part of her wanted to lash out, to scream at them, telling them they had no idea what she'd been through, what kind of torture she'd endured from her husband, but she knew that was exactly what they wanted her to do. They were trying to find her Achilles' heel, to get a reaction out of her, but she wouldn't give them the satisfaction.

After that, the courtroom seemed like a haven of peace. At least for now. She knew that once she took the stand, she wouldn't be able to ignore the questions as she had with the reporters. She'd have to answer them and endure the attacks that James's attorney would inflict upon her. She just prayed that she'd have the strength to get through it.

Reminding herself to take slow, deep breaths, Isabelle waited for the dreaded moment when she would be called to the stand and sworn in. It came sooner than she expected.

The only other time in her life when she'd ever been more nervous was the night she ran her car into the river and caught a plane for England. But sitting on the stand with James's sneering face in front of her, and his Ivy League pit bull of an attorney ready to attack, came uncomfortably close.

"Mrs. Dalton," James's attorney addressed her, "if I may call you that . . ." Isabelle nodded, trying to find a position that helped relieve the ache in her back. "Isn't it true that on the night of March 15 of this year, while your husband was out of town on business, you changed your appearance, then during a severe rainstorm, pushed your car into the Charles River and hopped a plane to England."

"Objection, relevance," Mr. Rakesh said as he hopped to his feet, scooting his chair back with a loud screech.

"I'm trying to establish credibility," Mr. Dupré shot back.

"Answer the question, Mrs. Dalton."

"Yes," Isabelle said, wishing she could help the judge and jury understand what drove her to such desperate actions.

Mr. Dupré seemed to change his mind and take a different approach. "Mrs. Dalton, is it true your family was poor when you were a child?"

"We didn't have a lot of money, but we always had a roof over our heads and food to eat," she replied.

"Isn't it also true that by the time you graduated from college your father had passed away and you owed $14,500 in school loans, not to mention a substantial amount of credit card debt?"

Isabelle felt like her dirty laundry was being displayed for the entire jury and audience to see. "Yes," she said, wondering what this had to do with anything.

"When you married Mr. Dalton, did he in fact pay off your loans and debt and provide you with a life of luxury? A large home in an expensive neighborhood, along with sports cars, designer clothes, and jewelry?"

"Yes," she answered.

"Is it true that you married him for money?" Mr. Dupré hit her directly between the eyes with his question.

"I object!" Rakesh's reaction was atomic in proportion. "Mrs. Dalton isn't on trial."

"Sustained!" the judge announced.

Dupré's tactics were obvious. He knew very well that his questions concerning her state of mind would invite Rakesh's objections, but Dupré had at least planted the seed of doubt in the judge's and jury's minds. Even though it had no bearing on the case, it would influence their feelings about the credibility of her testimony.

"Mrs. Dalton," Dupré came back at her. "Did your husband at any time, by his actions, or by anything he has ever done or said, give you absolute reason to believe he is involved in the illicit smuggling of diamonds into the United States?"

Isabelle opened her mouth to answer.

"You are under oath," Mr. Dupré reminded her.

"He never said anything, he never did anything," she answered.

Mr. Dupré smiled and looked at James triumphantly.

"But I have every reason to believe he is involved because of the evidence already presented to the court."

"We have no way of knowing those jewels weren't planted," Dupré countered.

"That's ridiculous!" Isabelle exclaimed. "Why would I do that? Where would I get that many rough diamonds?"

"You've already proven your thirst for revenge against your husband," Dupré said.

"Proven! How?" Isabelle asked incredulously.

"Objection, your honor." Rakesh's reaction was swift. "He's badgering the witness."

"Counsel, finish your line of questioning," the judge ordered.

"No further questions," Dupré said, taking his seat.

Dupré was done? That was all?

Isabelle didn't know what to think. Was it a good sign or a bad sign that his questions had ended so quickly?

Shaking head to toe and fighting with all her might to keep her composure, Isabelle made her way towards her seat, passing the table where James and Mr. Dupré sat.

"You're dead," James mouthed when her eyes involuntarily met his.

Drawing upon every bit of strength she had, she made it back to her seat. Along with the throbbing in her lower back, small twinges of sharp, shooting pains grabbed at her abdomen from deep inside. Trembling, she sat down, taking in several long breaths to calm herself and ease her pains. She would never give James the satisfaction of seeing her break down and cry.

Holding her chin up, she took her seat and let Ethan take her hand in his.

"Are you all right?" Aunt Sophie asked with alarm. "You look as though you're ready to pass out."

Isabelle swallowed, feeling the pains ease and release their deathlike grip.

"I'll be fine," she whispered.

Ethan squeezed her hand tightly and said, "You did a first-rate job up there. He was brutal, but you held your own."

Ryan reached over and patted her knee.

Isabelle was just grateful to have it over and to be feeling better. But seeing the slump in Rakesh's shoulders, she found herself doubting the outcome of the trial. The faces of the jury were impossible to read. Perhaps the four women in the jury box would feel compassion toward her and know that she had been a desperate woman trying to get away from a horrible husband. But the only thing reported about James during the investigation of Isabelle's "death" was his devastation at the loss of his wife and what a devoted, loving husband he'd been to her all the years they were married. No one knew the truth. They thought she was a kook, and using her for a witness just made Rakesh look like a fool.

"Any further witnesses?" the judge asked Rakesh.

"I wish he'd put me on the stand," Cynthia whispered to Isabelle. But Isabelle knew that surprise witnesses weren't allowed in court, contrary to how movies and television presented it.

The defense called their next witness, Mr. James W. Dalton.

James stood up and strode to the front of the room. Isabelle noticed he wore his most expensive suit and tie. He looked every bit the part of a successful attorney; too suave, too debonair to stoop to any criminal action.

But the judge and the jury had no idea just how low James could stoop.

Isabelle felt like a balloon with a pinhole-sized leak in it. Slowly, the hope and faith she had in the judicial system that truth would prevail, drained from her, leaving her feeling deflated and disappointed.

Mr. Dupré and James parlayed questions and answers with the grace and finesse of Fred Astaire and Ginger Rogers, a well-choreographed, completely rehearsed testimonial allowing James to bask in the glow of maligned innocence. The whole scene left Isabelle nauseated and worried. She had no doubt in her mind that he would walk away that day, free.

And then he would find her. He would hunt her down no matter where she hid, and he would kill her. He'd threatened to do it for many years; now she'd given him a good enough reason to go through with it.

Father in Heaven, she prayed an earnest plea for help. *He can't get away with this. Please . . .* she begged, feeling tears come to her eyes, *Please do something before it's too late.*

"How do you explain the excessive amounts of deliveries of Beanie Babies to your home?" Mr. Dupré asked him, addressing the key element of the case against him. "As often as once or twice a week."

"My dear mother is completely obsessed with her collection of Beanie Babies. And I have merely tried to help her complete her collection. I'll admit, at first I did it out of duty. She's not comfortable hunting around on the Internet, so I offered to help her. But after I got involved, I have to admit," he flashed a charming smile at the jury, "I got hooked on it myself. The pursuit is as much fun for me as actually receiving one of the Beanie animals in the mail. And when I realized how valuable some of the Beanie Babies are, especially the retired ones, collecting them became an obsession for me also."

Isabelle wanted to yell out, "Hogwash!" but didn't want to show further evidence of her "crazy woman" image.

"And you're telling us that Africa is a hot spot for acquiring Beanie Babies?" Dupré asked. The audience behind them chuckled.

James also chuckled, proving once again to Isabelle, that the entire thing was an act. "The economy is suffering a great deal there. Yes, Beanie Babies are plentiful and available. While on business there I met a man who was trying to sell his collection to feed his family. I felt sorry for him and paid him generously for the Beanie animals he had. People there are desperate and will sell for an unbelievable price, well below what they could get for it in the United States. If I'm guilty of anything, it's taking advantage of the buyer's market down there."

"And the diamonds?" Dupré asked pointedly.

"I don't know anything about any diamonds," James said, his expression so straight, his eyes so directly focused on Dupré, that had Isabelle not known otherwise, had she not seen them for herself, she too might have believed him. "I'm an attorney who deals with international issues. We have clients in Africa. I go there on business trips occasionally. And that's all."

"That did it," Ryan said in a low voice. "We lost."

I'm dead, Isabelle thought.

"That will be all," Mr. Dupré said, thanking Mr. Dalton for his testimony.

The room remained silent while the judge made some notes on a pad. When he finished, he looked up and opened his mouth to say something, but at that moment the door to the courtroom opened and into the room charged James's mother.

Chapter 26

Carrying a lumpy garbage sack over her shoulder, Marlene Dalton stood at the back of the room.

The crowd reacted with gasps of surprise and frantic whispers.

"Order in this court!" the judge barked. "Order!"

The room grew silent. Someone moved over offering a seat on the aisle to Marlene. She sat down in rigid silence, glaring furiously at her son.

"Your honor," Mr. Rakesh addressed the judge. "I would like to make a motion to reopen. My witness is here now and she appears ready to testify." He glanced back quickly at Marlene, who nodded and glared at her son.

"Objection!" Dupré cried. "They could have concluded for the day to get their witness here. They've already rested."

The judge looked at Rakesh.

"What testimony has your witness got to offer?" the judge asked.

"She has knowledge of the defendant's involvement in the smuggling of diamonds and has evidence to prove it," Rakesh explained.

"What evidence does she have?" the judge asked.

"Diamonds," Rakesh stated loudly.

Expelling a weary breath, the judge drummed his fingers in contemplation.

"Call your witness," the judge announced.

Mr. Dupré thumped the table with his hand, and received a stern look from the judge. Dupré quickly wiped the expression of frustration from his face. A streak of electricity raced through Isabelle's veins, sparking new hope.

After Marlene was sworn in, Mr. Rakesh began his line of questioning.

"Mrs. Dalton," he said from behind the lectern. "We're glad you finally made it."

Marlene nodded and kept her eyes trained on Mr. Rakesh.

The first thing Mr. Rakesh did was establish Marlene's relationship with the defendant, getting some preliminary questions out of the way.

Isabelle's heart raced and her palms grew sweaty. Did she dare even hope that Marlene was here to help their side? To actually testify *against* her son?

Marlene denied having any knowledge of her son's dealing with anti-government factions in Sierra Leone. She claimed she also had no knowledge that he was involved in anything even remotely illegal.

"Then why, may I ask, did you come through that door ten minutes ago, carrying a garbage bag?" Rakesh asked her, obviously as anxious to hear her answer as anyone.

Isabelle glanced over at James and saw him glaring at his mother. But Marlene didn't even give him the satisfaction of being intimidated by him. In fact, she didn't even look at him.

"Because my daughter-in-law bravely came forward and helped me see what kind of person my son really is," Marlene said, looking directly at Isabelle, with a kindness in her eyes Isabelle had never, ever seen before. Isabelle returned the look with an encouraging smile.

"And what kind of person is that?" Mr. Rakesh asked.

"May I have my garbage bag, please?" Mrs. Dalton requested.

"The state would like to offer Exhibit A to the court," Rakesh said.

The bailiff brought the bag forward and assisted her in opening it. Mrs. Dalton began unloading every shape, type, and color of Beanie Baby imaginable. After about twenty of the animals were lined up along the railing in front of her, Marlene looked at the judge who asked, "Would you like to explain all of this?" He motioned toward the animals with his hand.

"I would love to. You see, your honor, my son got me started on collecting these Beanie animals several years ago. And even though I told him many times that I wasn't really that fond of the animals, he still added to my collection on a regular basis, and many times I found myself wondering why he was so fascinated, almost obsessed, with collecting the animals.

"Of course, I understand, some of them are actually worth quite a bit of money, but even all of them combined don't amount to enough money to interest my son *that* much."

"Go on," Mr. Rakesh prompted.

"Well, I just kept tossing the little animals into my locked display cabinet, as my son told me to, when I realized that James hadn't given me any of the animals lately. Not that I cared, mind you. But I didn't think much of it until you and my daughter-in-law visited me."

"Yes," Mr. Rakesh said.

"I know I wasn't very cordial at the time, but it's a difficult thing for a mother to learn something like this about her own child."

"And what did you learn about your son, Mrs. Dalton?" Rakesh asked.

"I learned that my son was in fact smuggling diamonds inside Beanie Babies out of Sierra Leone."

The audience gasped and whispered excitedly.

Isabelle squeezed Ethan's hand, waiting for Dupré to object, but it didn't happen. A quick glance at James and his attorney, both sitting with shoulders slumped, told them it was over.

"How did you arrive at this conclusion?" Rakesh asked her.

"I did as my daughter-in-law suggested. I opened one of the animals." There was a moment's pause while Mrs. Dalton looked at her son, then picked up one of the Beanie Babies. Producing a small pair of cuticle scissors from her pocket, she sliced open one of the cuddly teddy bears and dumped the contents into her hand, holding it up for the judge, jury, and audience to see.

"I haven't opened up every one of these Beanie Babies, but each of the ones I have opened contained no less than ten diamonds."

A flush of red colored James's neck and face.

"Thank you, Mrs. Dalton," Rakesh said to Marlene. "That will be all."

Giving Isabelle a wink as he sat down, Rakesh, for the first time that day, relaxed back in his chair.

It was a feeble effort to cross-examine the witness. Dupré couldn't trip up Mrs. Dalton and she wouldn't fall into his tactics of intimidation. She was awesome, as far as Isabelle was concerned.

"Mrs. Dalton, your son is an upstanding citizen of this community and a valued member of one of the most prestigious law firms on the East coast. His record is clean to the point that he hasn't even had a speeding ticket since he received his driver's license. He pays his taxes on time, and he donates blood to the Red Cross and money to the local homeless shelter. And you want this court to believe that this man, James Dalton, is guilty of smuggling illicit diamonds into the country?"

"Yes I do!" she stated. "He used me!"

"Mother!" James lunged from his seat, but his attorney held him back. "You don't know what you're saying."

The audience buzzed with the drama set before them.

"She was right!" Marlene pointed at Isabelle. The older woman held up the still-heavy bag and let it fall to the floor with a resounding thud. "I knew you were using other people, but me? I'm your own mother!" The woman broke down in tears.

Again, a rumble from the audience pushed the judge over the edge.

"Order!" he demanded. Then, after drawing in a deep breath, he said, "Counsel, approach the bench."

Both attorneys went forward and discussed something with the judge.

Seething with vein-bulging fury, James kept his eyes on the judge. Marlene remained in her seat and Isabelle wished she could go to the woman. For the first time in her life, she felt sorry for her mother-in-law.

The two attorneys returned to their seats, and James and Dupré bent their heads together in anxious talk. Rakesh and his assistant sat back in their chairs and watched with amusement.

"Mr. Dupré," the judge prompted with a warning tone.

Mr. Dupré stood and addressed the judge, the confident tone missing from his voice.

"No further questions, your honor," he said.

Cynthia flashed Isabelle a thumbs-up and Ethan gave her hand a squeeze. Ryan smiled broadly with satisfaction, and Aunt Sophie rested her hand on her heart as if in silent prayer.

Even though the jury hadn't announced their verdict, there was no question in anyone's mind, least of all Isabelle's, that James was guilty.

The jury was excused from the courtroom to deliberate over the verdict. Ryan said he'd seen juries take days to decide; he'd also seen juries arrive at a verdict within hours.

This jury didn't even take that long.

Making plans to find a deli or coffee house nearby where they could grab a bite to eat, Isabelle and the others were getting ready to leave just as the announcement was made that a decision had been reached.

Shutting her eyes briefly, Isabelle prayed for the strength to accept whatever the outcome. James was guilty, she knew it. Even his own mother knew it. But would the jury, primarily made up of local businessmen, believe it?

The courtroom was filled with tomblike silence. Isabelle waited, barely breathing, for the verdict to be read. Everything could change in the next minute. Her life would drastically improve, or it could become the nightmare she feared.

A man in his mid-fifties with graying hair stood to read the verdict. This was it. The moment of decision. The pivotal event that had power over Isabelle's future.

"We, the members of the jury, find the defendant, James Witherspoon Dalton, guilty . . ."

The man went on, but Isabelle had heard the one word she needed to hear. James was guilty! James, the man who thought he was above the law, the man who thought his way was the only way, was guilty. Guilty!

Ryan threw his arms around her, then Ethan, Aunt Sophie, and Cynthia did too. Isabelle laughed with relief as tears of joy filled her eyes. It was over.

A humiliated and angry James was led from the courtroom, and Isabelle watched him. James seemed more of a stranger to her than a husband as he left with an armed escort. Just before he stepped through the door that led from the room, he turned and gave Isabelle an icy glare, a look that at one time used to send fear through her heart. But now, that look no longer had any power over her. He was no longer a threat to her. James Dalton was finally out of her life.

Rakesh not only rejoiced in the personal victory of winning the case, but the victory of knowing he'd done something to help the tragedy that was going on in his country, to his people. He swore it was just the beginning, and from the look in his eyes, Isabelle knew he meant it.

Rakesh assured her that a divorce would be a simple matter, given that she wanted nothing from James: no money, no furniture, not even her personal belongings. All she wanted was her freedom. He gave her his promise that she would receive it. She deserved it.

"Stop by my office before you leave for England, and you can sign the divorce papers," Rakesh instructed her.

While still in the courtroom, the group exchanged congratulations, then decided to go out to dinner and celebrate the victory.

Isabelle still wasn't feeling well, but was hopeful that the trial had been the cause of it. She would feel better now that it was over.

"I need to stop by my office and take care of a few things," Rakesh said. "Why don't we meet at the Blue Heron Restaurant in one hour?"

"Excuse me," a voice behind Isabelle said.

Isabelle turned and found her mother-in-law standing behind her.

"Marlene," Isabelle exclaimed.

"Hello, Isabelle," Marlene said guardedly. It was obvious by the mascara streaks on her face and puffiness of her eyes that she had been crying.

"That was a very brave and amazing thing you did today," Isabelle told her.

Marlene drew in a sharp breath and nodded. She blinked several times as tears shone in her eyes.

"I can't even imagine how hard this must be for you," Isabelle said. The rest of the group stepped away to give them some space so they could talk privately.

"James was my pride and joy. I was always so proud of him. But he was born with the burden of great expectations. Perhaps the pressure of success and living up to the 'Dalton' image was just too much for him," she said, shaking her head slowly as she tried to make sense of it all. "His father and I pushed him very hard. Maybe a little too hard," she admitted.

"He made his own decisions," Isabelle told her, trying to comfort the woman. "No one forced him to do what he did. He made that choice himself."

"I know you're right," Marlene said. "It's just so difficult to accept."

Isabelle's heart went out to her mother-in-law.

Marlene continued. "I wondered many times if James was up to something. I couldn't put my finger on it, but the way he evaded my questions about his trips and wouldn't go into detail about some of his clients made me suspicious. But it was this obsession he had with Beanie Babies and the way he always tried to make me out as the one who collected the ridiculous things. . . . It didn't make sense." Marlene wiped at the corners of her eyes with a lace handkerchief. "I didn't want to accept the truth. It was staring me in the face but I just kept ignoring it. That is, until you and Mr. Rakesh came and visited with me."

Isabelle didn't know what to say. She felt sorry for the woman but was speechless.

"You confirmed my suspicions. My son used me. Not only did that show to me just what kind of person he was, it told me just how much he really cared for me—not at all."

"I'm sorry," Isabelle finally said, knowing it wasn't much, but it was the best she could come up with.

"I owe you a tremendous apology," Mrs. Dalton said.

Isabelle looked at her curiously.

"It didn't come out in the trial today," she said, "but I also had my suspicions that my son was being abusive to you."

Isabelle wished she could spare Marlene any further pain, but she couldn't lie to her either. "Yes," she said with a nod. "He was."

Marlene closed her eyes as if feeling a renewed pain, then looked at her daughter-in-law. "There was always a look of fear in your eyes. You flinched whenever he made a sudden movement. And the cuts and bruises," Marlene said, her voice filled with compassion. "On the outside I believed your excuses for all of those injuries, but in the back of my mind I knew there was more. And then, when I heard you had died in that car accident, part of me was relieved that you wouldn't have to suffer from his hand again. But part of me . . ."

"Yes?" Isabelle prompted her.

"Part of me was ashamed that I'd never tried to help you and that I'd never been a good mother-in-law to you. I realize now that I missed out on a chance to have a relationship with someone very special." Marlene braved a tremulous smile.

Even though Marlene's words couldn't erase the years of loneliness and pain with James, they did offer a soothing balm to the emotional wounds that still hadn't healed.

"Thank you," Isabelle told her. "It means a lot to me to hear you say that."

"Will you stay in Boston now?" Marlene asked.

Isabelle shook her head. "No. My home is in England, with my aunt and my brother."

"I didn't know you had an aunt and a brother," she said.

"Neither did I until I left James," Isabelle told her honestly. "I've got a good life in England. I'm very happy there."

"I can tell," Marlene said. "I see it in your eyes. You seem different, more confident, stronger. You're even lovelier than before. It's partly due to your new look—that stunning red hair—but I think it's more than that." Marlene smiled with admiration. "I think it's because I finally see what a truly beautiful person you are, inside and out."

"Thank you, Marlene," Isabelle said, feeling a twinge in her lower back. She pressed the heel of her hand to the base of her spine to ease the pain.

"I'd like to stay in touch," Marlene requested. "I know I can't make up for all of those years, but I'd like to try if I could."

Isabelle drew in several breaths as a different pain, sharp and stabbing, wrenched her insides.

"Isabelle?" Marlene's forehead wrinkled with concern. "Is something wrong?" She hurried to Isabelle's side and held her as Isabelle doubled over. "Somebody, help me," Marlene cried out. "Hurry!"

Ethan was the first to run over. "Isabelle," he cried, wrapping his arm around her. "What is it?"

"Oh, Ethan," Isabelle gasped, then she collapsed in his arms.

* * *

When Isabelle came to, she was in a strange, dark room, with an IV attached to a vein in her arm, her mouth as dry as the Sahara.

Water, she thought with desperation, *I need water.*

She knew she was in a hospital room, but the thick, dull feeling in her head wrapped all details and reasons in a thick, heavy fog.

With the force of a locomotive, it hit her. It had to be the baby.

She grasped the handrail on the bed and found the remote. Noticing one of the buttons had the outline of a nurse on it, she pressed the button. Fifteen seconds later a woman rushed into the room.

"Did you call for a nurse?" she asked.

"My baby," Isabelle cried. "Is my baby all right?"

The nurse's eyes flashed alarm for a moment, then she said in a placating tone, "You'll need to talk to the doctor. I just came on shift. I'll go see if I can find him."

"Please," Isabelle pleaded. "I have to know."

The nurse rushed from the room, leaving Isabelle alone with her fears. She tried to tell herself that everything was okay. Now that the trial was over, things could be normal.

The door to her room opened and in walked Aunt Sophie and Ryan. Right behind them was Ethan.

"Aunt Sophie!" Isabelle cried when she saw her aunt. "I'm so glad you're here. What's going on? Why won't they tell me about the baby?"

Aunt Sophie placed a kiss on Isabelle's forehead. "I don't know how to say this," she started but couldn't continue.

"Isabelle," Ryan approached her, taking one of her hands in his. He looked at Aunt Sophie, then back at his sister. "You see . . ." then he stopped.

The door opened, and in walked a young man wearing a white doctor's coat and a stethoscope around his neck. He checked the file he held in his hand then looked up at her. "Isabelle Dalton?"

Isabelle nodded.

"Hi, Isabelle, I'm Dr. Warburton. How are you feeling?"

"I feel fine. Can someone please tell what's going on? How is my baby?" she demanded, raising her head and shoulders off the pillow.

The doctor paused for a long, drawn-out moment.

Isabelle glanced around the room, noticing that all eyes were on the doctor. It wasn't good. Whatever had happened was obviously not good.

"I'm sorry," the doctor said, "but there was nothing we could do."

Chapter 27

The mid-afternoon sun felt good on her skin. Isabelle relaxed in the chaise lounge chair and read her book, basking in the sun's warmth.

It felt good to be home. The flight back to England had been long, and Isabelle had returned to Swan Cottage exhausted and relieved to finally be there. Here, surrounded by rolling green hills, lush countryside, and her loved ones, she hoped she would be able to start healing. When she'd first arrived in England, she'd struggled to make sense of her marriage and her life; she'd learned of an unexpected pregnancy, had learned to accept it, and now would have to learn to live with its loss.

She had no appetite, and even though she was tired, she couldn't sleep. Her concentration was nonexistent and she had no motivation to do anything. Even though she was consumed with grief she still had a desperate hope that things would eventually get better.

A constant prayer, a continual pleading, filled her heart and mind. She needed strength, both physically and mentally, to get through this. Ethan and Ryan had given her a priesthood blessing full of promises and the assurance that her life was in God's hands and that He was very aware of her and loved her. All that He asked of her was patience in her suffering, hope in her lack of understanding, and faith in her time of trial. He would not leave her side, and all would be well.

When she thought of losing the tiny child that had grown inside of her, and she realized how much she had come to love and cherish that tiny being, she felt as though she would wither and die. She was full of questions. What had gone wrong? Why had the baby died? And most of all, how did she go on now?

But she of all people knew the answer to that question. She'd survived the death of her father and mother, her marriage to James, and her escape from him. Just as she had gotten through it all, she would get through this, too.

Sometimes the grief lifted long enough for her to gain some insight, to grasp some perspective. Perhaps the answer was as pure and simple as the fact that the time for her to have a baby just wasn't right. One of her greatest fears in having James's baby had been that the child would be a link that kept them connected. Now, there would be no ties. She was totally, completely, and utterly free from him now. And even though for the sake of having her precious child, she would still suffer a lasting tie to James, there was some measure of gratitude in her heart knowing that he had absolutely no claim to her anymore.

"Isabelle?" The voice seemed to come from a distance, but when Isabelle opened her eyes, Ethan was standing right in front of her.

"Ethan," she said softly, smiling. "What are you doing here?"

He knelt down on the grass next to her so their faces were only inches apart. "I came to see how you were doing."

She reached up and placed her hand on the side of his face. "I'm fine."

He placed his hand on top of hers, grasped it firmly, and kissed the palm of her hand. "I've been worried about you. Is there anything I can do?"

She knew if there actually was anything he could do, he would do it. "I just need time. I'll be fine."

"What are you reading?" he asked.

She held up a copy of the Book of Mormon her aunt had given her.

He raised his eyebrows. "How do you like it?"

"There's so much that's familiar to me," she said. "Even though I don't remember studying it much when I was young, I still remember the words . . ." she looked at the book, "and the feeling I used to have when I read it."

She held the book to her heart and swallowed. "Already it's given me so much hope and answered my questions. I love reading about the Tree of Life and most of all . . ." she cleared her throat, "most of all I'm learning just how much the Lord really loves us. I've never known that, I mean, really known that, until now."

Ethan smiled in understanding.

"I look back and see the Lord's hand guiding me through my life, giving me strength, giving me courage." She blinked sending tears down her cheeks. She laughed and wiped at them. "Sorry. It's just that it overwhelms me when I think about it."

Ethan reached up to her cheek and caught a tear with his thumb.

"How do other people get through hard times without this knowledge?" she asked him.

He shook his head. "They struggle and they wander through life wondering what their purpose on earth is."

"I'm so glad I have this. Understanding gives me so much strength." She patted the book. "And peace."

They watched as a pair of birds danced playfully on the grass, twittering and chirping merrily.

"Are you feeling up to a little outing?" Ethan asked with some hesitancy. "There's something I'd like to show you."

She looked into his eyes. Eyes that were so full of caring and devotion that words couldn't express the feeling any clearer. How could she turn down those eyes?

"Okay. What is it?" She let him pull her to her feet.

"It's a surprise," he said, wrapping a protective arm around her and leading her around the side of the house to his car.

With the windows rolled down, the clean scent of country air filled Isabelle's lungs. The familiar sights of the farms and houses and lovely village brought with it a sense of security and belonging.

Isabelle gave Ethan a smile. "It feels good to get out."

He gave her a wide grin. "I'm glad to hear you say that. I've missed spending time with you."

"I've missed spending time with you, too. And I haven't even seen Ian Scott since that first day we got home. How's he doing?"

"He's fine. He misses you, too, and he's anxious to show you how well he can skate on those roller blades we brought him back from Boston."

"Does he wear his helmet and pads?" she asked, dreading the thought of the child getting hurt.

"Every time. He does wonder why we didn't buy a pad for his bottom, though. He says he needs one there worse than on his elbows."

Isabelle laughed and noticed that Ethan was driving up the

street toward the day-care center. She hadn't felt up to going back to work quite yet.

She was surprised when Ethan pulled up to the school.

"What are we doing here?" she asked, gripping her seat tightly.

"I told you, there's something I want to show you," Ethan said.

With some reluctance, Isabelle let Ethan help her from the car. They stepped inside and Isabelle immediately noticed how quiet it was. "Where is everyone?"

"Maybe they're resting or having reading time. Let's go see."

Climbing the stairs Isabelle noticed some of the new artwork on the wall and admired the bulletin board that had been redone with lily pads and frogs. Maggie had been busy while she was gone.

At the top of the stairs Ethan paused. "You go first," he said, and she pushed through the door to the large activity room.

"SURPRISE!"

The welcome nearly blew Isabelle backwards through the doorway and down the stairs.

Standing in front of her were all the children from the school, Maggie and her assistant, Aunt Sophie and Ryan, other friends and neighbors, and even Dr. Holmes.

A large banner hung on the wall that read, "Welcome home, Miss Isabelle. We missed you."

"What is this?" Isabelle asked, feeling dizzy with excitement.

"It's a welcome home party for you," Maggie said, stepping forward to give Isabelle a hug.

"I was only gone two weeks," Isabelle said.

"But we missed you and we're so glad you're home. Right, children?" Maggie turned to the children, who cheered and clapped.

Ian Scott raced forward and gave Isabelle a giant hug, and she was soon mobbed by the rest of the children.

Growing warm inside, she looked around her at the wonderful people who had come to mean so much to her in such a short time. And she felt blessed. Yes, she had been asked by the Lord to endure a great deal, but she had triumphed. She had grown stronger and was a better person for everything she'd experienced. Her challenges weren't something she'd ever have asked for, or even wish on her worst enemy, but she'd survived them and had grown and learned many valuable lessons in life. And for that, it was all worth it.

Overwhelmed at the love surrounding her at that very moment, she blinked back the tears filling her eyes and they rolled down her cheeks.

"Don't cry, Isabelle," Ian Scott told her. "This is a happy party."

"I know," Isabelle answered him. "These are happy tears."

"They are?"

"Yes, sweetie, they are."

"I'm glad you're back," Ian Scott said. "I missed you."

Isabelle looked at his face, with his cute, impish nose and thickly lashed brown eyes and smiled. "I missed you, too."

After another hug, she joined the rest of the group and the party swung into action. A large "Welcome Home" cake and all sorts of snacks and goodies filled one of the banquet tables. There were games and singing and even a talent show by some of the children. Isabelle couldn't remember a time when she'd been happier.

That evening, after all the excitement had died down, the family, along with Ethan, Ian Scott, and Dr. Holmes, gathered in the backyard. Ethan brought fish and chips over for dinner, and as they ate they relaxed in the lengthening shadows.

"That party was fun," Isabelle said. "It was nice of everyone to go to so much trouble."

"The children at the center were the ones to come up with the idea," Aunt Sophie told her. "Maggie thought it was a great idea, and with a little planning and some phone calls, pulled it all together."

Isabelle smiled. "It meant a lot to me."

"Did you see Danny Cedric from the newspaper there taking pictures?" Aunt Sophie asked.

"Why in the world would someone from the newspaper be there?" Isabelle wondered.

"This is front page news," Aunt Sophie told her. "You've become a celebrity in town, my dear."

Isabelle laughed. "Me? A celebrity?"

"You have to admit," Ethan said. "You've lived through quite a bit. I'm sure many people will be fascinated by your story."

"They certainly are," Ryan told her. "Being the first one to report the events of the diamond conflict story and expose James is going to result in quite a boost to my career. I'm sorry you had to go through all of this," he said. "But it certainly didn't hurt my future any. Thanks, sis."

Isabelle rolled her eyes and gave him a smirky smile. "Glad I could help."

A sound in the distance broke the conversation.

"Is that barking?" Aunt Sophie asked, straining to make out the noise.

"It is," Ryan said, getting to his feet and looking toward the hill where Dunsbury Castle seemed to glow in the golden rays of the setting sun.

A hopeful look crossed Aunt Sophie's face, then she quickly forced the thought from her mind and started to clean up the containers of their dinner. "Is everyone finished?" she asked.

The barking got closer. Aunt Sophie froze. Then, slowly, she turned, just as Romeo limped through the bushes and into the yard.

"Romeo!" she cried, bursting into tears. The dog hobbled over to her. He licked her face and wiggled in a wild show of excitement.

"I don't believe it," Ryan said. "He came home."

Isabelle had tears in her own eyes. James had never admitted to doing anything to the dog; she'd just assumed it. But if it hadn't been James, then where in the world had the dog been?

Romeo made his rounds with the guests and Ian Scott giggled as the dog licked his face and yipped happily.

"Where have you been, boy?" Dr. Holmes asked the dog as he examined the straggly pooch more closely. "I believe his leg is broken. He looks thinner and his hair's full of burrs and mud, too."

Ryan stroked the dog's matted fur. "You've been through a lot, haven't you, boy?" he murmured. Looking up at the others, he said, "I guess we'll never know where he was, but he sure seems happy to be home."

The dog returned to Aunt Sophie, settling comfortably on her lap.

Romeo's return was a tiny miracle in and of itself. His return seemed to represent much more than just coming home. He brought hope and joy back with him, giving a renewed faith in small miracles and in life itself. Not only for Aunt Sophie, but for Isabelle, too.

While challenges were a big part of life, a part of life no one wanted, Isabelle knew they were also what made life the growing, enriching experience that brought people closer to God. She knew it had brought her closer, and for that she was grateful.

Ian Scott talked Ryan into going over to the pond and feeding the ducks and swans. With Romeo sleeping soundly on his pad outside the back door, Aunt Sophie cleaned up the meal, assisted by Dr. Holmes, who had been a frequent visitor around the cottage since their return from the states. Isabelle wondered if Aunt Sophie's absence had made his heart grow fonder. She hoped so. Nothing would please her more than to see her aunt find love again. And she couldn't think of a more wonderful person for her aunt to fall in love with than Dr. Holmes.

"Is there anything I can get you?" Ethan asked as he scooted his lawn chair closer to Isabelle's.

She shook her head. "Everything's perfect," she said, admiring the streaks of color from the setting sun as it painted the clouds in glorious hues.

Ethan looked at the sky also. "That's quite a sunset."

"It would be even prettier from the castle," Isabelle said.

Ethan looked at her. "Are you up to it?"

"I think so."

"I can always give you a piggyback ride if you get too tired," he offered.

"Now that would be a sight," she said with a laugh, picturing the image in her mind.

They made their way across the stretch of lawn to the pathway leading to the castle. The climb was more strenuous than Isabelle remembered, but the exercise felt good and the rush of fresh air seemed to help fuel her muscles.

"Almost there," Ethan said. "You need to hop on my back?"

Isabelle laughed. "I'm fine. We're almost there."

Hoping to catch the final glory of the sunset, they hurried to the castle, to the crumbling stone steps, and up to the top. There they stood, overlooking the patchwork of fields in the valley below. As the brilliant colors peaked and glowed, then slowly faded into a blush of pink and hues of purple, Ethan slipped an arm around Isabelle's waist and pulled her close. Isabelle rested her head on his shoulder and thought again of her great blessings and amazing new life. She never dreamed that she could have a life so wonderful, that she could step out of the shadows of loneliness, pain, fear, and heartache into the glorious light of love and family, of a heightened awareness of her Creator and

Father in Heaven, and actually have joy and peace in her soul.

Ethan turned her toward him and looked down at her upturned face. Neither of them spoke for a moment, but their hearts communicated the feelings they had inside.

"Thank you for being there for me," Isabelle finally said. "You've helped me through so much."

"I will always be there for you, Isabelle. I love you," he said.

Isabelle looked at him questioningly. He had made no secret of his feelings, but he had never expressed his love for her so clearly and unmistakeably.

"I do," he said. "I know you need plenty of space and time, but my heart was so full I couldn't hold the words in any longer."

Isabelle smiled, the grin on her face trickling warmth throughout her entire body.

The words filled her own heart to the point of bursting.

"And I love you," she said softly. "You're my knight in shining armor. You helped rescue me from a dragon named James and now, here I am, on a castle that belongs to me." She laughed out loud. "I feel like a queen. It doesn't get any better than this."

He lifted an eyebrow. "Are you certain about that?" He leaned down closer to her."Well, I guess it could get a little better," she said dreamily.

Smiling, Ethan leaned toward her and kissed her, sealing with their lips their confessions of love. The kiss lingered for a moment longer, followed by a hug that Isabelle wished could last forever.

"Make that *a lot* better," she said.

Ethan chuckled, then leaned back so he could look at her, giving her a lopsided grin that stole her heart completely.

"Why am I so happy when I'm with you?" she asked.

"I don't know, but I feel the same way. It's wonderful isn't it?"

"I can't believe you're willing to put up with me." She looked at him quizically.

"Isabelle, to me you really are a queen, and I promise I will always treat you like one."

Surrounded by his love, she blinked as tears stung her eyes. She couldn't believe she could feel so loved, so treasured and cherished, as Ethan made her feel. She wasn't naive enough to think her troubles were over, but she knew that with Ethan by her side, they would face together whatever challenges came their way. And they would live happily ever after.

The End

ABOUT THE AUTHOR

In the fourth grade, Michele Ashman was considered a "day dreamer" by her teacher and told on her report card that "she has a vivid imagination and would probably do well with creative writing." Her imagination, combined with a passion for reading, has enabled Michele to live up to her teacher's prediction, and she loves writing books, especially books that uplift, inspire, and edify readers as well as entertain them. (You can also catch her daydreaming instead of doing housework.)

Michele grew up in St. George, Utah, where she met her husband at Dixie College before they both served missions, his to Pennsylvania and hers to Frankfurt, Germany. Seven months after they returned they were married and are now the proud parents of four children: Weston, Kendyl, Andrea, and Rachel.

Her favorite past time is supporting her children in all of their activities, traveling both inside and outside of the United States with her husband and family, and doing research for her books.

Aside from being a busy wife and mother, Michele teaches aerobics at the Life Centre Athletic Club near her home. She is currently the Missionary Specialist in the Sandy ward where her husband serves as the bishop.

Michele is the best-selling author of seven books, a Christmas booklet, and has also written children's stories in the *Friend.*